Simon Williams

Salvation's Door

BOOK V OF THE AONA SERIES

The Aona Series by Simon Williams

Oblivion's Forge
Secret Roads
The Endless Shore
The Spiral Heart
Salvation's Door

Foreword

This is the final volume in the Aona series, a fact that fills me with a sense of accomplishment and a certain dread. The story that the books have told thus far, and which concludes here, has moved far beyond the events of Oblivion's Forge. Readers have told me that the Aona books confound expectations of the genre, to which I'm sometimes tempted to reply that it may well depend on which genre you feel that the series belongs to.

Myself, I don't have much time for such limitations and so if the books happen to straddle different genres then that's fine with me. If they have found a home in your imagination as well as on your bookshelves, then my work is done.

I want to thank the people on the various social networks I inhabit who have taken the time to offer encouragement and feedback and taken an interest- and all the readers and reviewers who have read and enjoyed the books.

Simon Williams

May 31st 2016

APHENHAST

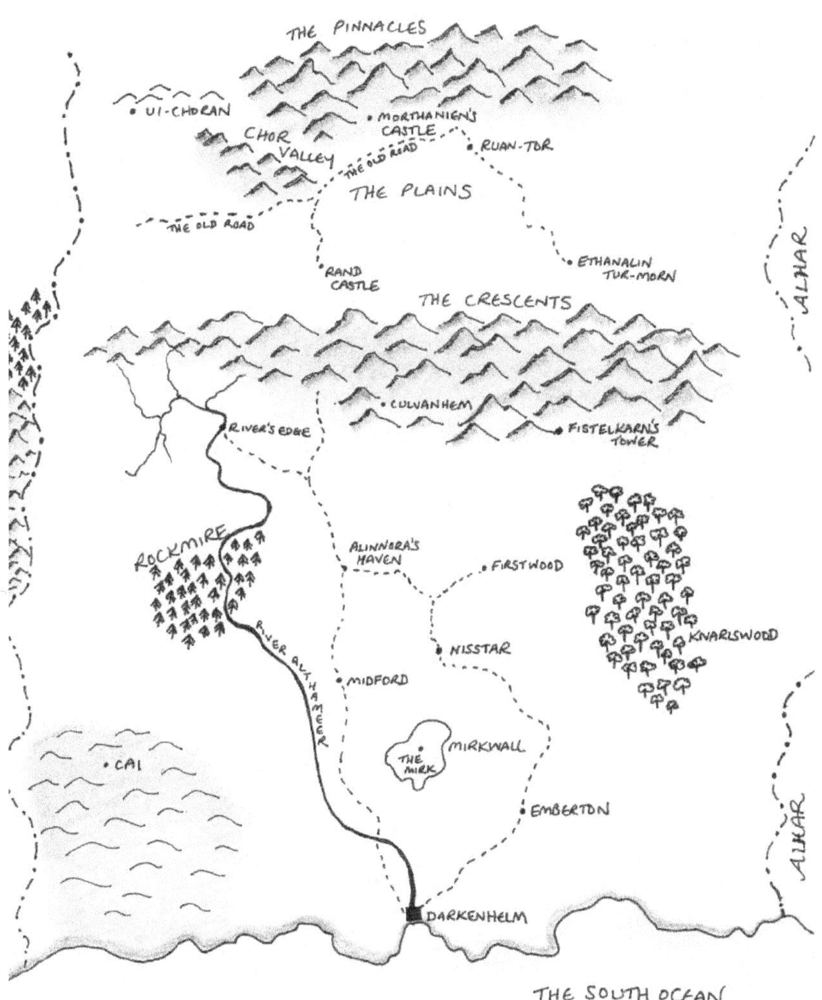

THE PINNACLES
UI-CHORAN
MORTHANIEN'S CASTLE
CHOR VALLEY
THE OLD ROAD
RUAN-TOR
THE PLAINS
THE OLD ROAD
RAND CASTLE
ETHANALIN TUR-MORN
THE CRESCENTS
CULVANHEM
FISTELKARN'S TOWER
RIVER'S EDGE
ROCKMIRE
ALINNORA'S HAVEN
FIRSTWOOD
KNARLSWOOD
RIVER ALTHAMEER
NISSTAR
MIDFORD
THE MIRK
MIRKWALL
CAI
EMBERTON
ALHAR
ALHAR
DARKENHELM
THE SOUTH OCEAN

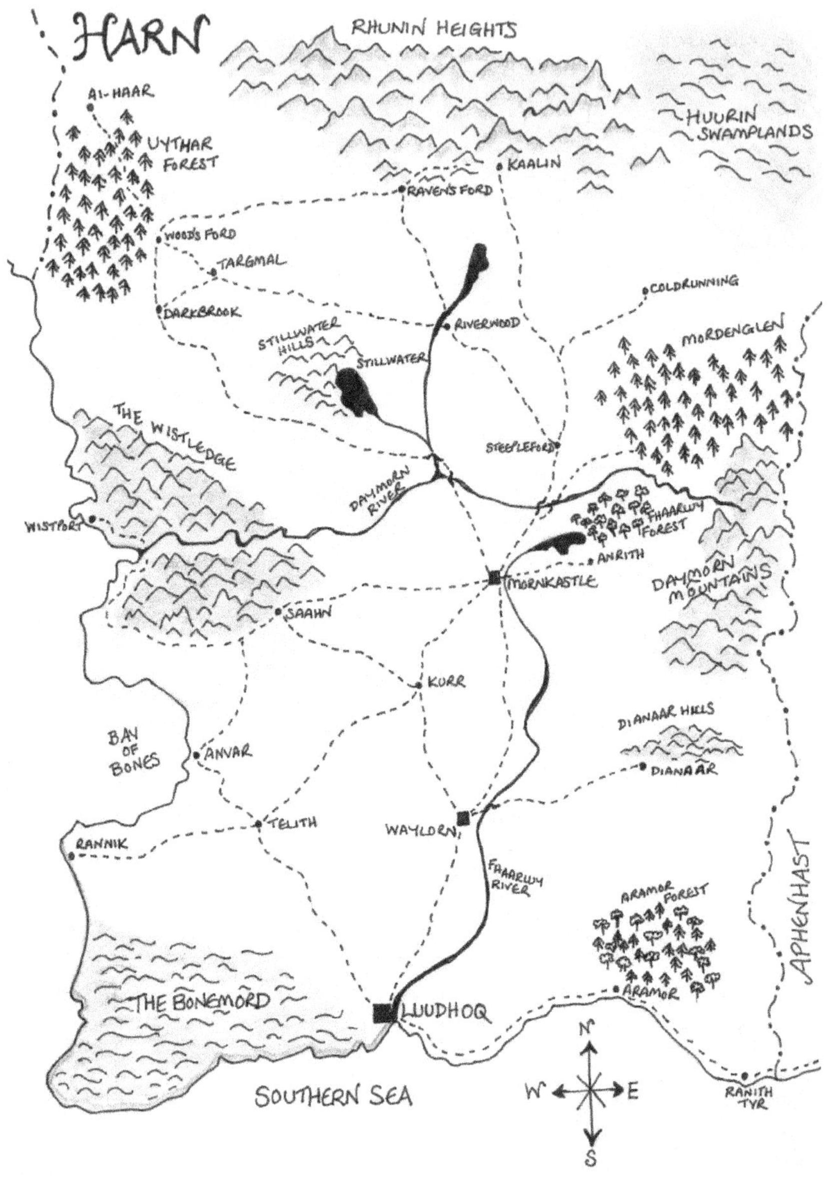

HARN
RHUNIN HEIGHTS
AI-HAAR
UYTHAR FOREST
HUURIN SWAMPLANDS
KAALIN
RAVEN'S FORD
WOOD'S FORD
TARGMAL
COLDRUNNING
DARKBROOK
STILLWATER HILLS
RIVERWOOD
MORDENGLEN
STILLWATER
THE WISTLEDGE
STEEPLEFORD
DAYMORN RIVER
FHAARLUY FOREST
WISTPORT
ANRITH
MORNKASTLE
DAYMORN MOUNTAINS
SAAHN
KURR
DIANAAR HILLS
BAY OF BONES
ANVAR
DIANAAR
WAYLORN
TELITH
FHAARLUY RIVER
RANNIK
ARAMOR FOREST
APHENHAST
THE BONEMORD
ARAMOR
LUUDHOQ
N
W E
S
SOUTHERN SEA
RANITH TYR

Prelude – The Unspeakable Rhythm

I

The wounded man limped over the muddy ground, dragging his less useful leg behind him as the tendrils of mist swirled all around. The tattered remains of his cloak flapped in the light breeze. The bitter taste of bile and blood tainted his throat.

He could remember little of any detail, nothing more than odd disjointed visions filled with the slaughter of thousands. The weeping, pleading masses had been herded into groups and then the shadows had appeared, dancing around them as the ground gave way or some unseen power crushed the victims' bodies slowly, pressing them to the wintry ground, grinding flesh and bone so that it became as one with the dark earth. The old sorcerer had watched, a rapturous smile upon his face as he gloried in the horrific, apparently pointless destruction. The wounded man wished he could forget that smile.

But there *had* been a point to the massacre. The shadows gained strength as the blood of thousands seeped back into the world. The terror of those who were slaughtered became the joy of that dancing darkness, but there was purpose to it all- he could no longer recall quite how, but at the time it had made a perverse sense.

Later the monstrous beasts had appeared, and were sent to do battle with the army that waited near the Stillwater. He had never imagined anything like these creatures. They were the one part of the nightmare that he recalled in near-perfect detail.

As he prepared to fight something had struck him on the head and he had fallen to the muddy grass. When he stirred later, most of the remaining fighters had been swallowed up entirely by the ground, pulled screaming into their own graves. Somewhere in the distance he saw faintly the horrific results of a battle in which he had not fought.

Many days had passed since. He had walked, pausing only to sleep fitfully for a short while, weep quietly to himself or drink from a stream or river if he was lucky enough to come across one. The pain on the left hand side of his head had subsided to a dull ache, and yet the wound had not stopped bleeding. It could not heal; part of his skull was missing. Despite his condition, somehow he had found the strength to keep wandering onwards, although he had idea where the path he followed might lead.

"I have a name," he whispered to himself occasionally. He didn't dare raise his voice any higher, not because there was no one there to listen but because he feared that the shadows would hear, even though he had seen nothing of them for days now. He couldn't be certain how many days.

The wounded man winced as pain flared up again for a moment in his head. He placed a trembling hand near to his wound and mumbled something incoherent to himself as he felt the raging heat it exuded. "Sorcery," he muttered as he staggered on along the muddy path, down towards the bottom of a scrub valley. Dead bracken and thick gorse bushes to either side rustled in the damp breeze as he made his way past.

When he reached the bottom of the valley, he saw two figures sitting by the edge of a river that meandered through the landscape. The hoods of their robes were drawn up. When he walked past, hoping that they would fail to hear him as he trod the soft ground, he chanced a look in their direction and saw that they were both busy eating something. He dared not stare for long enough to determine what their meal might be, but he caught a glimpse of raw, pink flesh, and perhaps a tiny foot and hand.

The wounded man picked up his pace a little more and threw frequent glances behind him until the mist closed entirely between himself and the two strangers. He whispered thanks to no one in particular and hurried along. His boots made squelching sounds as they partly sank into the soft, marshy ground. His legs trembled violently with the effort.

Not long afterwards a sudden flash of pain scythed through him, and he sagged to the ground. Lights and colours danced at the edges of his vision. He thought he could hear people approach, indistinct figures that appeared out of the mist and crouched down near to him but which he still couldn't make out. Pungent odours of smoke and cooked meat made his dry, sore mouth suddenly flood with spittle.

"Don't eat me," he whispered as the pain subsided. His vision faded further as his new companions gathered nearby. Someone knelt next to him and he felt foul, steaming breath upon his open wound. A moment later he uttered a pitiful, ragged shriek of agony as a tongue dragged its way across the exposed flesh of his brain.

"How did he live for so long?" he heard a woman's voice ask.

"There can be only one reason," a man replied. "The Gods of the Light protect him. I see the fervour in his eyes."

The wounded man sat up. He swayed back and forth and would have fallen had one of his companions not firmly held him upright. His vision flickered madly, but he could nevertheless make out that three people peered at him. One of them, a middle-aged man, feasted upon the cooked flesh of some creature. Half of the animal- he couldn't be entirely certain what it was other than a large hunk of meat- remained on the spit over a smouldering campfire. Two others, a boy with thick, greasy hair and a fat woman perhaps a little younger than the man with the food, stared at him with undimmed curiosity.

His stomach rumbled almost painfully, and the man grinned and wiped juice from his lips and chin. Then he leaned forward to offer a piece of meat along with a swig of water from a flagon at his side. The meat had a strong aroma of spice and herbs. "Even now, we must eat," he said, watching as the wounded man chewed slowly and with difficulty. How long had it been since he had eaten anything? "The Gods of the New Morning demand that we retain whatever strength we can as we travel ever nearer to the doorway."

The wounded man stared blankly at him. The phrase *Gods of the New Morning* felt as if it ought to mean something to him, as had *Gods of the Light*. For a moment an opaque image came to him of indistinct figures that stood like hapless spectres in a village street. They swayed in the dirt and called to something unseen, their voices ragged with emotion. It meant nothing to him. But *Gods of the New Morning* did.

Before he could think about the wisdom of doing so, he uttered a returning phrase, one that he felt matched it. "The Great Light of the East."

They each smiled at him as if he was a child or animal that had finally performed a longed-for trick. The fat woman clasped her swollen hands together and exclaimed, "He truly *is* one of the chosen!"

"I already said as much, woman." The man with the meat scowled at her before he turned to the wounded man once again. The grin returned with almost frightening speed. "You are one of us now. A member of the family, you might say. It's decided."

"It is?" the wounded man queried faintly.

"You'll come with us to the old circle where the doorway will be. The way between the worlds is thinner at the circles. But you may already know this. You may have been to the circles in your dreams."

The wounded man said nothing. His head had started to throb again. *Am I dying?* he wondered. *Am I already in some unknown afterworld? A place of constant travel to circles through doorways, or through doorways arranged in circles, or...*

His train of thought vanished, replaced by nothing. *I was dreaming before this moment,* was his first thought after that. *Everything that happened was just part of an ongoing nightmare.*

But what happened before the nightmare?

He tried to remember, but couldn't. He could still not even recall his own name. Meanwhile the battle, the monsters, everything that had happened before he stumbled through the mist, now had become vaguer than ever as if that same mist had seeped into his head.

"My name is Irrin," the man continued. "This is my wife Daina, and this is our son Gyreth. We've travelled many leagues already, from out of the west- not far from the Wistledge. We don't have far to go now. Not many leagues. You may ride on the cart with us. There are others, a dozen more. And we have captives. Those who turn their heads from the Gods."

"Why do you keep prisoners? Do you hope to sell them?"

Irrin laughed at that, and Daina crept so close that he could smell her hot, salty breath and the putrid odour of her ample flesh. "Did you enjoy your meat?" Daina murmured. "Would you care for a little more?"

Irrin picked up a couple of chopped meat chunks and placed them under his nose. "It must be days since you last ate."

The wounded man gratefully picked up the offerings and crammed them into his mouth. His desperate hunger allowed no room for any other thought. Daina offered him some water to help wash the meat down. She watched him continually and leaned provocatively forward to provide an unwanted view of her vast breasts hanging down within her loose shirt, thickly knotted veins bulging from the pockmarked skin. She looked to Irrin, who was busy pissing on the fire to put it out, apparently oblivious to the fact that he also splashed the meat on the spit. Daina gave the wounded man an odd, sly look, then stuck her tongue out and licked all around her lips. He thought it looked far too big, swollen and marked with clusters of sores as if afflicted by some disease.

The wounded man looked away, but Daina whispered something to him just as the rain began to fall. He couldn't understand the language she used. Might it be some hard Wistledge dialect?

Where was the Wistledge? He couldn't remember. West of here, Irrin had said.

"Time to ride," Irrin said eagerly, and Daina hauled the wounded man to his feet with the help of the silent Gyreth.

Slowly they made their way along the muddy track and down a gentle grassy slope towards a wider stony road where carts and a number of horses and riders waited. One of the carts was little more than a wheeled container with stout iron bars, attached to the back of the second cart. Inside it six prisoners had been placed. These pale, emaciated creatures stared listlessly as the wounded man and his new companions approached. They stank of blood and excrement. Two were missing an arm and a third had no lower left leg- it had been severed high up on the thigh, and far from cleanly. No attempt had been made to heal them as far as he could tell. One of them spoke silently to himself. None of the others uttered a word.

"They don't see the light," Daina told him as if that somehow explained their treatment. "They can't walk through to the world beyond because they don't see the light. How can something exist if you don't believe in it?"

That makes no sense, he thought.

But I don't think that matters anymore.

II

As they rode, Irrin told him about his past life before the journey they had undertaken. The wounded man listened as best he could, although waves of pain would crash through his head sometimes, so powerful that they caused him to cry out. Irrin offered neither sympathy nor the attentions of a healer, if indeed they had one amongst them. Instead he pointed to the agony as evidence of some kind of intervention by the Gods of the New Light, or the Great Light, or the New Dawn. The phrases appeared to be entirely interchangeable.

"I was once a carpenter," he said. "I shaped objects with wood. It therefore makes sense that now *I* am being shaped, in the image of the Great Light. You remind me of someone."

The wounded man stared at him for a moment without comprehending. Finally he asked "Who?"

"I don't recall certain things as well as I ought." Irrin smiled as if proud of the fact.

Abruptly Irrin reached across and stroked his companion's cheek almost tenderly. The wounded man flinched and looked away as Irrin asked, "Are you fearful?"

He thought quickly. "Only of the darkness, the enemy of the Great Light," he said.

Irrin looked seriously at him for a moment. Then he laughed so hard that the wounded man thought he might tip forward or over the side of the cart. "Should I not be?" he ventured after a while.

"No," Irrin told him, having recovered sufficiently to speak and pay attention to the road ahead. "You should not."

They lapsed into silence for a while, but Irrin did not seem to be a man who found comfort in long silences. Abruptly he burst into song, his voice an ugly throaty rasp that occasionally gave way entirely. The wounded man could not recall having heard the song before, but then he could recall no other songs either. He tried to ignore the noise and gazed steadfastly ahead- not that there was anything much to look at except the muddy, pitted track that stretched mournfully away before them.

But eventually the scenery changed, if only a little.

He thought the indistinct grey shapes that came into view ahead of them were the first oncoming soldiers of an enemy army. *That army!* he thought madly. *The army of monsters!* Panic spread through him and he stood up. He almost fell from the cart as he gesticulated wildly at the shapes. He tried to shout a warning, but the words that came out of his mouth sounded like pure nonsense. *Why can't I even speak properly?* he thought desperately even as Irrin hauled him down and put a comradely arm around his shaking body. "The language of the Gods," Irrin whispered, and the wounded man shuddered even more as he felt the man's hot, stinking breath in his ear and against his cheek. "So blessed," Irrin continued. "There's nothing to fear and everything to anticipate. Look! Before us stand the stones of the old circle, where the doorway will be opened. The Gods await us on the other side. We will welcome them into the world to herald in the birth of an Age."

They reached the stone circle soon afterwards. It measured perhaps fifty paces across with as many as thirty great slabs of rough-hewn rock that marked the circumference. Each one stood at least as tall as a man on another man's shoulders and six or seven hands thick. The wounded man wondered how such weighty structures had been brought to this place.

The carts were left outside the circle, and the prisoners hauled out and made to walk across the damp grass into the centre. The wounded man watched as Irrin, Daina and Gyreth and all the others removed their clothing. "You too," Irrin said to him. Curiously the chill that had set into his bones abruptly vanished as he stripped. The air felt warm and still, humid as late spring, and in a moment or two he had begun to sweat. He glanced across and saw Daina looking him up and down with a strange hunger in her eyes.

His companions began a dreadful cacophony of shouts and screams, and they danced and cavorted under the damp sky. He stood helplessly and watched as the scenes became ever wilder and more obscene. After a while he heard a low, steady rhythm, barely audible, as if a vast bass drum was being played somewhere far away.

Then, to his shock he realised that his heart now beat to that exact same staccato rhythm. *What's happening to me?* he thought desperately. The pulse grew steadily louder and slower, matched exactly by the tempo of his heart. Everything slowed down- the movements of the dancers, the cries of terror from the prisoners. The air became yet warmer. The drizzle intensified, hissing on the ground and turning the area to mud in moments. The wounded man thought he saw steam rise from the sodden ground.

The air in the middle of the ring of stones shimmered and his view of the stones behind it became distorted, as if he looked through an invisible but distorted mirror. He saw the muddy water on the ground begin to run in small rivulets towards the middle. He felt what he thought were tears roll down his cheeks, but when he wiped at his face he saw afterwards that his hand was stained red. The others also bled from their eyes, and from their ears. Scarlet lines traced a multitude of paths down their naked bodies, smeared and diluted by the unyielding rain.

I feel no pain, he thought, astonished. *My blood leaks out of me, yet I feel no pain. Am I healed?* He looked down at his body, and saw more streams of blood running down his chest, stomach, groin and legs, coaxed from his body by some unseen force. The slow rhythm grew louder still, so powerful that he feared his eardrums might rupture. His vision swayed alarmingly and his view of the distortion ahead grew ever more skewed.

The wounded man sank down onto the mud. It felt oddly warm, and it stank strongly of something he could not identify at first. The day darkened, and the mood of the celebrants around him began to change. Their ecstatic, swaying dance became something yet more frenetic, as if an unseen puppeteer pulled at a multitude of strings to which they were tied. Their shrieks became harsh, even agonised. Several people collapsed to the ground and flailed helplessly, unable to rise.

Rotten flesh, he thought suddenly. *That's what the stench is.*

But when he looked fearfully around all he could see was the mud, the rain, bodies that writhed in the filth. As he raised his head further he saw the sky lighten somewhere above, as if the sun might yet burst through the mass of seething cloud. He shielded his eyes from the light as it became ever more intense. The people who had brought him here struggled to heave themselves from the ground, and the wounded man saw to his horror that worm-like tendrils- roots, perhaps- had emerged from out of the soaking mud and fastened themselves around their wrists and ankles, even their waists.

Yet their bodies still moved forward, slowly but surely towards the central light. They shuddered to the unspeakable rhythm that boomed throughout this place. He heard bones snap, legs and arms break, yet still the bloodied, damaged bodies drew nearer to the epicentre of this mayhem, pulled by a stronger force than that which had hoped to pull the pallid bodies of the dancers into the earth.

The wounded man sensed shapes within the light, even though he could not look directly at it. Terror gripped him, worsened when he saw things he couldn't hope to describe slip from out of thin cracks and holes in the ground and swarm towards that hovering brilliance.

I'm not one of them! he heard himself scream, or perhaps the voice only sounded within his own mind. *I'm not one of them! Spare me!*

He had no idea if he pleaded with the light and the indistinct figures that he could now see within it like black flames silhouetted against the brilliance, or the entities that slipped from out of the deep furrows in the earth.

Something pulled him forward, nearer to the light. He saw that the prisoners held in the middle of the stone circle no longer had any skin. A few had collapsed in on themselves, others huddled like sacks of meat that gleamed wetly in the mud. They looked as if they had melted into shapeless heaps of flesh in the sudden heat.

The wounded man's eyes bulged and his skin rippled as he was pulled closer, until inevitably the things from within the earth burst forth to arrest his progress. Perhaps because he was not *one of them* as he had so desperately pleaded, he had not been pulled as close to the light as many of the others, and when the roots or tendrils- which felt like nothing more extraordinary than cold dirty hands- stopped him, he was brought to the ground where he lay, still staring towards the light.

Inexplicably, it was at this point that he suddenly remembered his name.

"*Ayvin,*" he whispered.

Immense pain soared in the right hand side of his head, and the vision in his right eye became red-hued and distorted, then non-existent. Something slid down his cheek, too heavy to be tears. He shook in silent agony, mouth wide open and lips bared.

Ayvin decided that the events he witnessed next- with the dim and narrow vision afforded by his remaining eye- were simply the consequences of the rampant madness to which he had succumbed. His grievous wounds, and his continued survival against the odds despite receiving no care for his injuries, had ensured his eventual descent into insanity. The people he had met, their crazed ritual and now the unspeakable forces that had pulled them apart, were all a product of his sickness.

Now figures stepped from out of the light and were attacked by shades and shadows that slipped from out of the crevices in the standing stones, from cracks in the ground, perhaps even out of the soaking sky.

Gods, he thought weakly, *fashioned by my dying brain. Fighting to see who shall claim me in the afterlife.*

But in his final moments, Ayvin realised that he was in fact quite incidental to the monumental struggle he witnessed, an irrelevant creature whose confused life leaked slowly away into the mud and rain, returning to and welcomed by the earth at last.

I – The Shattered Doorway

I

The portal stood black and broken, its energy dissipated. A great crack split it from top to bottom. The device had clung faithfully to life for longer than it ought, sending back sporadic images of the lush nirvana to which its coordinates pointed- as if to mock the broken woman who lay upon the cold stone slabs of a condemned world.

Perhaps the great power of Aona had then determined the usefulness of this ancient technology was at an end, and so it had eventually shut down.

Phaedra wept tears of rage and despair, her torment worsened as her body and mind slowly healed. At first, when her sight returned she could recall nothing of any use. Her memory, her cognitive skills, her capacity for reason had all been damaged, lost in the maze of her traumatised brain. But the essence of each trickled slowly back as she shuddered in agony, the attendant healing process slow yet inevitable. After she regained the ability to move, sit up, then stand and finally to walk with painful slowness to the portal, her hand moved like a lost creature along the dials and switches. Phaedra's red-hued gaze, still blurred and incomplete, turned imploringly to the mirror-screen. Images of the starkly beautiful world she had glimpsed remained etched indelibly on her mind. Even the damage inflicted by Garret could not dim them. But her eyes saw only her baleful reflection in the broken mirror surface of the portal.

Time passed; days, perhaps. Her body began to heal more swiftly. The pain ebbed a little.

Daniel had not been so lucky. If she moved her head a little way she could see his remains, spread over half a dozen paces or more. Before she finally turned limped from the chamber, Phaedra took one last lingering look at the smear of gore and bone that was all that remained of her lover's head. The flesh had barely moved in the time she had spent here. Maybe he would heal, but it would not be soon. Would she come back to see for herself? Perhaps. But then, the *marandaal* would take Harn long before then, and perhaps every other corner of the world.

"It... would be... miraculous." The last word took an eternity to utter. Phaedra repeated the statement twice, and uttered a low wail of frustration. Her powers of speech had not yet properly returned.

She stepped through the rubble of the wall that she and Daniel had hoped would conceal their work from the other five, and made sedate progress towards the upper parts of the fortress. Curiously, she could think only of the possible time of day and weather conditions that she might find. Day or night? Dawn or dusk? Would sunlight slant through the many arched windows, or would rain or sleet lash against the ramparts?

These banal possibilities were, after all, as important as anything else now.

Phaedra did not intend to encounter Issele and Anya as she wandered listlessly through the Fortress of the Seven. She had hoped never to encounter any of her comrades again, having decided to shut herself away in her quarters- once she had finished walking randomly throughout the fortress- and wait for the world to end.

But Issele called to her as Phaedra traversed the marble tiles of a cold and desolate hall. She stopped and turned to face them, although a shrill voice in her head demanded that she hasten onwards and through the opposite archway, never to be seen again. It vaguely occurred to her that this was the first time she had ever seen just Issele and Anya together.

"Where are they?" Issele strode across the floor towards her. Anya followed at a more measured pace. "Where *are* they, Phaedra?"

"Who are you talking about? Anyone in particular or everyone in general?" Phaedra inwardly marvelled at her glib tongue. *Never mind my private hell,* she thought. *No matter the situation, I still retain the same veneer. Issele, even if we persisted for another thousand years you'd never know me. And my speech has recovered just in time to bait you.*

Issele's stare was pure malevolence. "Are you going to tell me?" She looked searchingly into the other woman's eyes for a moment, and her expression grew predatory. "There's something wrong with you, Phaedra. Have you fallen from your balcony again?"

"Oh no. Something far worse than that, you'll be glad to hear." Phaedra felt sudden pain leap through her spine and a reddish flicker in her left eye, but despite the searing agony she managed to give Issele a sly look. "Would you like to know where Garret is?"

"It would be interesting to know where he's hiding himself," Anya spoke up as Issele opened her mouth to reply. "After all, he's never retired from the world for this long before."

"Garret has retired from Aona permanently," Phaedra said bitterly, and she proceeded to tell them everything about the scheme that she and Daniel had devised, ending with Garret stepping through the portal into the world they had located. "And now it's quite broken," she said finally. *Just like Daniel,* she almost added. "Go and find it yourselves if you want. The chamber remains unsealed. All the energy this place lent us has been used up. I suppose it didn't care *who* went through the gateway."

Issele made as if to strike her, but her arm remained held in the air. Her lips trembled and to Phaedra's astonishment tears appeared in her eyes.

Anya finally said, "Are you quite certain that…"

"Yes. It's broken. All the power has gone. Look for yourself; I know you will anyway. The world gave a chance to me and Daniel, and we would have taken it. But instead..."

Abruptly Issele turned and ran. The other two women watched her until she was out of sight.

"Well," Phaedra said quietly, "it's been a pleasure as always, Anya. Look after Issele, won't you? I do worry about her sometimes."

She walked away and headed slowly in the direction of her chambers. When she finally opened the outer door and walked from room to room she observed the immaculately tidy furnishings and realised that her servant had come to clean and dust them probably every day regardless of Phaedra's apparent disappearance, no doubt for fear of being found out and punished if she didn't. Even the fire in the hearth had been replenished and stoked recently.

Phaedra sat on the edge of her bed and wondered why her rage at the vast injustice fate had dealt her had all but disappeared. She felt only exhaustion. What would Anya, Issele and Omir do now? Had the city fallen into chaos yet? How far were their enemies from the gates of Luudhoq? She cared about none of these things.

For a moment Phaedra's vision became unbearably bright, then faded almost to nothing before it finally returned. A throbbing pain started up on the left side of her head and became so powerful that she thought her skull might burst sideways. When it ebbed away at last she decided to try to sleep. So clumsily that she wanted to scream her frustration, Phaedra slowly removed her clothes and inspected herself in the mirror, sourly admiring the physical recovery reflected back at her.

She quickly tired of the evaluation. Turning away, she went to lie down on her clean white bed and stare up at the ceiling, before finally her eyes closed.

Phaedra dreamed, as she often did, of her unreachable childhood in the old world.

Issele could not bear to visit the chamber where the dead portal remained. She screamed enraged nonsense when Anya suggested that she at least take the time to validate Phaedra's story, but Anya made sure to find the portal and check everything meticulously. Her steady gaze took in Daniel's remains, the crack and stain on the other side of the wall where Garret had flung Phaedra, and finally the silent, unresponsive instrumentation. It occurred to her then that if all seven of them had worked together to coax their old technology into life and perhaps harness whatever inexplicable power Aona loaned them, then they might all have had the chance to step through, one after another, to the world that Garret presumably now explored. *But we forgot how to collaborate long ago,* she thought, *and it would have been better for every known world throughout the universe if we had never worked together, never created that spark that then energised itself, the trigger that gathered momentum until it became unstoppable. The* marandaal.

Although it's a little late for me to care about the fate of worlds.

When she found Issele the next day, sitting in one of the smaller courtyard gardens in the fortress grounds, Anya told her what she had found.

"He *went without me,*" Issele hissed venomously.

The statement struck Anya as odd. "Of course he went without you. He hated you."

Anya put the matter of the portal- and Issele- to the back of her mind, and directed her energies towards the gathering of information from beyond Luudhoq's walls. One or other of the High Watchers would come to her regularly with news about the chaos that had spread throughout the south, much of it instigated by Watchers but some also by groups of outlaws and thieves who had seized the opportunity they'd long waited for- a largely lawless nation. The great army of folk from the distant north hadn't even bothered to attack and ransack Mornkastle. They had no need to; Mornkastle had fallen into almost as much mayhem as the smaller settlements. Refugees from other places poured into the city. The remains of the ruling Council- and the secret Council, although the difference was irrelevant now- had, accordingly to some reports, retreated to their fortress and nothing more had been heard from them. But their whereabouts was no longer relevant now that their hold on Mornkastle had slipped forever.

Perhaps they're dead, Anya thought. *They may as well be.*

She went to one of the Water Halls and used the power-amplifying effect of the far-seeing waters to witness events as far away as Mornkastle itself. In the brief moment during which the far-vision worked, Anya saw a broken, smoking ruin. Even the Council fortress had been destroyed. She glimpsed only a few people, and no Watchers. *They've moved on,* she realised. *Or they've turned against one another. Soon there'll be nothing left but rubble, ash and bodies left to fester as the spring warmth comes.*

Three days later she met with Omir and Issele. Omir had reacted to the news of his great rival's disappearance much as Anya had expected. He had raged; he had demanded more information, even when Anya patiently stated that she had none to give. He had spent a long time in the deep chamber from where Garret had stepped out of the world, presumably in a vain attempt to wake the technology. Finally he had calmed himself with murder, which was entirely expected.

"What have you found?" Omir asked her.

"I used the far-seeing waters," Anya said as she turned from the window, "and took myself to Mornkastle. I saw the inevitable results of chaos, as expected. As we already know, some Watchers have turned against the people or against one another, and others have fled. A few have killed themselves, which in my mind is the most interesting choice. But all I saw lay in ruins."

"Humans kill themselves all the time for much less," Issele pointed out. "That's the way things have always been."

"Indeed they do, and the Watchers have, I suspect regained some of their humanity. Despite all our efforts. Despite all *your* efforts, Omir."

"If it hadn't been for my work, we would never have had centuries of law and order," he stated coldly. "We used the machinery we had left to make what we could. I have never pretended that the Watchers were perfect."

"Order breaks down over time. We've observed that again and again if you cast your mind back long enough. Anyway, it would appear that matters continue to move quickly. The army of monsters and witches continues to move south. They have left Mornkastle to bleed to death, which is an eminently sensible choice. They had no need to invade it, although I expect the *orkar* in their midst took some convincing."

Omir pondered the matter. Finally he said, "They cannot be trusted."

Anya's lips twitched in a half-smile. "Who? Our enemies?"

He looked intently at her. "Our *Watchers*. Two of them here in Luudhoq had to be destroyed, if you recall."

"Yes," she said. "I recall the example you made. But what do you propose?"

"We know that there have been instances of Watchers engaged in random or even subversive acts. How do we restore order? Perhaps by removing the source of the chaos."

"The Watchers are not the only source of chaos with which we must contend," Anya pointed out. "One might say they're nothing more than a symptom of something deeper."

"I don't follow."

"You must have sensed that everything is not as it should be, even within the fortress. Instruments have been failing for a long time now. The Hall of Measurement has become little more than a junkyard. Doors refuse to close or open. Windows break without warning. Servants have died of no known cause. I don't expect you even notice servants, but surely you must have detected... an innate randomness to recent events. Someone died in the middle of the main gardens three days ago. A large stone fell from the sky directly on top of him and crushed his skull."

"And that wasn't your doing or Issele's?"

"No. I have better things to do with my time. The stone fell from directly above him as far as I could tell, from the sky."

"A meteorite. It's not unheard of. Although I suppose given the failed instruments you mentioned, it might not have been detected until..."

"The stone was identified as a block from the foundations of this fortress. Somehow it had disappeared from low in the wall of which it was a part, to materialise high in the sky above the grounds."

Omir laughed at that, but Anya continued, "Do you not find it surprising that the order and discipline that held the Watchers together for so long has fallen apart so swiftly and so completely?"

Omir said nothing.

"But you're right," Anya continued. "They can't be trusted. If the weapon can turn against the hand, it's no weapon at all. Soon the monsters from our dreams will come to lay waste to Luudhoq. We must have absolute, unquestioning obedience and loyalty from everyone. It goes without saying that the High Watchers will stand by us, and the people of the city will do as they are told. They haven't the wit or courage to do anything else. But the Watchers... we should have known it would all come back to bite us, Omir. All those decades you and Stephan spent coaxing that sporadically useful technology into some kind of use, creating monsters more often than Watchers… can you truly say you knew what you were doing? Even when it worked?”

He ignored the question. “We’ll destroy them. We need only the originals. They will remain absolutely dependable.”

Anya looked thoughtful. “One of them is to report to me at sundown today, here. I suggest you both attend, and I will find Phaedra and ask her to as well. You never know- she may even contribute something useful to our discussion. Regardless, I suspect we will gain some insight into what the Watchers have been doing.”

At sundown, one of the High Watchers came to Anya as she waited in the hall with Omir, Issele and Phaedra. She was surprised that Phaedra had agreed to attend, her curiosity having won over her dispassion for important matters.

With the four of them in the meeting hall, the High Watcher spoke, its calm monotone echoing harshly through the large chamber.

“Three Watchers are known to have committed crimes. One. Unauthorised killing of eight human citizens. Two. Unauthorised killing of five human citizens. Three. Unauthorised killing of seventeen human citizens.”

“Oh. Separate instances of the *same* crime then,” Issele said. “Presumably they have been apprehended and dealt with.”

“As per the law, they were located and destroyed.” The High Watcher then added, “We have a suggestion regarding these Watchers.”

“Continue,” Anya prompted it. She was a little surprised that the High Watcher had not said this during their previous meeting.

The creature continued, “In light of these events, we have observed the Watchers more closely. We see them as unpredictable resources, dangerous and counter-productive to your stated aims of repelling the advancing enemy force from Luudhoq at all costs.”

"This is the view of you all?" Issele asked.

"It is. The matter has been discussed and agreed."

They have had a discussion on such a matter without our knowing? Phaedra thought, a flutter of unease in her stomach. *How can that be? They were designed to obey explicitly, not to interact with one another on a high level.*

But the others did not appear to recognise the anomaly. "And what *is* your suggestion, precisely?" Anya demanded.

The cold eyes surveyed each of them in turn. "That all the Watchers be destroyed, either by our hand or by the Seven. They are not necessary for the successful defence of Luudhoq, nor for the destruction of the invaders that you now call *marandaal*. Our powers combined are more than sufficient to destroy our enemies."

It still refers to us as seven, Phaedra realised. *Does it even know that Garret is some unfathomable distance away, perhaps on the other side of the known universe? Does it know that Daniel is still as good as dead, even as the force that made us all immortal tries to mend and fuse his broken pieces?*

The Watchers are just a symptom of the chaos, she thought, *and the High Watchers' inevitable response is to attempt to eradicate them. However logical that idea might seem, I can see only that it will give rise to further chaos. All attempts to restore order will now simply create further mayhem.*

It's time at long last for things to simply run their course.

Phaedra almost questioned the High Watcher at that point- she wanted to know what made it quite so certain that their combined powers would be enough to destroy the oncoming enemy, no matter that they knew so little of its nature. But she said nothing. *It isn't my place,* she decided. *Oh, I'd love to know what strangeness has seeped into its harsh logic, to make it utter such words. But that's just a symptom of a wider phenomenon.*

Anya sent the High Watcher away and lapsed into thought. Omir almost spoke, but then appeared to remember that Phaedra still remained in the room. "Are you going to vote on this matter?" he asked icily. "We never can guess your intentions from one meeting to the next- those you choose to attend."

"Me? No, I think I'd better not," Phaedra said. "After all, it might result in two on either side, and then we'd have to fight over it. Do you miss your fights with Garret, Omir? I suspect he doesn't miss *you* very much."

Without waiting for an answer, she turned and left.

III

The afternoon decayed at length into a dull and close, misty evening. Phaedra wandered to a library that neither she nor- as far as she knew- any of her comrades had visited for a hundred years or more. After a short while she located the section that contained their own written notes, made perhaps ten or twenty years after their arrival in Aona. The ancient boxes that contained reams of observations and findings were covered with dust, and more awaited her when she prised open one of them.

As she thumbed through the ancient papers, she came across one that arrested her attention immediately. She had almost forgotten all about it.

"Comparison with the old world," she read aloud, and immediately wondered why they had taken so quickly to calling their former home the *old world* and never referring to it by its name. "The orbit around the sun takes three hundred and sixty five point three two of our days. The rotation upon the axis takes exactly one of our days."

Why did we never consider any of these strange facts properly? she wondered. *Because we were too busy building our empire, too busy making gods of ourselves. Of course, it could all be pure mathematical chance. But what* was *the probability that Aona would turn out to have these characteristics? And the advanced people of this world- surely they must have originally arrived here through the Gates, but how is it that they have no record of that time? How could something so momentous have been erased from their histories?*

She put the paper back in the box. Her appetite for browsing forgotten relics had deserted her. It was, after all, too late in the day to ponder the great mysteries of the world.

Phaedra found an odd restlessness grow within her, which became only greater with the onset of darkness. Later that night she made an abrupt decision to leave the Fortress for a while and head out into the city.

As she slipped through an unguarded side gate, choosing to bend the bars by sheer force of will, it occurred to Phaedra that this was the first time she had ventured outside the Fortress of the Seven in at least thirty years. She tried to remember the reason for her last excursion but couldn't, any more than she knew why she had decided to head out into the city now. Boredom, she supposed. Many unspeakable acts had been carried out because of nothing more than simple boredom, and this was simply a mundane walk through the city night.

Few people were out and about at this late hour. Phaedra lowered the brim of her hat, pulled her cloak tightly about herself and strolled along one of the narrower streets that led down towards the main square and the guild halls. Cold, wet mist dampened her clothing in moments.

She passed by half a dozen people in total before she reached the first of the guild halls a while later. Of course, none of whom had recognised her. Why would they? She had been virtually a recluse for more than a century, and in any case no one had ever painted a likeness of her. Some of the others had had statues or other constructs made of themselves, something that struck her as a peculiar vanity.

Phaedra had never been one for public appearances. *I'm a creature of the shadows*, she thought as a seventh person shuffled by, wrapped up in whatever little concerns occupied his mind. *I've barely existed in recent times- oh, except for my fanciful hope of escape from this condemned world- and soon I won't exist at all.*

She reached the main square and gazed moodily in each direction. The more distant buildings stood beyond her sight, concealed by a sea of thick mist. The near architecture loomed indistinctly to her left and right, a conglomeration of half-shapes lit here and there by shuttered lanterns.

Phaedra began walking again, but as she did a figure appeared out of the mist and headed straight for her. "Don't run," she heard the man say. In a moment Phaedra saw the predatory smile upon his lips and the glint of steel in his hand.

"I won't," she said, and waited as her brief flurry of unease- the result of her momentary thought that this might be a rogue Watcher or even a High Watcher- was quickly replaced by a vaguely irritated contempt.

When he was no more than a pace away and reached out to grab at her with one hand as the other drew back the blade of his knife, Phaedra seized hold of his arm and crushed it. The flesh and bone compacted under the force of her grip. Then she snapped his lower arm with a swift motion and tossed the ruined arm to the ground as he sagged to his knees in front of her, agony and astonishment in his eyes.

"It wasn't your lucky night, was it?" Phaedra said softly. "Do you know who I am?"

He opened his mouth and uttered a faint, agonised croak.

"Well?"

Her would-be assailant remained incapable of speaking, and in any case no recognition leapt in his eyes. Phaedra felt an inexplicable sadness come over her. She had helped rule Harn for a thousand years and even this wretched would-be rapist didn't recognise her. She had brought order from chaos, light from the muddied and superstitious darkness of a long-ago age, only to be barely remembered. She had hidden herself away for decades, finally venturing forth when the hour was already too late, to taste a world that could no longer be saved even if she cared about saving it.

Phaedra aimed a kick at the man's head. Her sudden anger lent her even greater power, so that his head exploded like a melon and splinters of bone and pieces of flesh flew backwards at least a dozen paces. The body fell backwards, and Phaedra stared hatefully at the faintly gleaming gore strewn across the damp cobbles.

After a while she walked on, but stopped shortly afterwards, her attention drawn to a large storehouse to her right. No light issued from its many windows, although that in itself was not surprising. But Phaedra imagined that the darkness behind these structures was something more than it appeared to be, and the more she stared at the windows the more certain she became.

It was difficult to know for sure while she peered through the mist, but Phaedra thought she saw one of the windows in the middle of the building become slowly wider and taller, even as the rest of the building retained the same dimensions. At the same time the space behind the window grew darker than ever, so much that Phaedra found herself suddenly reminded of the portal inside the Sanctum.

Supposing that this is the beginning of a Gate, right here in Luudhoq? she thought, taking several steps backwards. *Might the end be coming sooner than we think?*

She then witnessed something that confounded her even further. From out of the enlarged window small black streams began to pour forth, and spread not only downwards but across the side of the building. *This is no Gate,* Phaedra decided, *but I have no idea what else it might be. Sorcery? What other explanation but one that explains nothing?*

As each rivulet or vein of blackness spread across the wall it split and moved seemingly at random, and made it look as if the brickwork it covered had vanished completely to leave nothing but a void behind. *Matter being eaten by nothing to become nothing,* Phaedra thought madly. Yet the building somehow remained standing and gave no indication that it might suddenly crumble away, its foundations and solidity vanished from the world forever.

Phaedra wondered, as she finally hastened away from the scene, how far and how swiftly this phenomenon might spread through the city. Perhaps it would limit itself to the structure it currently assimilated, or it might spread like an unstoppable river across the architecture and infrastructure of Luudhoq, eating the very ground upon which people walked. *What world will I wake into tomorrow?* Phaedra asked herself as she made her way hurriedly back towards the Fortress of the Seven. *Will I wake at all?*

Much later, she dared to cross over to the window of her bedchamber, and found the city landscape- what little she could see of it- unchanged as far as she could tell. The faint opaque glow of lantern light loomed through the blanket of mist that still suffused the sky. When she opened her window she heard no sounds of panic and terror. No great swathe of inexplicable darkness had eaten the middle out of the city.

That will come soon enough, she thought, taking a deep breath of the damp, chilly air. *No matter what I saw tonight, some things remain certain.*

II - The Price

I

Kian reached out to grab Nia's hands and stop her frantic shaking. Nia stared in her direction but Kian could tell that she wasn't looking at her at all. *I have no idea how to help her,* she thought, and called out, "Anlerran!" Her friend had considerably better healing skills and had become used to dealing with Nia's outbursts.

More people had gathered nearby. A stout *orkar* man brought a flask of sourgrass near, but Nia reacted violently to the smell and almost knocked it from his hands. She clawed at something invisible in front of her and gave vent to a scream so wretched that Kian wanted nothing more than to run as far away as possible. Cursing to herself she looked around and called to Anlerran again. Where was she?

"Fetch Anlerran," she said impatiently when Iyoth finally arrived. "I can't help Nia. I never was much of a healer."

"You take after your father," he said dryly and walked away towards Anlerran's tent.

Others arrived while he was gone. One of them was Garrok, who Kian turned to. "Nia said that Yui is here. The child who was imprisoned by the Seven and who plagued Nia's dreams."

Garrok gave her a considering look. "A child of considerable power, from what I've heard."

"Undoubtedly." Kian flinched as Nia suddenly grabbed her arm and held her head against it, weeping. "Someone should guard Nia..."

"We longer need her." Kian looked and saw Kelandra step from the shadows. The Watcher gave Kian a cool look and turned to Garrok. "If Yui is here or approaching the camp, then find her and make her safe. You may wish to make use

34

of your ironmasters. I don't know why she has come to us-
other than in hope of a safe haven- but no doubt we'll soon find
out."

No sooner had Kelandra uttered those words than two
guardsmen arrived, breathless from running. "A new arrival,"
one of them said. "A young human child and her father and a
woman. Hastians, all three of them. They claim to have
escaped from Luudhoq and demand to speak to those in
charge."

"Well, then bring them here," Kelandra said. Kian
thought that she detected a slight hesitancy to the Watcher's
voice. *And so there ought to be,* she thought. *Did she not turn
the child over to her masters the Seven- with Nia's help, of
course?*

Kian hauled Nia to her feet with considerable effort.
Nia was almost as slim as the *du-luyan* girl and no more than
a head taller, but she felt like a dead weight. *I need Anlerran's
help, and perhaps Ileana's as well, particularly if Yui intends
to have her vengeance,* she thought. Glancing at Kelandra,
Kian felt certain that the Watcher might step aside and allow
Yui do whatever she wished. She and perhaps the other two
Watchers blamed Nia for the truth of their origins as much as
they did the Seven, which Kian thought defied all logic.

"I will take Nia to Anlerran," she said, but neither
Kelandra nor Garrok heard her, or perhaps didn't bother to
respond. Nia was not their concern. Both were looking in the
direction where the sentries had dashed back towards,
waiting for Yui and her companions to arrive. Kian looked
around and saw Ileana arrive. "Ileana, help me," she
implored.

As Kian and Ileana headed off towards Anlerran's
tent, half-carrying Nia, they met Iyoth coming the other way.
His expression was grim. "What is it?" Kian exclaimed.

"Anlerran isn't in her tent, and there are no recent
tracks around it," he said. "Her *illeagh* dog is sleeping within,
and I can't rouse him. If I was to wager I'd say someone has

used the Powers to enter the camp undetected, and taken her without the alarm being raised. This night is as bright as any in the last few tennights." He glanced up at the full moons, which were still close together in the sky, although Archaon had begun to drop towards the horizon. "Whoever did this was confident of getting in and out without being seen or even sensed- weaving spellcraft so as to pass unseen and unheard amongst us to steal her away."

Kian stared at him, dumbfounded. "That's... no, that can't be..." But at the same time she recalled how she had faintly sensed someone using the Powers when she went to Nia a short while ago. *I should have investigated,* she thought grimly. *I should have!*

Elluron demanded that the entire camp and surrounding area be searched for Anlerran. The best trackers were sent for leagues in every direction to search for any hint of a trail once the first glimmer of dawn arrived. But as Iyoth had feared would happen, shortly after sunrise each of them returned without anything to report.

Culos woke from a slumber which had no doubt been deepened by Anlerran's kidnapper. That morning he howled so desolately that the sound became unbearable to anyone within earshot. But even he did not set off to try and find her. Apparently no trail had been left to follow, even for the *illeagh* hound.

Angry discussions erupted about who or what could have taken the young witch, but they quickly reduced down to two possibilities- that the *kin* had somehow found a way to get in and out unseen- or Ruhal or someone carrying out the nefarious task on his behalf had done the same.

Aware of but not understanding the chaos into which they had arrived, Yui, Phyqor and Alexia were taken under guard by four of the *orkar* ironmasters and allowed to eat, drink and finally sleep. The following day they were questioned, but Kelandra and the other Watchers kept away and Elluron was beside himself with rage and grief, so it eventually fell to Ileana as a practitioner of the Powers who might understand Yui, to talk to them.

Yui spoke of how they had escaped Aphenhast, their capture and their eventual escape from Luudhoq. The calm and matter of fact way in which she told their story made Ileana's skin crawl. The other two said only a little. The child's eyes looked dark and her face pale and drawn as she described how she had managed to rescue both Phyqor and Alexia and then draw the three of them into the Green Road from their place of hiding deep in the warrens of Luudhoq. Ileana listened in fascinated silence and reflected on the power that the girl must hold to have done these things. She found herself reminded of when she had pulled Anlerran and Kian with her into the Green Road just before the great battle at Stillwater. *And Yui is only a child,* she thought. *How strong might she become given time?*

Yui also mentioned that she had dreamed of a Gate in the Green Road, and Ileana caught her breath for a moment. *Vornen sensed a Gate within the tower on the island when we were there,* she thought. *Could it be the same one? I'll need to tell Garrok and Kelandra, and Elluron if he'll listen. It may be important.*

Finally Yui gave her a long hard stare and demanded to know, "Is Nia hiding from me?"

"I expect so," Ileana admitted.

"Everything that happened to us is Nia's fault."

Ileana thought quickly. What might happen if Yui decided to unleash her considerable powers on Nia? How able was she to control them? Ileana thought back to her days in Ethanalin Tur-morn, always having to keep her own abilities hidden from those around her, able to unleash them only when she was somewhere out in the surrounding lands, hidden away. Her struggle to maintain a veil over her true nature had been bad enough, a never-ending battle against her own self. If she had ever let that other side consume her and directed the Powers at another person, especially when she had been Yui's age, then in all likelihood they would have erupted out of control. Who knows what kind of devastation she might have caused?

Regardless, I can't let her exact her revenge on Nia, Ileana decided. *In a sense, Nia helped put us* all *in the position we're in, for better or worse. She may yet prove to be decisively important again. I don't know how all this will end but I can't allow a vengeful child of Yui's strength to release her spite, no matter what happened to her.*

"I agree that Nia has much to atone for," she said carefully. "But I expect she also did what she thought was best for Harn- or for the South, at least."

"Nia did only what was best for herself," Alexia retorted immediately.

"Well, that may also be true." Ileana looked back to Yui. "You mentioned that she had seen one of your visions for herself."

"I think so. I didn't mean for her to," Yui said guardedly.

"Be that as it may, if that happened then perhaps she realised how important they might be. Her task as she saw it would be to find a way to entice you to Luudhoq and tell Kelandra everything that she knew. Of course, her involvement in imprisoning your father and Alexia- in different ways- was wrong. But Nia has certainly suffered- in the past, and now. She told Anlerran and Kian of the nightmares that you caused her, and they in turn mentioned it to me some time ago."

"I didn't do anything," Yui said quickly, but when Phyqor turned to look at her she shrugged and quietly added, "I just wanted to scare her in her dreams, that's all. She deserved all of it."

"And so her punishment has been meted out now, wouldn't you say?" Ileana suggested. "There's no need for anything more."

Yui shrugged. "I don't care what happens to her. But I'll leave her alone if that's what you want."

"It is. For the sake of us all." Ileana forced a smile and hoped that the full extent of her relief didn't show. "Thank you for telling your story, Yui. I myself know what the Green Road can be like. The three of you have shown immense courage in escaping Luudhoq and finding your way here."

"I expect you'll want to know why we came here," Alexia said. "The truth is, something or someone gave me the names of some people when we were in the Green Road, and in fact *you* were one of..." Suddenly the Hastian woman frowned as if she had only now realised something. She looked around and then stared at Ileana. "Where is Ilumor?"

II

The night of their arrival, Ilumor had become separated from his companions without knowing how or why. Somehow the *orkar* guards who had accosted the others had not even seen him, nor had his companions noticed that he was no longer with him as they were lead away.

He made his way along the perimeter of the camp, past the countless tents and fires and groups of fighters. Most of them were *orkar* but he reckoned more than a third of them were human. He observed much drinking, eating, singing and an occasional fight. The urgent sounds and sharp odours of fornication emerged from a few of the tents.

Ilumor passed by all this even as the sheer overwhelming chaos of the camp assailed all his senses. He walked under a heavy cloud of thought and faint hope that now his task had been successfully completed, he might finally be granted the freedom to return to his Lords. After all, he had somehow walked away and his disappearance had gone unnoticed. There had to be a reason for it, he told himself.

As he walked he noticed that the ground underfoot changed and become drier and looser now that he had reached the edge of the camp. Before him lay the dark of a moonless night. Had both Archaon and Ildar set already? He recalled that both moons had been high in the sky only a short while ago, but perhaps the camp was larger than he had suspected and he had walked for half the night.

Ilumor shrugged tiredly and kept walking. His eyes would adjust to even the blackest night soon enough.

He walked over scrubland and across low grassy hills. At one point he had to wade through an icy, fast-flowing stream. Finally he stopped, having heard a curious new sound up ahead. Its odd familiarity made him increase his pace until he arrived at a sandy shoreline that sloped gradually down to a vast sea.

Impossible was his first thought, but a longer look convinced him that by Aona's will or otherwise he had slipped through reality's veil to find himself at the Endless Shore.

Is this my fate from here on? he wondered. *To pass from place to place without knowing my destination, as if I had as much sense and substance as the air itself?*

He recalled the immeasurable time he had spent trapped in the Silver Road, and shuddered.

The sky above now held points of light- stars that he knew were not stars at all, unless they were the ghosts of heavenly bodies from a distant age, hung out and displayed for some unfathomable reason. Their faint illumination glittered weakly on the calm waves that rolled against the infinite shore.

As he walked slowly along, Ilumor noticed that not everything appeared as it had before. Occasionally the waves would stop moving completely, as if all the water in the ocean had suddenly frozen. Then their motion would continue as if it had never been interrupted. Ilumor stopped to observe this phenomenon for a while, perplexed. Then he noticed that in places along the shore the sand would occasionally move to create small whirlpools, in the centres of which holes formed, even darker than the sea. Ilumor stopped to watch them and idly wondered what might happen if one such event formed with him as its epicentre. But none did, and he smiled bitterly to himself, considering that to keep him upon the shore was Aona's plan for him at the moment. He could not simply disappear. He was not an innate part of this increased randomness, only a visitor.

He walked on for an indeterminate length of time. Hours, days, tennights could have passed by. He didn't tire, nor did he become thirsty or hungry. After a while he saw a young man sitting cross-legged on the sand up ahead, several paces from the water. As Ilumor approached he saw that this man stared thoughtfully at the distant horizon where the unending ocean appeared to meet the sky of unknown stars. *Who is this?* he wondered as he stopped a short distance away. *One of the higher* kin, *clearly, but I don't recognise him.*

The young man glanced across and regarded him in silence for a while. "What are you?" he asked finally.

The question confounded Ilumor. "I stand high amongst the *kin*," he said. "My name is Ilumor. You should know that name."

"I do," the other man confessed, "but I don't recognise you, and you are not *kin*."

Ilumor felt the light stir within him for a moment and wondered if his new companion could see it in his eyes. If so then he gave no indication of such knowledge. Ilumor stood indecisively for a while. Should he kill this man for his insolence? Should he keep walking? Was this yet another test?

Finally he sat down a few paces away, facing the ocean. "My name is Ferrin," the *kin*-man told him. "Perhaps you *are* Ilumor, or were, but you are no longer *kin*. I don't say that to insult you. I say it because I knew it to be true when I first saw you."

"Then how is it that I still walk this place?" Ilumor retorted.

"That, I have no answer to."

"And why are *you* here?"

Ferrin favoured him with the ghost of a smile. "I am here to meditate on the nature of life and death, and eternity- something I had a penchant for even in the days before I was raised to be *kin*. Soon, I will go to the eastern edge of Mordenglen to do battle with the starspawn." He regarded Ilumor for a while and then frowned, clearly puzzled by something. "What is it?" Ilumor demanded.

"You were brought here and now you can't leave. I sense as much."

Ilumor opened his mouth to deny the statement but found he could say nothing.

"Yours is a strange path indeed," Ferrin commented. "I can't fathom it." He got up, nodded in farewell and walked slowly away.

Ilumor watched the *kin*-man until he had gone too far to be seen. Then he turned to regard the ocean and contemplate its inky depths once again. *Walk into that darkness and drown,* he told himself hatefully, but he did not- or perhaps could not, still tethered to life by his tormentor.

III

A cold wind blew across the camp and disturbed the ash from the previous night's cook fires. Men and women cursed and drew their cloaks more closely about themselves. The greater part of the winter had passed and was less severe this far south, yet this day felt unnaturally cold.

Iyoth observed Elluron's grief and rage from a distance. He had said nothing to the half-*illeagh* and had no plans to- he could think of nothing useful to say, and therefore silence was no more useless than words- but inevitably, as he sat by his tent sharpening his weapons he imagined himself in the same situation. *Had Kian been spirited away, I would be the same,* he thought. *Worse. I would have abandoned all control and sense. I might already have set off after Ruhal- for surely he is behind this- and hunted him down. But as we've already established, no trail can be found. Ruhal must have an accomplice, someone with a considerable talent in sorcery. Even the* illeagh *dog has been fooled, and now paces restlessly around the camp.*

This can't continue, Iyoth decided abruptly, putting one of his longknives to one side. *Elluron is one of the three who accepted the responsibility of leadership, yet he's in no position to lead. Meanwhile my daughter mourns not only a friend but someone with whom she shared an important connection. Already our situation is dire. Kelandra and Garrok have no trust for each other- they cannot lead together without Elluron. And while we wait the land to the south descends into bloodshed and chaos.*

Abruptly he got up and strode away, unwilling to spend a moment longer wasted on the contemplation of such misery. In all likelihood there was nothing he could do about the situation, but he would try.

Iyoth found Lura wrapped up in a blanket and sitting on an upturned weaponry box sipping from a silver flask. When he sat next to her he could smell the pungent, bitter odour of sourgrass. He almost grabbed the flask from her to pour the vile liquid away.

"It's not yet noon," Lura remarked, slurring her words. "But I'm doing well. I'm warm and I can laugh at the world." She prodded his arm. "But *you*, Iyoth- you're cold and you laugh at nothing."

"I find no humour in our situation," he said quietly. "I need you to do something, Lura."

She glanced at him, amused and suspicious in equal measure. After a moment she reached out a hand to stroke his cheek but he slapped it away. "Listen to me. You did Anlerran a great wrong..."

"Oh, don't speak to me of great wrongs," Lura retorted. "You're no better than me. We're nothing but murderers for hire, only I can't recall the last time I was paid for anything. No, I tell a lie. Several *orkar* have paid me in sourgrass for a few things..." She scowled at his look of thinly veiled disgust and continued more sharply, "So now you claim to be a creature of morals?"

"I won't beg you," he said stonily, "but if you care anything at all for the world, and if you know how Anlerran could have been taken, you should tell Elluron. Or if you cannot bear to tell him, then tell Garrok or someone whose company you can bear."

"I had no part in it." Lura took another swig of sourgrass. "I don't know who Ruhal found to kidnap her. It had nothing to do with me."

Iyoth stared meaningfully at her. "Interesting. I didn't even mention Ruhal."

Lura shrugged and looked away.

"I think you *do* know who helped him." Iyoth wasn't certain at all that Lura knew, but he allowed himself to be led by gut instinct. "Count yourself lucky that Elluron doesn't yet think the same." Iyoth got up and strode away.

Lura waited until he was out of sight, then downed the rest of her drink and threw the flask to the ground in frustration.

Elluron's face looked pale and sickly in the faint lantern light. Lura waited uncertainly at the tent entrance until finally he looked up from his maps and calculations. "What do you want?"

"I want to help," she said bluntly. "If Culos can find Anlerran's trail..."

"What trail, Lura? If one existed, he would have already gone."

"Perhaps he cannot go unless others go with him. It may be that Culos can only attack creatures of the Old Dark. If, as some say, Anlerran was kidnapped by Ruhal or an accomplice, then that may explain it. Or maybe he somehow understands that if she's too ill or wounded to walk, someone will need to help her."

"I for one mark this as the work of Ruhal, rather than a bold move by the *kin* or the *choragh* themselves. And I lay much of the blame for this at Garrok's feet."

"Let me be the one who goes with Culos, if he can somehow find her trail."

"Why you of all people?" Sudden anger flashed in the half-*illeagh*'s eyes. "What do you know about this, mercenary? I'll have the truth from you, too late though it is."

"I've given the matter some thought," Lura said. "I can think of only one man who would help Ruhal in this situation- and only then in return for money."

"Go on."

"Ruhal has a brother. His name is Jerrim. They've been on poor terms for many years, but Jerrim is a coldly practical man. If Ruhal promised him enough money, he would help. Jerrim is a loner, with no particular allegiances. And he has a considerable talent for sorcery. Enough perhaps to enter the camp and kidnap Anlerran, especially if the Powers have grown stronger in him. The strength of our witches has grown further in recent tennights. The same may have happened to many others, wouldn't you say?"

"Ruhal had only a few coins left when we searched him after his treachery," Elluron remarked. "How would he pay his brother?"

"He has a little money hidden in unlikely places. Distant places. I don't know where they are, but once he told me that it was all part of his preparing for the worst. Perhaps that desperate moment has arrived."

As Elluron pondered her words, Lura continued, "Let me take one of our witches. In fact, as this situation is Garrok's fault as much as anyone's, demand a favour from him. The most powerful of his ironmasters to accompany me. As for Ruhal- I have known him for longer than anyone else here. If he'll listen to anyone it'll be me. And if this isn't

Ruhal's work at all- though like you I suspect it is- then the strongest of Garrok's ironmasters may be able to overcome any *kin* that hold her. If not, we'll return and report what we've found."

"So you say." Elluron stared thoughtfully at her.

"If I fail, you'll be well rid of me," Lura continued, but he shook his head and gave her a disgusted look. "Spare me your self-pity, woman. If you really want to help and if Culos can lead you to Anlerran, then so be it. You may have to wait until after this war for your payment, however."

"I neither expect nor want payment." Lura wasn't sure whether she did or not, but the words came tumbling from her mouth regardless.

"What kind of mercenary are you?" A faint, tired smile creased Elluron's lips for a moment.

"A drunken one." Lura laughed tiredly then managed to draw herself upright. "I'll be sober soon enough though, and I'll lay off the sourgrass until Anlerran is rescued."

"So be it. I'll speak with Garrok. If he agrees, an ironmaster will come to you and you will leave after first light tomorrow. Maybe he can help you to stay sober. And if you make a mess of this, Lura, and Anlerran is harmed or killed as a result- then don't come back." He looked down suddenly, apparently engrossed in his maps again, and Lura took that as her prompt to leave.

As she breakfasted on the cold remains of last night's meat the following morning, Lura looked up to see a formidable-looking *orkar* woman standing nearby, clad in studded leather armour with a grey and brown cloak draped almost carelessly over it. "You're Lura," she said stonily.

Lura nodded, and swallowed the food in her mouth before replying. "And you are?"

"Merine Haal, ironmistress. I've been commanded by Lord Garrok to accompany you on your search for Anlerran."

"Iron*mistress*?" Lura shrugged. "I suppose that makes sense. Well Merinne, how would you rate our chances?"

"Of locating her or bringing her back alive? Those are two very different things."

"Both," Lura said uncertainly.

The *orkar* woman sat next to her and eyed the rest of the cold meat. Lura sighed and offered her some, then waited as patiently as she could while her companion devoured her breakfast. "From what I've heard the dog found her before, when you were in Steepleford," Merinne said thoughtfully afterwards. "I expect Ruhal told Lord Garrok about it some time ago."

"That was a little different," Lura pointed out.

"Perhaps. But I see no reason why the hound can't do it again, unless some *very* powerful sorcery has hidden their trail. The mystery to me is that he's waited here unsettling folk with his mournful howls, and not set off after her already. Maybe he can only kill or maim creatures of the Old Dark."

"That was my thought also. And our chances of bringing her back alive?"

"I suspect we'll have to kill both Ruhal and his co-conspirator, assuming he is behind this," Merinne said, "unless you really believe you can convince Ruhal to let her go. Do you? Or did you overstate your diplomatic capabilities when you spoke with Elluron? Lord Garrok reckoned perhaps the sourgrass had warmed your confidence a little too much."

"It has that effect. That's one of the reasons I drink, Merinne."

"Hmm. Be that as it may- you may have known Ruhal for a long time, Lura, but when a man turns- or a woman for that matter- all those years and memories mean nothing. He is damaged, probably beyond repair."

"He is not a weapon or a machine," Lura scowled.

"I observed him from a distance on occasion. He looked to me like a man who could not deal with the pressure and expectation of leadership, yet he clung to it grimly regardless.

A part of him knew he had nothing else even as he tried to convince himself that Anlerran was somehow his. A dying man will grab at anything to save himself. A man dying inside will do the same."

"Well, that's true enough," Lura said sadly.

"Are you prepared to kill him if you must? Or were you hoping to leave that unpleasant task to me?"

Lura found herself lost for words in the same instant as she admired the eloquence and insight of her companion. The idea that she might have to kill Ruhal- one of the few genuine friends she had ever had, quite apart from everything else that he meant- filled her with unspeakable horror.

"I'll do whatever must be done." Somehow the words struggled out of her mouth, and she couldn't be entirely sure that she believed them. Merinne nodded, apparently satisfied.

Lura felt oddly ashamed. *Merinne has far less reason than I to go on this mission,* she thought. *She's only obeying the orders she was unfortunate enough to be given, yet she readily accepts all the possible outcomes. Whereas I simply lie and say whatever sounds right for the situation.*

Then again, she silently added, *maybe it's easier to be following orders. What did Ruhal mean to you, Merinne? Were you at Wistport? You may have been, but I don't remember. I don't care to remember much about that day.*

Lura got up, stretched and winced as her muscles protested and her shoulder joints cracked. *I'm too old for all this,* she remarked morosely as she rubbed sleep from her eyes. *In fact, I ought to tell Elluron I've changed my mind and just walk away from all this. Find myself somewhere to wait for the end of the world.*

But instead she walked with Merinne over to where their horses had been saddled up. Elluron waited for them there, along with Culos who paced back and forth in agitation.

Lura went over to the dog and squatted down. "Can you lead us to Anlerran?" she asked, and flinched as he uttered a loud bark. The intense look in the hound's dark eyes unsettled her. She wondered for a moment if he would simply tear Ruhal's throat out if and when they found him.

"I'd say he can," Merinne commented dryly.

"Good luck," Elluron said as they were about to ride off. "And thank you."

Lura nodded and looked steadfastly ahead, not able to think of anything to say.

She caught sight of Iyoth and Kian as they reached the edge of the encampment, and slowed her horse as they waved. "So you're doing it," Iyoth called out.

"Nothing much else to live for," Lura retorted, giving the *du-luyan* man only the briefest of glances. "It has nothing to do with what you said yesterday, in case you wondered."

She thought she saw a smile on his face. "Good luck to you both," he said finally.

We'll need it, she thought. Glancing back a moment later she wished that Iyoth was with them. *But this is not his to make right,* she reminded herself. *It's mine.*

Kian and Iyoth watched as the two riders and dog disappeared into the distance, heading north-west. After they had vanished from sight, Kian turned to her father. "What did you talk to her about?"

"I appealed to her conscience," Iyoth said. "And a part of me wishes I hadn't."

IV

The softest of rain drifted down from a dull and leaden sky. It made barely a sound on the canopy that the two men had erected with a leather skin over sticks.

They were brothers, but had lived apart for many years. The elder, Jerrim, had been cast out by their mother more than twenty-five years ago. The younger, Ruhal, had become Warden of Mordenglen, a title and responsibility for which he had long been groomed. Weak in the Powers, he had nevertheless shown himself to have numerous strengths in other areas- considerable self-belief and charisma as well as a passion for defending those who lived under his jurisdiction. He had also developed an uncanny ability to rally people to whichever cause he took up as his own. Although he had never held jurisdiction over the far west, he had launched the battle for Wistport and brought about the eventual liberation of the port in the event of weak, indecisive leadership from local Wardens. The pirates of Anvar were routed, many of them butchered in the streets they had claimed as their own, their ships sunk or set ablaze, their reputation torn apart.

Yet Wistport had marked both Ruhal's zenith and the beginning of his downward arc. Some amongst his fighters had emerged from the red haze of Wistport with the blood of innocents on their hands. They had raped women, children and men, they had slaughtered simply because they could. Some of these were human, a few were *luyan*, some were *orkar*. The reputation of the *orkar* suffered the greatest because of the unspeakable crimes committed by a relative few of their number. Ruhal was hailed as a liberating hero in some corners and reviled in others, especially the southern parts of the Free Territories where the Wardens were in thrall to Inerdyr.

More recently, as the dark rumours from Aphenhast in the distant east grew into unavoidable truths he had once again gathered a force of those close to him- although now they were fewer in number- in order to attempt to unite all Harn to face of this existential threat.

But one by one they all betrayed me, he reminded himself as he sucked at the *kyush* pipe and felt the pungent smoke swirl down into the depths of his lungs and through the dark pulse of his blood. His vision swayed for a moment, and Jerrim appeared larger and more angular than he ought, his eyes swollen and red-rimmed, the veins in his hands like the jutting roots of an ancient tree. Ruhal raised a hand to ward off this apparition, and heard his brother utter a harsh, mocking laugh as his vision slowly returned to normal.

All of them, he thought, returning to his inner monologue. *Sarros. Lura. Kelandra and her fellow Watchers. Even Jahar would have done sooner or later, had he the chance.*

All except Anlerran, faithful even through the desperate hurt that Lura chose to inflict upon us both.

"It's a long way to the Wilderness even on horseback," Jerrim commented casually.

Ruhal coughed and wiped sweat from his forehead. "It's a long way to most places."

"There's nothing there, you realise. Once you ride between Uythar and the northern tip of the Wistledge, a few leagues later you'll see for yourself. It really is a place where one abandons all hope. Perhaps that's what you intend." He took a puff of *kyush* and laughed suddenly. "But I suppose it doesn't really matter where you go. You'll never be able to escape yourself."

Ruhal shrugged, ignoring the jibe. "Maybe the starspawn will claim all Aona. But it will take time. I'll do what I can with the time I have left."

"As you huddle together in the harsh desert night? Such a delightful picture." Jerrim looked across at Anlerran, who still lay unconscious on the grass. Her wrists and ankles had been tied, which struck Ruhal as entirely unnecessary. Jerrim had already shielded her from the Powers- and without those she was incapable of presenting any sort of threat to him. *And she'll be glad enough that we took her away from all our enemies,* Ruhal quickly reminded himself. *They would have used her as nothing more than a weapon with which to wage war on the* marandaal- *a hopeless war.*

"You paid me less than half the amount we agreed," Jerrim complained. "If we were not brothers, I would have killed you for lying to me."

"You've killed for much less in your time, and I'm sure familial bonds would never stop you," Ruhal observed. "But the remainder will be paid at the end of our journey. That much I promise. We already talked about this." He inhaled his *kyush* deeply once again, and bowed his head for a while, listening to nothing more than the faint roar and pulse of the blood in his veins as he closed his eyes and tumbled through the darkness in his head.

"I hope that's the truth, Ruhal," Jerrim said, and then added cheerfully, "If it isn't, I'll kill both of you. But for the moment I'm still concerned that a party of would-be rescuers may be sent, even as far as here. I imagine the little witchling is quite precious to them. They shouldn't be able to find us of course, but they may come across us by accident. It depends how many they send and the number of groups. There's no warding against ill luck, wouldn't you say?"

"Ill luck has ruined me," Ruhal lamented.

Jerrim found that amusing. "If you say so, dear brother."

Anlerran had slowly regained consciousness as Ruhal and Jerrim talked. She listened to their conversation, kept her eyes shut and remained as still as she possibly could. Frantic, desperate thoughts rushed through her head. Jerrim, who she felt certain was the man who had captured her, was a sorcerer of considerable strength, and even now that he had shielded her Anlerran could feel his malign presence. He was not *kin*, just a renegade- a mercenary warlock of sorts. *I should have warned everyone that Ruhal would come back for me or send someone,* she thought miserably.

She tried to think back to the moment of her capture, but couldn't remember much at all. A movement in the darkness of her tent, her failed attempt to grasp the Powers, panic rising inside her, and then... nothing. Somehow Jerrim must have made his way in and out of the camp without anyone noticing- not even Culos or her father, never mind Kian or Ileana or the Watchers. How could he have managed such a thing?

Anlerran tentatively reached towards the Powers in her mind, and could tell instantly that the shield remained in place. It felt like a weight that pressed against her from all sides, an almost suffocating presence. She couldn't even begin to work out how to remove it. *I didn't even know such a thing was possible,* she thought ruefully. *But I have to keep hoping there's a way out of this.*

A little later, Ruhal gently shook her shoulder. She knew he was about to try and rouse her, for the odours of sweat and *kyush* became stronger as he loomed nearby. "Anlerran?"

"She may take a little while to come to," Jerrim spoke up, but Anlerran had already decided to stir. Blearily she opened her eyes and saw Jerrim for the first time. *He said they were brothers,* she recalled, *and he does look a lot like Ruhal. Even more than I expected. Yet he's different- he doesn't have that crazed, passionate look. Instead he's cold, merciless. Ruhal stumbled from one irrational episode to the next; I expect Jerrim plans for every eventuality.*

Anlerran noticed that their campfire, although made from wooden twigs, was completely smokeless. She didn't need to have use of the Powers to know that they were at play here.

"We are similar to look at, Ruhal and I," Jerrim said with a smile as he interpreted her look. "Not identical as you can see, but close enough. In fact, Ruhal- ever the sensible and practical one in our younger days- has become more and more like me in recent times. I'd go as far as to say he's *worse* than I ever was. Would you agree, Ruhal? More interestingly, do you think our mother would agree?"

Ruhal stared at Jerrim. "I didn't choose this path. It was forced upon me."

"It was forced upon Anlerran, certainly," Jerrim said, and winked at her.

"I wish all this could have happened differently," Ruhal sighed. He turned to Anlerran and his hand reached out to stroke her cheek. It felt warm and damp, as if he suffered some kind of fever. Anlerran forced herself to look into his eyes, trying not to shrink back too much for fear of angering him, and he smiled at her. To Anlerran the expression looked both sad and deranged.

"Well, I'll let you murmur your sweet nothings to each other," Jerrim said cheerfully. He got up and wandered off a short distance, perhaps to look out in case they were being followed.

"Circumstances change so quickly," Ruhal murmured. "It seems that only a moment ago I was being held prisoner by your father and everyone else who turned against me."

And now you're holding me prisoner, Anlerran thought. *There's a cruel irony.*

"Ruhal, it pains me to be shielded from the Powers," she murmured, firstly having made sure that Jerrim was still busy in his contemplation. "I would never run away from you or harm you. Maybe you can ask Jerrim…"

But Ruhal had already shaken his head, and interrupted her. "Jerrim doesn't trust you, Anlerran. He doesn't know you as I do. My brother is a hard and calculating man."

"And a sensible one," Jerrim called out without turning to face them. *The Powers enhance his hearing,* Anlerran thought. *I should have known. I must be careful not to try that again unless he wanders off somewhere further away for a while. But I don't think he will.*

"I will pay my brother his due when we reach the vicinity of Uythar," Ruhal continued. "I have some gold hidden there."

"So you say." Jerrim looked round and grinned almost as if he relished the prospect of *not* being paid.

"He will release the shield then, and we'll continue on our way," Ruhal explained.

"If she behaves herself," Jerrim added. "Don't even think of escape, Anlerran. We both value you too much to ever let you go. In different ways."

"She may well want to escape *you,* but why me?" Ruhal rejoined, and Anlerran almost joined in when Jerrim laughed.

"I'll release her when I have my payment and we've reached our destination," Jerrim added for good measure when he returned. "That's the situation, Ruhal. One of the effects of the Powers- not that you'd really know- is that you are always acutely aware of what others can do with them."

"Anlerran wouldn't harm you if I..."

"Is she not one of the three witches who burned Inerdyr alive?" Jerrim cut across, giving his younger brother a hard stare. "Or do I have my facts wrong?" When Ruhal hesitated he continued sharply, "I won't change my mind, so don't beg me again. Begging disgusts me. Even now you're better than that- aren't you?"

The night passed, warm with the promise of spring. The following morning dawned bright and clear with the cover of cloud having rolled away westwards. After feeding her some of their breakfast, Ruhal said softly to Anlerran, "I must apologise."

Anlerran looked guardedly at him. "Apologise?" *Where would you even begin?* she thought.

"We should never have gone to the Rhunin. I realise that now."

"Ruhal, I led us there. Do you remember?" She bit her lip and hoped that he didn't consider her words a transgression.

But Ruhal was too caught up in his own explanation. "If we'd chosen another path- if we'd remained in the middle north and raised our army from within the settlements, we would never have encountered your father. It was because of *him* that all this happened. It was because of *him* that we ended up here this day, as fugitives."

Anlerran nodded slowly a couple of times and tried to look as if she was mulling the matter over and arriving at the same conclusion. The act appeared to work, because he continued, "Yes, do you see? He drove a wedge between us, and matters were never the same after that."

"They never were," Anlerran agreed faintly.

"He couldn't bear to see you with anyone else, and so he had no choice but to usurp me. I know my method of getting you back was crude, but think on this- sooner or later he would have made you his. He would have lain with you, perhaps to create more part-*illeagh* children. I saw the way he looked at you. He longed to plant his strange seed in your womb."

You live in a world where your delusions are the only truth, Anlerran thought. *You create suspicions to fuel your hatred and to justify your actions, and then you embellish them with ever more fanciful notions.*

With an effort she looked at him. "Would he?" she asked tremulously. "Do you think he would have done?"

"Undoubtedly." Ruhal's smile was righteously grim but Anlerran could still detect a glimmer of triumph in his eyes. "There is little that Elluron would not do. What, after all, do we truly know of his nature? Remember that he abandoned you, his infant child. It was up to me to help take you to a place of safety, to occasionally watch over you from a distance over the years, and then rescue you from the Old Dark when it rose in Mordenglen."

Anlerran imagined him watching over her as she grew up and felt sick inside.

"Then there's Lura," Ruhal added quietly, and Anlerran willed herself to remain calm. "She came to me when I was weak, in a deliberate attempt to destroy everything we had. I should have resisted her, but Lura can be persuasive, even though she's a no-good drunk and much of the time she's ruled by her anger. Well, I don't need to tell you. You have seen Lura for yourself."

Yes, I've seen Lura for myself, and she is more or less what she is. Anlerran fixed her attention on the trees and surrounding grassland, even the distant storm clouds that might reach them before evening. She had to do something to hide the fury that stirred within her once again. *You, on the other hand, seem to be many people. And that inner darkness you spoke of has washed over you now like a black tide. I see very little of the man I thought I knew. Instead I see a desperate, irrational fugitive who'll say anything at all to keep alive the myth of his own innocence.*

That evening, after another day's ride they crawled under the canopy just as the first fat, heavy raindrops began to fall. Later Anlerran's wrists were untied, and she was fed some broth and dry bread from the men's rations. It tasted foul and some of the vegetables used to make it were rotten, but she forced it down, reminding herself that she had no idea when or if she would be fed again.

Jerrim had a little to drink from one of the large skins of cider he had shown Ruhal earlier. Anlerran hoped that he would drink enough to make him at least less capable and watchful- she retained a faint hope that the shield might break or be breakable- but she suspected that Ruhal's brother was too sensible to allow his attention to slip when he had so much at stake, and she was proved right. Ruhal, however held no such inhibitions, and he became increasingly erratic as the evening passed, to the point where eventually he slumped forward, muttering senselessly to himself and occasionally looking up, startled by something imaginary. At one point he even scrambled to his feet and staggered out into the rain. Anlerran watched through the gap in the tent fabric as he stood with arms outstretched and screamed at the sky as if he had dared an unseen force to do battle with him.

Jerrim glanced at Ruhal's antics with wry amusement before fixing his cold gaze on Anlerran. "I do hope I'm invited to the wedding," he said.

V

Lura stared out from the shelter afforded by the tall poplar trees, lost not so much in thought as in memory. The steady roar of the rain, heavy against the upper leaves, melted into the background as she recalled the very different sounds of a bustling city scene in the distant past on a very different day.

She had met Ruhal for the first time in Mornkastle, eighteen years ago. He had looked out of place in the city, she remembered thinking. He had been part of a group of young men with the Warden of Mordenglen of that time. Less muscular than he later became. Less at ease with people.

Less angry. Less unpredictable.

The Warden had sought swords-for-hire to help police the southern perimeter of the Mordenglen district. That area had fallen into a state that would then have been considered lawlessness but which these days would have passed for normality. His men were there to help select the most useful from those men and women who hoped for employment. Lura had been selected and ended up spending more than a tennight firstly under Ruhal's tutelage and then, once the Warden was satisfied with her progress, as a compatriot and equal.

He called me beautiful, Lura recalled. *It took him almost that entire time, but he managed to say it eventually. I even believed him. I glowed when he looked at me and stammered those words. I felt as if I'd been lifted up in the air.*

I'm not beautiful now. In any case the ugliness inside people starts to show after a while, no matter how they might look.

"Are you hungry? You don't look it."

Lura roused herself and looked across at Merinne, who had unwrapped a few portions of salted beef. She offered her some of the meat and Lura took it, realising that she was hungrier than she had expected. Despite the growing dread in her stomach, she managed to eat. Merinne also gave some to Culos, and the great hound gulped it down in barely more than a couple of bites. Afterwards he stared intently at Merinne as she ate her own portion.

Lura felt a little better with some food inside her. She reached for her flask of sourgrass, but Merinne grabbed her wrist firmly. "No," she said, her voice like stone. "If we rescue the girl, you may drink yourself into oblivion if you wish. But not until then. Did you not promise Elluron that you'd remain sober until the task is done?"

Lura thought of arguing with the *orkar* woman, but an unsettling picture came to her mind of Ruhal watching in distaste as she drunkenly begged him to release Anlerran, even offering to lay with him one last time before he put her out of her misery.

Once the rain had eased off a little later, Merinne left to scout ahead. Culos went with her, leaving Lura alone with her dismal thoughts.

They returned with the sky almost fully dark. The clouds had lifted in the west and several stars gleamed in the open sky.

"We are nearer than I thought," Merinne said as she sat down. Culos settled between them with a sigh that Lura thought sounded frustrated.

Lura felt a knot tighten in her stomach. "How near?"

"A league, no more than that. I sensed the Powers being used- or rather, a kind of construct that someone had made to shield someone from using them. Like a net placed over someone and then tied. Not something I have come across before."

"Jerrim," Lura said immediately.

"More than likely. Anyway I took the precaution of masking my own sorcery as best I could and watched the three of them from a distance for a while."

"Is Anlerran hurt?"

"She didn't appear to be, although it was difficult to tell from where I hid. I think we need to move quickly tomorrow morning, at first light, and make sure Jerrim is dealt with first. If I can break the spell he's wrapped around Anlerran then perhaps she can then help us. Not a precise plan, but it's all I have." Merinne added a little more of their wood to the fire. "You should sleep awhile," she commented. "I'll wake you later."

Lura wrapped herself up in one of their blankets and lay down, but sleep would not come. After a while she suggested to Merinne that the *orkar* woman sleep in her stead, and watched enviously as Merinne fell asleep within moments.

Lura stared into the flames for what could have been an age, lost in thoughts that circled endlessly through her mind. *I can't do this,* she told herself many times, but she knew the awful truth- that she was already doing it and that it would end in her death.

So be it, she thought savagely as the small hours wore on. *Let the end come quickly, because I'm done with it all.*

The following morning, they continued along the path and eventually came to an area where bracken-infested scrub sloped down towards the base of a shallow valley. From this point as the land dropped gradually away the vegetation thinned out towards the grassy plain below. Their motion had made no sound, an effect of Merinne's sorcery that she had employed to quieten their progress.

Next to a rocky outcrop in the valley Lura saw a small camp had been set up, maybe two hundred paces away. Flames licked around the pile of wood that had been made for the campfire, but Lura noticed that no smoke rose from it at all, although the fire had been made from twigs and small branches.

Merinne glanced up into the clear dawn sky where several of the brighter stars still lingered. "Good. The air is as calm as possible, not even a hint of breeze."

"Will that help us?" Lura queried.

Merinne nodded. "That's my hope. With any luck they won't even see us until we're there." When Lura looked doubtfully at her she continued quietly, "A spell that my people only seldom use, and only then in battle against an especially dangerous foe. Remember, we must prevent Anlerran from harm if we can. If we reach the camp without being seen, we must act quickly and decisively. I will deal with Jerrim. You must ensure Ruhal cannot harm Anlerran, no matter what."

Lura tried to imagine how such power could be brought to bear. *Is she truly the strongest of Garrok's ironmasters and ironmistresses?* she wondered. *Was his remorse so strong?*

Their walk down the slope and as far as the camp passed in a blur for Lura. Her fear had vanished- no doubt only temporarily- replaced by an odd, calm detachment. She barely noticed as Jerrim suddenly noticed them and seized the Powers. As Merinne and Jerrim became locked in a battle of wills, Ruhal stared perplexed at Lura. "What are you doing?" he demanded. "Why are you here? Do you want to die?!"

"Disarm yourself," Lura heard herself say, as she glanced quickly at Anlerran. Had Merinne been able to release her from Jerrim's shielding? Lura had no talent in the Powers so couldn't say one or the other. "I don't want to kill you, Ruhal. Lay down your weapons."

Suddenly Lura felt the air nearby buckle and somehow become heavier, and her vision swayed. Out of the corner of her eye she saw Merinne sag to the ground, and Jerrim step towards her, although he moved slowly and appeared to struggle to stay upright.

Then Anlerran moved suddenly, her arms outstretched towards the wounded Jerrim, who turned to face her but too late. Something invisible slammed into him and snapped his body backwards and nearly in two. Lura heard the sickening sound of his bones break before he fell.

"Jerrim!" Ruhal screamed. "No!"

Lura tried to stay on her feet. The sudden release of the Powers had caused the air to swirl one way and the other at random, as if tiny dust devils came in and out of existence. "Ruhal, please..." she began, but the violent wind tore the words away. Regardless of whether he had heard or not, Ruhal charged at her and Lura retreated, forced into desperate defence as he hacked wildly and screamed nonsense at her. Lura glanced at Anlerran for a brief moment and shouted her name. *I can't stop him alone,* she thought as Ruhal continued to advance, inflicting wounds on her arms and another in her side which slowed her down. But Anlerran looked frozen with fear and indecision. "Kill him!" Lura shrieked, knowing that she was done for if Anlerran failed to help her.

The wound in her side bled profusely. Blood soaked through her shirt. The pain made her slow to react and Ruhal pressed onwards with murder in his eyes.

Somehow Lura summoned the strength to launch a counterattack and cut him on his arm. Ruhal screamed with rage and lunged forward, careless as to the consequences, and Lura saw her chance. She side-stepped and with every last remaining ounce of strength delivered a scything stroke that cut through his belly and side. Ruhal howled in anguish and fell to his knees. He opened his mouth but could utter no words. The wind dropped to an eerie, absolute calm at the same time.

"Put an end to him," Lura heard Merinne murmur weakly from behind her. "Make it a quick kindness."

Lura grimaced and gasped with the pain of her side wound. She could barely breathe without being gripped by agony. Again she looked to Anlerran, but the young witch sat with her head bowed and eyes closed. Perhaps whatever effort she had expended in overcoming Jerrim had left her spent.

Ruhal had lost hold of his sword. Lura kicked it into the longer grass nearby and stared down at him as he swayed on his knees. He neither begged for his life nor conceded defeat. "She's *mine*," he spat, flecks of blood and spittle around his mouth. "Why are you... here? They'll never..." He grimaced in pain as blood leaked between the fingers of the hand that clutched his stomach. "Go back, Lura. You're not... not a hero..." Agony gripped him again. Finally, he looked up and said through clenched teeth, his eyes wide and mad: "*I never loved you.*"

"You're lying," she whispered, and he laughed at her.

Lura swung her sword at his head in a slow arc. It cut through his jaw and sent blood and bone through the air. She collapsed to the ground and heard Anlerran's cries of anguish as her consciousness faded.

VI

When Lura came to, she had been wrapped in a thick blanket and propped up against a tree. A small fire had been lit, and Anlerran and Merinne sat by it. Culos prowled some distance away, restless and sombre.

She reached down and felt a tightness around her middle. Her wound had been thickly bandaged, and she could smell healing ointment. Anlerran and Merinne turned to look as she tried to sit up a little straighter. Anlerran said nothing, and Lura had no idea what the girl might be thinking. All sorts of dreadful expressions mingled when she glanced at her.

"How is the pain?" Merinne asked as she saw Lura stir.

"It could be worse."

63

"I found the bandages and an ointment I recognised amongst Jerrim's belongings," Merinne explained. "I'm no healer myself, but with any luck it will do until we arrive back at camp."

"You could have let Ruhal go," Anlerran said quietly.

"No." Merinne shook her head. "We could not. Ruhal was some way past the point at which men negotiate. What do you think would have happened if we let him go? What would you say happens when you grant mercy to madmen?"

Anlerran said nothing.

"We are about to fight the *marandaal,* Anlerran. An enemy that does not comprehend surrender, weakness, dialogue. People will die in their many thousands. This isn't a time of kindness."

The young witch remained silent for a short while. Finally she nodded tiredly and said, "I used to think that the time for kindness was whenever it might be needed most. But you're right. I never truly knew him, yet he was not the man I met in Mordenglen, nor even the man who ventured with us into the deep Rhunin and the lair of the *illeagh.*"

"Where is his body?" Lura asked quietly.

"I made a small pyre some way from the edge of the woods," Merinne told her, "and placed a ward so it could not be disturbed. When you're able to, we'll go to cremate him. And Jerrim too, if you wish."

"Ruhal's family have always buried their dead," Lura pointed out, then smiled thinly as a thought occurred to her. "That said, cremation removes any chance that they might return to this world as *diafagh.* And dead men have no say in the matter. So let's burn them both, and burn the past with it."

Lura could barely look down at Ruhal's broken face as she and Merinne lifted him onto the pyre. *Will I see it in my sleep every night for the rest of my life?* she wondered as they placed Jerrim alongside his brother.

Merinne lit the wood with the help of a scattering of firepowder, and flames leapt eagerly to claim the bodies. The three women stepped back from the heat and watched as the brothers burned to ash. Finally, when only embers and the harsh white contours of bones remained, they turned and left.

Lura wondered bleakly to herself what emotions would assail her next. But as they rode slowly away south, she felt nothing at all- only an emptiness that stretched away forever in her heart.

They finally arrived back in the camp around mid-afternoon. Lura was barely able to stay awake and had to be helped from her horse and taken swiftly to the hospital tent. As word of their return spread and people swiftly gathered around, Elluron caught Anlerran in a hug that almost took her breath away, then shouted for healers to attend. "I had thought you gone," he whispered in her ear as he helped slowly bear her away to recover.

"So did I," Anlerran murmured with a faint smile. She almost slumped against him, exhausted.

"We'll set more guardsmen and a couple of ironmasters around you from now," he continued grimly, but she shook her head. "No, father. I'm at no more risk now than anyone else. Ruhal is dead at Lura's hand."

"I'll thank her when she's recovered."

Anlerran shook her head grimly. "Were I you, I'd never again speak of Ruhal to her."

The following day, Lura felt well enough to walk around. Her wound healed quickly, helped by the attentions of *orkar* healers. *I reckon I'll be as slow as an old grandmother for a while though,* she thought, wincing as she took a walk around the edge of the encampment in the morning sunshine. In the distant north-west, storm clouds massed but here it felt almost spring-like.

She saw Iyoth walking towards her, and stopped, although her heart began to race. *What is wrong with you?* she tiredly asked herself.

"You heal well for a human," Iyoth commented.

"Thank you. You're polite for a *du-luyan*," she retorted, and couldn't help but smile when he laughed out loud. "You're also in unusually good cheer," she added.

"And why not? You rescued Anlerran, so my daughter is happy. You also managed to come back without a limb or even your head missing. I'm impressed, Lura."

"Thank you." She almost added, *Maybe you're impressed enough to lay with me later?* but managed to stop just in time and remind herself that Iyoth was probably the only man in the camp she could call a friend. *Don't ruin a good friendship like you've ruined everything else!* she savagely berated herself.

"I know what the emptiness is like," Iyoth added bluntly.

Lura had no idea what to say to that unexpected insight so she just nodded and carried on walking, full of hope and dread that he would walk with her.

But he didn't, and she spent the day in the dismal company of her own thoughts, and the memory of a long-ago summer in Mordenglen when her world had been a place of bright hope.

III – Fear From Within

I

Many years had passed since the last time Arin allowed himself to even think of the Powers. Brought up in the South, where anyone found to possess a hint of such talent was arrested and summarily executed, he had learned from a young age to hide them from everyone. Arin had concealed them so well that even Watchers would not have discovered his true nature. As time went on masking the Powers became second nature to him.

But sorcery- both the strange darkness that was synonymous with the Free Territories and the equally mysterious magic wielded by Watchers- had never been far from his thoughts over the last few days.

He and Elina had fled the manor house along with everyone else when they learned of the chaos that swiftly spread from the centre of Telith. The other servants had gone their own ways, most of them in the hope of finding their families and then putting as much distance as possible between themselves and the town. Elina had no family, so she had stayed with him.

How could the Watchers allow this to happen? had been his first question, but it had soon become evident that the Watchers were the cause of the mayhem. Some had gone mad, abandoned their duties and killed people at random. Some had fought each other. A few had fled Telith, although no one knew where they were headed. To the sounds of screams and the ominous sight of flames from burning buildings as fires took hold, he and Elina rode north-east along one of the smaller roads. The acrid stench of smoke drifted into the sky behind them.

They had travelled for two leagues north-east, when they saw a lone figure in the middle of the road ahead.

Arin brought his horse to a halt and motioned for Elina to do the same. The cloaked figure had been facing away, but now turned slowly to regard them. "It's a Watcher," Elina whispered. "We've no chance if..."

"Wait here." Arin dismounted, and stepped forward cautiously. Something told him that if matters took a turn for the worse then he would be better defending himself on foot rather than having to try staying astride a frightened animal.

"No, my lord! You can't fight it!"

Arin barely heard her. He began to walk slowly towards the Watcher. "Folk in the town are saying you have all abandoned your duties, my lord Watcher," he said politely, trying to quell his fear. Ordinarily he would never have dared to speak to one of the peacekeepers of Telith without being prompted, but protocol hardly mattered now. Yet he couldn't be sure that the Powers within him, completely hidden for so long, would come to his aid if needed. *What are you doing?* an anxious voice in his head demanded. *Turn and find another path! This creature can kill you in an instant!*

"Is it true?" he asked. "If it is, may I ask why?"

The Watcher walked slowly towards him. The sun slanted down to illuminate the lower half of his face, while the brim of his hat shaded the hard blue eyes that stared intently at Arin. Inexplicably, he grinned. Arin had never seen a Watcher so much as smile before. Inside, he struggled to control the Powers as they began to burn through every part of his being. "My lord Watcher, Telith lies in chaos," he said. "The town is burning."

"And the people with it," the Watcher added. "Fire holds no prejudice. I myself listened to the screams of the dying."

Arin stared at him. "I don't understand. Why has the town been abandoned? Why are people being executed or burned alive? Have orders been received from the Seven? Or..."

Without any warning the Watcher's expression became one of cold, venomous hatred. He ran straight at Arin.

The Powers leapt from Arin's body in immediate response and slammed into the ground between them, transforming the patchy earth to deep mud into which the Watcher began to sink. As his adversary strained to reach him, Arin concentrated on removing the heat from the air around the Watcher. After a short while frost began to cover the Watcher's body, but even as it did Arin felt pain soar through his body and a constriction around his heart as the Watcher stared balefully at him. He fell to his knees, unable to breathe and helpless as the agony intensified. Shapes and colours danced at the edges of his vision.

Then Elina rushed past him as he fell forwards. "No," he whispered as he managed to lift his head up to see her swing her axe straight at the trapped Watcher's head. As the blade cut through the Watcher's face, Arin's crippling pain vanished and he swiftly redoubled his efforts. More frost began to coat the Watcher's head, only to evaporate immediately in the pale morning sunlight. Elina hacked at the Watcher again, even as she almost sank in the softened ground. This time the Watcher's head split in two and the blow severed part of the skull.

Elina staggered back as Arin got to his feet and slowly made his way over to her. The two of them stared at the exposed brain of the dead Watcher. Thin, coloured threads wound their way through the glistening flesh. Parts of the brain even appeared to glow. Arin had never seen anything like it before.

Elina wiped the axe blade as clean as she could on the grass. Her hands shook. She glanced fearfully at Arin, and when he made as if to try and comfort her she backed away, then walked swiftly back to her horse and jumped up into the saddle. She kept her eyes fixed upon him as he caught up with her.

"I need to explain something to you," he began, but Elina interrupted. "I don't know what you are, Lord Arin, and I don't wish to know. Maybe I should take my chances on my own."

"I'm no longer lord of anything," he pointed out, but Elina had already urged her horse onwards, thankfully not in the direction of the town. He followed, wondering how he might explain what he had done and if he would even get the chance.

A little later as they stopped at a fast-flowing stream for themselves and the horses to drink from, Elina said grimly, "We killed a Watcher, my Lord."

"I'm not your *lord,* Elina. We're simply two people without a home, like many others."

Elina took a swig of cold water, shuddered and said nothing.

"You saved my life," Arin pointed out quietly after a short while. "I'm in your debt."

"If we'd ridden the other way and done what we could to avoid him, none of this need have happened," she pointed out.

"He would probably have attacked us anyway. They've gone mad."

"Did you know that for sure? I don't see how you could have done. I think you couldn't help yourself. Something-some part of you- made you confront the Watcher."

Arin didn't want to think about that.

"Maybe all the Watchers have become lightdreamers, and now they're intent on spreading their insanity to hasten the end of the world," Elina said. "I saw five lightdreamers together a tennight ago when I was at the market in Telith. Folk have seen more and more of them now even this far west. Maybe Watchers are not immune to that madness."

"It's possible." Arin frowned. Elina's theory was plausible and deeply troubling.

"What did you do to it?" Elina asked. "Something happened to make him fall into the ground, and then I saw *frost* form on his face. *You* did that."

"I have a certain... talent in the Powers," Arin said quietly.

"I knew it. You're a sorceror." Elina shuddered and looked away. "A warlock. You deal in the forbidden arts."

"Elina, what happens to anyone south of the Never-Built Wall who is found to have the slightest ability where such things are concerned?" he asked.

"The Watchers take them away. Everyone knows that."

"They take them away and execute them. That has been the law as laid down by the Seven for centuries. So anyone with strength in the Powers learns from a young age that if they want to survive they need to find a way to hide their nature. I found such a way, so that even Watchers would be unable to detect the truth about me."

Elina shook her head in disbelief. "I can't believe that for the last six years I've been working for a warlock."

"I can't guarantee you much, Elina, but I can safely say it hasn't affected your employment in any way," Arin remarked dryly.

"Are you like those mad ones in the north, who can curse you with no more than a look and a sign in the air?"

He sighed. "No one can curse another person so easily, Elina. The Old Powers are only what they are, neither more nor less. A tool in the wrong hands is very different to the same tool in the right hands, but it's still nothing more than a tool."

"Perhaps." Elina looked far from convinced.

"This fear of sorcery is something that the Seven have instilled in people over long centuries through the Watchers and those who work as their spies and enforcers. As you know, one of the first things taught to children in our schools- those fortunate enough to attend such places- is that the Old Powers are inherently evil, a mad sorcery used by the forces of chaos and depravity beyond the Never-Built Wall. It's all part of ensuring that the folk of the south remain pliable yet wary of the threat from the so-called wild lands."

"They *are* wild. The truce in Mornkastle exists for a very good reason. Even *I* know that, and I didn't go to school for more than two years."

"Do you really think the sky turns dark and the dead come swarming out of the ground as soon as you set foot beyond that arbitrary line?" Arin almost shouted.

Elina cringed. "I've heard stories..."

"Everyone hears stories. Worse than that, everyone listens to them. A vile rumour spreads faster than a good one, and it's always been thus."

"There may be others like you," Elina ventured after a short while. "Others who have managed to hide their abilities somehow."

"Yes," Arin agreed, "and I think it's time that we found them."

Elina scrambled to her feet and stared at him in disbelief. "Why would we want to do *that*?!"

"Because," Arin said patiently, "much of the South has more than likely fallen into chaos, and in such times it may be wise to seek out others who are the same, for common protection. At the least it's a risk that may be worth taking."

"But how would you even do that?"

"I can sense others with strength in the Powers. I've been able to ever since I can remember. Even those who can hide their abilities from normal folk, or Watchers, come to that. It isn't always easy, but I can do it. I can remember dozens of times when I looked at a person and knew they harboured forbidden sorcery. So if we come across such people, then we should do whatever we can to encourage them to join with us."

Elina shook her head. "I'd rather we didn't."

"Elina, if you want to stand a chance of surviving this madness, I advise you to stay with me and whoever we find." Arin saw the poorly-concealed look of fear in her eyes and relented. "These are troubled times no matter where we go. Like it or not, our best chance of survival may lie with others like me."

She nodded reluctantly. "I hope you're right. But I'm not sure I believe you."

II

Over the next tennight they came across settlements gripped in chaos as Arin had expected, and one that had burned almost entirely to the ground. They found a few other places where the villagers had tried to organise themselves into some kind of ramshackle militia. They would be no match for a single Watcher, but Arin didn't have the heart to tell them that. In each village he looked for people who might possess a trace of talent in the Powers, but found no one. Luckily they encountered no Watchers either.

Arin began to wonder if they might be looking in the wrong places. *Would any folk with sorcerous abilities have revealed themselves even now?* he asked himself. *If I had grown up in one of these close-knit villages where superstition is a cornerstone of life I would likely have fled given the chance, and made my own way. Then again I'm alone except for Elina. If I had a family I would have taken them with me somewhere, and hidden away.*

But where would such people flee to?

They found a man busy ransacking one of the storehouses in an abandoned village through which they passed. He hastily filled his pack with food, working as quickly as possible. A horse stood tethered and waiting fractiously nearby, already burdened with a couple of suspiciously full saddlebags.

As he heard their approach, the man- thin and lined and with tanned skin- pulled a dagger from his belt. "I'll be gone in a moment," he said warily, his sharp gaze flitting between the two of them. "There's enough here for you both as well. Too much for me to carry it all. No need to fight for it, is there?"

Arin noted the look of desperation in his eyes and raised a hand to placate the stranger. "We had no intention of fighting you for it. Haven't we all seen more than enough bloodshed to last us a lifetime?"

"There'll be more," the man said grimly. He added a bundle of saltmeat, dried fruit and grain to his pack and threw a look back over his shoulder as he continued, "I've ridden all the way from Mornkastle. Have you heard about what happened there?"

"The Watchers turned against the people?"

"Yes, but many say that it all *started* in Mornkastle. An army has marched from out of the distant north. All manner of creatures form its ranks. *Orkar* beasts, witches and warlocks, terrible creatures of chaos..."

"Witches and warlocks? People who wield the Powers? Are you certain?"

"Certain as I can be. The Lord Warden of Mornkastle himself made a speech about it. He warned that the enemy would ransack the city and that everyone should be prepared."

"And did they?"

"I don't know. Maybe they have by now. Truthfully, I don't think they needed to attack the city to bring it to its knees. No, they used sorcery instead, to sow seeds of chaos within Mornkastle without assailing the city walls. I saw it myself before I fled. They must have done something to the Watchers. I don't know what it was or how they did it; I don't care to know. But some of the Watchers turned on the people. Others just left the city either on their own or in small groups. Some even killed themselves." The man shook his head grimly. "Now, I *know* that some powerful weave of sorcery must have been brought to bear for such things to happen. The Watchers' oaths have been binding without fail for centuries. But some evil has reached out and maligned them."

"You may be right," Elina spoke up, "because the same has happened in Telith, and maybe every town and city across the land. Every settlement that we've seen, be it large or small has fallen into chaos."

The man stopped attending to his saddlebags and looked worried. Arin dismounted and wandered over to the storehouse as the man fastened his backpack and got back on his horse, still looking worriedly in Elina's direction. "Avoid Telith, if you're headed west," Arin said, noting that the rider had already turned his horse in that direction. "Avoid everywhere you can."

The man from Mornkastle nodded his thanks and rode swiftly away along the dirt track.

Over the next few days Arin and Elina encountered several more wandering refugees. Two of them were from Mornkastle and told much the same story that the first man had given, along with other rumours from around the middle lands. "You seem intent on finding this marauding army," Elina commented as they stopped to rest and eat at noon. "Is that wise?"

"I don't know if it's wise or not, but it's an option we should consider. If they are more or less what people are saying then for better or worse, I am one of them- or I could be."

"How is a landowner of Telith like a lawless hedge-witch?" Elina pointed out. "You're a civilised man, Arin."

"I fear the time of civilisation as you and I have known it may be at an end."

Later that afternoon Arin and Elina drew close to a ruined castle set on a low hill next to scrubland. Arin recalled that its name was Hevvin's Mount, although he couldn't recall who Hevvin had been. The rambling structure had stood abandoned for centuries, although it had been built well and its walls were mostly still intact even if the roofs had caved in here and there.

As the path ahead narrowed and they slowed so they could ride in single file, Arin thought for a moment that he could sense a presence of some sort up amongst the ruins. He drew his horse to a halt and peered towards the great fortress. *Yes,* he thought suddenly, and he could feel the Powers begin to stir quietly within his body in response to a poorly-masked concentration of sorcery somewhere within the castle.

"What is it?" Elina glanced warily at him.

"There are people up there," Arin said quietly. "Some of them are like me."

"Then let's be away from here before they see us," Elina implored.

Arin shook his head. "They'll more than likely know we're here. We should speak with them, ask them to join us. Or join *them* perhaps, if they'll allow it."

"But what if they…"

A faint rushing sound came through the air and a split second later an arrow struck a rock next to them. Elina squealed and calmed her horse, then looked fiercely at Arin. "Let's get out of here!"

She cursed loudly as Arin swiftly dismounted and took a couple of steps towards the castle. "We mean no harm," he called out as he raised both arms, "but we need shelter. Can you help us?"

"What are you doing?" Elina hissed. "Let's get out of here!"

"I'm like you," Arin continued loudly. "I know what you are, and I'm the same."

From one of the dark archways of the castle two figures stepped forth, both of them armed with shortbows. Arin was taken aback to see that they were young boys, perhaps no more than seven years old. One of them was human, the other *luyan*.

"Go away!" the human boy shouted. "Go away or we'll fill you both full of arrows!"

Arin took a single, slow step forward. "Please," he implored, and bent down to place his dagger and longknife on the ground. "We'll disarm ourselves." He turned slowly and motioned for Elina to dismount. She stared helplessly at him. "Have you lost all sense?"

"Please, Elina."

Elina dismounted, cursing under her breath and shaking her head. Reluctantly she took the axe that had dispatched the Watcher from her belt and placed it on the ground. "We're about to become their prisoners," she murmured as the boys cautiously approached, whispering furtively to each other. "And there'll be more of them waiting inside the castle, I'll wager."

"I already know there are," Arin said, then quietly added, "They're frightened, Elina. Can you not tell?"

The human boy glared at them. "Step back. No, further." Once they had retreated to his satisfaction he turned to his companion as they stopped a dozen paces away. "Take their weapons," he said, with his bow still levelled at Arin. "If either of them try to run, I'll shoot them."

The *luyan* boy tentatively approached, his disconcertingly pale eyes flitting between Arin and Elina. He snatched up the axe, dagger and longknife and scrambled back, trying to look behind and forward at the same time, and almost tripped over a protruding tree root in his haste.

"Now walk the horses ahead of us, around the side of the castle," the human boy demanded. "You try and run and you know what will happen."

"We're not going to run," Arin said quietly as he and Elina began the walk up towards the old castle. "We have food," he added as an afterthought, but neither of the boys appeared to have heard him.

They were commanded to lead their horses into the stables half-concealed around the back of the castle and then to walk back around to the main entrance, a pair of wide wooden doors which had partly rotted away with age and damp.

Much of the area within the castle lay wild and overgrown. Tendrils of ivy and other creepers curled and coiled around ancient statues, columns and the rotting remains of furniture. Throughout the dismal hall into which they were told to walk, burial headstones loomed out of the partly flag-stoned floor. Arin recalled that burials were much less common than cremations throughout the South, so it struck him as unusual that this large internal bonefield would have been built here. The roof was riddled with gaping holes and much of the remaining structure looked dangerously unstable. The rubble and debris scattered across the flagstones was testament to that peril.

Arin and Elina were commanded to walk into the middle of the area, which was clear of headstones. At the same time some of the other children Arin had already seen lurking in the shadows came forward, most of them armed with rudimentary weapons of one sort or another. Bright-eyed and watchful through their adornments of dirt, they ranged in age from about five or six up to sixteen, seventeen and eighteen. Arin, who had begun to wonder if only young children occupied this place, relaxed a little. Perhaps this community of grubby refugees had structure to it, a leader or some kind of hierarchy.

As he had suspected, an attempted cloaking had been put in place to try and mask the Old Powers the children harboured. But the effort was hasty and poorly-conceived. Arin could tell from a quick glance which of those who now gathered around himself and Elina had some magical abilities. He reckoned about three quarters of them. Those who held no trace of sorcery appeared to be the siblings of those who definitely did. He saw one boy- an especially strong example, no more than eight years old- standing by a little girl who clutched at his arm and behind the two of them an older girl in her teens. Their collective stance and acute likeness convinced Arin that these three at least had the same parents.

There are no parents here, he observed. *Why should that be? Are all these children runaways? I suppose people of such an age may be more likely to run away, but so many in one place? What brought all of them together? How did they find one another?*

"I can tell that most of you hold the Powers," he said softly. "I do also."

"We already know," one of the older boys said. "Maybe you're no better at hiding it than we are."

Arin nodded, and tried to hide his surprise. "My name is Arin and my companion is Elina," he continued, but already a murmur of unease had rippled through the gathering. The children were far more interested in the danger his presence might pose to them.

"You shouldn't have let them in, Irrik," one of the older children scowled at the human boy who they had seen first. Tall and thin, she had an unhealthy, sallow appearance. Anger flashed in her eyes as she continued, "You were told to shoot them if they didn't go away! Why didn't you?"

"I tried," he protested. "I tried but they... they wouldn't leave. It was Ryn's fault." He prodded the *luyan* boy, who immediately pushed him back, and within a moment they were squabbling and had to be dragged apart.

As he observed them Arin found it odd that *luyan-* and Ryn was one of four here- and humans would hide together, given their distinct and separate communities.

"We have to decide what we're going to do with them," someone spoke up, but those words only provoked fresh argument. *They don't have a leader,* Arin realised. *Maybe no one wants to lead, or maybe no one wants to be responsible if something terrible happens.*

If I can convince them that we intend no harm, I should lead them.

The thought of being at the head of a ragtag army of child sorcerers was at once both ridiculous and frightening. Arin almost dismissed the idea out of hand, but then a sobering thought occurred to him. What would happen to them if they remained in hiding, leaderless and arguing over everything? Sooner or later, they would be found. Perhaps by allies of this army that had emerged and come down from the north, but more likely by Watchers.

"You won't be able to stay here forever," he told them.

"Why not?" one of the children demanded. "We had to hide here because of the Watchers. They've started killing everyone."

"What will you do if the Watchers come here? A whole group of them? Some of you are strong, but I don't think all of you together would be able to kill more than two or three. Supposing a dozen Watchers found this place?"

An uneasy silence followed his words as they looked at one another. After a short while one of the older children, a boy of about sixteen or seventeen, stepped forward. He looked angry. Perhaps he saw Arin as a usurper. "What would *you* suggest we do? We have to avoid all the towns. The little ones can't walk far. We've no choice but to hide."

He makes good points, Arin thought, and decided to put the matter to one side for now. "I don't expect you have much food. We have some in our saddlebags with the horses. You all look as if you need it as much as we do, so it might be a good idea to retrieve those provisions before some passing thief finds them."

The boy turned to three others near him. "Go and get their saddlebags. Anything useful, bring it here. Food or weapons or whatever you can find."

As they hurried away, the boy gestured to the ground. "You may as well sit. You might be here awhile."

A fire was built and lit inside a perimeter of stones in the centre of the hall. Arin was glad of the warmth but found that it made the shadows around the edges of the place appear darker. The three children who had left to retrieve the saddlebags returned a while later with some of their provisions, which were placed with those the refugees already had.

Arin was surprised a little later when Ryn came to sit nearby. The *luyan* child didn't say anything but just ate his helping of stew and stared straight ahead. Under the grime covering his pale countenance he had a haunted look to him.

"Do you have any family anywhere?" Arin asked eventually, and immediately wished he hadn't.

The little boy shook his head. "Watchers came and killed them. I hid and then I ran away afterwards." Ryn uttered the words flatly and without any trace of emotion, but after he had eaten he put the bowl down, wiped at his eyes, then got up and walked away.

Arin took his map from his backpack and studied it. They should head north, he decided at first, perhaps beyond the Never-Built Wall if they could. But straight north would take them towards the lands near to the Wistledge, from where unpleasant rumours had emerged about the *du-luyan* communities. *North-east then,* he mused. *That might lead us towards Mornkastle or maybe just south of it, but we'll avoid the city itself. North-east and then straight north.*

He mentioned his idea to Elina, speaking quietly so that – he hoped- no one else could hear. "Is it likely to be any safer anywhere else?" she replied doubtfully. "This castle has lain abandoned for many decades. These children have hidden themselves away here precisely for that reason. They hope to avoid the horrors of the world."

"The horrors of the world cannot be avoided," Arin pointed out. "Besides, they're not ordinary children. Most of them hold the Powers to one degree or another. A few have immense ability. But they're afraid and they have no leader-certainly I don't think that boy truly leads them, no matter that he likes to issue orders when he can. Sooner or later they will use their strength in anger, but they have little idea what consequences will result when that happens."

"A lost soul leading other lost souls," Elina murmured, and he looked sharply at her. "What do you mean by that?"

"I have known you for years, Arin. You're a good man, but you're lost. These last few days I've begun to realise why that might be. Do you really want to lead these children and act as some sort of protector and mentor? Or are you seeking some sort of purpose to your broken life? The life you've never been able to live properly because of your nature?" She looked down. "I apologise. I misspoke."

"No." He sighed. "You didn't. Those are good questions, Elina, and I suppose the answer must be yes to both of them. But I could be leading them to their doom without knowing- if any agreed to come with us. Would they be any better off in our company?"

"No one can know," she said.

On an impulse Arin stood up and said to those near enough to hear, "Bring everyone who isn't here into this hall. I have something important to tell you."

"Who do you think you are?" one of them called across. "You're lucky you're not full of arrows."

"You're lucky you have food for a few more days, which we shared with you," Arin retorted. "But I'll not argue the point. Just bring everyone here and listen. There are events elsewhere in the land that you need to know about. The knowledge itself will do you no harm. Do as you will with it."

After a moment two of them went to find the other children who were scattered around the castle. When everyone- at least, Arin presumed everyone was present- had finally gathered in the hall, he said, "A great army has come from out of the north and is camped near Mornkastle. These people are marching south, perhaps to claim Luudhoq itself."

"I've heard about that," one of the girls piped up, and another echoed the statement. Arin pressed on, "Some of the people within that army are witches and warlocks- folk who are strong in the Powers, just like most of you. They understand how it is to live life as you have had to."

That may not be entirely true, he realised as they stared suspiciously at him. *It isn't a crime to harbour such talents, north of the Never-Built Wall.*

"How do you know this?" one of them asked finally.

"We've travelled all the way from Telith," Arin said, "and we've met several people along the way on different days, who told a remarkably similar story."

"Anyone could say that," she pointed out. "Anyone could tell a lie when they know there's no disproving what they say."

"True, but I've no reason to lie to you. I'm telling you this because you cannot stay here forever..."

"Why not? Have you seen a better-guarded place anywhere round here?"

Arin was about to reply that the castle was far too large for them to adequately guard all the way round, when they heard the sound of someone running through the corridor beyond one of the archways, towards the hall. After a moment a girl of perhaps eleven or twelve years with scruffy blonde hair appeared, gasping for breath. Even in the dim light Arin saw the look of utter panic on her grubby face.

"Watchers!" she exclaimed. "There are *Watchers* out there and they're coming up the path towards the entrance..."

The gathering descended into chaos.

III

Arin acted out of instinct. All rational thought fled his mind, and as the Powers raced within him he let the sorcery fly throughout the great hall to cover the exits and lessen the noise within the place. Soon many of the children realised what he had done, and he was shocked when they looked expectantly to him. Even the older ones were frozen with fear.

No matter their powers, their innate terror of Watchers and what they might do consumed them utterly.

"Some of you will need to come with me," he said, "and the rest of you must stay here, together." At the back of his mind, a voice urged him to make quick, strong decisions. *Whatever you do, don't hesitate,* he thought. *Hesitate and they'll no longer believe in you. At this moment, for some reason- maybe it's because you used the Powers to cloak the sounds in the hall and they realised what you'd done- they believe in you. They'll follow you. Show any fear and that will end.*

"You," he said, pointing to one of the older boys. "And you." He gestured to the girl who had been arguing with him only a moment ago. "You as well." Both of them were strong. He turned to Elina, who had made as if to come with him. "Stay here," he said.

"My place is with you, Arin. Where else would it be?"

"If there really are Watchers out there, then there's little you can do to help."

"Really? You mean like the last time you encountered a Watcher?" She stared meaningfully at him.

"Please, Elina. Stay here and try to keep everyone as calm as possible. I hope that the cloaking has worked, so they won't be heard or seen. But I can't be sure. We'll return as soon as we can."

He turned to see Ryn step forward. "I'm coming too," he said stonily. "They killed my family."

"No, Ryn. I need you to stay here." Arin bent down and whispered in the boy's ear, "Elina will need looking after. She doesn't have the Powers like you and I. Will you look after her for me, until we return?"

The boy thought for a moment and then nodded reluctantly. Then a look of alarm leapt in his eyes. "What if you don't come back?!"

"We will. I promise you."

Even as his heart sank at how easily he had made a vow he might not be able to keep, Arin gestured for the two he had chosen to come with him. "Lead on," he whispered to the girl who still waited agitatedly at the archway. She walked ahead along the passageway and towards the entrance of the castle through which he and Elina had entered. She stopped before they reached the main doors into the courtyard, and instead beckoned them over to a passage over on the left, where a couple of arrow slits were carved into the wall. "Look," she whispered, and invited Arin to peer through the aperture.

At first he could see little in the murky night, but after a moment his Powers-heightened sight adjusted, and he saw three faint shapes make their way slowly up the track towards the castle entrance. They had no need to light the path ahead, and he in turn had no need of a light source to see them by. Watchers gave out less heat than humans would, but still enough for him to see where they were and how quickly they approached.

The caution that they clearly exercised caused his heart to sink. If they didn't suspect that a danger of some sort awaited them here, then they would have surely approached far more quickly. As it was they walked slowly and paused on occasion, scanning left and right. *They must know that there's prey for them here,* Arin thought. *But they must also know that that prey is dangerous.*

All three of the children with him were powerful, but they were surely unfamiliar with using their innate sorcery. They would have learned to hide it from a young age, something that Arin knew was counterintuitive. Such magic existed to be used; it was not and never had been intended to be concealed from the world. Had they ever used their talents in anger?

"We're going to have to kill them," he whispered, "and the three of you will have to use the Powers. I can't tell you exactly how- you're going to have to tell yourselves. You'll have to unlock every little bit of force that you can muster and direct it at these Watchers. I will do the same."

"I'm scared," the younger girl whispered.

"Truthfully, so am I." Arin forced a smile. "But we have no choice." He turned to the others. "Be ready. Let it free. I will…"

He never completed the sentence. The great wooden doors exploded inwards, and a harsh, blinding light suffused everything. As he fell back and hit the ground, Arin heard the terrified screams of his companions. A high-pitched sound cut through his head, and he clapped his hands over his ears, although the noise did not abate.

Arin looked dazedly to one side. The boy lay dead several paces away, a huge splinter of wood through his head. His eyes stared sightlessly up as if in bewilderment that death could have come for him so soon. A little further away, the older girl knelt on the ground, shuddering and weeping tears of blood. Her eyes appeared entirely dark red.

He looked towards the broken entrance and it was at that point that he realised something that should have been impossible.

At least one of the Watchers was *wielding the Powers*.

Arin staggered to his feet, dimly aware of the other child standing to the other side of the entrance, a faint shimmer of sorcery around her. At the same time, even through the intense light he could see three forms steadily walking right up to the entrance.

I can't take down all three, he thought. *I can barely think. I don't think I've the strength to destroy even one of them.*

But the sorcery that had always been a part of him had other ideas. It soared through and out of him, and an invisible hammer of force struck the approaching Watchers. The light disappeared so suddenly that for a moment Arin could see nothing at all.

After only a moment, he felt the barrier between them bend and finally shatter, and the Watchers appeared in the entrance, little more than silhouettes against the night sky. Arin stretched out an arm towards them and aimed the swirling energies directly at the head of one of the enemy. *Cold,* he thought. *It shouldn't take much to make this cold night colder still.*

The Powers responded immediately to his thought, and the Watcher reached a hand to his head, stooping slightly. Then he fell forwards and lay still. At the same time, Ildar emerged from behind the clouds, and by the harsh moonlight Arin caught his first detailed look at the two other Watchers. One was male, the other female. Both wore dark cloaks.

Frost began to form on the male Watcher. *Colder yet,* Arin silently commanded. *So cold that his heart becomes still.*

But just as his foe sagged to the ground to join his comrade, Arin felt an agony like nothing he had ever experienced before build inside his head. His vision became brighter and distorted, then began to fade at the edges. The female Watcher stepped towards him and stooped down. All he could see now was her face, hard and merciless eyes burrowing into him as he fought against her. *She's the one using the Powers,* he thought. *How can that be? How can a Watcher...*

Suddenly the pain disappeared, and the Watcher began to shudder, her spasms becoming worse as she stood unsteadily and turned slowly to face the girl. She took a hesitant step towards her, then another. *No,* Arin thought desperately. He tried to get up but couldn't.

The Watcher took a third step and then burst into flames.

Arin shut his eyes and rolled desperately out of the way as she fell to the ground. He gritted his teeth and managed to get up and limp slowly over to the girl, who stared transfixed at the burning Watcher. As he looked into her eyes he could see the flames of their foe dance madly, sometimes orange, sometimes blue, or even green. For a while they were both too exhausted to do anything but sit and watch their enemy burn.

"What's your name?" he asked her a while later, when the fire had burned out and the remains of the Watcher smouldered on, a curious hybrid of ash, metal and blackened remains of flesh.

"Lumi," she said without looking at him.

"Well Lumi, you saved my life."

She gave him a sudden sharp look. "You saved *mine*. But Ester and Luc..." She looked to the lifeless forms of the other two and shrugged tiredly.

Arin looked towards the broken doorway. "I don't think there are other Watchers out there, but they may yet come."

"We can't destroy them all. They're too powerful. I don't think I can even stand up."

Weak though he was, he managed to help her to her feet and together they made their way back through the dark tunnels towards the central hall.

Arin barely heard the sounds of hysteria and grief around them when they finally reached their destination. The noise faded gradually as he sank to the ground and a strange warmth and stillness seeped through his veins. He tried to keep his eyes open but could not. For a moment he thought he saw Elina sit by his side, but she looked blurred and indistinct. He tried to open his mouth to speak to her but it might as well have been sewn shut.

His sight faded to nothing before he could so much as utter a whisper.

When Arin woke his first thought was that he had been left alone in the ruined hall, so quiet had it become. Then he saw a small group of children a short distance away. A movement to his right made him turn his head, and he winced as sudden pain flared up. He saw Lumi sitting nearby and reading a small, tattered book. She looked up and saw that he had regained consciousness. "Elina!" she called out.

Arin couldn't see Elina anywhere at first, and felt so dazed that he didn't notice her until she was just a few paces away. *I'm far from well,* he thought dully. *My sight comes and goes. The slightest movement causes agony.*

"How are you feeling?" she asked, squatting down beside him.

"Terrible," he said, and looked across at Lumi. "She seems to have coped far better with using the Powers than I did."

"Maybe it's because you're old," Lumi ventured, and Arin laughed weakly at that, then grimaced as the act caused pain to flare up in his temple again. *Maybe there's a touch of truth to that,* he thought. *If I'd had the chance to use and hone my abilities down the years, I might not be lying here like a cripple now.* But aloud he said, "I'm forty-three years old, Lumi. I know that must seem quite ancient to you, but some people live for much longer."

Arin sat up with Elina's help, and managed to pull his cloak on. The fire had been stoked up and replenished and a group of sombre children sat around it, but he could feel only a fraction of its heat. "I'll get you something to eat," Elina said, and bustled away.

Lumi put her book down and glanced across at him. "I tried to sleep," she said, "but I had nightmares about the Watchers, and my heart wouldn't stop racing."

"How long has it been?" he asked.

"A day. It got light and now it's got dark again. Ester and Luc were buried in the grounds to the north. We had to use the Powers again to soften the earth."

Arin nodded sombrely. "Did you know them well?"

Lumi shrugged. "Not really. I don't think I know *anyone* that well. I don't have any brothers or sisters here, or friends. Maybe that's why they leave me on guard so often. I don't mind being alone."

"You did well," he told her. "I was as good as finished. If it hadn't been for you, that Watcher would have made her way through into the castle, and who knows how many might have perished."

"I just did what I had to," she mumbled, and picked up her book again. This time she appeared to concentrate more fully on it, a studious frown upon her face. *She doesn't want to talk about what happened,* Arin thought, *and who can blame her?*

"Did your family get murdered by the Watchers?" she asked tentatively a while later.

Arin wasn't sure what to say. "I didn't have any family," he told her finally. "Just a few friends. Elina's all I have left."

Lumi nodded. "That must be sad. Not having any family or children of your own, or anyone to be in love with."

"What good did being in love ever do anyone, Lumi?" one of the other children called across, and she scowled at him.

Arin had nothing to say to that, but an image of Loren suddenly bloomed in his mind - not that that had been her real name, he reminded himself. More than anything, he remembered the strangely haunted look in her eyes. *I should have asked her to stay,* he thought. *But I knew she was on the run. She would have been caught if she'd remained in Telith.*

Then he asked himself: *I wonder where she ended up? And why do I still think of her after all this time when I don't even know if she's still alive? If she is, she could be anywhere in Harn or even beyond. Certainly she'll have continued to flee north, possibly even far beyond the Never-Built Wall.*

Arin sighed and put such thoughts firmly to one side. He sat up gingerly, grimaced and took a deep breath, marvelling at how weak he still felt. *The sorcery comes more easily to me now,* he thought, *after having been kept hidden away for so long. But it takes so much from me each time- and last time more than ever before.*

Lumi remained restless, and after a short while she put her book down. "Do you think that other Watchers know when some of their kind are killed?" she asked, a troubled look on her face. "I once heard that they're all linked together somehow as if there's a web of sorcery around them, and when that web gets moved or broken in some way they all know about it and those who are closest come to investigate." She shuddered and looked away into the shadows. "Like spiders."

Arin thought about that for a little while. It was a plausible idea, and the possibility made him uneasy. "I don't know if they are or not," he said finally. "But did you notice that the last of the three- the female Watcher- was using the Powers?"

"I did. Is that unusual?"

"Watchers have *never* been able to use the Powers, Lumi. Down all the centuries, there has never been a documented case of any of their kind seizing them. Don't forget, one of their main purposes has always been hunting down sorcerors, witches, magicians, whatever you want to call them. People like you and I."

Lumi frowned. "That doesn't make any sense then."

"No. It doesn't. Anyway, going back to what you said. I don't know if they will realise that three of their number have been destroyed, but we should assume that sooner or later more Watchers will come here anyway."

"What do you think we should do?"

"I think you should all leave. Of course, there are many risks involved with doing that, but it may be that we can reach this army. You'd be amongst others like yourselves there."

Elina had come back with some dry bread and saltmeat, and caught the last part of their conversation. "An army is no place for children," she said firmly.

"It's no place for anyone with a choice in the matter. But we live in dangerous times. What would you have them do, Elina? They may repel further attacks by Watchers- or other enemies, of which I'm sure there's no shortage- but more will die, and sooner or later they'll be overcome. Some of these children don't even *have* the Powers to protect themselves with. They depend on siblings or friends. But what if their protectors are killed? Who looks after them then? I know that to seek help and shelter within this force from beyond the Never-Built Wall is a far from ideal solution, but I see no other."

"I would go," Lumi interrupted. "I don't have anyone here. So it doesn't matter where I am. I'd rather be somewhere where I stand a better chance of staying alive."

"And I think that chances are you would stand a better chance there," Arin said.

"But most of them won't want to go, and you can't force them," Lumi warned.

Arin chewed thoughtfully on a hunk of bread. It was brittle and so dry that it drew every last bit of moisture from his mouth. How much more food did these children have left before they were forced to risk heading out to nearby settlements to forage and steal? "I have to give them the opportunity and explain why it makes sense. Then everyone can make their own choices."

Elina was not done yet. "And what if we're attacked by Watchers while we're out in the open? Remember, we won't be moving quickly. They'd need to ride more than one to each horse. I don't know how many horses they have here but I doubt there are more than a few..."

"There were two," Lumi said, "but we decided that they'd be more useful for meat than for riding, so they were butchered. We still have the Watchers' horses though."

One of the boys in the group by the other side of the fire had listened to their conversation, and spoke up. "I'm not going," he said, shaking his head. "This is my home now. It's *our* home."

"A broken castle riddled with graves and shadows?" Arin said, and swiftly realised that he had spoken out of turn.

The boy glared at him and retorted, "Well if you don't like it you can leave. Some of us already think that the two of you brought the Watchers here, that they were hunting *you* and wouldn't have stopped here if you'd just ridden past. So maybe you should be careful about what you say."

"If it hadn't been for Arin, the Watchers would have got past the entrance and all of you would probably be *dead*," Lumi shouted.

The boy sneered at her. "You think these two are going to be your new mother and father? You just live in your own silly little world! You don't have anyone and you never will!"

Lumi scrambled to her feet and ran from the hall in tears. Arin listened as her footfall faded into the mournful silence of the castle.

Later on, as more of the children returned to the hall, Arin decided to at least warn them of the consequences of staying here, in the light of the attack by the three Watchers. As they gathered, he sensed a certain restless reluctance amongst them. *Perhaps they're here out of courtesy because they know I helped them,* he thought. *They'll listen or at least appear to, and then they'll choose to stay. As that boy already said, this is their home now no matter what it looks like.*

But eventually it will be their burial ground- or it would be if Watchers bothered to bury their victims.

He decided to get straight to the point. "More Watchers will arrive sooner or later. Yes, you might say that with luck they might never come here- why would they unless they already knew you were here? But I have something to tell you about one of the Watchers that we killed. That Lumi killed, in fact." He looked around to see if he could spot the girl, but she was nowhere to be seen. *Is she guarding some lonely outpost?* he wondered. *Or has she hidden herself away somewhere? Might she even have run away?*

"That Watcher was not simply using the strange sorcery known to their kind. She was also using the Powers. I believe that is why they didn't simply ride past. She must have sensed all of you within the castle, despite your efforts to conceal your nature. And that, to put it simply, is why it cannot be safe for you to remain here."

Amidst the collective murmur of unease that immediately rose, Arin continued, "The safest place for you all is with others like you."

"You mean the army that attacked Mornkastle," one of the older girls said. "We've all heard stories about those people. The sorceror Inerdyr set his own army against them but they were destroyed, and so was he."

"I heard about that too," a boy standing next to her added. "They've marched through all the villages in their way and killed the people who weren't able to escape."

"I heard that it's mostly made up of monsters," a younger girl piped up. "Big monsters that like to murder and rape and eat human flesh even while their victim is still alive!"

"They're called *orkar*," the first girl told her. "They're going to rampage throughout the south and burn down all the towns and villages, and even big cities like Waylorn. Some people say they'll even conquer Luudhoq."

"That won't happen, the Seven and the High Watchers are far too powerful. Even the dark magic of witches can't destroy Gods," someone else answered back, and within a moment the discussion had descended into a shrill argument.

"Quiet!" Arin shouted, and to his surprise they ceased their squabble sufficiently for him to be heard properly as he continued, "Many tales are told about the *orkar,* mostly in order to make sure people remain frightened of them. Undoubtedly they are formidable creatures, and they may seem barbaric to us in the South, but they are not quite the monsters that they're made out to be, no matter what you've been told. Perhaps this army does intend to conquer the south. However, you'll be safer amongst those who understand you rather than those who wish simply to destroy you. And even if you don't believe that, do you really think you'll be safe here?"

"He's just trying to scare us," someone further back in the hall said.

"I have no reason to scare you." Arin looked for the owner of the voice but he couldn't quite make it out in the gloom. "I assure you that one of those Watchers seized the Powers. If one can, then there will be others who can. That means you are not as hidden away here as you thought."

He let them reflect on that for a moment, and then he spoke up again. "Who amongst you will come with us?"

They looked at one another, and none of them spoke. Arin's heart sank. *Not a single one of you?* he thought. *If you remain here then you'll die here, I'm certain of it.*

Then he heard a voice he recognised. "I'll come with you."

Ryn pushed himself through until he was in the front row, and walked over. Arin smiled faintly. "You're wise beyond your years, Ryn. Anyone else?"

"This is the only home we have," the boy who had spoken a short while ago said. "It's all we have left, and we won't risk it for you or anyone else who comes here." Speaking a little more loudly he addressed everyone who had gathered in the hall. "Why would any one of you go with these two? We don't know them. Maybe they're slavers."

"We are assuredly *not* slavers," Arin sighed. He looked around. "Will no others amongst you see sense?"

"You can take Lumi if you can find her," one of them spoke up. "She already said she wanted to leave."

"You should probably go now, before you bring any more Watchers here," someone else added.

With a heavy heart Arin packed a little of the provisions from one of the saddlebags, leaving the remainder for the children. If luck favoured them then they could find more from the next settlement they chanced upon. "Good luck to you all," he said quietly, as he turned away from their steady, distrustful gaze.

Arin, Elina and Ryn walked through to the stables at the rear of the castle, where they found their horses still unbutchered. They had even been given some grain and water. "Are you sure you want to come with us, Ryn?" Elina asked the little boy as the three of them led the horses around the side of the castle in the early morning sunlight.

"I hate it here," he told her. "It's dark and cold and it's haunted."

Arin wondered if he should search for Lumi before they left, but as they passed near to the front entrance where the great wooden doors still smouldered in the gathering light, Arin caught sight of the girl sitting on the ground, a small backpack slung over her shoulder. "I don't want to stay here," she called across as she got up and walked over to them.

"Do you have everything you need?" Arin asked her when she reached them, and in answer she simply opened her pack and showed him its contents. Arin was confounded when he saw that she had filled her pack mostly with books and only a few provisions.

They waited for Lumi while she went to claim one of the other horses from the stables. Arin wondered if the girl would be able to ride the tall creature, but it soon became clear that she had ridden many times before from the ease with which she leapt up into the saddle after swiftly preparing it. Elina helped Ryn into the saddle behind her. "You'd better hold on properly," Lumi warned.

"You'd better not go too fast and throw me off," he replied pensively.

Three days of fine, cold weather preceded a deluge. As cold winter rain began to hammer down around noon on the fourth day, Arin and his companions took shelter in the thickness of a woodland where tall pines stood close together. As they waited in pensive silence, occasional fat raindrops and the dull roar of rainfall far above served to constantly remind them that the storm had not yet passed.

"Are they really going to march south and destroy all the big cities like Waylorn and Luudhoq?" Ryn asked suddenly. "Can't the Seven do something about them? They're Gods. They must be able to do something."

Arin looked up and regarded the boy in silence for a moment. This was not the first question Ryn had asked about the matter since their departure from the castle. Arin suspected that the boy had done little but dwell on the matter. Arin wondered for a moment why Ryn was concerned about those places- he hadn't thought a *luyan* child would be even remotely interested in the fate of human towns and cities. Almost all the major towns in the south were human settlements.

"Do you want them to destroy those places?" he countered.

Ryn stared at him, confused that his question had been answered with a more complex one. "Yes, if it means the Watchers all die," he said finally.

"Many people will die, not just Watchers," Elina pointed out.

Ryn shrugged. "I don't care. I just want it to all be over. And I'm tired of all this riding. It makes me feel sore all over. I just want to sleep forever." He stared resentfully down at the ground, lost in whatever dark thoughts consumed him. For one black moment Arin wondered if he had made a grave mistake in convincing the two children to travel with them. Would their lives really be any better under the protection of this army of renegades, militiamen and witches, assuming the four of them got that far? Might they have been better off if they'd stayed with the others in the castle? It was impossible to say. Both of them had been alone in the uneasy crowd of which they had been a part, but now they journeyed with two strangers towards a fate that none of them could predict.

"I'm hungry," Ryn spoke up, a sudden hint of hope in his voice.

"We're *all* hungry," Lumi pointed out. "If we eat everything we have now then we'll have nothing for days further ahead and then we'll just starve."

Ryn scowled unhappily. "Well I'd rather die with some food inside me."

Maybe we should have gone north to cross the Never-Built Wall as soon as we could to avoid the Watchers, Arin thought as he half-listened to the children's dismal conversation. But his mind retained a disquieting sense that to head north would have been equally dangerous. *The Old Dark,* he reminded himself. *The* choragh *and those who do much of their work. They're not the mythical subjects of scare-tales- they're real. Those who serve them would quickly find us if we ventured into that region. It wouldn't surprise me if Ryn and Lumi also knew that much, on some deep level.*

No, we can't go that way.

He shuddered and looked towards the shadowy depths of the woods, convinced for a moment that some silent unseen entity watched them.

Once the rain stopped a while later, they emerged from the cover of the trees and Arin picked up the water flask he had left out in the open to catch rain. They rode on along the track, the horses' hooves squelching in the mud as they plodded wearily onwards, heads bowed against the weather.

The following day, as Arin and Elina consulted their maps after the meagre breakfast they had all shared, Lumi sat on an old tree stump and buried herself in one of her books, intent on taking the opportunity to read before another day spent on horseback. But a short while later she happened to look up to see Ryn staring at her. When she looked back he asked her, "Why are you always reading?"

"Because I've always liked to," she said.

"I wish *I* could read," Ryn confessed.

Lumi considered for a moment. "Maybe if we ever get where we're supposed to be going, I could teach you," she said. "Everyone should know how to read."

Ryn gave an embarrassed little smile and nodded. Then, abruptly he asked her, "Did you have a mother and father?"

"That's none of your business," she retorted. Why did he always have to ask such rude questions?

"*I* did," he said softly, and she relented a little. "I don't remember them very well," she told him finally. "They died when I was five, and then I was brought up by my grandfather."

"What happened to him? Did the Watchers get him?"

"No." Lumi felt the memory stir in her mind, still bright and painful. "He just got ill. He's dead now," she said, and reached for one of her books again. Books made the world go away, she reminded herself, even if it was only for a little while. Unfortunately they couldn't make annoying little *luyan* boys go away.

She read a couple more pages but found that she could no longer concentrate properly. It wasn't even the fact that Ryn sat nearby and occasionally stared at her with those oddly pale, almost translucent eyes. She sighed and looked across at Arin and Elina. *Why did they choose to help us?* she wondered worriedly. *Does Arin hope to be paid for handing over two children who hold the Powers?*

Although the thought made her uneasy, deep down she didn't believe he would do that. If anything Arin and Elina were in just as much danger as Ryn and herself. They were probably in *more* danger now. *They shouldn't have taken us with them,* she mused, tracing a finger along the spine of her book. *They should have just left, or never have even stopped at the castle. They would have been nearer to somewhere safe by now, with only themselves to look after.*

She opened her book once again and began to read.

After Arin and Elina had agreed on the path to follow for the next few days, and they prepared to pack up and head onwards, Lumi finally put her book down and uttered a sigh that sounded almost contented. Arin thought he saw her smile for a moment, although the expression quickly faded. "You would have liked my library," he commented.

Lumi looked up and stared at him. "You had a *library?*"

"I did. That was one way in which I was lucky, you could say. But I had to leave everything behind."

"So did I," Lumi said. "Maybe it was easier for me, because I didn't have much to begin with."

Yes, Arin thought. *I was probably luckier than anyone I know.* "Where did you live?"

"Meadowbrook. It's a small town just east of Telith." She paused and then continued after a moment, "I lived there with my grandfather. But then he died and I lived on my own."

"On your own?" Arin repeated doubtfully.

She nodded. "I made sure I went to the school so I could learn more and be even better at reading. When I heard about what had happened in Telith and someone said that Watchers were heading towards Meadowbrook I just ran away. I knew I had to go on my own. I didn't have anyone else."

Arin suppressed a shudder at the oddly matter of fact way in which the girl had given her story. Was she simply hiding her grief or had it hardened into something else?

"When you have the Powers it's like a horrible, nasty secret that you can't tell anyone about," Lumi confessed after a moment.

He nodded sadly. "Yes. That's exactly what it's like. I learned from a very young age- even younger than Ryn- to keep it all hidden away. It was the only way to survive. But you already know that."

"I remember when I first knew that I was different," Lumi said. "I was sitting outside and playing in the dirt with one of the wooden toys that my grandfather used to make. I don't know why, but I remember I picked up a couple of small stones in my hands and I just decided I would try to do something to them- make them change shape or make them hotter. I never thought that I couldn't do it. I just knew that I could, and that was that."

"What did you do?"

"I held one in each hand and concentrated on heating them up, so that they could keep me warm. It was a cold day in the spring. But they just got hotter and hotter, except that they didn't burn me, even when they were glowing hot. I remember staring at them, wishing I could make them go cold again. I didn't know what to do, so in the end I just put them down and went inside and hoped that no one would see them. They cooled down in the end, but it frightened me." She paused. "That's when I knew I could make something happen but didn't know how to stop it from happening."

Arin smiled faintly. He remembered doing something not entirely dissimilar. He too had experienced that moment of horror and complete loss of control that came after the initial euphoria.

"What will happen to us?" Lumi asked bluntly.

Arin considered for a moment and decided to simply be honest. *She's old enough for the truth,* he thought. *In many ways she's old beyond her years.* "I don't know," he said. "I won't lie to you and say everything will be fine if and when we reach these people. It might not be. But sometimes in life there are no good choices, so you have to make the one which is the least bad. That's what I hope we're doing."

But later that day, Arin was reminded that sometimes no matter what choice had been made, bad luck could be just around the corner.

As they rested by the side of a wide grassy track that skirted a woodland of tall chestnut trees, they heard riders approach. Arin hoped that they might have time to untether their horses and head into the woods, out of sight and hopefully out of earshot. But the newcomers arrived sooner than he had expected and drew quickly to a halt. Arin's heart sank as he observed their cold-eyed, hungry look- the gaze of opportunistic hunters making the best of harsh times.

The six riders gathered around the companions in a semi-circle, and one of them- a lean, dark-eyed man with pockmarked skin and sores on the backs of his hands, stared at them for a long while. "Well, I had a feeling our luck would turn sooner or later," he said finally, in what sounded like a heavy Anvarian accent. A couple of his men sniggered. "I assume that all four of you wish to remain alive. Am I correct? Please nod your heads if you agree."

When they warily did so he grinned, revealing a mouth of crooked, stained teeth. "Then this matter should soon be sorted." He fixed his attention on Arin, and at the same time loaded a crossbow with a deftness that indicated his ease with the weapon. "You seem like a sensible man. We've no need for you, and I happen to be in a good mood so you can be on your way. Your companions, on the other hand, are *exactly* who we need. Men like us who earn a hard living on the road... well, we all have certain appetites. I'm sure you understand."

Arin's expression remained neutral but the look in his eyes became hard as stone. The man with the diseased skin leaned forward and peered at him. "Did you not hear me?"

Then Elina suddenly stepped forward. "Take me if you wish. You don't need the children." Her voice trembled.

"I do," one of the riders spoke up, and laughed as they looked at him. He was a youngish, portly man with a flushed countenance. "The girl, anyway. The *luyan* is good for nothing but meat."

Everything then happened with horrifying speed. The leader of the outlaws pointed his crossbow at Elina, and simply fired without warning. The bolt went straight through Elina's chest. She fell on her side to the ground with nothing more than a faint gasp, the bloody end of the bolt protruding from her back.

"I don't have time to argue or bargain with you," the man continued, and he turned to his comrades. "Fill this man full of arrows. He's chosen his fate."

Arin had already tried to summon the Powers again, but he found that he couldn't. He stared helplessly at Elina's body as blood seeped from her. "Please…" he whispered. Why should he have been rendered so helpless now when he needed his abilities the most?

I wish I could have kept the children safe, he thought numbly. *What a sorry, pointless end this is. Why did I take them from the castle? What was I thinking?*

He closed his eyes and hoped that the end would come quickly for them all.

But the moment passed, and nothing happened to him. Instead, he sensed the Powers being used nearby. In an instant they blossomed into a furious, intense force like an invisible fire. He opened his eyes and looked across at Lumi and Ryn. Then he stared at the bandits, who swayed helplessly in their saddles as if caught by invisible creatures that pulled them this way and that. Those who had prepared their weapons dropped them to the ground. The horses whickered and thumped their hooves in fright and their riders fell to the ground, unable to stay in the saddle. As the panicked horses galloped away, Arin saw smoke rising from the mouths of the fallen men. Their skin began to blister and peel.

Then they burst into flames.

Fire, he thought. *Lumi's speciality perhaps. Maybe Ryn's also.*

As the children finally relinquished their hold on the Powers and stared open-mouthed at what they had done, Arin ran to them. He managed to get to Ryn just before the boy swooned and fell forwards. The three of them stood together and watched as the bandits writhed in agony, becoming nothing more than ashen husks.

As the flames finally died out, Lumi leaned to one side and vomited. "I hate it," she whispered. "I hate how it feels."

"I'm sorry," Arin said quietly as he turned away from the grisly remnants of their enemies. "I couldn't summon anything. I don't know why. You shouldn't have to do what you did."

"It doesn't matter. We killed them." Lumi looked across at Elina's body, her eyes red with despair. "But it's our fault that Elina's dead. You shouldn't have taken us with you, Arin. I was afraid something like this would happen, and now it has."

They buried Elina in a secluded spot at the edge of the nearby woodland where it overlooked a wide grassy valley and farmland. Arin stood over the unmarked grave for a long while and wished desperately that he could think of something to say. "You were a true friend," he said finally. "You deserved better."

"Shouldn't we put a marking stone here for her?" Lumi ventured.

Arin shook his head. "I would have liked to, but I suspect that to mark a grave these days might make it more likely to be disturbed."

"Because of grave robbers?"

"No, Lumi. Something worse than grave robbers." Arin got to his feet. "I hope she remains at peace."

"It's all our fault," Lumi said, and angrily wiped away a tear that had started to roll down her cheek. She took a deep breath and forced herself to look at him. "Ryn and I should go our own way now. Maybe we'll go back to the castle. We should never have come with you. I'm sorry about everything."

"Lumi, listen to me." Arin turned away from the grave and continued quietly, "Both of you, listen to me. This is important. Elina and I stopped at the castle because I could tell there were people who held the Powers hiding inside. That was my choice, but it was something I felt I had to do. And when I saw all of you, I knew that I had to warn you about the dangers of remaining there, and tell you all that you had a choice. I didn't know for sure that this would be a better or safer way. But my point is this. I *chose* to give you the chance to come with me. If anyone is to blame, then I am."

He looked solemnly at Lumi and Ryn as they tried to understand what he had told them. "Here's something else to think about. You both saved my life earlier. There isn't any doubt about that. So we'll stay together and look after one another. Do you both swear that we'll do that?"

The children looked helplessly at each other. "All right," Lumi said finally. "I don't really want to go back to the castle."

"Neither do I," Ryn added immediately.

"But you know we'll only bring you trouble," Lumi continued.

Arin shook his head. "We'll hear no more about it."

A little later he reached tentatively for the Powers and found that he could grasp the sorcery and bring it forth. While the fact reassured him, he remained concerned that he had somehow been rendered helpless when he'd needed his strength the most. *But it's been so many years since I'd used it at all,* he reasoned. *No wonder it's less than reliable after all this time being almost crushed out of existence.*

The companions travelled slowly for the rest of the afternoon with both of the children still exhausted. Ryn in particular was withdrawn. *I shouldn't be surprised,* Arin silently reflected. *He's helped to burn a group of men alive, and he can't be older than seven years.*

The three of them said little as they rested for the evening. A gloom had settled upon them, and conversation felt pointless. Later, when Arin woke Lumi around dawn so that he could get some sleep while she kept watch, Lumi saw Ryn stir just as Arin started to nod off. When she finally heard him snoring Lumi said quietly, "He's so lonely."

Ryn frowned in puzzlement. "Of course he's lonely. He's only got us and he begged us to stay. And he lost Elina."

"Yes, but I think he's been lonely for a lot longer than that. Maybe he just loses everyone he cares about. It happens to some people."

Ryn shrugged. He didn't understand what Lumi's interest was in whether or not Arin was lonely, and wondered if she got some of her strange ideas from the books she read. He got up and went over to one of the packs to rummage around for rations. "Don't eat too much," Lumi warned him.

"I'm only small," Ryn protested. "There's no way I could eat as much as you or Arin."

"I think you eat twice as much," Lumi retorted, wondering to herself how the little boy could fit so much food inside his slight frame. *And I thought the* luyan *people ate less than humans,* she silently remarked.

Lumi soon became absorbed in her own thoughts as she watched the sky lighten, fearful of the unknown future.

IV

Their luck changed for the better later that day. They searched for food in an abandoned farmstead next to a river that ran through the valley that they had followed, and found plenty to keep them from going hungry for a tennight. Thereafter they made quick progress over the ensuing days. Arin listened to the rumours and stories that ran rife through the few inhabited villages they passed through, and he learned that they drew ever nearer to the invading army. Some people from the villages had apparently decided to flee west, but others had made the decision to join the invaders. The choice depended very much on which rumours people chose to believe.

Finally, late one morning they caught sight of the vast army, now a half-dozen leagues south of Mornkastle.

"I'm scared," was the first thing Ryn said as the companions drew to a halt and surveyed the enormity of the gathering before them. It looked like a forest of tents and smoking wood fires, with people threading their way around the encampment, and was larger than any of them had imagined.

"Everything will be all right," Arin said, but Ryn just held onto Lumi more tightly and Lumi gave Arin a quick, nervous look that betrayed only a little of the fear she felt.

When they reached the camp a little later, two guardsmen armed with shortswords and dressed in tattered, well-worn leather armour approached. "You seek to join us?" one of them demanded. Listening to his accent, Arin reckoned he was from the far north-east of Harn.

"We do," he said. "We may be of help to you. We have some capability with the Powers."

The man smiled knowingly. "Is that so? Would you care to know how many folk say that? Many want to join us. It's winter and we have food and shelter. Protection from Watchers too."

"At least take us to someone who can verify the truth of what I tell you," Arin persisted. "If we're found to be liars then I'm sure you can turn us away."

"I will. And I'm not saying you can't stay if you make yourselves useful. But if it's not through sorcery, it's likely to be through servitude. Can you cook? We need more cooks. Or do you have any healing skills? We need healers too."

Arin shook his head. The soldier sighed and ushered them impatiently on, through the perimeter and into the camp as his comrade and two others led their horses away. "Stay by my side," Arin warned the children as they set off.

As they were led through the camp, Ryn caught his first glimpse of an *orkar* and turned to Lumi. "What are *they*?" he exclaimed.

"What are what?"

"Those huge creatures. They look like monsters."

"They're called *orkar*," Lumi said. "They come from the far north of Harn. I've read about them."

"They're scary," Ryn commented.

He was dumbfounded when Lumi suddenly grabbed his hand and held it tightly as they walked along. "What are you doing?" he demanded, and tried to pull away from her, but for such a slim girl she was surprisingly strong. "This is a big place and you could get lost," Lumi warned, "so I *won't* let you go."

"You can't do that!" Ryn scowled up at her, but a moment later he had forgotten all about his attempts to escape her clutches. In fact, although he wouldn't admit it, he felt glad that she held his hand as he stared in wide-eyed bewilderment around the camp. The stench, the chaos and the frightening things he saw made him wish for a moment that he was back in the castle, even though none of the others had really cared about him. *Anyway, the Watchers would have got them,* he reminded himself. *Even though Arin and Lumi killed those that found the place, more Watchers would have come, just like Arin said. We had to leave. I just wish that we didn't have to come here.*

Ryn shrank back fearfully as he saw two *orkar* soldiers argue and then start to hit each other. He felt the Powers stir inside him in response to his own worry, but with an effort he managed to quieten them. The sorcery that lived inside him had been much more active recently. He wondered if that had to do with him spending so much time firstly with the other children at the castle, and then with Arin and Lumi, both of whom were *really* strong in the Powers.

The larger of the two *orkar* managed to wrestle his adversary to the ground, and aimed punch after punch at his head. Ryn didn't want to look, but he couldn't help but stare in horror. Eventually the larger *orkar* man was dragged away by several of his comrades, but only after the one on the ground no longer moved. Ryn wondered if he was dead, but he had no time to find out as Lumi walked him firmly onwards, picking up the pace as Arin told them to hurry along.

Further on he saw a short line of people queueing to defecate into a hole that had been dug in the ground. Ryn looked quickly away and wondered to himself why humans were all so disgusting, although Lumi looked just as revolted when he happened to glance up at her.

He saw other things going on that he couldn't understand at all, including at least half a dozen people who gathered together and openly wielded the Powers. What were they doing? he wondered. Were they practicing how to control them?

He asked Lumi what she thought. "Maybe they are," Lumi agreed. "But it's none of our business."

As they hurried along after Arin however, Ryn felt a cold certainty that soon enough it *would* be.

They were led to a group of people by one of the larger tents in the middle of the camp, and the soldier spoke to a young human woman with long brown hair. When she looked at them, Ryn took a step back and almost tripped over.

"Yes," the woman said clearly, looking at each of them in turn as she spoke. "All three of them." She looked to her companions, who nodded in agreement.

"I don't want to be a part of this," Lumi said quietly to Arin, "and neither does Ryn. We talked about it."

Arin nodded. "I understand. I don't think anyone *wants* to be a part of all this."

Lumi's eyes widened in sudden, misguided hope. "Oh! So we can go then? I think we should. I mean, you should come with us as well if you want to, and..."

"They won't let us. I'm sorry, Lumi- but that's just the way it is. Besides, the Powers are gifted to us for a reason. The *marandaal* stand poised to invade and destroy Harn..."

"I don't care about Harn!" she almost shouted as the people to whom they had been taken stared at her. "Well I don't," she continued vehemently in a quieter voice. "I lost everyone and everything I had. It can burn and die for all I care. What use am I going to be in this stupid war? I'm only eleven years old! And Ryn is only six..."

"I'm *seven*," the *luyan* boy said indignantly.

"I just want to leave," Lumi continued. Her voice shook with emotion. "I want the three of us to leave and get as far away as possible from here. We'll use the Powers against them if they try and stop us! You've seen what I can do. I'll do it again!"

"Will you?" Arin rejoined. "They work when they need to work, against your enemies. That's my experience of the Powers, and I've been around for quite a few more years than you have."

"Stop talking to me as if I'm just a small child!" Lumi snapped, and looked down at the ground, biting her lip. She wiped angrily at her eyes. Ryn looked just as miserable. Arin felt the blackness of despair fall like a shadow across his heart, coupled with a hard, brittle fury. In his ignorance he had told himself he was their rescuer, but in reality he had taken them from their sanctuary to be nothing more than tools of war. They knew it, and he should have known it as well. When he looked into the eyes of those to whom they had been taken, he felt the three of them being measured, their usefulness carefully weighed.

Sometimes, he reminded himself, *there are no good choices left to make.*

IV – The Song of Their Blood

I

Jaana watched Lyya's lithe form through half-open eyes as the *luyan* woman sat up, stretched and finally got to her feet. One shake of her translucent hair and it settled immaculately into place in a stream down her back and shoulders. Jaana doubted that any *luyan* ever required use of a comb.

Many things about Lyya were different now. Her instincts had evolved to become *kin* senses, and the world had opened up a little further and deeper for her. That had been five days ago, and still Lyya held about herself an air of bewilderment and wonder, tempered with fear. She would get used to it in time, Jaana reasoned- however much time they had left.

To think that not so long ago, I felt just as helpless and lost- no, more so, Jaana reflected. When I met Lyya for the first time I'm not sure I even knew who I was any more. Certainly I had no idea what I wanted to be. I'd lost my path and I had no idea if I'd ever find another one. At least now I have a purpose. Back then, I feared life as much as death. Now I feel no particular fear for either- that must be one of the secrets of true freedom. That, and to have an overriding purpose.

As she stirred, Lyya turned to her. "I saw *diafagh* a short while ago, stumbling lost through the undergrowth. Two of them."

Jaana shrugged. "What of it? You've nothing to fear from such things. You'll see many other miracles before all of this is done. Many of the *kin* and anyone else who holds the Old Powers will be heading east for the final confrontation."

"The dead are not miracles, Jaana. They belong at peace under the earth, or as ash in the four winds."

Jaana suppressed a groan of frustration. Lyya's new knowledge and *kin* senses remained at odds with the *luyan*

111

doctrine she had been raised to believe in. But little could be done about that contradiction. Lyya would remain and fight alongside her, and that was all that mattered in the end.

She sat up and pulled her shirt on. Over the last several days the weather had become noticeably warmer and more humid. Some of the trees had even started to bud, and Jaana had noticed an abundance of flowers in several clearings through which they passed even though spring was still in its infancy.

A spring that many of us won't live to see, Jaana thought as she looked in her pack to see how many rations they still had left.

"How far are we from the wall?" Lyya asked pensively.

"Still several days, perhaps longer. You sound almost eager."

"I'm eager for all this to be done with, if that's what you mean. There's no hope for either of us. Not now."

"That depends very much on what you mean by hope. There is hope for Aona, and therefore there's hope for everyone and everything. The struggle for this world is not about you and I, and certainly not the flesh we inhabit. Isn't there an old *luyan* saying- *Death is but the beginning*?"

"Death is a doorway, not the end," Lyya corrected her.

"Then there is always hope. Hope is eternal," Jaana pointed out.

Lyya laughed at that.

After a quick breakfast the two women headed east, as they had since leaving their shelter. Their ultimate aim was to reach the eastern edge of Mordenglen, where the Border Wall marked the barrier between Harn and Aphenhast. Of course, it was not so much a wall here in the North as a vast chaos of rubble and entangled vegetation, but Jaana had seen for herself the powerful natural defences that Aona could bring to bear everywhere along this line of half-fallen stonework when she entered Harn for the first time. The wall, or rather the natural sorcery that had made the wall its home and infiltrated the surrounding vegetation, would do whatever it could to defend the land.

Later that morning, as they headed along a narrow, winding path with close-packed conifers on either side, Lyya muttered something to herself, put her pack down and wiped at her brow before removing her shirt. Jaana watched as she tore a strip off the fabric, tied it around her breasts and stuffed the remainder into her pack.

"You remind me of when we first met," Jaana murmured.

Lyya turned to her, a sudden gleam of something in her eyes that Jaana interpreted as hope. Lyya reached out to stroke her cheek, and Jaana's suspicions were confirmed when her lover continued, "We don't have to do this, Jaana. Nor do we have to join anyone else. We can go somewhere, hide and..."

"...live happily ever after?" Jaana gave her a hard little smile. Had Lyya still not accepted her eventual fate? "We cannot turn away from what we have to do, Lyya. Why do you still think we can? That isn't the destiny of those chosen to save Aona. Try, if you still think you can fight against your fate. But you should know that Aona's essence flows within you now. Head west and you'll find yourself walking east soon enough, unable to work out how it happened. A backward track will only lead you full circle. We have only this path to walk, Lyya, and the sooner you accept that the better it will be for us both."

As she witnessed the now-familiar despair in her lover's eyes, Jaana grabbed her arm fiercely, suddenly angry at Lyya's continued reluctance to accept her fate. "Would you rather die with me or live without me? I would *never* want to spend long remaining days in lonely silence, waiting for death to come- not if I couldn't be with you. I would rather know you were at my side as we fight the creatures of the void. I know you would make the same choice."

Lyya bowed her head and eventually gave a reluctant nod. "It should never have come to this," she remarked sadly.

Jaana kissed her on the lips and reminded her, "But it did. Ours is a noble purpose. You must always remember that."

Although the air was warm, still they glimpsed patches of mist that lingered in the lower reaches of the great forest through the morning, silvery tendrils that reached slowly out towards the areas where sunlight fell. Everywhere the two women looked, signs of early spring were abundant in the form of flowers budding and even opening, or small creatures scurrying through the undergrowth.

As the shadows lengthened late in the afternoon, Lyya stopped at a fork in the path and suggested that they rest for the night rather than press on. Although she was used to physical exertion and as fit as anyone she knew, in recent days she had often felt exhausted for brief moments- a temporary effect, Jaana assured her, of the changes wrought within her body as the Old Powers worked their magic. That exhaustion had always been accompanied by a feeling of utter desolation and a desire to simply collapse and sleep, to make this grim existence disappear for a while.

"In a while," Jaana said. "We'll head down this way." She pointed to the path on the left hand side, which led down towards the depths of a shadowy ravine.

Lyya peered doubtfully down the slope. "Are you sure this is the quickest route? Should we not skirt around this area or at least look for a shallower part of the valley?"

"I don't intend to take the quickest route," Jaana explained. "You'll see why in good time."

As they began to make their way along the path Lyya hesitantly pointed out, "There are others down there. Others like us. I can feel their presence."

"So can I, and in fact, that's why I led us this way. But as you said, they're like us and so there's nothing to fear. Your *kin*-senses are building all the while, Lyya. I wondered when you might sense the others nearby."

The path twisted one way and the other as it threaded its way down the steep slope of the valley. At times the way ahead became perilously narrow, and both women almost lost their footing several times. Their uncertain progress dislodged dirt and small stones that tumbled down to the valley floor and river far below. "Now they'll certainly know we're coming," Lyya said at one point as she steadied herself.

"Of course they will. I would expect them to. It works both ways, Lyya."

The *luyan* woman stopped for a moment and looked up at the patch of darkening sky above the canopy of trees. A faint, sharp sliver of red appeared caught in the silhouetted tangle of branches- Archaon, which had risen a short while ago. *How many more times will I see it?* she wondered. *Or see any of this? How many more times will I wake?*

Lyya took a deep breath and continued on along the path. Not for the first time, she told herself that it was pointless to contemplate such things now.

Darkness lay thick throughout the deep valley when they finally reached the river, where the path continued along near the water's edge. But their *kin*-senses used what little light fell this far and strengthened it. To them the night appeared almost as if Ildar's full face shone down upon them from a clear sky. Lyya's existing *luyan* ability to see well in the dark and to detect the heat of any creatures large or small that might be wandering nearby made her awareness almost as total as it would have been during a bright day, although that did nothing to allay her unease.

Jaana led the way upstream, striding with new-found eagerness as if the other *kin* were now very close. Perhaps they were. Lyya could not yet tell exactly how near or distant they might be, but she followed with trepidation and wondered to herself if they were as safe meeting with these people as Jaana had assumed.

Soon the river widened. Up ahead a small waterfall fell thirty or forty hands into a tranquil, wide pool of water. Sitting by the river's edge and looking out over that pool were three *kin*. They turned and got to their feet as Jaana and Lyya approached. Lyya felt a momentary stab of fear as she looked at them, and calmed herself with an effort. Two of them looked ordinary enough at first glance- a slim, nondescript man with dark hair and a younger man- more boy than man, she thought after a moment. The third, a female, looked anything but normal. *She has no skin,* Lyya observed as she stared at the *kin*-woman. *And the heat that comes from within her- it's far greater than the others. Why would she be remade in such a way? What purpose does such an abomination serve? How does she even remain alive?*

"My name is Ferrin," the older man said after a moment, apparently satisfied with his initial appraisal of the newcomers. "This is Leon- and this is Ithia. We numbered more than this, but our other companions now serve our Lords elsewhere."

"I'm Jaana. This is Lyya," Jaana replied. "We were headed towards the Border Wall, but we sensed that other *kin* were nearby so thought we might travel with you, if you permit it. You *are* headed the same way?"

Ferrin smiled at that. "Who isn't?" He motioned for Jaana and Lyya to sit, and as he and his companions did likewise he added, "I suspect the battle to end them all may come soon. A relief, in a way. My companions and I have travelled far and done much in the name of our Lords, but soon the greatest test of all will come. The struggle for which each of us was remade."

Lyya barely repressed a shudder at those words.

"And what of your story?" Ithia spoke up. Her eyes fixed on Jaana, bright and intent, but to Lyya's surprise Jaana glanced in her direction and gestured for her to speak. "Why don't you tell them our story, Lyya? It might sound more interesting coming from you."

"Might it?" Lyya swallowed and thought quickly. She couldn't decide how or where she ought to start. "We met in the forest of Knarlswood, in Aphenhast," she began, but Jaana laughed and shook her head. "That was a different life for both of us, Lyya, and it doesn't matter now. Begin from the time we were at Inerdyr's castle."

"You were acolytes of Inerdyr?" Ferrin remarked. He seemed surprised and slightly amused at that.

"For a while," Jaana admitted, and gestured for Lyya to continue.

Lyya reluctantly retold the story of how they had travelled with Inerdyr's army as far as the Stillwater. She recalled as much as she could of the journey and the horrific aftermath, the sacrifices she remembered seeing, the untold thousands who had perished either on the way to the battleground or during the battle itself, which still remained indistinct in her mind like a nightmare shrouded in fog. She mentioned the lower *kin* she had seen fighting and then being routed by the army of witches, *orkar* and northmen.

"I remember only a little of what happened," she confessed, "but then I remember I somehow found and followed Jaana's trail. Inerdyr's enemies let her go."

"They let her go?" Ferrin raised an eyebrow. "Why would they do that?"

"I don't know. I didn't see it myself..."

"I tried to offer them a truce," Jaana interrupted. "I tried to show them the extent of their own stupidity in their refusal to ally with us. They would have none of it, and I thought my time was done. But then one of their number said he would send me back to our Lords- as if they exist in only one stronghold! He suggested that they would be enraged at my capture and humiliation as he called it- never mind the fact that I was one amongst many who had been defeated, and that this was a battle only, not the wider war. He also said that they had no wish to wage war upon the *choragh* until the *marandaal* were banished from Aona- and then only if they still claimed dominion over the Younger Races. Those were his words."

Ferrin laughed at that. "How gracious of this man! He seeks to offer terms of peace to the ancient protectors of Aona?" He looked thoughtfully at Jaana. "I assume he was one of their leaders?"

She nodded. "But not a human man, not entirely anyway. I'm not sure what he was."

"Who do you suppose killed Inerdyr?" Lyya asked.

Ferrin shrugged. "Does it matter? I wondered the same thing for a while. As it turned out, the mad sorcerer of Mornkastle was not key to any of this. Inerdyr thought in his conceit that it would never be necessary for him to become *kin*. And even when he was remade, he proved himself to be a far from reliable ally. If you'd care to know my theory, I would say it could have been the work of the witchlings- the Descendants as they like to call themselves, although of course we're all descendants of powerful practitioners."

Jaana frowned. "How could they have reached him without our Lords destroying them in the process?"

"Now that's a more difficult question, and one that I've asked myself more than a few times." Ferrin paused and then said quietly, "I don't like to make guesses, Jaana. I like structure and as much certainty as possible. But if I were to hazard a guess, I would say that they found a way to use the Green Road."

"Then *we* ought to have found a way to reach that place," Jaana replied, taken aback. "How could we not have been granted the ability to go where they went, and use the ability to move quickly to destroy these renegades?"

Ferrin said nothing to that.

After a moment Lyya added quietly, "Eventually I found Jaana in eastern Mordenglen. I wasn't *kin* at that point, but she remade me."

Ferrin nodded appreciatively. "Quite so. You would have done anything to remain at her side, clearly. It's right that the two of you should be the same as you face the same enemies."

"Were you afraid?" Leon spoke up suddenly. "I was, when it happened to me. Sometimes I still am when I recall it."

"The defenders of the world have nothing to fear but defeat, Leon," Ithia remarked, and stroked his cheek fondly. Remarkably, the boy didn't even flinch at the touch of raw flesh.

"As Ithia said, the only thing to fear now is defeat," Lyya replied carefully, and then lied, "I certainly no longer fear death." *I only wish for it all to be over,* she almost added. *A sleep I never have to wake from.*

They lapsed into silence for a while longer. Lyya tried to imagine what it would be like to finally face the *marandaal* after all this time. She couldn't even picture them in her mind. Jaana had said they might appear like shapes fashioned from light, but also that they could alter their appearance at will. *They sound more like an unspeakable destructive entity forged in the depths of the Existence than any kind of creature,* Lyya thought. *How is it that they exist? Were they truly created by humans tens of thousands of years ago as some say? I know that humans are mostly destructive beings, but why would even they do such a thing?*

Later, Jaana lay down to sleep and Lyya did likewise, having noticed that both Ithia and Ferrin had done the same. Leon, meanwhile, sat on a boulder with his feet and ankles in the cold water of the river, silent and apparently lost in his thoughts.

II

When Ithia's eyes flickered open to behold the dawn, they immediately met Leon's steady gaze. The two *kin* stared at each other for a moment and a kind of wordless understanding passed between them as it had for many days now. Then Ithia sat up and stretched, and remarked, "Most days, the last thing I see before I sleep is you sitting beside me. Then I see you again when the dawn light wakes me. It's as if you haven't moved."

"More often than not I haven't," Leon confessed. "I no longer need to sleep, so I sit and use the time to think."

"What do you think about?"

"How strange it is- this path that we follow. How different to the lives we once led. Sometimes I even wonder what comes after us."

"I'm not sure what you mean."

"Soon we will fight in the greatest battle of this Age. We'll more than likely perish."

"We change and in time become something else," Ithia corrected him, and tried to banish the disquieting knot of unease that tightened inside her.

"It won't be as it was. Nothing will. A new power will rise. Something that no one has ever seen, or foreseen."

Ithia moved closer and pressed a finger to his lips. "Do not say such things," she chided him, "or if you must, make sure you don't utter them when Ferrin can hear you."

Leon looked guardedly around, but Ferrin had gone hunting- or perhaps sought out a suitable place for his daily meditation- at first light. As the first note of birdsong rang out he had risen and departed, and he had not returned without their knowing. The two *kin*-women were still asleep.

"I had a dream," Leon said.

"Leon, you said that you no longer slept."

"But I can still dream. It was like a vision, Ithia- from some distant Age yet to be."

"And what did this Age look like?"

"Dark stone, noise and squalor. Ten million people in walled cities where once a hundred thousand lived. A kind of sorcery I can't even begin to describe. And presiding over it all..."

"Don't." Ithia's voice cut across his abruptly. "I don't want to know. I don't need to know. It isn't a world that we will ever witness. It's just a forbidden window."

"If it's forbidden, then why did I have this dream? Why would it be permitted?"

Ithia thought for a while and then said quietly, so that their new companions would hopefully not hear if they had since been awakened, "If the Existence is like a circle and you sit upon that circle for long enough, sooner or later you may see the same things. Events come and go, and perhaps over many millennia they repeat, although in different ways. Glimpses such as yours may appear to be windows into the unknowable future, but perhaps they are also fragments of the past. This, perhaps, is how sometimes people claim to know the future."

"What great power could allow this, or make it happen?" Leon wondered.

She smiled at that. "That's hardly for the likes of you and I to know, and it's only a theory, an idea about how the Existence works. I heard it a long time ago and for some reason it remained with me. But it's just an idea, Leon. If I were you I'd forget about your dreams of distant Ages. I don't know why it happened, but it doesn't matter. If time wears thin on occasion and allows you to see through the veil, so be it- I'm not entirely surprised that such things would happen now. But you're a witness to the destiny of people you will never know, just as they will never know you."

"Nor the sacrifice we all made," he added in a low voice, but he could say no more on the matter, for Ferrin was on his way back, strolling along the riverside path with an easy calm that neither Leon nor Ithia knew.

V – Dreams and Despair

I

The humming sound and the heat in the air became unbearable as the lightdreamers turned to face Fauli and Parril. Nothing of consequence looked out from behind their eyes- no intelligence, no reasoning- and yet some instinct within them had sensed Parril's involuntary summoning of the Powers, which had disrupted the vital stage of their ceremony.

Fauli saw dark shapes and swirling colours form in the air. The lightdreamers screamed and shouted, enraged. Even in their madness they appeared to understand what was happening. The dark space in the air between them shimmered and flickered as if the forces invoked by the boy sorcerer had disrupted it. Most of the lightdreamers began to shake uncontrollably and then fell to the ground. One of the few who managed to remain on her feet rushed at Parril, her features twisted into a malevolent rage. Parril appeared not to even see the woman run straight at him but Fauli stepped into her path and cut her down before she could reach them, her longknife a deadly blur. The woman sagged to the ground clutching at her neck in a futile attempt to stop the gushing of blood.

The Gate shimmered and shook in the air, and the heat around them continued to grow. The shapes and colours darted around the lightdreamers and then disappeared. A moment later the Gate winked out of existence, and the seasonal chill suddenly returned.

All the lightdreamers lay dead at the lake shore, except the one who Fauli had killed, whose blood still leaked from her unmoving body to stain the damp grass.

Parril collapsed suddenly, and Fauli knelt down to help him. *I'm not sure what he did just then,* she thought, *but*

I'm fairly certain that he just saved us from an incursion by the marandaal. *What else would step through a Gate fashioned by lightdreamers?*

Trying not to contemplate the enormity of what that meant, Fauli hauled the boy to his feet as gently as she could, desperate to be away from this place even though the Gate had apparently disappeared and the lightdreamers had all been destroyed. Gates and the Powers and lightdreamers were not matters that she understood anything about, and she had no desire to discover any more than she already had.

She felt a sudden intense pain in her side and saw blood seeping through her shirt under her cloak. *How did that happen?* she wondered. *None of them could have got close enough to me.* Then she saw a wicked-looking throwing star in the grass, slick with her blood, and she grimaced. *How did I not even notice that? Some kind of sorcery? I would normally have seen it and cut it down in mid-flight.*

"You're bleeding," Parril murmured as he noticed her wound.

"I'll live," Fauli retorted with considerably more vigour than she felt.

They made their way slowly onwards. Fauli tried her best to ignore the pain. Their path took them through the damp woodland, and when it forked Fauli opted for the wider, flatter trail. By the middle of the afternoon they had emerged into more open land covered in shrubs, bracken and grassy hills. Parril stopped suddenly and said, "We should warn people about the lightdreamers."

Fauli laughed weakly. "What people, Parril?"

Ignoring her jibe he continued, "If one group can make that Gate appear then there must be others, mustn't there?"

Fauli silently agreed with him, but she cautioned, "The main towns are mostly south of here, so that's where we should probably head. But we need to stay away from Mornkastle and the surrounding area. If the authorities there discover who you are- or *what* you are- then you'll be captured.

123

Perhaps they'll even return you to Inerdyr if they know that his men are looking for you. Everyone has a price and I imagine yours is quite high."

Parril shuddered.

"Anyway, we need somewhere to stay awhile," Fauli continued. "You're not well enough to travel any great distance."

"What about you?" he pointed out. "You're badly wounded. I saw the blood."

In answer, Fauli pulled up her shirt enough for him to see the wound. It still hurt, but it had long since stopped bleeding and had even started to close up. Parril stared incredulously. "How do you heal so quickly?"

"All *du-luyan* do," Fauli said. "It makes one more reason for the folk of the other Races to hate us. Certainly humans are jealous of us in that respect."

"I don't hate you," Parril declared. He finally dragged his eyes away from the wound. "Why would I? You saved me from capture. And even if you hadn't, I wouldn't..."

Fauli raised a hand wearily. "Thank you, Parril, but let's talk about how we don't hate each other after we find somewhere to rest."

They headed south and skirted along the edge of the woodland for a league or more until finally they reached an open grassy plain bordered by hills to the east and further south. Parril had needed to rest three times already, and as they paused at the edge of the woods he collapsed to his knees once again, head bowed and palms pressed against the damp grass. Fauli observed him worriedly. He looked as pale as a *luyan* and shook noticeably.

As she squatted down at his side he looked at her, hair blowing across his wan face, and said tiredly, "Go without me, Fauli. You don't owe me anything. Go."

Fauli shook her head, wondering how best to address an impetuous twelve-year-old boy. "I'm not leaving you. You may remember that *you* saved *my* life not long ago. You're also perhaps the closest person I have to a friend, Parril- no, the *only* friend I have."

"Really?"

"All the others are dead, or as good as. But that's a story for another time, if you truly want to hear such a tale. Anyway, I'm not about to abandon you now. The next farmstead or cottage that either of us spots, we'll go there and beg shelter."

"It might not be safe," he warned.

"We've no choice. I don't fancy your chances without some rest and healing."

"Thank you," he mumbled, and as she helped him to his feet Fauli wondered briefly if he had thanked her for refusing to abandon him, or simply jested about her bleak assessment of his situation.

Luck was not entirely against them that afternoon. As the light began to dim Fauli's sharp eyes caught sight of a cottage and stable in the distance, nestled near the bottom of one of the rolling hills that rose from the grassland. By the time they had reached the buildings, night had fallen and dim lantern light could be seen behind the curtains of one of the ground-floor windows. In the stable a horse whickered softly and pricked up its ears as they drew close.

"If you sense anything of the Old Dark here," Fauli said softly, "then be sure to tell me."

Parril just nodded tiredly.

Fauli knocked on the door and after a short while they heard someone walk into the hallway and draw back the bolts. The door opened slowly and a man in his middle years peered out at them, holding a lantern to one side. His lined face looked full of shadows and what little hair he had left clung to the sides of his head.

He said nothing but immediately noted Parril's condition and waved them inside. Fauli didn't know whether to be relieved or worried that he so readily ushered them in.

But she reminded herself that they had nowhere else to go. They had little choice but to trust in fate.

The two of them sat Parril down in a back room which the householder lit with a couple of other lanterns. He stoked up the fire to push back the shadows further and then remarked, "You would rather have stayed hidden, no doubt."

Fauli said nothing, and hoped that her unease didn't show. "I couldn't let him die," she said quietly. Parril had already fallen asleep, she noticed. "Can you help him?"

"I believe so, with any luck. I don't suppose you want to tell me how the two of you happened to be travelling together. But I can guess."

"We'll go if you wish," Fauli said quickly. "We don't want to bring you bad luck."

He shook his head. "You don't have to do that. I'm no friend of Inerdyr." He nodded, perhaps seeing a subtle shift in her expression. "Yes. I've met a few others who have fled his army over the last tennight or so. You're not the only ones by any means. Besides, you're here now, and that makes me an accessory, doesn't it? You covered your tracks as best you could, I expect."

"We tried." Fauli's tone was guarded. Then she remembered that she had no idea if Inerdyr's men were still looking for them. She suddenly remembered having seen a small group of Tracking Beasts back at the camp, and shivered. Presumably the creatures hadn't been sent to hunt them down. *We'd have been captured by now,* she thought, *and I would have been executed. Nothing can throw those creatures off the trail. Why were they not sent after us?*

She glanced worriedly at the boy. "He looks worse than before."

"He'll live, with any luck. I'll mix up a potion for him which should help. But what he needs most is rest. I don't suppose you've had time for much of that since you escaped." He added softly, "Are the rumours of the Old Dark true, would you say? That it runs like a poison through Inerdyr's army? Others have said so."

"I know very little about such things," Fauli confessed. "All I can say for certain is I felt something malign that affected people. There were many fights, and some people died as a result. Others became paranoid, convinced that friends or family members plotted against them. It was a place of fear and madness. It might eventually have affected the two of us had we not escaped." She shuddered. "It *did* affect me in truth. I suffered dreams every night that were full of death, torture, shadows that were people and people that were no more than shadows."

"Hmm. I'm not surprised. Stories have been told in secret about the mad sorcerer for many years, long before Inerdyr gathered his unwilling army together. Stories of madness and torture and unspeakable acts of depravity. Of course, no one dares to say such things openly. I keep an eye on events out to the west of here, as best I can. I heard the stories of the army being raised from the folk of the settlements long before I met people who had escaped from it. The Wardens have no spine; they readily let Inerdyr and his henchmen gather their people and use them howsoever they wish."

"I've seen far more of the Old Dark than I ever wanted to," Fauli said. "Something certainly ran through that army-some evil presence. But I saw lightdreamers there also, preaching their madness before they were beaten to death."

He nodded. "Most of those people will be dead before they reach the Stillwater. But I suspect that's part of the plan. Inerdyr's masters are not called the Blood Lords for nothing. The power of sacrifice is stronger than ever now with the starspawn already destroying Aphenhast in the east, and the *choragh* gaining in strength accordingly." He looked appraisingly at her. "Are you going to give your names? You don't have to, of course."

"Fauli," she said after a moment's reluctance. "And this is Parril."

"Mine is Ienin." He glanced at Parril as the boy stirred drowsily. "Let's get you both something to eat and drink and then you can rest."

"You seem remarkably trusting of two desperate fugitives," Fauli said as he wandered into his kitchen to prepare the promised potion and some food, and she sat in one of the chairs opposite Parril. She couldn't help but sigh contentedly. She hadn't sat in a chair for more days than she could remember.

"Do I?" He glanced back and smiled to himself. "If you meant me harm, Fauli, you'd be dead already - both of you. That much I can assure you. And the same goes if I meant *you* harm, which I do not."

Is he some kind of hedge-warlock? Fauli wondered. *Clearly he's more than he appears to be. Then again, isn't everyone these days?*

She watched as Ienin roused Parril sufficiently for the boy to swallow some of the thick, green-coloured potion he had mixed up. Parril coughed and grimaced at the taste but managed to keep it down. Later on, Ienin served them a dinner of root vegetable broth with some hunks of bread, washed down with golden ale. Fauli had to stop herself from gulping everything down too quickly. Parril, who still appeared wan and pale, ate and drank slowly and fell asleep again as soon as they had helped him back to his chair afterwards.

"Where will you be headed when he's well enough?" Ienin asked after the plates had been cleared away.

"South." Fauli paused, the worrisome image of the lightdreamers strong in her mind. *I have to tell him,* she decided, and so she gave the details of their encounter with the lightdreamers. Ienin listened soberly until she had finished and then pondered the matter for a while.

"If others are able to come together and open another Gate, that would be calamitous," he said finally. "They must be stopped. But I'll wager that if Parril even so much as grasps the Powers before he's recovered properly, then he's likely to perish. Regardless of what you've told me, he must rest and recover first. He may be needed to find and stop other groups of lightdreamers from what they're doing. Of course, there are lightdreamers throughout Harn and possibly the entire known world by now. Neither he nor anyone else can stop them all."

Ienin gave them both blankets for wrapping themselves in for the night- the fire had burned low in the hearth and much of its warmth had fled the sitting chamber. After he had left for bed, Fauli sat wrapped in her blanket and watched the glowing embers, her thoughts drifting from the past to the present and finally to the unknown future. *How much longer will I keep cheating death?* she wondered. *All my old friends are long gone. I miss them as much as ever, and I've no purpose, no reason to continue. I'm only alive now because Parril happened to come along at the right moment. But does that mean anything or was it simply fate and nothing else?*

Parril stirred drowsily. His eyes opened momentarily and he looked across at her. "Thank you," he murmured.

"Will you be thanking me a tennight from now, I wonder?" Fauli replied. He didn't reply, and after a moment she realised that he had fallen asleep again.

II

Parril recovered slowly, so they remained at Ienin's house for another six days. Fauli helped with whatever work and chores she could, determined to pay Ienin back for his hospitality in some way.

On the morning of the seventh day, Fauli and Parril departed Ienin's house. Dense clouds gathered in the sky and held the promise of rain. "I have no money to give you, which

129

shames me," Fauli said awkwardly as they bade each other farewell.

"I chose to take you in," he replied simply. "Good luck to you both."

They headed south-west with the sun rising slowly at their backs. Parril walked with a determined step and Fauli marvelled silently at his new-found resilience. By the time they stopped for lunch, however, his thoughts seemed to have drifted towards the length of the journey ahead, for he asked, "How far do we need to travel, do you think?"

"As far as the first town we come across, provided we're well south of Mornkastle," Fauli responded.

"But that could be... that could even be as far as Waylorn," he protested.

"I doubt it. Roads lead to towns, as you know perfectly well. Sooner or later we'll come across a road, and we'll follow it."

Two days passed with neither event nor mishap, and around midday on the third day the path they had been following joined a wider dirt track. *Our luck may be turning,* Fauli thought- and she turned out to be right, although it appeared to be for the worse.

She heard the *orkar* men only an instant before they stepped from out of the cover of the trees to either side of the track. Two stepped out in front of them, clad in hide and leather armour, and when she turned to look behind she saw another two standing in the track. Fauli had never met an *orkar* in her life, and judging by Parril's reaction neither had he.

One of the two in front of her turned to his companion and said something in their own language. The other man nodded and pointed to Parril.

"You will come with us," the *orkar* who had spoken said.

Fauli and Parril had their wrists tied behind their backs, and were then made to walk in the middle of the group of *orkar*. The track left the wooded area after a while and continued west across open grassland.

After a while Fauli caught sight of a large encampment in the distance ahead. As they drew nearer she saw that this was a vast army- but certainly not Inerdyr's. Shielding her eyes from the sunlight, she surveyed the area for a while. There were hundreds of *orkar,* but also many humans and even a number of *luyan.*

As Fauli watched the masses of *orkar* guarding and wandering through the camp, she wondered where this army had come from. Surely these were enemies of Inerdyr and his people. *Do they plan conquest over the South?* she silently asked herself.

The *orkar* guardsmen nearest to them watched warily as their entourage reached the edge of the camp. They exchanged words with the four who had captured Fauli and Parril, and then one of them walked swiftly into the camp.

As they waited in pensive silence, Fauli allowed her gaze to wander around the area. Here and there cooking fires smouldered, some with meat of one sort or another sizzling and dripping over them. The aroma of food mingled with the heavy odours of sweat and the waste from privies that had been dug around the area felt curious and unpleasant to her sharp sense of smell. For a moment, when the breeze turned a certain way she could also detect the odour of rotting flesh. *No worse than any other large army though,* she reminded herself, *and certainly no worse than the one from which we escaped. These are ordinary sights and smells by comparison.*

"Will you stay with me?" Parril asked at her side.

"I will if they let me." When alarm leapt in his eyes she added, "We've come this far, Parril, and we have nowhere else to go. Let's just see what luck has in store for us, and deal with whatever happens."

A short while later a woman wearing a dark grey cloak made her way towards them, flanked by two *orkar.* Fauli watched as she approached and suddenly became certain that this was not a human but in fact one of the feared Watchers of Luudhoq. Not having met one before, she nevertheless had heard them described often enough to recognise the creature. With an effort she met the Watcher's cold eyes and for a moment thought that they changed colour slightly. *My imagination,* she decided, but wondered at the same time if the sorcery wielded by such creatures might allow for such a thing.

She thought for a moment about the message that she and Parril had intended to give to whoever they could. Might those in charge of this army be able to do something about the lightdreamers? On an impulse she said, "We have something important to tell your leaders. I don't know what you intend to do with us, but you need to let us speak with them."

The Watcher regarded her for a moment. "Come with me," she said abruptly. Fauli and Parril stepped uncertainly after her through the mud, and two of the *orkar* who had captured them walked to either side. The Watcher led them briskly to a large pavilion tent inside which a number of people were gathered. Their attention was focussed on a couple of large maps spread out on the ground and forced down with stones in each corner.

Fauli scanned each of them in turn. Could these people the commanders of this army? she wondered. They were an odd-looking group to say the least. She saw two more Watchers, two *orkar* warlords, even a *du-luyan* girl.

Then her eyes widened in shock. *I know that girl,* she thought, staring at the young *du-luyan* female, who looked warily back at her. *Or at least I've met her before. She was that thief we found ransacking Fistelkarn's tower. What is she doing here of all places?*

"Who are these two, Kelandra?" the larger of the two *orkar* rumbled.

"They were found by one of your scouting groups and brought to the eastern edge of the camp a short while ago," the Watcher said. "I'm told the boy has some strength in the

Powers, but I'll let the experts among you decide if that's true or not."

"He does," the *du-luyan* girl spoke up immediately. "He's strong. Very strong."

Parril coloured and looked down at the ground. Fauli moved slightly to stand even closer to him- not that she could stop them doing whatever they wished with the boy.

"Well, that's half their story. They also insisted that they had something important to tell us." Kelandra turned to Fauli. "You have before you everyone with authority and command, ready to listen. Say what you have to say."

Fauli took a deep breath and considered her words. If she rambled like a madwoman or failed to convince these people then their journey would be in vain, and no one would believe them until it was too late. *Be calm,* she told herself, *and just offer the truth. You can do no more.*

"We were caught up in Inerdyr's army," she began, "but we managed to escape. In fact the two of us escaped separately and met later, but that doesn't matter." She decided that these people didn't need to know about the *diafagh*. "As we travelled we came upon a group of lightdreamers out to the north-east of here, engaged in some sort of ritual at the shore of a lake. I took one look, marked it as the sort of insanity they are known for and suggested we hasten away. But Parril sensed that something else was at play- a powerful force had been awakened, and somehow the lightdreamers had caused it, or were a part of it."

Fauli glanced quickly around, satisfied to see that she now had their full attention. Knowing glances were exchanged, but no one spoke. With new-found confidence she pressed on, "We felt the air become much warmer. A strange sound started up. I don't know if it came from the lightdreamers or something else. And then we saw a dark space form in the air. At first I didn't know what it was, but then..." She glanced at Parril, who folded his arms and shuddered at the memory. "A Gate was being formed," she said finally. "But Parril used the Powers against the lightdreamers, and somehow that broke the spell. Then the Gate just... vanished. All the lightdreamers died.

"We've been travelling south in the hope that if we mention this to the authorities in the first town we find, they can do something about it. We don't want to be a part of this war, but you had to be told about the danger. If lightdreamers have somehow gained the ability to create and open Gates, if the *marandaal* can somehow influence them in such a way..." She left the sentence unfinished, but she could tell simply by looking around that she had already said everything she needed to. Everyone gathered looked ill at ease.

Finally a pale looking man with violet eyes spoke up. "The matter will be discussed. Thank you." He turned his attention to Parril. "You'll remain with us. There are people here who can look after and train you." To Fauli's bewilderment he turned to the *du-luyan* girl. "Kian, you can help arrange it."

So she's a sorceress as well as a thief? Fauli thought as Kian nodded in acceptance. *Well, maybe that's how she knew Parril had some talent in the Powers.*

"What about me?" she heard herself ask, and instantly grimaced at the plaintive tone of her question. *Why would they care? Maybe they'll just let me leave. Part of me wants to be away from here.*

"Your people are known as formidable warriors," the man noted, "and we have only a few amongst us. If you can fight, you have a place here. But you should be aware that eventually we must face the *marandaal*."

"She is a trained weaponswoman, so she will *certainly* be of use to you," a voice spoke up from the entrance. Fauli turned quickly to see who had spoken, and blinked in shock. The speaker was not only a *du-luyan* man, but one who she recognised, albeit from many years ago.

"Iyoth," she said quietly.

"You know me as well?" He seemed amused.

"And your reputation," she said guardedly. "Everyone knows you, or *of* you. Did you return to Cai?"

"I did." The thin smile vanished abruptly. He crossed the tent to where the *du-luyan* girl stood. "This is my daughter, Kian."

I should have known, Fauli almost retorted. *The assassin and the thief.*

Iyoth addressed everyone. "This woman Fauli is a trained weaponswoman, as I said. Most of her childhood was given over to that training. She was an orphan, you see. People in that sort of situation are often selected for such a role. They have less to lose, and sometimes that gives them more focus. Anyway, she completed her training and then left to travel. As far as I'm aware she never went back."

"No," Fauli agreed. "I didn't." For a moment she felt a curious darkness open up inside her, a weight into which she could fall and be crushed. As Iyoth had bluntly pointed out, she had no family. She had never had a family. The few friends that she had made died in the act of trying to warn the authorities in Aphenhast about the coming of the *marandaal.*

No one, she thought, over and over. *No one left. No one. Gods, let me be gone from this place.*

Iyoth was not yet done with his unwanted accolade. "Very few complete their training with full honours. Fauli did. Dare I say it, she may well be more than a match for me with a blade in hand. Any sort of blade." The assassin looked her up and down. "Perhaps not a two-handed greatsword. Anything smaller though."

"This was all years ago," Fauli said weakly. She couldn't be sure whether or not she was protesting. *Does it even matter?* she thought.

"Stay," she heard Parril murmur at her side, and for some reason that plea brought her out of her grim thoughts of the past. After a moment Fauli gave him a weary smile. "Why not? I have nowhere else to be, and no one to answer to."

VI - Unaccountable Faith

I

Is she reaching out to me, or am I going mad?

This thought had plagued Alexia for days.

She stood and looked out across the open grassland as far as the distant horizon. *I see Aona's light so often now,* she thought. *At least, I think I do. Or am I simply imagining things? Did the journey render me insane somehow? Did it damage me in some subtle way that only now manifests itself?*

Alexia couldn't decide where the truth lay. She had spent many nights lying awake, tormented by the fear that time had started to run out, that although she had reached the people whose names had been revealed to her in the Green Road, she now had no idea what to do.

She also worried that people had started to gossip and spread rumours about her. Phyqor and Yui had both noticed her staring off into the distance for long periods of time on numerous occasions, but she reckoned half the people in the camp also had by now. They would observe her and draw their own conclusions about her state of mind.

She remembered Yui's words during their journey north to reach this place. *You brought part of it back with you.*

Alexia shuddered and wondered if that might be true. But what could she possibly do about it? Might there be something that she now had to do? Did her glimpses of the mysterious light mean anything at all or was it simply a strange after-effect, a taint or residue in her mind?

She wandered east of the encampment to the edge of a small woodland. To the north the land sloped gently upwards to the summit of a large grassy hill where birds wheeled around on the stiff air currents. The path she had followed now divided. One way meandered towards and then up the hill while the other took a route alongside the edge of

136

the woods before it dropped into a steep valley whose sides were worn partly away by the recent rain. After a moment's hesitation Alexia took this path. But as she reached the tree line she stopped, certain that she had caught a murmur of fleeting words carried in the breeze. They did not come to her in a language that she could understand.

She calls to me.

Alexia would have dismissed the idea as nonsense only a few months ago. Now she was not entirely surprised when the path before her brightened and each and every facet of the surrounding woodland burst with new detail as she walked. "Are you doing this?" she whispered. Despite everything she plainly saw, she wondered again if some latent madness afflicted her. *I doubt anyone walks the Green Road and remains entirely unscathed,* she thought with a shudder.

The light grew steadily stronger until the way before her became utterly obscured in that brightness. Finally Alexia stopped and turned to see the woodland lit only by weak, wintry sunlight and foliage shifting almost imperceptibly in the light breeze. In comparison with the path down which she had walked it looked almost drab, as if an invisible cloud loomed over it.

"What do you need from me?" she whispered plaintively, for perhaps the tenth time in as many days.

But as on every previous occasion, no answer came.

That night Alexia dreamed that she had found her way back to the Green Road. In her dream she aimlessly wandered the streets of the desolate city which she thought of as Luudhoq's shadow.

At first the city appeared much the same as before. Broken buildings rose sharply into the half-lit alien sky. Great cracks opened up momentarily in the ground to reveal either complete darkness, sickly green-hued light or flashes of savage white brilliance. Here and there, entities that behaved like furtive creatures but which could have been anything moved through the harshness of the shadows.

But Alexia soon observed that parts of the city had caved in completely. Sinkholes had appeared and caused nearby structures to collapse into them or to be pulled nearer, as if the fabric of this place poured slowly away into these chasms to be lost forever. Alexia dared not go near to these, but she knew without needing to approach them that each such abyss had become effectively infinite in depth, the matter that it had claimed still crumbling away as it fell forever through dark space.

"The cycle must continue, or everything will be lost," a voice spoke up from behind her.

Alexia turned slowly to see a being that bore her image, except that it looked drained of colour. Whether it was the same creature that she had met before she couldn't tell. *I know this is a dream,* she told herself. *I don't have to be afraid.*

But before she could even react, the creature reached out its hand and touched her cheek. Alexia flinched and recoiled as a sharp image came to her mind of a Gate inside the Green Road, a black portal into which Aona's essence slowly leaked away. It felt so real, so *near* that Alexia became certain it would pull her towards it and perhaps even destroy her if she reached out towards it. *This must be the Gate that Yui dreamed of,* she thought. *It's real. A hole eating away the centre of the world from the inside out.*

She turned her head and tried desperately to banish the image from her mind. "I know nothing of Gates," she protested. "Why must it be me?"

In an instant the touch became a hard grip, as strong as iron and as cold as ice. She felt herself being drawn back towards the creature like a helpless puppet. The eyes in the harsh visage burrowed into her. Alexia tried to speak but she could hardly frame a single thought.

Why were you chosen? Why did I reach out to you? This time the voice slid through her mind, and Alexia cried out.

Because you and your kind are the chroniclers of the Ages. Few hear my voice; those who do must write the story of the Age they witness.

"But... the Gate..."

On the other side, you will understand.

Numb with cold and fear, Alexia nevertheless tried to reason what this conduit or messenger had said to her. "What do you mean, the other side? Must I walk through it?"

You will understand in time. But you will also understand the price.

Abruptly Alexia's eyes flickered open. The finer detail of her dream faded away as she sat up and shivered in the cold night air. Through the fabric of the tent she could see Archaon's pale reddish glow. Nearby, Phyqor stirred and saw that she was awake. He moved nearer and placed an arm around her. "A bad dream?" he murmured.

Alexia nodded, took a deep breath to calm herself and managed to smile. "You will have known more than your share of those," she whispered and glanced at Yui, who still slumbered deeply just across from them. The child's mouth was slightly open and she snored gently. Alexia thought she looked oddly peaceful.

Phyqor gave her a concerned look. "The Green Road?"

"Intuition or a lucky guess?"

"I know you, Alexia. And I know that it's occupied your mind for a long while now."

She pulled her blanket around herself as a draught of cool air burst through a small gap in the tent and caused a ripple of goose bumps on her arms. "I think I know what I have to do now," she said quietly. "But you won't like it."

He opened his mouth to ask her, but she shook her head. She could barely look at him. "Tomorrow. In the light of day."

Alexia managed to sleep only fitfully for the rest of the night, and she woke again before first light. The memory of her earlier dream remained in her thoughts as she watched the daylight slowly appear around her. As the sun rose and she watched sunlight dance upon the tent covering, the name suddenly came to her of the man who could sense the formation of Gates.

"Vornen," she murmured. She knew who that was- a Hastian man, accompanied more often than not by a woman also from her own land. She was from Darkenhelm judging by her accent, Alexia thought, whereas Vornen was from much further north.

Vornen will be needed, she mused. *He can locate the Gate. And we need one other. One of the witches who travelled the Green Road to kill Inerdyr. Someone who can lead us both through the Green Road without becoming entrapped by the evil that lurks there.*

That morning, after she had dressed and breakfasted- not that there was much breakfast to be had- Alexia sought an audience with the leaders. In the event she was allowed to see only the fearsome-looking *orkar* warlord. Not knowing what quite to say, and mindful of the man's impatience, she mentioned only that she had information about a Gate within the Green Road, and that Yui had also dreamed about it. Judging by his sharp reaction, this was something he had heard about. Perhaps Vornen also knew about the Gate and had already mentioned it to them.

"I will convene a meeting today," he said, and waved her away. One of his lieutenants had just been admitted with news and information that appeared to interest the *orkar* chief more, and he was already muttering and shaking his head over an unfurled map when she left.

Around midday Alexia, Yui and Phyqor were summoned to the large pavilion tent where the meeting had been convened. Alexia looked around and saw Vornen with Amethyst and Ileana. Anlerran and Kian stood a little further away. The Watchers were also present, and Alexia felt a little knot of hate tighten in her stomach as she glanced at Kelandra's serene face.

The man called Elluron- who Alexia had heard was half-*illeagh,* something she could scarcely believe- stood and addressed everyone who had gathered.

"The matter of the Gate in the Green Road, which three people present here have declared exists, must be dealt with," he began. "Vornen sensed it when he, Amethyst and Ileana walked the Green Road to escape from Inerdyr. Independently of this, Yui, Phyqor and Alexia"- he gestured to Alexia and her companions- "who arrived here a few days ago, also spoke of a Gate within that place. Yui told Ileana that she dreamed about it. But now Alexia has something further to say on this matter."

Alexia swallowed and looked nervously around. She hadn't expected to be prompted to say anything so soon, nor had she worked out what she might say. For a moment she recalled those dread-inducing occasions long ago when she had to fulfil dreary duties as one of the Princesses of Aphenhast, and reluctantly spoke in public.

But I have to do this, she reminded herself. *I have to at least tell them what I know to be true. Then they must do as they will.*

Hesitantly Alexia began to tell the story of how she, Phyqor and Yui escaped from Luudhoq, and their descent into the Green Road, drawn there by Yui's powers. Perhaps Ileana had relayed to the others parts of what Yui had previously said, but Alexia spared no detail. She related everything she could remember from the time that the three of them were hiding together deep in the warrens of Luudhoq, not neglecting to mention Yui's dream of the Gate much later on. Finally she described her own dream from the previous night, although she wished again that she could describe it more vividly than she managed to. *If I had a chance to write it down then my story might have been more persuasive,* she thought, frustrated as she paused for a moment. *I was always clumsy with the spoken word.* Eyes stared back at her, some of them curious and attentive, others disbelieving.

"I will know what to do when I find it," she said finally, and felt everyone's stare upon her as she repeated those words. "It must be destroyed," she added- but of course they surely already knew that, assuming that they believed in its existence.

Incredulous silence followed. Nothing could be heard except the wind sighing outside. Glances were exchanged- either worried or simply dismissive.

Garrok finally spoke up. "Well? Do you intend to enlighten us further?"

"It will be destroyed by someone who steps through it, and into the very heart of the world." Alexia paused and then continued, "The Gate within the Green Road is a wound that will widen, even spread eventually to the outer world. It will eat everything from the inside out given enough time- or perhaps the *marandaal* will find a way to reach it, and hasten that fate."

"Could this gate even be the work of the *marandaal?*" Kian asked.

Alexia shrugged. "I truly don't know. It may be that Gates are made for no reason whatsoever- that they're simply a response to an imminent danger such as the *marandaal.* I suspect they pre-date those beings. But we know that sooner or later the *marandaal* find their way through Gates, regardless of their origins. What's happening in the Green Road is like a disease that weakens and cripples an entity, allowing an attack by another disease." She sighed inwardly at the many blank looks that were sent her way and between those gathered.

"How could you possibly *know* that the act of stepping through the Gate will destroy it?" Kelandra demanded. "Will you also know what to do if you step through? What then? You seem knowledgeable on the subject- very knowledgeable given your history as nothing more than a family member of a dynasty that no longer exists."

"Alexia had little to do with her family even before their fall," Phyqor spoke up. "She was a scholar of many matters, particularly history and philosophy. Her legacy has nothing to do with her intellect."

Alexia flashed a quick, grateful smile in Phyqor's direction, but she still couldn't think of anything meaningful to say.

Then Vornen spoke up.

"We all know that the *marandaal* have already made use of Gates in their conquest of Aona. Whether that means they created the Gate of which Alexia has spoken, no one can say- but they may well have the ability to control Gates to an extent. The powers of the *marandaal* are quite beyond our comprehension- how, for example, do we explain the emergence of lightdreamers- who are afflicted by visions of the *marandaal,* their minds tricked into thinking of these destroyers as gods? Surely the *marandaal* created this sickness for a reason. As Fauli already attested, some lightdreamers appear to have gained the ability to hasten the birth of Gates and join Aona with the void for brief moments. Sooner or later, if they are able to maintain those links between the world we know and the unknown abyss, they may become strong enough to welcome in their new gods themselves."

"And given your own knowledge," Kelandra asked him, "what would you say happens if someone steps through a Gate?"

"Often, vast amounts of power are used up when Gates are made ready for *marandaal-* or other creatures- to step through them," Vornen explained. "When they are breached, they close or disappear, perhaps because they detect that someone or something has passed through them and their purpose is complete. In fact, closure and disappearance are the same thing where Gates are concerned.

I know this to be true. I've seen it happen far more often than I ever wished to."

"You make them sound like live creatures," Anlerran said.

Vornen turned to look in her direction. "I wouldn't dare to presume what makes something alive or not. Are the *marandaal* creatures? Or are they a disease, much like whatever vileness may be eating the world from the inside out?"

"It felt so real in my dream," Alexia said quietly. "I stood before it, watching and waiting, and I *knew* that for the sake of Aona this hole in the fabric of the world had to be closed. But when I saw the Gate, surrounded by the light of the world, I could feel her pain and rage and even fear- the fear of being alone in an Existence where life has been destroyed, worlds turned dark. Already Aona has started to die because the *marandaal* reach through the Gates into the world we know, the one we can see and touch. I don't know why *I* was the one to have this dream."

Because you and your kind are the chroniclers of the Ages, came a whisper in her head.

"And so you believe you can find and close this Gate?" Kelandra's tone of voice indicated clearly that she could not bring herself to believe it.

"I will know how to pass through when I reach it. That's all I'm absolutely certain of. I can't describe how. And I have no idea how it can be found."

"It might simply annihilate you if by some miracle you did find it," Elluron pointed out. "It may even hasten the destruction of Aona herself."

"It has to be done," Alexia insisted. "I've no doubt of that."

"Because of a dream," Kelandra said flatly.

"No ordinary dream." Alexia met her stare boldly, anger giving her sudden courage. "Do you remember when Nia told you about the strength and power of Yui's visions,

Kelandra? You were convinced sufficiently to have her given over to the Seven."

"What if we do nothing and the *marandaal* emerge inside the Green Road?" Garrok argued as Kelandra was about to reply.

"That may be the purpose of this particular Gate," Alexia said. "Perhaps they have forced it into being, or perhaps it simply came into being as so many others probably have across the known Existence." She looked around at everyone and added, "Of course, even though I know what to do if and when I reach the Gate, I don't know how to find it to begin with, nor am I confident of traversing the Green Road without some misfortune happening to me."

"Some people say that you know how to find Gates, Vornen," Kelandra spoke up.

"Not exactly, and not by choice," he told her, "but in the past I have been drawn helplessly to them, unable to choose any direction other than that in which the Gate lay. I lost that curse for a while but it returned, less strongly than before. I sensed the Gate Alexia spoke of when my companions and I journeyed through the Green Road. I knew where it was at that point in time." He paused. "In honesty, I can't say if it was the *same* Gate. But it seems likely."

Everyone listened as Vornen gave his account of what had happened as he, Amethyst and Ileana made their way through that netherworld to escape Inerdyr. Alexia listened to his description of the mysterious tower on the island and how he would have been pulled towards it and perhaps into it had it not been for his companions. She shuddered, and wondered if the same might happen again.

"Then you might be able to locate it a second time," Garrok mused.

"I may be able to," Vornen admitted. "I could sense it during much of our previous journey. It moved sometimes, but I could still tell where it was. I think I could find it, given time." He paused, suddenly having realised what he had just said- and perhaps unwittingly volunteered for.

"It isn't that simple, Vornen." Ileana shook her head. "The trickery of that place worked its way into your mind, and will do so again. Neither of you are likely to survive the dangers of the Green Road- not just the two of you. You would need someone else, someone who understands the place better, who knows how to walk it and hopefully avoid the worst dangers. I can do that."

"No, Ileana." Jak grabbed her hand. "There's no need for you to go as well!"

"Yes, there is," Ileana told him. "If Vornen and Alexia go without anyone else, they're likely to become ensnared in that place to be lost forever. Besides which, three can look out for one another far better than two. That's the simple truth, Jak."

"I won't let you!"

"Jak, grow up!" Ileana said more forcefully, and his eyes widened in shock. Lost for any sort of response, he finally turned and stormed away. After a moment Ileana cursed under her breath and followed him. Vornen glanced at Amethyst, who stared down at the ground and said nothing.

"Are we to put our hopes in the three of you?" Kelandra's smile was bitter. "A young girl barely grown, a woman who claims to have tasked in a dream with closing down a Gate- were you not so lucid I might have thought you'd become a lightdreamer- and a man who by all accounts has done nothing of consequence in his life except witness Gates open and close? I see any evidence that three of our number venturing into this Green Road will do anything for our cause."

Ileana returned without Jak. Kelandra immediately gestured to her and added, "We cannot afford to lose Ileana on this fool's errand. The idea must be dismissed, for that reason more than any other."

Silence followed. "I agree," Garrok said finally, and looked to Elluron, who nodded. "We cannot allow this risk to be taken. Alexia has no strength in the Powers. It may be that her time spent in the Green Road- which by all accounts was a torment- has caused this delusion."

"It's no delusion," Alexia almost shouted, but the leaders had made their decision and considered the matter dealt with. The meeting was called at an end.

Yui and Phyqor said nothing as they accompanied Alexia away from the meeting. Alexia herself felt so distraught that she was almost unable to think.

But after a while, her resolve hardened.

I'll find a way, she decided. *I'll find a way or I'll die finding it.*

II

Later that day, with the onset of dusk Alexia peered outside their tent to find the guardsmen close but not close enough to hear a quiet conversation. She turned to the others. "I have to find a way back to the Green Road," she whispered. "I need to go and speak with Ileana and Vornen."

Phyqor felt his heart sink. "You heard what they said. The idea has been dismissed. If they find out that you're trying to do this without their knowledge..."

"Someone else could go," Yui added, although even she didn't sound convinced, and when she looked at Alexia a moment later her expression changed, as if she had suddenly noticed or sensed something different about her. "You *did* bring part of it back with you," she said softly. "It means you can see things that other people can't. Sometimes in your dreams and sometimes when you're awake."

Alexia smiled faintly. "I've thought from time to time that I was going mad, Yui."

"She chose you," the girl said emphatically.

"That's as may be. But I don't know *why* I was chosen."

"Perhaps it's because you're a student of the world," Phyqor remarked. "For as long as I've known you, you've consumed knowledge like no one else. Who knows the story of Aona as well as you do?"

"There are untold centuries in the First Age that even I know nothing of," Alexia protested, blushing a little. But once again she recalled those words Aona's conduit had told her in her dream- *You and your kind are the chroniclers of the Ages. Few hear my voice; those who do must help to write the story of the Age they witness.*

She took her knife from her belt and crawled to the back of their tent. "Alexia, this is madness," Phyqor protested quietly as she cut a slit in the fabric wide enough for her to squeeze through.

"You can't go back there without us," Yui pleaded.

Alexia peered out through the gap she had made. There were no guardsmen to be seen on this side, nor could she see anyone else looking in her direction. She pulled down the hood of her cloak. "I'll be back after I've talked with them," she whispered, and made her way out as quietly as she could.

It occurred to her as she walked through the twilit camp that she had no idea where to find Vornen and Ileana. Alexia felt despair begin to grow within her, and she was on the verge of giving up for the evening when she glimpsed Vornen walking through the camp just up ahead.

She caught up with him, and lifted the hood of her robe enough for him to see her face when he turned. "I need to talk with you and Ileana," she said.

Vornen looked quickly around. "You'll have to talk with Amethyst as well," he said with a faint smile, and gestured to a camp fire some distance away. Alexia saw Ileana and Amethyst sitting by it.

She accompanied Vornen as he made his way back to his companions. The three of them were in a relatively quiet part of the camp, and Alexia relaxed a little although she kept her face hidden from casual observers as Vornen bade her be seated.

Alexia decided to get straight to the point. "Will you help me?" she asked, looking to Ileana and then Vornen. Amethyst gave her a stony stare and looked away. The woman bristled with anger and fear. *I don't blame her at all,* Alexia thought.

Ileana swallowed nervously. "If we go against our own leaders..."

"What will they do to you?" Alexia quickly rejoined. "As far as I can tell, you're one of the most important people here. I, on the other hand, have everything to lose. I'm nothing to them."

Ileana looked to Vornen, then to Amethyst, but Amethyst stared pointedly away and said nothing.

Only a moment could have passed before Ileana spoke, but to Alexia it could have been an eternity. She closed her eyes, and imagined a coin falling through darkness. By her answer, Ileana would determine how it landed.

"I believe everything you said," Ileana murmured eventually. "I believe that we have to find a way to locate this Gate. But we may never return."

"I will come with you," Vornen added.

Ileana suddenly looked somewhere behind them, listening intently. "We need to go now. I think they've realised that you're not with Phyqor and Yui. There'll be *orkar* fighters here in moments. Ironmasters too, probably." She gestured towards the nearest edge of the camp. "We'll head that way."

Amethyst grabbed the girl's arm. "You haven't even thought this through, Ileana!"

Ileana shook her head. "I don't have time to think it through. But I have to do this."

"Ileana and I have survived the Green Road before," Vornen added. The commotion some distance away had become louder. Lightly he added, "Even *you* managed to, Amethyst."

She laughed humourlessly and wiped at her eyes. "The two of you seem to have conveniently forgotten that on the last occasion you didn't have to actually step through a Gate, not knowing what would happen to you on the other side or whether or not you'd be simply snuffed out of existence."

Ileana hugged her closely. "You have done so much for me."

"I kidnapped you," Amethyst said, half-joking and half-crying.

"You made it possible for me to trust," Ileana told her solemnly. "I can't even begin to tell you how important that is."

"Tell me when you come back," Amethyst managed to say. She caught Vornen in a fierce embrace. "You had better look after her, and look after yourself," she whispered. "I won't lose you!"

"*No,*" he said forcefully just before they kissed. "You won't."

Ileana turned expectantly to Alexia, who looked dismayed. "I wanted to say my farewells…"

The girl shook her head. "No time!"

After the three of them had left, Amethyst stood in disconsolate silence, her mind whirling with desperate thoughts. The two people she had left in the world- two people she loved more than anything- had been torn away from her in an instant.

The warmth from Vornen's lips fled her own to disappear into the night. Amethyst sat and closed her eyes, alone in her despair, oblivious to the commotion that soon erupted as *orkar* and human guardsmen arrived. She only raised her head when she heard Jak's voice nearby. "Where's Ileana?"

Under cover of full darkness, Ileana, Vornen and Alexia followed the least-populated route out of the camp, and took the opportunity to take provisions from an unguarded store.

Then they hastened away and into the gloom of the hinterland beyond.

They were more than two hundred paces beyond the perimeter when Ileana stopped and turned to face her companions. Archaon's faint light shone sporadically as it rolled in and out of thin cloud. "Are you ready?" she whispered.

Alexia and Vornen both nodded, although they were not. They never would be, and if they didn't do this now then it would only become more difficult. Vornen tried not to think about Amethyst sitting alone by the fire.

At Ileana's behest the three of them linked hands. "Don't let go, whatever you do," she warned. After a moment Vornen closed his eyes, although he couldn't say why. Perhaps it was the fear of seeing the world he knew melting away to become something else- or of what he might glimpse in between one reality and the other.

After only a moment he felt himself fall through the darkness, and soon nothing surrounded him but the hands he tightly held.

III

Garrok's features contorted with rage as he shouted his frustration, but Kelandra didn't bother to conceal her contempt at the *orkar* warlord's fury. "What's done is done," she pointed out. "We certainly can't send anyone after them. Alexia and Vornen are of no consequence, and we will simply have to deal with the loss of Ileana."

Garrok was not done. "I had men keeping watch over Alexia through the night. I suspected she would not be content with our refusal. But more guards should have been posted."

"Be that as it may, we have other things to discuss. The fact that Yui has now joined us is fortuitous. It's time to make use of the child's special talent, and discover where and when Gates will appear."

"Are you certain that she can do that?" Elluron asked.

151

"The Seven did not interrogate her almost continuously for many days without being certain. In truth, I knew it when Nia told me- although I can't say how. Nia also felt the power of the child's visions herself."

"And do you intend to interrogate her in the same manner as your former masters?" he asked, giving her a level stare.

The Watcher smiled. "You may be surprised at the subtlety I've learned in recent days."

Amethyst took a deep breath of the cold air, tinged with the smells of luncheon being prepared across the camp along with less pleasant odours- leather, mud, weapon oil, faeces and others that she couldn't guess at. As she picked her way through the mud she wondered to herself why life persisted in landing blow after crippling blow no matter how hard she struggled. *How fate twists itself into ever greater knots,* she mused. *Alexia had a dream that was more than a dream, or so she alleges, and now the two people I have left will be taken away from me. Why did Vornen have to remind everyone that his Gate-sense has stirred again? If only he'd stated that whatever talent he had in that area had disappeared, and left it at that. And why did Ileana have to join in? Why couldn't the two of them have kept their mouths shut?! Then Alexia wouldn't have come to take them away from me. She would have had no one to drag into her crazed idea. And why did they even agree to go with her?!*

But somehow in an instant last night Vornen and Ileana had committed themselves to the task, a journey through a waking nightmare to a place that would in all likelihood swallow and destroy them.

Amethyst balled her hands into fists as the rage and grief almost overcame her. The sight of army camp life simply continuing, as grimly banal as ever, only made her feel worse.

It all felt quite surreal. Alexia had been second in line to the throne of Aphenhast, a woman known by name to everyone in Amethyst's home city of Darkenhelm, if not necessarily by sight. If her sister Maria had perished, which was surely more than likely, Alexia would have become Queen- unless the priesthood in Emberton engineered a way to seize power for themselves, which again was probable. Still, no such machinations mattered now. Darkenhelm, like every other city in Aphenhast, no doubt lay in ruins.

She wondered once again what had happened to her parents and sister. Had they somehow fled the city? Were they in hiding somewhere?

With an effort Amethyst pushed that underlying worry to one side. She could do nothing for them, she told herself forcefully.

Amethyst couldn't bear the possibility that she might lose Vornen and Ileana. Her family in Darkenhelm might have somehow escaped the *marandaal,* but her companions were also her family now. In different ways they had stirred up feelings that at times threatened to overwhelm her. *Who would have thought I'd love and need them so much?* she wondered. *Not so long ago I thought I'd never need anyone for anything. I was determined to spend my life in exploration and adventure. That certainly didn't turn out as planned.*

She glanced up as someone approached. It was Jak, and he looked as miserable as she felt. "She didn't even say farewell," he said quietly.

"They didn't have time," Amethyst said, and at the same time wished that they'd been caught before they could go.

"I think Alexia's mad. The Green Road made her mad," Jak declared.

"Maybe, maybe not. But we have to face facts. They're gone and all we can do is wait and hope for their return. Ileana did what she thought she had to do."

"I don't know how I can forgive her," he mumbled.

Amethyst sighed. Why were boys all so helpless and short-sighted? "You love her, don't you?"

"Of course I do!"

"Then she shouldn't need your forgiveness." Amethyst turned angrily and walked away, unable to speak further without her voice giving way.

That same morning Phyqor and Yui were taken to the leaders' tent where the reason for their being summoned became immediately clear. "Yui, we need you to help us find where the Gates may appear," Elluron began.

Yui's eyes widened with fear. "No! I won't do it! I won't!"

"We need you to help us." It was Kelandra who spoke, but Phyqor thought that her voice sounded oddly gentle. "We can't defeat the *marandaal*- the creatures from the void- unless we know where and when the Gates will appear. Will you help us? Please?"

But Yui grew even more panicky, perhaps at the mention of that name. She began to scream and wail. Phyqor comforted her as best he could, and when finally the child's distress had reduced to a quiet sobbing Garrok spoke up, but not patiently. "She must be made to understand how important this is. If need be, we'll put her in the necessary trance and force the detail of the visions from her."

"That's what the Seven tried to do, and it failed to work," Phyqor told him. "Doing that could drive her so far into herself that you will never get anything more from her, no matter what barbaric methods you use. You don't even have any idea how her visions work."

"Perhaps Phyqor can talk with his daughter alone today about the importance of her help," Elluron said quickly, and both Garrok and Phyqor relaxed a little.

"I will try," Phyqor said, "but she will not be forced. And if you harm her..." He left the rest unsaid, and taking Yui by the hand he turned and left without being given leave.

Well, that may be our last hope fading, Nia thought from outside the meeting tent. *But I might have said the same if I was Yui. It was frightening enough to behold her visions from my own perspective. To her they must seem entirely real.*

And one day soon they will be.

That afternoon Nia happened to cross one of the fields at the border of the encampment, hoping to find somewhere quiet to contemplate in peace. She saw Yui and Phyqor sitting on a boulder and staring towards the sunset. They appeared to be oblivious to the half dozen or so *orkar* soldiers who stood some distance away, ever watchful. Perhaps they had been tasked with ensuring that the pair of them didn't try to leave. *I expect everyone's being a little more vigilant now after Alexia, Vornen and Ileana vanished,* Nia mused.

Something about the girl's manner made her stop and look and then walk nearer to them, although she feared what the child- or her father- might do.

"May I speak with Yui?" Nia found herself asking him.

Phyqor stared incredulously at her. "What could you possibly have to say to my daughter? Have you not caused enough harm?"

"I've caused more than enough harm," Nia admitted. "But I would like to speak with her anyway, if I may." She moved the folds of her cloak aside, took her two daggers and handed them handle-first to the mystified Hastian man. "Here. These are the only weapons I have. Would you care to search me for any others?"

"I'd rather not have to touch you," Phyqor responded coldly.

"As you wish. May I?"

Phyqor looked to Yui, who simply shrugged. "Nia wouldn't dare to try and harm me. Those *orkar* over there would kill her straight away." Even as she spoke two of the *orkar* walked a little nearer.

As Phyqor got up and stood nearby, only to begin pacing pensively around after a moment, Nia sat and turned to the child once again. She wasn't at all sure what to say, but in any event Yui spoke first.

"I just want to die."

The words sent a chill through Nia's heart. They were the exact same words that she had uttered to herself when the same age- and younger, and older, many times- during her time at the orphanage and on a number of occasions later.

"I often thought the same thing when I was your age," Nia ventured at last.

"Did you." Yui folded her arms and turned slightly away from her.

"Yes. I didn't live in a palace. I wasn't the daughter of a handsomely-paid architect. I never counted a princess amongst my friends. I never really had friends."

"Why should I care? You don't *deserve* friends, Nia. I thought Alexia was our friend but then she just went back to the Green Road without even saying farewell."

Nia sighed. "Maybe I don't know what it's like to be you. I don't have your powers, or indeed any powers any more. But I've a pretty good idea of how you feel."

Yui shrugged disinterestedly.

"You have a father who loves you," Nia continued. "All I know about my parents is that they gave me away to an orphanage."

Those words suddenly got her attention. "That's strange," Yui commented. "Why would they do that?"

"I have no idea. Maybe I interrupted whatever plans they had for their lives. Maybe they just hated me. It doesn't really matter now, although when I was younger I thought about it all the time."

"How old were you when they gave you away?"

"Too young to remember. The first place I can recall properly is the orphanage." Nia took a deep breath. "And the things that happened to me."

Yui frowned. "What do you mean?" Looking at Nia's expression she added, "Oh," and looked down at the ground, a flush to her cheeks. Uncomfortably she asked, "What is it you want, Nia? To feel sorry for you? Because I don't and I never will."

"Nor would I expect you to. All I'm saying is that you're not the only one with problems to face. I have had nightmares most nights of my life, Yui, even before the special ones that you made for me. But *you* have an incredible gift. You can use it to tell people where and when the *marandaal* might force Gates into this world. *You* have a chance to save everything. And if you do, that means you and your father and Alexia get to live out the rest of your lives."

"Alexia's gone," the girl said disconsolately.

"But she'll be back." The words continued to tumble from Nia's mouth even though she didn't believe them herself. "Alexia has done the bravest thing you could possibly imagine. She has gone into the Green Road to find and try to shut down the Gate that will otherwise destroy everything. She did so because she knew that if she didn't, no one else would be able to. But that didn't make it any easier. I'm sure she was frightened- only a mad person would claim to be otherwise- but she went ahead and did it anyway, for the sake of the world and everything we have left.

"Even so, Alexia's effort will be in vain unless we also find out where and when the other Gates will appear, here in the world that we all know. If we know that, then we may have a chance to defeat the *marandaal* as they emerge from the Gates. But you're the only one who can help us with that, Yui. Just like Alexia is the only one who can close that Gate in the Green Road, when her companions guide her there. So even if you care nothing for the world, do it for her. This is the single most important decision you'll ever make."

Nia took a deep breath. She couldn't be at all certain that she even believed her own words. If she didn't, how could she possibly convince anyone else? And why by all the Powers had she even tried? Only a short while ago she had thought it better to give them a wide berth and find a route around.

Yui stood up and looked across the field for a moment, then set off towards the camp. Phyqor threw Nia a curious glance and then hurried after her, and after a short while the *orkar* soldiers made haste after them. Nia watched the entourage leave for a moment and then headed her own way. *I should have left her alone,* she thought bleakly. *I've probably made things even worse.*

As Nia trudged across the muddy grass, she came to the sudden realisation that she had no purpose here anymore. She had revealed the secrets of the Watchers and the people of the Bonemord, and if her companions thought to keep her in order to find a use for her shapeshifting ability then they would be sorely disappointed. Nia was convinced that it had disappeared forever, and had even hinted as much to Yui.

I'll pack and leave, she decided as a few flakes of wet snow began to drift down. *Not that I have anything much to pack.*

She overheard a conversation between two Darkbrook men as she walked past their section of the camp.

"…and he said this Lord Arin and his companions are about as strong as the witchlings we already have," one of them was saying. "Might make all the difference. Three of them with the Powers. Makes you wonder who else in the South has hidden their abilities away all their lives…"

"Could be dozens," his companion commented, and took a contemplative puff of *kyush*. Then he reconsidered. "No, hundreds."

Nia walked past them without pause, but the name echoed persistently through her head. *Lord Arin.* Arin of Telith had been a lord of sorts, albeit a minor one who had fallen into disgrace. Could he be here? That said, the Arin she had met hadn't been a sorcerer as far as she knew.

Why does it matter? she asked herself forcefully. *Why are you still thinking about him after all this time? Do you really think he's spared a thought for you since he last saw you?*

Nevertheless she looked around the camp of the Darkbrook militia until she finally caught sight of Teryn sitting by himself at a campfire and carving what looked like wooden dice with a small knife. "What can I do for you, Nia?" the commander asked as she cautiously approached.

"I heard the men talking about a group of people who've joined us," she said airily.

"People join us all the time, and others leave," Teryn shrugged. "You know that."

"They happened to mention a Lord Arin. Is this Lord Arin from the town of Telith?"

"He is." Teryn gave her a shrewd look. "But what is it to you? Do you know him? Wouldn't surprise me *who* you knew- Nia of Luudhoq, spy for the Watchers."

"Oh, my time of helping Watchers is long behind me," Nia said with a smirk. "These days you can't be too careful around them."

"There's a fact," Teryn commented.

Seeing that he had apparently forgotten his question about Arin, Nia took her leave of the Darkbrook man and strolled away as casually as she could considering the barely controllable emotions his words had stirred within her.

Only when she lay down to sleep a while later did she finally manage to convince herself that her best option would be to crush and forget everything she felt about Arin and leave all of this behind as she had planned. *I thought I'd learned this lesson,* she thought. *But it seems I'm forced to keep relearning it.*

IV

"I'll do it," Yui said quietly as she settled down to sleep that evening. "I'll give them the pictures of the Gates if that's what they want."

Phyqor stared at her in surprise. "Are you certain?"

His daughter pulled her blanket over herself. "Yes. It's not because of what Nia said though. It's just that she reminded me of Alexia and what *she* is doing to help. I suppose she couldn't come back to us because they found out that she'd gone. She had to leave when she did."

Her father thought for a moment. He didn't know whether to be relieved or fearful, and he felt both at the same time. *Thank you, Nia,* he thought- and a moment later, *Or damn you, Nia. I can't decide which.*

"I'll be with you the whole while," he assured her. "I won't leave you."

"I know," Yui said. "But I'm still scared."

And I won't be able to make you feel less scared, Phyqor thought. He moved to sit closer to her and stroked her hair as she closed her eyes and began to drift off to sleep. *I never could. I'm helpless in the face of everything you are and everything that's happened to you. All I can do is stay at your side.*

"I want Alexia to be my mother if she comes back," Yui murmured drowsily, and a moment later she was asleep.

The day's discussions about the forward march were already well underway the following morning when Phyqor and Yui were admitted to the command tent. As all eyes turned to them, Phyqor gestured for Yui to speak.

"I will help you," Yui said. Her voice was quiet but everyone could hear the tremor to it.

The sense of relief amongst everyone was palpable. "Thank you," Elluron said as a murmur started up amongst the others. "And thank you also, Phyqor."

"I didn't speak with her," he admitted. "She made the choice herself." He wondered if he should mention Nia, but decided not to. "I will need to be with Yui to calm her and to keep her from becoming lost in the visions."

"You can do that?" Garrok frowned.

"I've managed to before. If I maintain my link with her and she remains aware of my presence it keeps her tied to the world, in a sense. If it becomes too much for her, then we stop and continue later, or another day."

"Ildoron will question her when she's ready," Kelandra said, and the other Watcher stepped forward/

Phyqor and Yui sat facing each other. He whispered words to her, so quietly that no one could quite make them out. She relaxed visibly. Then she closed her eyes and breathed slowly and deeply for a long while- so long in fact that Phyqor could hear restless murmurs amongst those who watched and waited.

Finally she began slowly to look one way and then the other. Her eyelids flickered rapidly and she reached out her hands as if searching for something. Suddenly her eyes opened, and a faint murmur sounded as everyone saw that her eyes appeared jet black. Those present who held the Powers felt the strength of the child's sorcery and a few took steps back, uneasy in the face of such a torrent of energy.

Ildoron knelt nearby to ask questions in tandem with Phyqor, his grim countenance half in shadow in the dimly-lit tent. Phyqor held the child's hand and said quietly, "I'm here, Yui. I will always be here. Can you sense me?"

"Yes." Her voice shuddered faintly. Then she whispered, "Don't leave me. Don't let go."

"I won't. You know I won't. What do you see around you?"

"The night sky. The moons are close together, but not touching. Ildar is near full, and Archaon just like a big red fingernail."

"Do you see anything else in the sky, near to them?" Ildoron asked her.

Yui flinched at the sound of the Watcher's voice but replied, "There's... a bright star just under Archaon's rim..."

"The light from that star, Yui. Does it appear to shimmer and glitter, or does it look still?"

"It's still."

"And how high is Archaon in the sky?"

"About as high as it gets, maybe halfway up."

Ildoron turned to the others and said quietly, "That's no star. It's a planet, which is called Hyyron in the south." He observed their blank expressions and added, "Another world that revolves around the sun, as Kelandra mentioned to some of you. Archaon and Hyyron will be in the configuration Yui described, nine days from now."

"How can you know that?" Kian asked.

"Some of your witches and warlocks are able to predict weather and seasonal variations with great accuracy. We have ways of charting and mapping the movements of celestial bodies." He paused. "You could say the magic of numbers which we use to predict such movements is innate to us."

Ildoron turned again to Yui, whose eyes, darker even than the night she had described, gazed into the vision in which she was ensnared. "Look around you," he said. "What else do you see?"

"There's a river near me. A wide river. The water's flowing really quickly... Father! Are you..."

"I'm still here, Yui. Always." Phyqor continued gently, "What else?"

"Mountains up ahead. The river flows towards a valley in the mountains. Towards the west." Yui paused. "The highest mountain has a spiky top to it."

"The Wistledge," Lura murmured.

"Look nearer to the river, Yui. Do you see anything there?"

The child turned her head this way and that and finally said, "Some old buildings. It looks like it used to be a village, but it's just ruins now. I can see the remains of a bridge on both sides. The middle part has fallen away."

"That sounds like Wester Ford," Lura spoke up again. "An abandoned settlement, about a league or so east of the

Wistledge. The Daymorn flows through the middle of it. No one has lived there for at least fifty years. It flooded too often, I believe."

The effect of Yui's vision had been chilling. To an extent, everyone near saw what she saw and felt as if they could step into that vision and become lost in its grasp.

"We must send a force there," Iyoth spoke up. "And anywhere else that Yui senses where Gates may appear."

Garrok shook his head. "How would we do that? We don't have enough people with strength in the Powers. Other Gates may form at the same time, or at least on the same day as others. "

"Then why do this at all?" the *du-luyan* persisted.

"Quiet." Ildoron turned again to Yui. "Come away from that place. Find another of the Gates. Whichever will open next, if you can."

Yui's head dropped, her eyes flickered and her lips moved as if she uttered soundless words. The atmosphere of foreboding became almost unbearable. Moments passed.

"I know where this is," she said suddenly. Her voice was quiet but clear. "I've been here before."

"Look around and describe it," Ildoron murmured.

Yui looked up, down and to both sides. Her eyes looked like black pools, absorbing everything. "This is east of the main square in the middle of Luudhoq, near the river," she said finally. "There's a bridge that goes across the river nearby. I remember seeing this place when we first came to Luudhoq. It's important. Something about it makes it easier for a Gate to form here."

Murmurs of unease rose up amongst everyone. Yui looked up, and the dim lantern light reflected in her eyes as she searched heavens that only she could see. "Do you see either of the moons?" Ildoron asked quietly.

"I can't see Ildar but I can see Archaon," Yui said. "It's only just risen, and it's half full. I can only see it a little, because there's some cloud in the sky. It's still not quite dark yet. I think it must be late in the afternoon."

Ildoron turned to the others. "That will be fifteen days from now."

Elluron spoke up. "This changes everything. I had hoped that events throughout the south would occupy what authorities remain in the region and mean that we might not have to contend with the Seven until after the *marandaal* are defeated. But if a Gate opens in Luudhoq, we need to be there to destroy the *marandaal* as they emerge."

"And how many sorcerors with sufficient strength do we have?" Garrok rejoined. "Nowhere near enough, if we intend to guard every area where a Gate might form."

"I thought our intention had always been to crush the powers of the Black Citadel," Lura said.

"That may well have been Ruhal's intention," Elluron replied. "But we face a single, total threat to our survival in the form of the *marandaal*. Still, if we must crush the Seven in order for us to be at the Gate when it opens, then so be it."

They questioned Yui for a short while longer and discovered that another Gate would open in the days ahead, just south of Anvar on the western coast eleven days hence.

"Can you find any others?" Ildoron asked, but Yui shook her head and slumped forward slightly. A moment later she was asleep in Phyqor's arms.

The matter of Luudhoq took up much of the remaining day. Arguments and counter-arguments were raised and heard over and again.

"We know that if a Gate does open within the city, and we are not there to face the *marandaal,* everything will be lost," Garrok stated at one point. "One way or another, we have to overcome the Seven and take Luudhoq."

"I always thought that was our plan," Kelandra remarked. "Certainly it was mine." She gave Elluron a lingering look, but he remained lost in thought.

"You have the ability to sense others of your kind, I believe," the half-*illeagh* man said to her after a while. He looked at each of the Watchers in turn. "Well?"

"It is stronger in some than others," Ildoron spoke up finally.

"And who is the strongest amongst the three of you?"

"I would say Alturus."

Kelandra nodded. "Alturus is perhaps the strongest of *all* the Watchers in that regard. He can sense others from a distance of several leagues or more- how far away they are, and the direction in which they're headed."

Alturus himself remained silent and impassive. "What do you intend?" Kelandra asked warily.

"We need to bring as many of the errant Watchers as we can to our cause," Elluron explained. "The south has been destabilised, and perhaps set ripples of unease through Luudhoq. But Watchers continue to roam the land, many of them with murder and vengeance on their minds. If we're to take Luudhoq, then we need them. We need to harness that hatred, direct it towards the Seven. In other words, we need them to be of the same mindset as the three of you. Alturus could seek them out."

"It should be possible to convince some of them," Ildoron mused. "We represent their best chance of vengeance."

"There are only three of us," Kelandra warned Elluron. "What if Alturus is killed by one of them, or a group? Would you risk our being reduced to only two?"

"Yes," he said simply. "Do you think we can take Luudhoq without them?"

"Perhaps." Kelandra shrugged. "Perhaps not."

"Alturus, you will seek and approach lone Watchers only. And you will not be alone. We will send an ironmaster and a master bladesman with you, so if you encounter other enemies then you should be more than capable of handling them. If you convince one Watcher to join you, you're then better prepared to convince a second, and so on. We'll give you a tennight to recruit whoever they can, as we press on towards Luudhoq."

Kelandra did not look persuaded. "Alturus, what do you say?"

The older Watcher smiled thinly. "I would welcome the opportunity to be away from the stink and squalor of this place. I will do my best to present a convincing argument for our cause. As Ildoron pointed out, we represent their best chance of vengeance."

"I will speak with Garrok and arrange for an ironmaster to accompany you." Elluron thought for a moment. "Iyoth should go as well. He's the best of our warriors, I would say."

"It may be hard to convince a Watcher who sees one of their own accompanied by an *orkar* sorceror and a *du-luyan* assassin," Kelandra commented dryly, but the matter had been decided. *So be it,* she thought, and left them. As she walked away, she wondered if the vengeance she longed for might have started to slip from her hands.

Iyoth was told of the task later that afternoon by a messenger from Elluron. He told Kian immediately, but she already knew, her Powers-sharpened hearing having picked up his conversation with the man who delivered the message. "Apparently I am the best they have," he said with a smirk. "What does that tell you about everyone else?"

"I've no doubt you're the best," Kian told him, "but don't let it go to your head." She looked away, trying not to let her worry show. Iyoth put an arm around her and kissed her on the forehead. "I'll do my best to stay away from mad Watchers," he said lightly.

"I would come with you but I don't expect they'd let me, especially after Ileana went against their orders," Kian sighed.

"We'll return in a tennight," he said, "with or without an entourage of vengeful once-servants of the Black Citadel."

Iyoth lifted her chin so that she looked at him. "I'll come back to you, Kian."

"You'd better. You're the only family I have," she said, trying to glare at him and wipe her eyes at the same time.

Iyoth went to see Lura afterwards. "I will be gone for some days," he told her abruptly.

Lura felt a prickle of unease stir within her. "Why? Where are you going?"

"I've been enlisted to help Alturus and one of Garrok's ironmasters recruit Watchers to our ranks." Iyoth shrugged. "Apparently they need someone devoid of sorcerous powers who can fight. I suppose I fit the description. Actually they could have chosen Fauli, but they picked me. I suppose I should be honoured."

"I wouldn't know about honour. When you are going?"

"Tomorrow morning. I'll be back in a tennight."

"I wish I could go with you," Lura told him without thinking.

He raised an eyebrow at that. "Really? I *have* become popular. Kian said the same thing. Does life in a marauding army bore you so much you'd rather spend your time in the company of a Watcher?"

"I'm alone in a crowd here. As you would be if you didn't have your daughter."

"True. Anyway, I thought I'd tell you."

"Why?" Lura demanded flippantly, and his expression hardened. "No reason," he retorted, and he turned to leave. Lura grabbed his arm, horrified at herself. "Don't go!"

"I have to go, Lura, if I'm to be any part of this…"

"No, I mean *now*. Stay with me awhile." She reached out and traced her hand down his cheek. "You're the only one here who means anything to me. I hate being alone with my thoughts. I think of you all the time."

For a moment he looked lost, trapped, taken aback. "Please tell me…" Lura swallowed, wishing she had never said anything at all to him. "Please tell me I mean something to you."

He didn't say anything. He took a step forward and wrapped his arms about her, pulling her close so her breasts crushed against his lithe form and she struggled to breathe.

A moment later they kissed, and for a while Lura entirely forgot the world and its cruelty.

When she woke the following morning, he had already gone. As Lura's hand touched where he had lain, she wondered if he feared farewells more than whatever enemies waited.

V

Jak had walked around the perimeter of the camp three times already that same morning, immersed in his misery and unable to think of anything but Ileana. Regretful thoughts chased one another through his mind. *She didn't need to go. She would have stayed if I'd been there when Alexia went to them. I would have convinced her. Why wasn't I there? Why did she have to listen to Alexia and be fooled by her?*

Will she ever come back?

Jak had volunteered to carry out errands and walk as often as he could in an effort to tire himself out so that he might sleep better at night. But the tactic hadn't worked. He had been plagued by ill dreams, many of them tainted with all sorts of violent imaginings concerning Ileana's likely fate.

I love her, he thought miserably, *but it wasn't enough to make her stay.*

He wished he could have spent time with her before. He decided that he would have told her how brave she was and that he knew she was doing the right thing. Somehow the words would have just fallen out of his mouth.

She *was* brave. Brave and mad.

He hadn't told anyone, but his dreams had grown steadily worse as more and more people had joined their army.

168

He had no idea why that might be. All these dreams concerned the new arrivals in one way or another. Sometimes they would be in great danger and no one would be able to save them. Sometimes they would simply go insane without reason and start to hurt themselves or attack their families and friends.

Jak sat wearily on a boulder in the north-western corner of the camp area, which also happened to be the most elevated position. From here he could look out over the sprawling expanse of tents, people, grass, mud, camp fires and every other piece of paraphernalia that came with a force of this size. He shielded his eyes against the low winter sun and watched the scene despondently.

It occurred to him that he could no longer tell the locations of the Descendants as well as he could previously. For tennights he had always been able to tell where Ileana was- ever since he had met her, the powers she held had burned in his mind as an invisible beacon, tugging at his senses. He had always had a keen sense for the Powers, and in Ileana's case he had welcomed the ability to tell where she was- it meant he worried about her less when she wasn't within sight. Of course, now he could no longer detect Ileana at all. She had vanished from the world.

He was also able to detect the locations of the others- Kian, Anlerran, Yui, that boy Parril who had arrived with Fauli the other day, and also the two children and man from Telith who everyone seemed to be talking about.

But now- and particularly from this location where he could see the whole encampment spread out before him- Jak found it more difficult to determine where any of them were. He sat and pondered the matter for a while, and then suddenly felt a strange, insistent pull when he stared at a small group of people near to where he sat, who were carrying pails of water and firewood. They looked entirely unremarkable- five ragged refugees from one of the midland villages they had passed near to, who had decided that they stood a better chance of survival here than in their settlement.

Two of them have some strength in the Powers, he thought. *I'm certain of it. It's only tiny, but it's there.*

He wondered idly how many others might also harbour such residual sorcery, and if it mattered. *They're much too weak to be of any use,* he reckoned. *Do they even know of their own abilities?*

But because he had nothing better to do he decided to wander around the camp, stop at various intervals and see if he could find any others like them.

To his bewilderment, he could. He counted up to fifty- most were human, but there were also some *luyan-* and then he lost count, so he went elsewhere and began again with others that he detected.

He walked all the way around the encampment until he arrived back at the boulder up in the north-eastern corner where he had started. The completed walk convinced him that his initial suspicions were correct. A small, residual vein of the Powers hid within at least two hundred of the humans and some *luyan* who had joined them during the march south. Perhaps in each case that gift was so weak that they didn't even know they had it. But it existed nonetheless.

He stopped, weary from his walk around the perimeter, and sat down on the boulder to contemplate what he had found.

Not one of them had even a tenth of Ileana's strength, nor that of Kian, Anlerran, Parril, Yui or other Descendants. None of these people could hope to match even the weakest of the sorcerers he knew about. But Jak reckoned that there had to be a reason why the Powers had been awakened in these people at this time. Maybe it had to do with the *marandaal* and the innate response of Aona and the Old Powers to the invasion- after all, as his father had once said, living creatures were all greater or lesser slaves to the mysterious forces of the world, and as the world changed so did the sorcery that ran like a river through it.

But why only now? The *marandaal* had first arrived many tennights ago. And why such a relatively tiny amount? What use could it be?

Jak wondered why he should have been the one who had made this discovery. *I always had a strong sense for the Powers even though I couldn't wield them myself,* he thought. *But surely there must be others like me, here amongst so many people.*

Perhaps there weren't.

But the reason didn't really matter. What did matter was that the leadership be told of this discovery as soon as possible. If they decided that what he had found was worthless, then so be it.

Jak had to wait to see Elluron, having decided that he was the least fearsome of the three leaders and the least likely to dismiss his story out of hand. He struggled to describe what he had sensed at first, but finally the words spilled forth in a rush. Elluron listened more attentively as Jak continued his explanation. When the boy had finished everything he had to say, Elluron looked thoughtfully at him. "Thank you, Jak. This knowledge may prove to be invaluable." He walked over to the nearest guardsman. "Find Kelandra and Garrok and ask them to attend me. And Merinne, the ironmistress. Her expertise may be needed."

When they arrived a little later, Elluron explained briefly everything that Jak had told him. "Jak has found perhaps two hundred already. But there may be more to find, if one of us walks with him through the entire camp." He turned to Merinne. "Can their strength in the Powers be magnified at all? Is that possible, would you say?"

Merinne shrugged uneasily. "From what I know of ironmaster training, an individual is born with or inherits a certain strength, and that is what they continue to have through their life- unless they somehow burn themselves out of course. The rest- by which I mean other factors that determine someone's overall strength- is simply down to training and teaching them to get the best out of themselves. However I recall something I learned from my training- a process by which a link can be established between two or more practitioners who are weak in the Powers, to achieve an effect greater than the sum of their individual limits."

"How easy is this to do?"

"It's dangerous and difficult, and has seldom been used. You may as well consider it a theory and nothing more. That said, according to this theory the greater the number of people who can be linked together, the greater the effect."

"Enough to be of use against the starspawn?" Elluron asked.

"Certainly, if all these people could be somehow linked together. That could potentially result in sorcery on a scale never known before." Observing his expression Merinne hastily added, "But you should know that this is something that has rarely been tested even amongst the *orkar* people. Our approach is straightforward. If someone is found to have the required strength, then they are trained and if successful then they become ironmasters or ironmistresses. If they possess only faint talent, then they find other occupations."

"Why not link them as you described?" Kelandra asked.

"Because we have never needed to," Merinne replied flatly. "The great war against the *choragh*, resulting in the eventual liberation of all the Younger Races, occurred before the Seven came to southern Harn, but you must know something of that era regardless. That was the last time when linking of everyone with a residual ability in the Powers would have been useful. But from what I know of that time, the Powers were wild and unpredictable and even for decades after the overthrow of the *choragh* the Younger Races struggled to control them. Linking was unheard of then, and since that time we have largely lived at peace in our own lands- or at least we have never faced a situation so grave that our dedicated sorcerors could not deal with it."

"But this can nevertheless be done or at least tested," Garrok spoke up.

"If they can be taught how to link together, then yes," Merinne confirmed. "Those of us who are strong in the Powers would need to teach them somehow. In any case they would need to learn not only how to link, but to do so without burning themselves out- not to mention others to whom they are linked- in moments. Furthermore, I expect they will be fearful when they realise the truth about themselves. If we decide to do this, some will die. It's inevitable."

"Why now?" Elluron mused. "Have their talents lain buried for their entire lives, or is this something new that's happened to them?"

"These people present a danger," Kelandra spoke up. As they turned to look at her she continued, "How do we know that this sudden emergence isn't the work of the *Old Dark* as you call it? The *choragh*? Would that not be an ideal way for them to destroy us from within?"

VI

As preparations were made to train and link those people with detectable traces of the Powers- despite Kelandra's misgivings- the leaders turned their attention to a suggestion made by some of the *orkar* ironmasters, to forge weapons with the Powers that could then be used by the greatest weaponsmasters.

"There are fighters amongst us who possess extraordinary talent and experience," Garrok mused. "Iyoth, for one. Fauli. Lura."

"You would gift Lura with a Powers-strengthened weapon?" Kelandra appeared surprised.

"I'd say she has earned it," Elluron commented. "Besides, if it means she and the others are able to stand in

173

the front line against the *marandaal* alongside those who can wield their own sorcery, I would consider it more a curse than a gift." Elluron smiled faintly. "Perhaps she will consider it so as well."

Garrok lapsed into thought. "Would you have me command the best of our ironmasters to create such weapons?" he asked finally.

"I would." Elluron considered. "I think a greatsword for Lura and scimitars for both Fauli and Iyoth. We need your magicians to do whatever they can, Garrok. But we'll bring our fighters together first and see what they think."

Lura and Fauli were both told about the intent to create Powers-forged weapons for them the following day, and it was suggested that they spar each morning using their preferred weapons in readiness. "I'm surprised you found a use for me," Lura commented, to which Elluron replied, "You have found ways to surprise *us* before, Lura. I'm sure you'll do so again."

I'm more than a little rusty were Fauli's almost apologetic words to Lura the first time they sparred together as preparation for their weapons.

But as they practiced again two days later Lura found herself astonished once more not only at the *du-luyan* woman's speed but also the smooth grace with which she moved and fought. *Catlike* might have been an apt description. Certainly if her skills were a little rusty they must have been unbelievable before. Fauli barely broke sweat at first, while Lura worked so hard in defence that she could feel perspiration trickle down her back, between her breasts, from her armpits and several other places in no time at all. *Powers, am I so unfit?* she asked herself angrily at one point as she desperately defended against a flurry of attacking feints by her opponent.

But she wasn't unfit, she knew. Her wound from the duel with Ruhal had healed almost completely, albeit with the help of *orkar* healers, and she worked on the same instincts that had always served her well in the past. True, she might be a shade slower now than ten or twenty years ago, but she was quick enough for almost anyone. Fauli, however, was like lightning, and Lura found herself continually forced into defence.

Finally they broke away as Fauli gave the hand signal they had agreed on beforehand when one of them suggested a rest. Lura was surprised and a little relieved that Fauli had called it before her. "You fight well," the *du-luyan* woman admitted.

"You're supposed to add *for a human*," Lura commented ruefully as she wiped at her brow, and then looked down at her shirt with a grimace of distaste as they sat together on an upturned provisions crate to slake their thirst. She felt certain that she sweated far more now than she used to.

"For a human," Fauli concurred, and Lura laughed. "You have a good deal more modesty about you than Iyoth, that's for certain. Then again, even his own daughter lacks the man's arrogance. Iyoth truly is one of a kind."

"You love him," Fauli said. "I would be careful."

"I…" Lura blinked. "How do you… I mean, why should I be careful? After all these years, I couldn't care less what other people think about who I choose."

"Nor should you, of course. But Iyoth has a poor reputation amongst his own people. He chose to become an assassin for hire and wander human territories."

"I know about Iyoth's reputation. I can't imagine there's much he hasn't told me by now. What about *your* reputation, Fauli? I cannot imagine that your people thought a great deal of your decision to leave Cai and travel, after you became a weaponsmaster."

"Possibly not." Fauli looked into the distance, a grim look on her face. "They expected me to remain and train others perhaps, or to defend the borders of our territories. Still, I didn't have anyone to leave behind. Something broke inside me, I suppose. Maybe I realised how few ties I had to Cai and its society. I never felt as if I was one of them. I had a mentor, but he was always distant towards me. Still, I ought to have expected it. *Du-luyan* society is uncomfortable with orphans."

"You've heard about what happened in Cai by now, I expect."

The *du-luyan* woman nodded soberly. "I suppose it doesn't matter what we- my race, I mean- think of Iyoth. Few of us remain. We have more important things to think about than one man." She shrugged. "Maybe fatherhood has changed him."

Lura suddenly wondered what the offspring of Iyoth and herself might look like, if they were to ever have children. *Powers know I'd have to work quickly at that,* she thought sourly. *I can't have more than a few years of child-bearing ability left in me, if that.*

"I made friends with some unlikely people," Fauli reflected. "But they were true friends. They're all dead now."

"As are mine. When Ruhal decided to fulfil his dream of a united Harn, he chose me and two others. We started all of this. But Sarros was revealed to be a traitor to our cause, Jahar was killed in a battle with the Old Dark, and Ruhal... well, I'm sure you've heard what befell Ruhal."

Fauli nodded. "That must have been the most difficult thing you've ever done."

"It should have been. But it passed by in a blur. I didn't feel as if I knew what I was doing. I only thought about it afterwards. And ever since."

They watched as Merinne approached from across the camp. The stolid *orkar* woman made her way unhurriedly across the mud. Lura saw that she held a two-handed greatsword in its scabbard, and a feeling of unease rose inside her. "Is that what I think it is?" she asked when Merinne was near enough to hear.

The ironmistress nodded. "It's for you, Lura. We think it should work well enough, although time will tell. Of course, there's no way of testing it properly unless you seek out those enemies it's intended to destroy. The *kin* and their masters have been conspicuous by their absence in recent days, and the *marandaal*... well, they will come when they come." She passed the sword over, and Lura immediately marvelled at the lightness and balance of the weapon. Instantly she somehow *knew* that armed with this blade she would be faster and stronger beyond her normal means, when she faced the Old Dark or the starspawn.

Merinne turned to Fauli, and unbuckled a curved scimitar from her belt. "This is yours, *du-luyan.*"

Fauli took it cautiously and stepped away several paces to test it with a few moves. "This is a special blade," she declared afterwards with a faint smile. "How long did it take to make these?"

"It took eight ironmasters every waking moment of the last two days. We have something for Iyoth as well, when he returns."

A sudden chill came over Lura as she imagined herself and Iyoth striding into battle against the *marandaal.* She wondered how long her luck would hold. *I'm the last of Ruhal's merry band of four,* she reminded herself. The blade gleamed in the pale sunlight. *Why am I even still alive? So many times I've been that close to death- whether by almost making a decision to end it all, or by poor choices in battle or elsewhere.*

"You can use these for sparring, should you wish to," Merinne said, misinterpreting her look. "It would take considerable magic to so much as chip either blade. Only an ironmaster can break them, and only then with great difficulty."

Lura put the sword back into its scabbard and tied it in her belt. "I only wish I was unbreakable," she said with a wintry smile.

VII

"Loren!"

Nia froze. *Only one man would ever call me that,* she thought. But she didn't turn at first. Instead she cautioned herself. *There may be some other woman with that name. It's common enough.*

But the call was repeated, nearer to her this time. Her heart pounded more and more quickly. Her mouth felt dry. Finally she turned, trying to keep a politely neutral expression on her face. But her efforts fell apart as she saw Arin with a young girl she had certainly not seen at his mansion, and an even younger *luyan* boy. Were they the sorcerors she had heard Teryn's men talking about? She suppressed a shudder at the thought of more children who bore the Powers walking around the camp. *We invite chaos at every turn,* she thought.

"Arin," she said faintly. "I... I see you've found a family for yourself." Suddenly, without thinking she added, "My name isn't Loren by the way. It's Nia."

"Well, I didn't suppose it was." Arin smiled. "I never expected to see you again. Nia."

"I never expected to live this long," Nia admitted, "but something always confounds those expectations."

An uncomfortable silence followed. Nia felt the curious stares of the children upon her. "So why are you here?" she asked finally, even though she already knew the answer. She tried her best to ignore the thoughtful look the girl gave Arin and then herself.

"We had nowhere else," he said simply. "There were others, but we couldn't convince them to come with us."

Arin proceeded to tell Nia everything that had happened since Telith had fallen into chaos. She feigned surprise at his confession that he- and the two children who he introduced as Lumi and Ryn- had a talent in the Powers. When he talked about the castle where the children had hidden themselves away, Nia felt all kinds of emotions stir within her. *An orphanage without masters,* she thought.

When Arin finished his story she managed a quick smile and said, "Well, that sounds like quite an adventure." Before she could stop herself she added, "I should apologise for Telith- and indeed for every other town and village that's been destroyed. You'll hear the truth sooner or later, so you may as well hear it from me."

Arin frowned. "How can any of this be your fault?"

"Because I knew the secret of the Watchers- how they came to be," Nia said bluntly. "I kept it to myself- and a few others- for as long as I could, but then it was decided that I'd kept it long enough. Truthfully I think some of those in charge here fully intended the mayhem that resulted. But it was my knowledge and my words that did the deed. The truth spread, and nothing could stop it. I expect by now everyone has heard it." She paused and observed their expressions. "Well, maybe not everyone."

Nia ended up telling the three of them far more than she intended to. They went to sit around one of the fires where luncheon was being served, and as they ate she described her escape from the Sanctum, her witnessing of the Watcher being made, her encounters in the Bonemord, her journey north and her fateful meeting with Xu'naal, followed by her capture and trial in Darkbrook and eventual encounter with Kelandra and her new companions. She even went as far as to describe the nightmares caused by Yui and the reasons why the child hated her so utterly to begin with. The words spilled from her mouth and she felt helpless to stop them. She paid no heed to the fact that others beyond her intended audience- several Darkbrook men and an *orkar* axeman- also listened in on her story.

The children listened attentively, fascinated and horrified in turn, their eyes round with excitement as they drank in the vivid sights and sounds of Nia's retelling. Arin, to her surprise, simply looked grim, perhaps even angry. *Now you know what I'm really like,* Nia thought at one point when she glanced at him, and she said as much after she finished her story. He didn't reply.

"That's the most amazing adventure I've ever heard," Ryn declared.

"It sounds a little *too* amazing," Lumi said, and Nia flashed a quick smile at her. "Do you think so? I only wish it was. Speak with any of those in charge here and they'll vouch for the truth of it. Most of it, anyway."

"And now you're here," Arin said softly.

"Yes. Now I'm here. Not by choice, of course. I don't think I've ever taken part in full-scale war out of choice. I always preferred to operate by myself, in the shadows. Best place for me, I reckon." Nia got hastily to her feet. "Well, I hope you all enjoyed the story. Good evening."

She turned and strode away, trying to appear relaxed but certain that she was walking far too quickly.

A little later, as Nia contemplated again whether or not to depart she saw Arin approach, by himself this time.

"I'm surprised you didn't bring your new family with you," Nia said airily as he sat on an upturned weaponry box next to the one she was sitting on.

"They're with two of the witches who are close to the leaders."

Nia laughed. "Is that wise? Those people are dangerous, you realise."

"I hardly have a choice in the matter. They wanted to explain the situation to the children. Anyway, I wanted the chance to speak with you alone."

Nia swallowed. "Really? Why? We've both said our stories. What more is there to say?"

Arin looked intently at her. "You've been running away your whole life."

"You barely know me, Arin. Don't presume to tell me what my whole life has been like. Anyway, I've had a lot to run from." Nia scowled at him. "It's none of your business. I shouldn't have said as much as I did, but there's one more regret to notch up. You know as much as you need to satisfy your curiosity, I imagine."

Arin half-smiled. "Hardly."

"Oh! Do you wish to know more about me? About my works of assassination, thievery and spying on the good citizens of Luudhoq, turning them over to the mercy of the Watchers whenever I was asked to? Or perhaps you'd like to go further back? To my childhood? You're lucky I didn't mention all that when your *family* were listening. That would have shocked them."

"Tell me if you want to tell me," Arin said quietly. "And if you don't, then don't."

Nia remained silent for a short while. "I don't think I can," she murmured finally. "It's just words, and words can't describe how I felt every single day. The terror, the pain, but worst of all, the knowledge that I was *nothing*. An unwanted child, discarded by its parents."

She had begun to shake again. *Powers, control yourself!* she thought, and just about managed to- but she couldn't speak. Her lips pressed tight shut. She closed her eyes, and after a moment a faint, desolate sound issued from her. She felt Arin's hand pressed against her own, but for a while she was no longer in the open air of the camp but enveloped by the dank gloom of the orphanage. No longer could she smell the routine odours of an army on the move. Instead she inhaled the sharpness of stale sweat, of skin and hair unwashed for many days, as she was held down in excruciating pain as a group of the masters took turns to rape her.

With an effort Nia opened her eyes and looked at Arin. "Loren was one of the girls who disappeared. I don't know why I used her name. She was never found, but there were some days when I thought she was one of the lucky ones. Maybe she escaped or maybe they murdered her, but either way it was a release. Maybe *that's* why I used her name."

Arin stared sombrely at the ground and said nothing.

"How I wish I'd been born with the use of the Powers," she added venomously, and he gave her a sharp look. "Be careful what you wish for, Nia."

"I would have killed them slowly," she continued, a far-away look in her eyes. "I'd have spent days and days tormenting them. They would have begged and pleaded with me to end their lives, long before I would finally do so." Nia frowned. "It's odd that I found two of those men, years later."

"How did you find them?"

"Kelandra sent me on a mission to assassinate two men who she had said were supplying and selling dangerous and illegal herbs from the South Ocean Islands. Some people had already been poisoned by them. Anyway, it turned out that these two men used to work at the orphanage. Selling herbs was the least of their crimes."

"Do you think Kelandra knew who they were? In relation to the orphanage, I mean."

"Perhaps. There wasn't much that Kelandra didn't know. Perhaps she thought it would make me better at my job, if I could gain my revenge on a few of those men. I'm not sure it did, but there we are."

Arin nodded. "I want to tell you something, Nia. I've thought about you every day since you left me."

Nia stared at him, lost for words. She was still struggling to reply when a sudden eruption of noise somewhere in the camp cut through their conversation. A shimmering could be seen in the air and an odd, continuous noise like metal scratching against stone. Then smoke and screams of horror rose into the air, and the encampment dissolved into chaos.

It took a long while for the mayhem to be brought under control. Half a dozen people who held a trace of the Powers were being taught to link, but at least two of them had lost control and the sorcery the six held between them had simply bloomed into unutterable chaos. All six were destroyed, wiped out by one another. Incredible amounts of heat and cold swept through the vicinity, killing or harming at least a hundred other people. The weather was momentarily affected, soft rain turning to shards of ice. The ground was scorched and turned black for a hundred paces in every direction from the charred remains of the trainee sorcerers.

Some distance away, Jak stared in horror and disbelief at the scene. *I caused this,* he thought wretchedly. *I pointed out those people. Now they're dead and their families are left to suffer, all because of what I did.*

Eventually he managed to tear his eyes away from the sight. He turned and ran, and when he reached the edge of the camp he continued running.

"Jak!"

Amethyst's voice cut through the still air, and Jak looked up, startled. He almost dropped the knife that he held.

Amethyst cautiously made her way down the slope to where Jak sat by the stream. "How did you find me?" he asked.

"I saw you running away." Amethyst glanced at the weapon. "What did you intend to do with that- or needn't I ask?"

Jak shook his head and flung the blade to one side. Amethyst retrieved it, placed it securely in her belt and sat by him. She had no idea what to say to him, but Jak spoke before she could think of anything.

"I've just had enough. I've lost Ileana, and now I've caused all those deaths. I did it, Amethyst. If I'd kept my mouth shut none of this would have happened!"

"You weren't to know." Amethyst thought for a moment and added, "They knew the risks. The leaders discussed it at length with at least one of the *orkar* ironmasters. They made the decision to go ahead and try to teach these people to link. Maybe they will still go ahead."

Jak threw her a look of disbelief and horror. "After all that?!"

"I suspect they will do anything if they think it will help them to defeat the *marandaal*. But let's put that to one side for a moment. You can do nothing about it. I firmly believe that Ileana and Vornen will come back from the Green Road. We cannot lose hope and we cannot lose belief in them. What if Ileana returns and finds that while she helped to seal the Gate within the Green Road, you had decided to put an end to your own life? Can you imagine how she would feel?"

"She wouldn't care. She went without saying farewell."

"She had no choice in the matter, as she saw it. Ileana believed in Alexia, and she must have thought she had good reason to, much as I can't fathom what that might have been. So we have to believe in her."

Jak said nothing.

"And like it or not, I have to help look after you until they return."

"I don't need looking after," he said angrily, but he wouldn't look at her when she said quietly, "You do, Jak. I need to look after you, and you need to look after yourself as well. If you feel like ending it all again, tell me. Do you promise?"

He simply burst into tears. Amethyst put an arm around him and they sat together for a while longer.

She didn't dare tell him that she too found herself within a hair's breadth of giving up hope for Ileana and Vornen. She felt cold inside as she contemplated their miniscule places in this bitter age. *I don't understand you and you don't understand me,* she thought, *and we've more than likely lost everyone and everything. What remains for us except a minor part in a last stand against an implacable, invincible enemy?*

For a moment she even considered using Jak's blade to hasten her own final sleep.

VII – The Unwanted Path

I

Iyoth tethered his horse to the nearest of the tall chestnut trees and unpacked his rations from the saddlebag. His mood was sour. He felt tired, angry and at odds with the world, none of which was in itself unusual, but he could still not get used to the reason for his anger- the fact that he had left behind far more than he could possibly have imagined.

Kian, he thought morosely. *I gave her away with barely a moment's thought all those years ago, and now I can't bear to be parted from her.*

And then there was Lura.

Iyoth stood still and looked out over the darkening landscape. One hand loosely held the reins of his horse. He let the memory of his last night with Lura consume his thoughts. *I would certainly never have thought that would happen,* he mused. *Nothing ever works out how one expects. I resolved to never become entangled and complicated in that way ever again. And as for it happening with a human woman... well, if a year ago someone had told me that would be my fate, I would have laughed in his face and slit his throat.*

But Lura is different, for all her many faults. What do I see in her that others don't? Do I just see through and beyond the damage her life has caused her?

As he helped his companions set up camp, Iyoth reflected that he had lived a bitter and unhappy life full of poor choices, and so had Lura- although perhaps hers had been more a product of circumstance rather than choice.

All in all, this was far from the ideal time to be selected for a dangerous mission that involved roaming the southlands of Harn in the hope of recruiting Watchers. *I should have refused the mission,* he thought. *They could have chosen Fauli. What does she have to lose? She never had a family. She appears to have no friends.*

But the thought only made him feel ashamed and even angrier.

As they settled by the fire a little later Iyoth glanced at the ever-taciturn Alturus. Had the Watcher recalled anything of the life he had presumably once lived? What might happen if he did?

"It's about time I showed you both some items I brought along," the *orkar* ironmaster Varin said. Iyoth and Alturus watched as he brought forth some odd-looking objects and laid them on the ground. Three of them were small and pebble-shaped, although Iyoth found to his surprise that he couldn't tell if they were made of stone or metal. "These are colourburst stones," Varin said, tapping one of them with his claw. He handed one each to Iyoth and Alturus. "Cast one into the air if we're apart from one another and need the other two to come to you. They float into the sky and then burst in a shower of colours which can be seen night or day, regardless of the weather."

"You *orkar* are full of surprises," Iyoth commented as he felt the weight of the colourburst stone in his hand.

Varin shrugged. "We reveal the products of our sorcery only when we have to. Garrok judged that these might be useful and I agreed. Now these"- he pointed to three small bundles that looked like tightly wound nets- "may not be of use against Watchers, but if we come across someone with strength in the Old Powers and need to subdue them, they will help."

"They appear to be nets, made from some extremely strong fibre," Alturus observed as he touched one of them.

"And so they are. They would be difficult for anyone to escape from. But if any sorcerer or witch is caught up in this mesh, it prevents them from drawing on the Powers. This is something new that we created. Merinne, the greatest of our kind, observed something similar that Anlerran's captor had fashioned in order to place a barrier between her and the Powers. She has worked on weaving a similar shield into this material for many days."

"Impressive," Iyoth admitted.

"Useful, potentially," Alturus echoed. "Of course, there is no particular reason why Watchers may not also hold the Powers, in addition to the sorcery bestowed during our... remaking."

Varin perhaps took too long to ponder that statement, for Alturus added sharply, "We were once human, Varin. And any human may harbour the Powers. I do not, as it happens."

The *orkar* man simply nodded. There was nothing else to say.

They cooked and ate the birds and rabbit they had caught earlier in the day, and agreed on who should take which watch during the night. The following morning, Iyoth woke to find that Alturus was already awake. The Watcher faced the south-west, unmoving.

Of course, Iyoth thought as he sat up and stretched. *They don't sleep. They have no need for it.*

But Alturus remained thus for a long while, and finally Varin said to him, "What is it, Alturus? A Watcher nearby?"

Alturus gave a barely perceptible nod.

"Finally. Something to do," Iyoth declared, but Alturus turned round and addressed them both. "No. Not this one. I'll go to him alone. I'll not convince him otherwise. He is... damaged. Unpredictable. Yet not beyond saving."

"All the more reason..."

"I'm stronger than him, Iyoth. I don't believe I will be in great danger. The test will lie in my ability to convince him of our cause, and in this particular case I will be better able to do so on my own."

"How far away is he?" Varin asked.

"Three leagues, more or less."

"Let us accompany you to within half a league," Varin suggested. "That way, if you're wrong, we can hopefully come to you if needed."

Alturus considered. "Very well," he said finally. "But we go now."

Varin put aside the leftovers from last night's dinner with a sigh.

II

We've done this before, Caul remarked gloomily to himself as he and Arian sat in the shelter afforded by a tall horse chestnut tree, one of a large number in the arbour of the abandoned mansion they had come across. *Last time we sheltered and rested as we fled our enemies, Arian trusted me to watch over her as she slept, and what did I do? I couldn't even keep myself awake, and those* luyan *hunters must have laughed silently to themselves as they stole up on us.*

But the *luyan-* at least, those had captured them and taken them all the way to the castle where the *kin* waited- were surely almost all dead. Caul doubted that more than several had managed to escape. Perhaps some had been turned to *diafagh,* forced to shamble with neither purpose nor thought through the grounds of the castle or the land around it, until someone brought the mercy of the Powers to bear upon them.

And what of our people? he asked himself. *How many survived after being scattered like the four winds? Has every Wistledge tribe been subverted by the Old Dark?*

He and Arian were far from the Wistledge now, and he doubted that any of the huntspeople of those tribes would pursue them this far, but they had no shortage of other enemies to contend with.

The owners of this mansion and its attendant outbuildings were long gone, but Caul and Arian had walked around the grounds and inside the buildings several times, determined not to be ambushed. Their inspection had revealed signs of a bloody struggle, although it remained unclear who or what the protagonists had been. Caul didn't care to know the recent history of this place. All that mattered was that the humans who had lived here- a landowner family and their retinue of servants, he guessed- had fled, and some of them had died. Perhaps those were the ones who had refused to flee or had put up resistance to the invaders of their home. Although the spray marks of blood on some of the inner walls pointed to a violent encounter of some kind, they had found no bodies anywhere within the buildings or in the grounds.

Caul mused on the matter only for a moment longer and put it to one side. The fate of his own people consumed him and he had no time for whatever happened to the humans of Harn.

"We need to take some food from the storerooms," Arian said abruptly. Caul was initially surprised by her words, but then reasoned that during the winter months there were few creatures to be hunted, all the fruit had long fallen from the trees and any root vegetables left below the ground in the fields would have frozen and spoiled.

"Even the food that humans eat is bearable in the absence of anything better," she reasoned, as if she had read his thoughts.

They made their way across the grassy lawn towards the nearest archway, and through towards the rear of the main building. Once again Caul's sharp senses picked up the odours of dampness and mildew mingled with the harsh but faded scent of blood. Incoming rain glistened on the sills of broken windows. Their footfall echoed sharply and their boots crunched on broken glass as they made their way through towards the kitchens.

"Maybe we really will have to escape to somewhere distant and raise a family," he said as he watched Arian rummaging through the meagre stores in the rooms behind the kitchens a little later.

She threw him an odd look. "I thought we agreed it wouldn't come to that."

"That hope has died," he said.

"I thought it might." Arian picked up a pack of wrapped saltmeat and sniffed warily at it. "But I think to bring children into a world like this would be a cruelty- don't you?"

"I hadn't thought about it that way," he confessed.

"If either the *marandaal* or the Old Dark hold ultimate power over living things, then it's time to die, not make new life," Arian declared morosely. "And what kind of life is this, spent picking through the humans' leftovers?"

"We may yet prevail," Caul pointed out, and she half-smiled at those words. "That's the resurrection of your dead hope, is it?" She gave him a long, considering look. "Would you like to be the father of my children, Caul? *Our* children? If we somehow defeat whatever long odds are stacked against us?"

"I would," he confessed.

"Even if I wasn't the last?"

He took a deep breath. Was now the right time to tell her? There would never be a good time. "You would be the only one, even if you weren't the only one," he said finally. "No matter how many others still lived. You always have been."

Arian smiled at that. *When was the last time I saw her smile?* Caul wondered. She opened her mouth to reply, but at that moment they heard a faint sound from somewhere distant within the building.

They made their way back along the series of corridors that ran adjacent to the exterior back wall. As they walked, Caul saw a figure standing in the rain out in the gardens, and silently he touched Arian's arm twice in a signal they had mutually understood for years. *Danger,* it meant- nothing more than that.

Beyond the side archway where they had stopped, rain hissed down into the lush, mature gardens of bushes, flowers and ornamental fountains and statues. A tall, angular figure stood on one of the small square lawns, bent forward slightly. The rain ran down the folds of its greatcloak and from the rim of the water-softened hat that covered almost all of its face.

It did not move, and for a moment Caul fancied that it might even be a statue that someone had inexplicably dressed in a hat and cloak.

At his side, Arian slid from her belt one of the longknives they had found in the weaponry store. Although the weapon made no sound, the figure in the garden slowly raised its head as if it had just woken up. Caul looked into its eyes and a shudder ran through him.

I can't tell what it is, he thought. His eyes told him at first that it was human, but his deep senses warned of something else.

Finally he understood.

"Watcher," he breathed, so quietly that only Arian should have heard him. But the creature must have heard or lip-read the word, for its cold blue lips creased in a smile, and as the cut-glass eyes observed the two *du-luyan* lurking in the shadows of the abandoned building it raised an arm and touched the soaked brim of its hat in mock greeting.

"*Du-luyan,*" it said softly. "Few of your kind remain."

Arian brought forth her other longknife and held them before her. "*Na kai-oth aal, an-huul,*" she murmured to Caul in their own language. *We should run as fast as we can.*

He was about to reply, but the Watcher said, "I speak your language. I speak all the known languages of the world. I can assure you- running will do you no good."

Arian spat on one of the stone slabs that patterned the floor near the archway. "Your way then," she said. "Take us if you can. We'll cut you to pieces."

"That, I very much doubt." The Watcher regarded them both for a moment, and walked a little nearer. "Look at you both. Fugitives, lost. Running from everyone and everything. No friends; no families. Living day to day like beggars or mongrel curs. I don't need to ask you anything to know the truth of your situation as it happens. I am much the same."

"The people of the Free Territories know you only as a servant of the Black Citadel," Arian said.

The Watcher laughed softly at that. "They know more about us now than they ever did, and so do we. I'm no servant of the Black Citadel as you call it. I serve only myself. I go where I wish. I take whatever I need from those I swore to protect and rule over." He looked them up and down. "You are hunted. I am a hunter. Luckily for you I have no interest in hunting your kind."

"Then what *do* you hunt?"

"Whatever I need to. Animals for food. Even Watchers need to eat." He smirked as if he had made a joke.

"And humans?"

"What do you care for humans?" he asked, a note of suspicion in his voice.

"We don't. There's little love lost between our races," Arian admitted.

The Watcher regarded her in silence for a moment, as the rain finally eased off. "A rage came upon me, and if I had the chance I might well have slaughtered a number of them," he said then. "But I had no such opportunity- whatever happened here was not my doing- and the fury passed. At least, it abated. That was three days ago." He looked at both of them in turn. "I suspect that neither of you have heard the truth about the Watchers. A single revelation that sowed the seeds of chaos throughout the land."

Arian and Caul looked uneasily at each other. The Watcher gave a barely audible sigh. "Would you care to know? You want to survive, don't you? You had better learn a little more of recent events in Harn. Your accents are Hastian. Cai, perhaps?"

Caul nodded. "Cai was taken by the Old Dark."

"Hmm. Many places and people seem to be taken by the *Old Dark* these days. I don't entirely understand what that is." The Watcher walked towards them and had got past almost before they knew it, although that shouldn't have been possible. "The library is still dry," he called back as he headed down a passageway and finally into a small library which stood at its end. As the two *du-luyan* cautiously followed, Caul whispered to Arian, "They are the law keepers of southern Harn. This is not how they're meant to be."

"We were never meant to be," the Watcher said without turning round.

By the time they walked into the library he was already seated at one of the tables, legs up on the table and arms folded. For a moment he appeared to be lost in thought. "Let me be brief," he said eventually. "Here's the truth of the matter. Some days ago now, it became known to my kind that we were not what we thought ourselves to be. Each one of us had believed without question that we were pulled from the Void through a gateway by the Seven, rescued from what would otherwise have been eternal darkness. Given life, you might say. Pulled from stasis into the light."

Caul and Arian exchanged wordless glances.

"No Watcher has ever recalled their existence in the Void, and as it turns out there is a very good reason for that. We did *not* come from the Void. We are not the ancient guardians of humanity, fashioned by the Seven or perhaps their ancestors. Our origins are, it would appear, rather more mundane. We are-or *were*- humans, from Luudhoq. So I suppose in a sense we *were* fashioned by the Seven. Remade, at least."

"How can that be?" Caul asked.

"How can it be? The Seven take human people from Luudhoq occasionally, for the sole purpose of turning them into Watchers using the sorcery they employ in the depths of their Sanctum. Their appearance is changed. The story of the Void is driven into them. They develop the powers for which Watchers are known and feared. If they survive the transformation, then they become one of the law keepers of Luudhoq and the South."

Caul and Arian exchanged dumbfounded looks. "And have you now turned against your masters?" Arian asked finally.

"*Masters*." The Watcher gave her a flat look. "Tell me, knifemaiden or whatever you call yourself, what would *you* do?"

Arian pondered the matter. "Are the Seven not immortal, and indestructible?"

"I would say that if something can be created, then it can also be destroyed," the Watcher said, "and that must apply to all things. All creatures. The Seven *appear* indestructible because they have not yet met their match. But the *marandaal* will bring about their ruin."

"They'll destroy everything," Caul pointed out.

"Perhaps. May that day come soon." He folded his arms and lapsed into thought for a while. "The name they gave to me was Seneth," he told them after a while. "Of course, I would have had another name, although I don't remember it. Perhaps in time I will, although that doesn't matter now. I've been a Watcher for a long time, and whatever life I had before my... *rebirth* is long gone."

"Do you remember anything of who you were?" Caul asked curiously.

"I have no precise memories in terms of time and place. No names. Only images." Seneth looked thoughtfully at them. "We have certain things in common."

"We do?" Arian echoed warily.

"As I said before, few of your kind remain. The Watchers heard reports of a battle just east of the Wistledge between two groups of *du-luyan*. One would have been local to the area, the other... somehow arrived from Aphenhast, though by not by any usual means."

"Most of our people were massacred, and if anyone other than us survived they're likely scattered across much of Harn by now," Caul explained. He proceeded to tell Seneth about the events that had led to their original retreat to the Silver Road, followed by their emergence in the lands of their cousins by the Wistledge. The Watcher listened patiently, offering neither question nor comment until Caul was done with the retelling.

Seneth suddenly looked up and beyond the entrance to the room, alerted by something that even Arian had not sensed. "What is it?" she demanded immediately.

"Another Watcher approaches this place," he said. "That may not bode well for any of us."

He got up and walked slowly back down the corridor. Caul and Arian looked to each other and then Arian motioned for Caul to follow her in the opposite direction, through another exit towards the back of the manor house.

It was in the grounds in that area that they suddenly came face to face with another, older Watcher. Grey-haired and severe, he gave them a cursory look and then walked straight past without a word. Caul and Arian stared at each other in disbelief. When they turned, they saw the two Watchers facing one another.

"Did you know how far and wide your infamy has grown, Alturus?" Seneth asked. As he spoke the rain began to fall heavily once again, but neither of the Watchers paid it any heed.

"I am not concerned with infamy," the Watcher Seneth had named as Alturus replied. "I am concerned only with the destruction of the Seven and the *marandaal*."

Seneth glanced quickly around. "I don't see any of your companions. How did you locate me? Are you alone?"

"I was sent to find lone Watchers and convince them to join us," Alturus said. "I came to you alone, but if you value your existence then you should return with me."

"I don't value it especially, and I have no intention of joining your band of rebels and renegades. Your notion of a united land will never come to pass. The Seven will never allow it, and you cannot defeat them. Leave that for the *marandaal*."

"We have no intention of leaving anything for the *marandaal*. Amongst us we have people who wield sorcery that you and I cannot understand, Seneth. I believe that united we *can* destroy the Seven. As for a united land, that will only happen if we take Luudhoq. We have no choice; it has been revealed to us that a Gate will open within the city sooner or later. It must be closed, or the *marandaal* annihilated as they step from the void."

Seneth appeared momentarily interested, then shrugged. "A moment ago, you said *if you value your existence*. I told you, I do not. I have been alive for eighty-eight years since the Seven remade me. You yourself must have lingered for longer still, for I remember I saw you in the first days after the event. Almost certainly no one I could have known would still be alive today. For you, the possibility is infinitesimal. What value can *your* continued existence possibly still have?"

"And yet here you are, still alive," Alturus remarked. "I'm not concerned with my own history and the fate of those still unknown to me. I *am* concerned with the task of overcoming the Seven and the *marandaal*. I'll gladly rest when my enemies lie dead or vanquished."

"How noble," Seneth commented. "But your fight is not my fight." He looked past Alturus at the two *du-luyan*, who were themselves dumbfounded to realise that they hadn't taken the opportunity to run. "If you're after recruits, those two look like worthy specimens, assuming you have a need for more folk who wield the mystical Powers. You said that you have some already, but I'm sure you could always use more."

Alturus turned round unhurriedly, to find that Arian already had one of her longknives raised. "We want no part in your war," she said clearly.

"Is that your weapon of choice?" Alturus said, a faint, hard smile upon his face.

"Take a step closer and you'll find out how good I am with it," she responded spiritedly.

"Are you certain they hold the Powers?" Alturus asked Seneth, one eye still upon Caul and Arian. "Detecting such residues was never my strength, although I seem to remember you had a certain skill in that area."

"I am certain. Both powerful." Seneth smirked, his cold eyes resting on both of the *du-luyan* in turn. "I'm *not* certain how you'll tame them, however. The female in particular is a wild creature."

"I've no intention of taming anyone." Alturus gave Arian a level stare. "What is it to be? I guarantee even an old Watcher such as me will be faster than yourselves. You'll come with me peacefully, or under duress."

"Neither," Arian said, and in one fluid motion she threw the longknife with as much strength as she could muster. It sped straight at the Watcher. Caul gaped in astonishment as it struck him straight in the eye and embedded itself deep inside his head.

Alturus sagged to his knees. His body shook. Slowly he reached out and began to pull the blade out of him without uttering the faintest cry of pain. Seneth looked almost as shocked as Caul initially, although he swiftly recovered his composure. With an uncertain smile he said to them both, "That was impressive. But you've done nothing except hasten your own deaths."

Arian and Caul looked at each other and fled towards the rear entrance into the manor grounds. Caul could not help but glance back once. He saw Seneth stroll away and into the shadow of the buildings, perhaps to do nothing more but sit and wait for his life to end. Alturus staggered to his feet, still struggling with the longknife that had stricken him. It gleamed in the rain as the Watcher grasped the blade and part of the handle. Blood and something that gleamed like silver dripped between his fingers.

"Do you want to die?" Arian snapped at him. Caul sped after her, and they ran on, deep into the surrounding woodland and beyond.

They heard nothing of Alturus, only the persistent hiss of rain.

But Caul already knew he would come after them, and he felt more certain than ever when a moment later bright colours lit up the sky for a short while, as if the Watcher had released some unknown magic with which to hunt them.

III

They dared rest only when they reached the other side of the woods, where dusk and a clearing sky waited. They could easily have pressed on in even darker conditions had it not been for their exhaustion. Arian sank to the ground with a sigh and sat wearily against the trunk of the lone tree nearby. In silence she looked out over a shallow valley that stretched away below and before them to the north. As Caul looked agitatedly back into the gloom from which they had emerged, she murmured, "We've crossed two rivers and taken lesser-used paths. We can do no more to hide our trail. Not until we've rested, at any rate."

Caul sat beside her, so tired that he barely felt the wetness of the grass. "They heal more quickly than any natural being," he pointed out. "He will undoubtedly follow when he can. And I'm not sure any trail can be hidden from a Watcher."

"I realise that, Caul. But we had no option other than to become his prisoner."

"Well, if he catches up then we've no option but the Powers. Speaking of which, I thought they might have been your... weapon of choice, as he put it."

"I was too tired, and I worked on instinct." Arian glared at him. She was clearly in no mood for a protracted argument. Caul let the matter go, and tried to think instead about the best direction for them to head in. But his head began to droop and he could barely put together a single coherent thought. Arian said quietly to him, "Sleep, Caul. I'll wake you in a while."

She shook him awake a little later, and once he was fully aware she drifted asleep, her head leaning slightly forwards and her arms crossed. Caul sat and listened to the sounds all around. Aside from Arian's faint, steady breathing, he could hear only the chirruping of crickets and faint rustles in the undergrowth now and again as small creatures made their way through the grass.

What now? he asked himself. *Can we escape the Watcher? If he catches us, can we defeat him? Or will he return to his army and recruit others to help hunt us down? If they are heading south, then we should keep going north-and-west, although not near the Wistledge.*

North would take them into the lands of the Old Dark eventually. They would be in danger from an altogether different source then, but at least they had some idea how to fight an enemy whose sorcery was familiar to them.

Caul wondered how long the Watcher would pursue them. Perhaps he would give up. After all, were there not other sorcerors to be found, who they could recruit for their war?

A little later, Caul caught a glimpse of something to one side- barely a shadow of a shadow, yet it was enough for him to quickly shake Arian awake. She sat up silently, alert in an instant. Caul sensed the Powers stirring within her as well as himself as he made a slight gesture towards the direction where he sensed that something approached.

But despite their keen senses, the *du-luyan* man was almost next to them before they even saw him properly. Perhaps it was because of his race that both Caul and Arian hesitated just long enough for him to do what he intended to do. A web of intricate netting shot from his outstretched hand and covered both of them in a moment. Caul reacted instinctively, lashing out with the Powers, his intention to make their foe a smoking ruin. But to his horror, he could do nothing. The sorcery within him remained as nothing more than an urgent spark, before it faded away entirely.

They both struggled furiously but neither of them could do anything except writhe pointlessly amidst the netting. Caul tried to cut his way through it and found that although it was flexible, the material was tougher than steel.

Finally he gave up and stared hatefully at the moonlit figure that loomed above them. He was shocked to realise after a moment that he recognised him.

"Iyoth," he whispered.

Iyoth frowned and looked at him, then at Arian. Finally he blinked in surprise and shook his head. "Caul. And Arian." His expression grew sharp, intense. "What happened at Cai? Where are all our people?"

"Do you really care to know?" Caul asked coldly. "When were you last there?"

Iyoth's smile disappeared. "More recently than you, I expect. My daughter and I passed through Cai as we travelled to Harn. It looked empty at first... but *kin* lurked throughout."

"You have a daughter?" Arian frowned. "I thought you had no family except Lerim."

"That's a story you don't need to know," Iyoth said shortly. "Tell me what happened at Cai. Leave nothing out."

Caul described the bloodshed as the *kin* attacked their ancestral home, culminating in the decision that he and Arian had helped take, for the sorcerers of Cai to open the way to the Silver Road. As the assassin had requested, Caul spared no detail, reasoning that Iyoth deserved to know the fate of his own people no matter whether he cared or not.

Iyoth listened expressionlessly, and when Caul had finished he remained squatting down and silent. "The Silver Road," he said finally.

"What of it?"

"You made use of it. You opened a way through and then directed yourselves to another place."

"It was far from exact, and it was dangerous. Many of our people died, and some would say we hastened their deaths." Caul frowned suspiciously. "You know our people have had the ability to reach that place for long centuries. What are you thinking?"

"You will have heard the rumours of the *marandaal* approaching the Border Wall to invade Harn," Iyoth told them. "But that is not all. I have travelled with a great army from out of northern Harn, and they have amongst them someone who can tell where and when Gates will appear. One will form within Luudhoq at some point, another near the Wistledge and a third somewhere near the far western town of Anvar. We cannot possibly send our sorcerers to every one of these distant places. But the Silver Road..."

"I won't do it," Caul said dismissively. "I'm already partly to blame for what happened to our people..."

"Then leading humans and *luyan* through the same place should matter rather less to you, wouldn't you say?"

They will more than likely all die, Caul thought, *and so will both of us.* But he held his tongue.

A part of him felt a measure of shame and interpreted his unease as cowardice. But Caul was a practical man. He knew the dangers that would face anyone using the Silver Road to traverse what would otherwise be great distances.

It isn't just that though, he reminded himself. *I still held a faint hope that Arian and I would be able to evade capture and somehow find a place to live out however many days we might have had left. How ironic that one of our own people has caught us and intends to drag us into his mad scheme. Are they truly so desperate?*

Arian could remain silent no longer. "You always were a hateful, vindictive creature. Cai became a better place when you left."

"That hardly matters now, seeing as Cai has since become the domain of the *kin*", Iyoth pointed out. "Regardless, I will take you back to the leaders of the army and put forward my idea. Then they can decide what to do with you."

"You're going to take us *both* back? How are you going to manage that? Why don't you just kill us here and now and save yourself the bother," Arian spat. "Do you really think we'll come willingly?"

"Such anger, Arian. I forgot to tell you- I am not alone. There are two others. They will come soon. One of my companions is badly wounded, I'll admit. We had to go to help him. Apparently two *du-luyan* attacked him when he encountered them. Two *du-luyan* whose trail was difficult to follow, though not impossible." Iyoth smiled knowingly as they looked to each other.

"I ought not to be surprised that you consort with Watchers," Arian sneered. "Is there a shred of honour in you?"

Iyoth laughed at that. "Where has honour got *you*, Arian?"

Their captor paced around nearby as he waited for his companions. A short while passed, until finally they heard the sound of footfall from out of the woodland and two figures came into view, one of whom they recognised.

Alturus stared coldly at them. If she was afraid, Caul thought, then she hid it remarkably well. He tried not to allow his despair to show as the Watcher and *orkar* regarded them in silence.

"How's your eye?" Arian smiled suddenly at the Watcher, but his expression remained unchanged.

The *orkar* man wore a thick cloak over his hide armour and his face was partly covered in intricate tattoos. It occurred to Caul that this was the first time he had even met an *orkar*. He would never have expected one to choose a Watcher as a companion. Or a *du-luyan* for that matter.

"Are you certain, Alturus?" the *orkar* asked quietly after a while had passed.

The Watcher nodded slowly and then said in a low voice, "I am certain." He spoke more slowly than he had before, and his words slurred slightly. "The ability... has gone."

Iyoth turned to Arian and fixed her with a cold stare. "You did this."

Arian shrugged disinterestedly. "He wanted to capture us. Now I suppose he has- with your help- but at least we went down fighting."

The *orkar* man went to sit near them. "Unfortunately, your spirited defeat has resulted in us having to abandon our task. We had hoped to locate more Watchers and bring them to our cause, but Alturus can no longer do this, and we have no time to assign another Watcher."

"I have a task for these two, Varin," Iyoth said. "They are able to open gateways into the Silver Road, and use that place to traverse great distances." He explained his idea to his companions, and Caul felt his heart sink as he saw both the *orkar* and the Watcher look at them with renewed interest.

Finally Iyoth turned his attention to his captives. "I'll release you, if you swear by all our ancestors and by the future of all our people, that you will return with us, not seek to harm us- that would end very badly for you- and help us to reach the locations where the Gates will open. You will also give up your weapons until we arrive back."

"If you think we can use the Silver Road in the way you suggest, you're insane," Arian snapped.

"We have no other options," Iyoth said simply.

"And since when did you care so much for the fate of the world?"

"I'm not here to answer your questions, Arian. Well? Do you swear, or shall we simply drag you along like potatoes in a sack?"

Arian looked helplessly to Caul, who shrugged. "At the moment, we don't appear to have a choice," he noted. With an effort he looked to Iyoth. "I swear it," he said reluctantly.

"As do I." Those three words sounded like the most difficult Arian had ever uttered.

Iyoth appeared satisfied by that, but Alturus said, "Wait. Let me warn you- if you attempt any attack, or attempt to flee, I will personally kill both of you."

"We need them, Watcher," Varin said. "Beating them senseless to teach them the error of their ways might be a better option."

"No." Alturus' eyes were fixed upon Arian and filled with a cold, relentless hatred. "If they move against us or try to escape, they die by my hand and slowly. They will scream for death long before I grant it. *That* is what will happen."

Varin shrugged helplessly and looked at Iyoth, who said to his captives, "You would do well to heed the Watcher's words in that case. I cannot stand in his way."

"I could try," Varin added, "but I won't."

The *orkar* man knelt nearby and pulled at the netting, which slipped from Caul and Arian and shrank so that it became nothing more than a small bundle that he tossed over to Iyoth. As Caul felt his grasp of the Powers return he quickly resisted the urge to use them. "What was that?" he asked Varin.

"A cloaking net. Very useful against errant users of the Powers," Varin replied.

The five of them continued north-east. As the sky began to lighten, Caul's mood remained as black as ever. *What a destiny*, he thought morosely. *And who would have thought Iyoth of all people would have fallen in with this motley force of witches, barbarians and orkar?*

Caul had hoped that Iyoth's idea would be dismissed out of hand as dangerous nonsense, but his heart sank as those to whom the decision would fall pondered and weighed the assassin's words. He sighed and looked down the muddy ground, wondering when they might be given something to eat.

"Given the impossibility of getting sorcerers to these areas in time to combat the starspawn," Iyoth said finally, "and given the need to attack them as soon as they emerge from any Gates that form, I see no other option."

"Here's an option," Arian spoke up immediately. "Why don't you just slit your own throat and be done with it, you treacherous son of..."

"Enough!" the *orkar* warlord shouted, and even Arian cringed. The *orkar* looked to Caul. "You appear to be the more reasonable one. We need your help if we're to reach these places before the Gates form. If the *marandaal* are allowed to pour through into Harn then everything is lost. Iyoth has asserted that you can open gateways in and out of the Silver Road and lead people through that place, to the areas that we need to reach. Does he lie? I would advise you to speak the truth. We have a number of people amongst us who are skilled at truthfinding."

"It can be done," Caul said reluctantly. "But the process is difficult and dangerous. It's likely that many of those we take with us will die before we even reach our destination. We know the Silver Road perhaps as well as anyone else alive, but the place presents grave dangers to anyone."

"Not only that, but it became more dangerous during the last time we were there," Arian put in. "To put it bluntly, the Silver Road has started to fall apart. Neither of us can say what it will be like now and what threats we will come up against. The Old Dark, no doubt, but other things as well."

"We need to send people strong in the Powers to three places," the *orkar* leader said. "To Wester Ford, near the Wistledge. To a place near Anvar. And another within Luudhoq."

Caul smiled grimly. "The first two may be reachable. But Luudhoq will not be."

"Why not?"

"To put it simply, Luudhoq does not have a presence in the Silver Road. It is not alone in that regard. Other larger settlements also have no effect on the patterns of that place, and therefore cannot be detected and reached through it. Darkenhelm is another such city. That's the way it has always been."

"You'll have to reach Luudhoq yourselves, as you'd no doubt already planned to," Arian added.

The *orkar* looked from one to the other, then turned to Iyoth. "Do they speak the truth?"

Iyoth shrugged. "I honestly wouldn't know, but as you said we have a number of people who are skilled at truthfinding. Perhaps they can find out. Maybe Alturus still retains that skill." He smirked as Caul and Arian looked warily at him.

"We can help you reach Wester Ford and Anvar," Caul said, "but only if we're strong enough to open a gateway into the Silver Road. We may be able to- our abilities have grown over the past few months- but it remains dangerous. More so than ever. We will need to remain together, Arian and I. For one thing, it will take the two of us to open a gateway and maintain it. The last time, we needed four, so even the two of us together may not be enough."

As if his caution had been entirely ignored, one of the others- a Watcher who Iyoth had named earlier as Kelandra- spoke up. "Very well. So be it. We'll let you eat, drink and rest, and tomorrow we'll decide who will travel with you. According to the information we have, the Gate at Wester Ford will appear first, a few days from now, and the one near to Anvar two days after that. We need you to reach Wester Ford, destroy the Gate when it opens there, and then use the Silver Road again to reach Anvar."

The Watcher motioned to a human man who stepped forward and spread out a map before them. Marks had been made at Wester Ford and at a location south of Anvar.

"We may not even survive the first battle," Caul protested.

"You may not," Kelandra agreed stonily. "But if you do, then pick yourselves up and travel to the next one. We have no one else who can do this. Meanwhile, as you pointed out, we will need to deal with Luudhoq ourselves." She glanced at the *orkar* warlord and then the pale man standing to the other side, who Caul had thought might be *luyan*. As he looked again at him he realised that he couldn't say what race he belonged to.

"Are we agreed?" Kelandra asked. They nodded, and Caul felt his heart sink.

"And to think I hoped to die fighting for our own lives, not for these people," Arian said in a low voice.

Arian watched the following morning, shivering in the cold breeze as the sorcerers from amongst these people- not that many of them were worthy of the title- were selected and organised. They were a motley collection of humans and a lesser number of *luyan* who held the Powers, although she judged that only a few of them were likely to be of any use. She almost said as much, but decided to keep her observation to herself. Two of them- the human boy Parril and Eraya, a *luyan* woman, were strong. As for the others, she wondered how long they would survive within the Silver Road.

She felt almost detached from everything for a moment, as if a part of her had already given up and expected the Silver Road to be their burial ground. Angrily she told herself to fight until the end, wherever and whenever that might be.

Arian saw Parril embrace a *du-luyan* woman after he was chosen. For some reason the woman appeared upset, although she tried not to show it. *I know her,* Arian realised in shock after a moment. *That's Fauli, the orphan who became a weaponsmaster and then left Cai forever.*

She smirked to herself at the thought of a *du-luyan* orphan adopting a human boy. Fauli glanced in her direction but didn't appear to recognise her. A moment later she turned and walked quickly away.

Parril took a deep breath and put on a brave face. To her surprise, Arian felt a certain grudging admiration for the human boy. She reckoned he might be tougher than he appeared, although Arian overheard him complaining that he hadn't even had breakfast yet. *They all complain,* she reminded herself, not sure if she meant males or humans, or both.

A short while later Arian and Caul stood next to each other, with their followers behind them. Everyone watched apprehensively as the two *du-luyan* bowed their heads and stood facing the east in silence. After a moment their arms reached out. Finally a harsh, cold glow of silvery light appeared in front of them. A murmur of unease rose up amongst those who had been selected for the journey. The illumination flickered, became larger, then smaller and finally large enough and consistent enough in shape to step through.

With the gateway opened, Arian stepped through and Caul held it open. Their followers- petrified though some of them were- finally walked through.

Within a short while they had gone, and the rip in the fabric of the Existence disappeared.

V

Nothing that Arian and Caul saw of everyone's reactions to this cold grey world surprised them in the least. They knew that not a single one of them was ready for this journey. Neither were they in truth, but most of these people had never even heard of the Silver Road before, let alone stepped into this murky realm.

It's only to be expected, Arian thought as they rested after walking for what might have been half a day. *These are people caught up in a nightmare, aware of their own mortality as never before. Well, we're not so different to them. I can't remember the last time that Caul and I weren't one false step away from an early grave. But all of this shows only one thing- how desperate the Descendants and the* orkar *and renegade Watchers and all those others are. They have no other choice if they're to stand any chance against the* marandaal.

Am I a Descendant of the First also? she wondered, not for the first time. *My strength has grown ever since the battle against the* kin *at Cai. I suspect that may have even happened* because *of what happened there. Iyoth and his daughter claim to be Descendants- not that Iyoth has any talent in the Powers as far as I'm aware. And that means that Lerim was as well- for all the good it did him.*

And what about Caul? Might he be a Descendant also? My family never spoke of any such heritage, and I don't think his did either.

She glanced across at him and then away when he gave her a questioning look.

Had we lived in peaceful times, we might have been wife and husband by now, she mused. *I would have agreed to it, if he had possessed the courage or forthrightness to simply ask. But I'd have to wait for the sun to turn dark before Caul asked such a thing. No, I'd need to put in the effort myself. But it would be worth it. I didn't realise how much I loved him until we were given this suicidal task. If by some miracle we both survive this, then I'll...*

Her thoughts were interrupted by a mournful, keening sound from somewhere out beyond the treeline, across the open land of silvery grass. She couldn't tell how far away the owner of that sound might be, and even when the noise was repeated a moment later Arian couldn't say if it had drawn closer or not. But her companions acted as one and assumed that it had.

"*Kin?*" Caul murmured, but she shook her head. "Something else. I don't think we want to find out."

They had already caught sight of *kin* during their journey. Fortuitously, all of them had been distant and headed along paths that were unlikely to cross theirs. Arian's instincts told her that attack was not on their minds- those that had minds to speak of. They were on their way to some far destination, commanded by their masters the *choragh* or perhaps other *kin* who stood above them in their strange hierarchy. Some hastened towards the Border Wall to fight against the *marandaal-* they were headed mainly in a near-opposite direction to her company, although direction in itself didn't necessarily mean a great deal in the twisted world of the Silver Road.

If they leave us well alone then we'll do likewise, Arian told herself. *We need to conserve all the energy that we can in order to make it towards a point from where we can reach this village near the Wistledge, if we're strong enough to open a second gateway.*

She remained worried that those *du-luyan* who had become *kin* or fallen in with them might await them somewhere near there. But there simply wasn't enough time to worry about and prepare for that as well. What would be, would be.

Arian listened intently for the sound she had heard to repeat, but only damp and oppressive silence surrounded them.

The companions headed on along the path. To one side the land fell away alarmingly into a wide abyss, the bottom of which could only be vaguely seen. Something that might have been a river wound through the base of the chasm, which Arian estimated could be more than ten thousand hands deep and at least a thousand wide. Certainly it was wider and deeper than any valley she had seen in the sunlit world.

On the other side, vegetation and buildings intermingled in a chaotic mess. None of the buildings looked like any she had ever seen. Some looked top-heavy or overbuilt on one side, structures that should have been impossible. Occasionally she saw something black and many-shaped creep through the spindly, silver-edged trees or along the various contours of the structures that sprouted everywhere from the ghostly forest. Something that sounded like wind sighed through this madness, but no wind existed here.

The companions had trudged through the eerie landscape for a while before eventually the strange, ethereal mist descended again. It blurred everything within its pallid silvery-grey shroud. Arian turned to ensure that everyone was still present, then she and Caul agreed that they should walk at the front and rear respectively.

Soon the landscape beneath became featureless, open moorland. Time passed in grey silence and their surroundings barely changed. Here and there it sloped up or down, and every now and then they noticed the darker silhouette of a copse or woodland or the harsh shape of a rock against the backdrop of mist. Arian wondered briefly what they might have been able to see had the mist not been a continuous presence, and decided that she would rather not know. *Kin* and other beings that she could not identify were nearer now, but perhaps the mist hid the companions from them.

She sensed that somewhere up ahead, the way to the area just east of the Wistledge was clearer. Arian had found that the longer she spent in the Silver Road, the more she could feel the swirling, invisible fabric of the place and the currents that drove it, and the more she could sense the parts that were somehow weaker and easier to breach. The Silver Road had rules, even if those rules had become less than reliable. She could tell which direction to go in order to reach a place from which a gateway might be created. What worried her was that even she and Caul together would not be strong enough to form and open a second gateway. No matter the abilities of their companions, the task of forming the way through to their destination would be down to her and Caul. Through history, only the *du-luyan* had ever properly studied the Silver Road and its curious effect of allowing sorcerors of sufficient strength to form gateways to and from that realm. Only their people knew intuitively how it could be done.

It took four of us last time, she reminded herself. *I'm astonished that we were able to reach the Silver Road again to begin with.*

Angrily she told herself not to allow seeds of defeat to take root in her thoughts. She couldn't afford for that to happen.

The companions struggled through the heath in silence. As the mist finally lifted the path led them to a valley where great cliffs of jagged black stone rose so high that their summits could not be seen. Here they encountered *kin-* but these creatures had become ensnared or trapped by elements of this ever-changing, ever-dangerous world.

Through the middle of the valley a river ran, but it flowed far more slowly than it ought, as if within the confines of its banks time moved more slowly or the laws that governed materials had been driven askew. A number of *kin*, some of them once human or *luyan,* could be seen within the ponderous flow. They struggled to free themselves, and the limbs of some had been already torn from their bodies. Arian wondered how they could have become trapped, and she motioned for the others to walk some distance away from the river.

One strange effect the river had forced upon them appeared to be the silencing of their voices. These *kin* could no longer speak or even cry out their rage or agony to the silent world they had hoped to traverse. Their mouths opened and Arian saw the hatred in their eyes as they beheld the companions who stared in horror and fascination at their plight.

Her attention was drawn to the nearest of these vile, unfortunate creatures. It turned its head to them as the companions walked past. One of its arms remained free, and Arian thought the *kin*-beast might reach out its set of long, almost spider-like fingers, but it didn't, perhaps unable to. Life only trickled through its form. The creature bared its teeth at her, and baleful red-rimmed eyes fixed her with a murderous stare.

"Are these *kin*?" she heard someone ask. Without turning round she said, "Yes. In time, you may learn the sensation that washes through your body when one or more of them is near. It's not a feeling that anyone would wish for."

"Should we kill them?" someone else asked, and this time Arian turned to face them. "We keep our strength for when and where it's needed most. Look at these creatures. They may well remain trapped here for all eternity."

"Then perhaps we should put them out of their misery," Parril pointed out, although he looked away when Arian told him, "I would rather that these abominations remain here and suffer for all time. Creatures like these slaughtered most of our people."

No one said anything else.

As they made their way on through the valley it gradually widened and revealed a landscape that sloped gradually away before them, towards seemingly endless grassland and forest. Arian kept her eyes fixed on a point ahead, about half of the way down the slope. *There,* she thought. *That will be the place.* Her Powers-deepened senses told her that the fabric of this place might be thinner there. She stopped briefly and looked back to Caul, who nodded and gave a faint smile. She could tell that he had sensed the same.

They gathered at that location. Arian felt the air begin to swirl around them as she and Caul concentrated on the location they needed and summoned what she could of the Powers.

As before, when the two of them together with Merithen and Rend had worked together, they concentrated on finding a path through to the abandoned village of Wester Ford, a place that they had been near to only once, as part of a diplomatic expedition years ago. They managed to visualise it, recalling how the mountains had looked that day- a sullen dark against the azure sky- the continual rush of the Daymorn river as it wound its way towards those peaks, and the ruined settlement itself, full of tumbled walls and thick with long decades of vegetation. They felt the Powers flow between them, so quickly and with such force that for a short while they struggled to control the emerging gateway.

A murmur of unease came from their watching companions as a shimmer of movement appeared several paces in front of them. It flickered and changed shape at first, then became a doorway of soft light that cut through the surrounding gloom. At the same time, Arian felt the path beyond it also move and change shape as it connected with the part of the Silver Road nearest to Wester Ford.

Arian took a deep breath and glanced at Caul. She judged that the gateway was strong enough to remain in place, and he nodded his agreement. She almost collapsed to the ground, and her legs shook for a moment as he held her up. "Step through, one by one after Caul," she said to them. "I will go last and ensure nothing follows us. And whatever you do, *keep walking*. Do not stop, no matter what you see or hear until you reach our destination."

Caul looked at her for a moment, then without warning leaned forward slightly and kissed her on the lips.

Arian blinked and tried to think of something to say, but he turned and a moment later he had stepped through the gateway.

Arian tried to clear her thoughts as the others followed in Caul's wake. Once the last of her companions had vanished into the light she stepped after them, and looked back into the Silver Road only once. *One more time and then I hope never to see this place again,* she thought. *It's a nightmare that's become worse than ever. How will it end? What does such chaos look like, when it reaches its natural conclusion?*

She saw the faint outlines of her companions ahead and walked in their wake through the light, steadfastly ignoring the strange flickers and shadows that danced at the edges of her vision, and the faint sounds that she couldn't even hope to describe.

Arian saw the cold, harsh glow of daylight through the other end of the gateway. Soon she had reached it and stepped into a chilly late afternoon. Rain spat down from a sky of heavy, dark clouds borne along by a stiff breeze.

In the middle of the ruined settlement, a large pile of burned bodies stood. The companions regarded the grisly scene in silence for a while, before Eraya spoke up. "Who do you suppose did this? The *kin?*"

Arian observed more closely the ash and char as it drifted in the cold breeze, then nodded. She could detect a residue of sorcery that lingered around the remains. The fire had undoubtedly been augmented so that even the lashing rain could not douse it.

"But I thought this place had been abandoned for a long time."

Arian glanced at the *luyan* woman. "Maybe these people were lightdreamers who had been drawn here."

Eraya shuddered and looked away.

"We should make what shelter we can here," Caul spoke up, "and wait. Tomorrow, the *marandaal* arrive."

"What if more lightdreamers come as well? Or the *kin*?" Parril asked.

"A good question," Caul said, but he had no answer.

VI

The companions used old wooden beams to make a rudimentary roof over one of the larger buildings in the village, and lit a fire in the remains of the hearth. As they huddled near to the flames and ate from their provisions, Arian found her curiosity stirred by Parril. "How do you know Fauli?" she asked him.

He blinked in surprise. "Do *you* know her?"

"Not personally, but I know *of* her. She was one of our finest weaponsmasters in living memory. She still is, I suppose. But she had a certain distaste for her own people."

"What do you mean?"

"She decided to leave Cai when she was barely full-grown."

"Fauli was an orphan," Caul pointed out. "She had no family and I don't think she had friends in Cai either."

Parril nodded thoughtfully. "I met her after we both escaped from Inerdyr's army. We became friends. At least, I think we did."

Arian smiled faintly. "She certainly seemed fond of you."

The following morning, as she emerged from their shelter and walked to the edge of the village where the river ran past, Arian noted that the breeze had become stronger. It also no longer blew directly from the north-east, but from one direction, then another and then yet another, seemingly at random. Arian had witnessed conditions similar to these before in the prelude to certain violent storms, but not quite as powerfully as this. Her skin crawled, simultaneously hot and cold. Already she could feel beads of sweat dripping down

217

her in places. *This is it,* she thought suddenly, and a feeling of dread built within her as she ran back to the others.

As the companions walked to the village perimeter, conditions worsened further. In one of the fields on the other side of the river, dust and earth had billowed into the air and was being swept around in an ever-tightening vortex. Arian had seen such dust-spirals before, but this was more powerful than any she had encountered. The air, thick with vile energy, continued to cast this way and that, as the wind became ever stronger. She glimpsed a darkness deeper than anything around it, in the middle of the field. Meanwhile the wind howled like a lost soul as it swept around the village. The storm widened and became stronger than ever in the areas outside the abandoned settlement, but as the companions watched fearfully the wind near to them dropped almost to stillness.

Lightning flashed through the sky and the patch of darkness before them grew larger, more defined. *The Gate,* Arian thought. *Soon they will come.*

Abruptly, light burst forth from the Gate, and as one the companions screamed and stumbled backwards, temporarily blinded by the brilliance. Arian could feel the pull of the chasm beyond the Gate intensify. The sorcery that seethed inside her responded with a mad surge and spilled forth in readiness.

The river, swollen with recent rainfall, churned and roiled near to them, agitated by the strange energies that now began to stir. Then it slowed almost to a standstill, its motion affected by the monumental forces at play.

The *marandaal* came from out of the tear in the world. *The light that steps from the void,* Arian thought as she glimpsed patterns of stars beyond the Gate.

Not one of the companions ran in fear. They could not have done had they tried. In this moment they were conduits, slaves to the forces that had always been a part of them, and that sorcery now poured forth in an unstoppable stream of strange energy that met the *marandaal* as they emerged from the void. A cataclysm of brilliance and shade tore through everything.

Arian saw a figure whose form shifted continually. She could not even tell whether it moved towards or away from her. Its surface shone like some kind of metal but it also behaved like a liquid that could float and change shape and move however it wished. For brief moments she could even see *through* it, although it distorted the view of everything that lay behind. Even as the Powers soared through her body, Arian felt this moment last forever as she beheld the inconceivable sorcery that held the *marandaal* together. It had no regard for the natural laws of things.

It came towards her, and she directed her raging sorcery at it, making use of the unnatural warmth of the air to direct thin darts of extreme heat at its ever-changing body. It paused and the shape rippled and blurred. Then it came for her again, more swiftly. Arian tried the same method of attack- she had no time to think of anything else- but it had no effect.

Then Parril was at her side, and the *marandaal* began to lean forward and slow down as if it faced into a howling storm, no matter the stillness of the air. Its shape changed more slowly than before. Arian threw a quick glance at Parril and saw veins stand out like roots on the boy's face and hands. They bulged so much that Arian thought blood would burst out of him. The air crackled with wild energy as the starspawn forced its way forwards. Parts of it began to tear from the body as the currents of power unleashed by Parril cut through it.

Amidst Arian's desperate thoughts came an idea. She concentrated again on the enemy, only this time she attempted to freeze the air around it. It slowed further and began to shake. Arian saw ripples form in the air, so strong that they distorted her view of everything in front of her. The *marandaal* changed shape more frequently with each passing moment.

Such was Parril's strength that even the *marandaal* could not withstand the two forces bearing down upon it, one like an invisible wall of razor sharp wire and the other a cloud of air colder than the deepest winter. The tremors that gripped its form became so severe that the creature could be seen only as a faint blur through the gloom.

Then it simply exploded, and Arian was sent flying backwards into the dirt.

When Arian came to, darkness had fallen. In the western sky she could see Archaon descend towards the horizon. Ildar had risen in the east and by its light the village looked almost like a place in the Silver Road. Arian shuddered and tried to sit up, but a sudden agony gripped her. Two figures knelt nearby, concern on their faces. She recognised them as companions of hers, but for a moment she couldn't even remember their names. *What's wrong with me?* she wondered frantically as her vision began to blur.

"Arian?" She heard Parril's voice, although she couldn't see him. Instinctively she reached out a hand and felt someone- presumably Parril- take it. "What happened?" she demanded. "Did we destroy them all?" *Of course we did,* she thought immediately. *They wouldn't have survived otherwise.*

"Yes." Something about his reply made her think he was holding something back. Panic gripped her. "Caul! Where is he?!"

"He's being tended to by Eraya. He's wounded, but not badly."

"And the others? Were they all killed?"

A few moments passed before he replied. "Almost everyone. There are two others. That's all."

Arian's sight gradually returned. She blinked and stared up at the boy. He looked away from her, shame in his voice as he continued softly, "I ran away. After we destroyed the first one, I picked myself up on the ground and I just ran away. I couldn't feel the Powers at all. I came back afterwards and almost everyone was dead. And there was nothing left of the *marandaal*. No bodies. How can they not leave bodies when they die?"

Arian didn't know what to say. "How... badly wounded am I?" she asked eventually. She still couldn't get to her feet or move her arms properly, but could feel no specific wounds.

"I'm not sure," he said. "I think you're exhausted. Maybe you just burned yourself out. It happened to me before. But this time I was stronger. I shouldn't have run away, but I had to."

"Help me up," she murmured.

Parril managed to haul her up into a sitting position, and Arian looked around. At the point where the edge of the village met the river, she saw the dark shapes of her companions' corpses, torn and ripped apart.

Of the *marandaal* she saw no remains, no evidence that they had even existed, and she shivered as she recalled Parril's question.

She struggled to her feet and Parril took her to see Caul and Eraya. They sat together and slumped wearily against the side of a half-ruined outhouse.

Caul staggered to his feet and embraced her. "We'll rest awhile, and then try to get to Anvar," he said quietly.

"Will we be strong enough?" Arian wondered.

Caul just held her more closely still.

VIII – The Melting of the Boundary

I

The march south continued for days. Everywhere the aftermath of the chaos that had gripped so much of the south was evident. They came across a number of burned-out and abandoned villages, and scenes of slaughter and atrocity were commonplace. A black mood developed amongst the leaders and their companions, due in no small part to setbacks such as Alturus' grievous wounding, and the violent horror that had resulted from attempts to link together people who harboured residual levels of the Powers.

They steered well clear of the city of Waylorn, but scouts were sent to observe the aftermath of that city's fall. They returned to report that as expected, the Watchers had abandoned their duties there as they had everywhere else. Some had turned on the citizens, and in the absence of law and order, some citizens had turned on one another. At least a third of the city had burned. No one authority now existed there, and battles for control raged on as black smoke rose relentlessly into the sky and the streets ran with blood.

Despite the failure of the mission to recruit more Watchers, half a dozen joined regardless as the push towards Luudhoq continued. Each one of them arrived by himself or herself. Where a reason was given for their decision, it was the same one in each case- that this force was the largest and most powerful throughout the south, outside of Luudhoq, and that it stood the best chance of defeating the Seven and taking the city.

But the leaders and those close to them had long since begun to doubt.

The weather grew increasingly unpredictable as they neared the far south of the land. Some days dawned warm and springlike, only for the temperature to plummet so that it may as well have been the depths of winter. On three days, thick frost covered the ground for much of the morning and dozens succumbed to frostbite. In between those times, so much rain fell that large parts of the land through which they marched were turned to muddy lakes.

As they rode to within five leagues of Luudhoq, Anlerran turned to her father, troubled by her thoughts. "No part of the south has remained untouched by the events of the last few tennights," she observed. "Have you seen any settlements left in peace? The truth we revealed has had consequences that have moved far beyond those we expected."

"Had it not, we would have faced small, well-motivated armies of Watchers time and again," Elluron pointed out. "As it is, more people have left than have joined in the past five days. If we were being attacked on all sides even before we reached Luudhoq, imagine how many more would have left."

"That isn't all. You can't have failed to notice the abrupt changes in the weather recently. Something is causing the natural balance of things to fail. I don't think it's simply the *marandaal*."

Elluron said nothing to that. When Anlerran began to speak up again, he said abruptly, "Let's fight the battles we can win, Anlerran, not the battles that we can't."

II

It struck Phaedra as oddly appropriate that the day when the city would in all likelihood be brought to ruin dawned with steady drizzle and a low murky sky of thick fog. *It rained a lot in the old world,* she recalled. *Often it wouldn't stop for many days on end. And after that came the drought, followed by the worst winter anyone had ever known. Our technology marched on in a haze of unparalleled achievement but we remained helpless against the elements.*

From out of the cloying mist came the lonesome sound of a longhorn being blown, a desolate monotone that caused a ripple of unease amongst the human defenders of the city. Along the battlements of the city walls the High Watchers stood unmoving, dark statues that faced the oncoming foe implacably and devoid of emotion.

Phaedra scanned the rows of defenders on the walls and behind them, and deliberately magnified her vision so that she may as well have stood alongside them.

Then a sudden, cold realisation came to her.

The Watchers, she thought as her vision swiftly took in the ranks of defenders for as far as she could see. *There are no Watchers anywhere.*

On a whim Phaedra decided to find her comrades and tell them. She was surprised that she had been the first to notice the Watchers' absence, and equally taken aback to find her comrades still in one of their meeting halls.

"Did they not desert Mornkastle?" Omir retorted. "They left that city to fend for itself- those that didn't turn against it. If they've vanished, then so be it. We don't need them. I would rather that we can depend on every defender we have than need to keep an eye on one troublesome element."

"But this doesn't make sense," Anya pointed out. "It's most unlikely that they all would have suddenly agreed upon a common course of action. Mornkastle is a case in point. Some Watchers turned against the human citizens. Others left, either in groups or on their own. A few killed themselves. My point is that this feels too much like a deliberate, thought-out plan, which is not what we should expect if many of them have decided to believe the truth of their origins."

Omir stared coldly at her. "What would you have us do, woman? Seek them out, hunt them down?"

"That's exactly what we should do," Issele said immediately.

"If they present a danger then some of the High Watchers must be enlisted to locate and destroy them," Anya agreed. "But we have our enemies to deal with first."

"They've certainly travelled a long way to meet us," Issele commented with a smile.

"I expect the Watches have fled, east or west from the city," Omir sneered. "Maybe a few remain cowering in some far-flung corner."

"If some of them chose to side with the enemy then they wouldn't be the first," Anya warned. "By the way, Omir- do you even know how your machinery worked? Did you ever pause to consider how strange it was that this particular piece of old technology could still be coaxed into occasional life, centuries after almost everything else passed into uselessness?"

He stared at her, lost for a response.

"Maybe you should have got rid of them when they gathered here in the Fortress days ago," Phaedra pointed out airily. When Omir turned to her she continued, "*You* dealt with two of them most impressively, Omir. I'm sure with a joint effort we could have wiped them all out in moments. Still, that's the benefit of hindsight."

Omir walked slowly over to her, dark eyes contemptuous as he looked her up and down. "This is a day of reckoning, Phaedra. Do you intend to fight alongside us?"

"I hadn't really thought about it," she said, which elicited a short laugh of cold amusement from Issele.

"You are a waste of space and breath," Omir said quietly. "You always were, even in the old world. What is it like to be you, I wonder? These days you appear to derive no enjoyment from the pain and plight of others, no satisfaction in power, nor do you find pleasure in companionship... except Daniel, of course. Poor Daniel. Yes, I learned of his fate. Such a shame."

A hint of emotion in her eyes must have given her away. Omir smiled and continued, "The end can't come quickly enough for you, can it? But we'll defeat this monstrous rabble screeching at our gates, and then we'll defeat the *marandaal*. And you, my dear Phaedra, will live forever and ever."

She thought about delivering a scathing response, but Phaedra was astonished to find that she had nothing to say. All she could feel was a vast, all-encompassing hatred that opened up like a chasm inside her, but for once no words accompanied that vitriol.

If she had been able to destroy the three of them in that instant- or better yet, leave them alive but in torment for all time- then she would have done without any hesitation.

But instead she turned and left, and as fate determined, that was the last time she saw any of them.

In one of the Water Halls, a Watcher named Gahelyn removed his hands from the pool and stood up, a faint smile upon his face. Everything, he judged silently, appeared to have fallen into place at the right time. His dream about the people of the Bonemord had turned out to be true. Even now they poured forth in a steady stream, heading relentlessly towards Luudhoq's western edge. Something had broken the web of sorcery that had long lain over the Bonemord, and the occupants of that dismal realm knew it. They would reach Luudhoq soon enough and eventually they would force their way into the city.

That I should have dreamt at all is miraculous, he thought. *After all, Watchers do not dream. But now every Watcher knows that he or she was once human and some, like me, have begun to dream. Emotions stir. Some of those emotions have been impossible to contain.*

But to dream of something that had not yet happened at the time, and then observe it happen- is that not an even greater miracle? How can that be explained?

We can never again be like them, he reminded himself. *The Seven stole everything from us. But one way or another, their little empire will fall into chaos, and we will at least have the small satisfaction of bearing witness to that fall.*

He turned to the other four who waited nearby. "The prisoners from the Bonemord have been released. They pour forth, no doubt with vengeance in mind."

"How can that be?" one of his companions asked.

Gahelyn shrugged. "I believe that the powers of the Seven are waning. I have even heard a few of the humans... the *people* out in the city streets dare to say the same when they think that no one is near enough to listen. Events happen now that would once have been thought impossible. The established order has started to unravel and that will continue until the process is complete. The Seven cannot stop it, and the force will do its work until spent." He paused and then added, "Those who emerge from the Bonemord- some of them are not unlike us. They were remade in a similar way. But they were not strong enough to withstand the process, their minds and bodies not reliable enough to become Watchers- and so they were instead imprisoned within the marshes, perhaps as an experiment. The Seven chose to keep them there rather than have them destroyed."

"Mercy has never served them any purpose," one of his companions noted.

One of the others asked, "And what do *we* do? What role do we play in the face of this?"

Gahelyn considered. "I have no plan," he admitted eventually. "I brought us here only to confirm my dream. I suggest we leave Luudhoq. After that... I don't know."

They looked at each other. *You four have dreamt also,* Gahelyn realised. *I wonder what yours were like, and if they contained some prophecy soon to be fulfilled. Or were you simply plagued by your unreachable pasts?*

A thought occurred to him. *If the Seven have become weakened, then it may be time for us to attack them. Whichever one of them we find alone first.*

He observed a shift in the direction of his companions' gazes, and turned to see Phaedra of the Seven idling at one of the arched entrances.

Gahelyn sensed his comrades' alertness even as his own body prepared for what might come. He didn't for a moment believe that the five of them together stood any chance of defeating one of the Seven, even if his theory was true. He hadn't discussed an actual attack with them. But he told himself that he would not run, nor would he surrender, nor would he join the effort to defend the walls against the baying hordes that massed north of the city. The five of them had already agreed that they were done with Luudhoq, done with the lies of centuries, and to the best of his knowledge every other Watcher had deserted his or her post and duties. Some had reacted with fury to revelations about themselves, only their fear of the Seven and the High Watchers staying their hand. Others had said and done nothing. But he suspected they would in time.

We can hurt her, perhaps, he thought. *She may be immortal, but what if we can damage her in such a way that she lingers on in pain for eternity? What if we can drive some spike of power through her brain, so that the merest thought makes her weep for the possibility of death?*

That would be worth our own deaths many times over.

But then Phaedra spoke, and her words confounded him.

"They're arguing about whether or not to hunt you all down. Is it wise to remain lingering in the Halls? If they happen across you, they *will* destroy you."

"And you?" Gahelyn murmured. He realised immediately that he had discarded the honorific for his mistress, but titles of any sort were laughable now. "What will *you* do?" *I'm asking the wrong question,* he told himself at the same time. *I should be asking her why she would warn us about the intentions of her comrades. Is the bitterness between them so great? Are they so divided? Might that be how we defeat them?*

He did not expect the woman to smile at him, nor could he determine the nature of the expression, even though reading the faces of others and being able to interpret their subtle changes was a skill innate to Watchers. *Madness?* he wondered. *Is she suffering from some kind of insanity?*

"You're interested in what *I* will do?" Her smile widened, sad and amused at the same time. "That's very touching. Tell me, have you recalled much of your former life, before the lie of the Void?"

Gahelyn felt a surge of anger, but with effort he maintained his composure. He was still unused to emotions of any kind. "A little," he said eventually. "Fragments of nonsense, nothing more. Points with no reference. Why do you ask? What is it to you?"

"Soon you may remember more." Phaedra traced a hand along the cool marble column nearest to her. "How ironic that *I* recall only fragments of my life in the old world, and I suspect I'll recall less still as time goes on- or at least I would, if I had that luxury."

None of the Watchers spoke. Phaedra's ramblings meant nothing to them. They watched and waited for her to move against them, but she merely raised a hand in farewell and then wandered away down one of the corridors as if she still had all the time in the world.

III

As the mid-morning fog began to lift from the damp grasslands, a lone infantryman made unhurried progress towards Luudhoq's northern gates, limping along the rain-soaked track. Omir, flanked by two silent High Watchers, watched from one of the turrets of a command tower as the man stopped one hundred paces from the gates and raised his gaunt face to study the lines of defenders on the wall and others clustered behind the bars of the vast iron gates.

"We do not seek to destroy Luudhoq," he spoke up. His voice was clear and powerful, no doubt augmented by sorcery. It cut through the dank air and a murmur rose amongst the people of the city as he continued, "We demand only that the Seven relinquish their power over the people of this city. A Gate will soon open within Luudhoq, and the *marandaal* will likely emerge from it. We have the power to destroy them when that happens. Your masters do not."

Omir's lip curled in derision at the messenger's words. *Is that the best they can come up with?* he thought. *They must know full well that we would never give them Luudhoq, no matter that the rest of the south has fallen into chaos. The rogue Watchers amongst them will have counselled accordingly. Order will be restored after we destroy the* marandaal.

So why have they sent this wretch to make a pointless demand?

The ranks of the army from which the messenger had walked stood so far back that even to Omir's sharp eyes they appeared as little more than a blur. Aside from the High Watchers, no one here would be able to see them at all. Perhaps their sorcerers had augmented the misty gloom somehow, causing it to linger around their fighters even as it lifted elsewhere.

He spoke, projecting his voice clearly so that the messenger and also the defenders across the nearby battlements and below in the streets could hear him.

"You already know that Luudhoq will never surrender to your marauding army of beasts and witches. Your kind have kept yourselves from the light of civilisation all these centuries, immersed in your wilful ignorance and superstition. The people of Luudhoq will not surrender to you. They will never give up their freedom." Down in the nearby squares and streets he saw several High Watchers urging the people near them to cheer in response.

The soldier nodded to himself as if he had expected those exact words, and then looked up directly at Omir. "We require the absolute and unconditional surrender of the Seven," he continued, his voice cutting clearly through the mist. "You, the people of Luudhoq, do not have to die this day. Nor do the Watchers. But your overlords the Seven and their High Watchers- if they will not give up this city and allow us to defend all Harn against the *marandaal,* we require their destruction."

Omir had heard enough. The enemy truly believed in their powers, and battle would be joined sooner rather than later. He had expected as much.

Concentrating on the lone infantryman, he unleashed all the frustration and hatred he felt and had nurtured over the long centuries. His effort began as an attempt to slowly crush the man against the ground- slowly enough that defenders and aggressors alike would see the true extent of his power. The man slumped forward for a moment as if bowing in acknowledgement of his adversary's might. But then he drew himself upright as trickles of blood made thick lines down from his ears and eyes and dripped from his chin. *The arrogance of the condemned man,* Omir thought, and both of his hands balled into fists. His foe should have crumpled almost to nothing in the face of such force, to become a heap of condensed flesh and bone, unrecognisable.

Instead the messenger disappeared, as if the mist had spirited him away.

An inevitable murmur of unease rose amongst those defenders on the walls and near the city gates who had beheld the vanishing. Omir stared incredulously at the space where the man had been and took a sharp intake of breath. What had happened? Some of the Watchers were skilled in cloaking, and it was entirely possible that one or more of the renegades would be. But he would have known if the messenger was still there yet hidden. He was not. He had actually moved to some other place, or perhaps had simply been erased from the world.

Omir quieted his senses and concentrated on the distant, shadowy ranks of the enemy, listening only to the sounds that travelled from that direction. Soon enough he could tell from the tone and cadence of those who had sent the messenger that his disappearance was entirely unexpected by the enemy also.

Omir returned fully to his physical self and thought quickly. Could this be an example of the growing chaos that Anya had described? Might further random events happen? Or might there be some hidden purpose to this, the agenda of an unknown force?

He could not afford to believe such things- certainly he had no time to be side-tracked by them now- yet he turned to the nearest of the High Watchers without knowing why. "What happened to their messenger?"

To his shock the High Watcher appeared to ignore the question. Omir almost repeated it, but something stopped him. *It cannot be explained,* he thought, *and certainly not by a machine. I am a God amongst people here, and I cannot explain it.*

Amongst the tumult of his thoughts he heard Anya, some way back from the main gates, raising her voice to address everyone for hundreds of paces. After a moment he could see her as well, walking amongst the rear ranks of citizens as they shrank away to give her space. "The enemy is predictable!" he heard her shout. "They use deceptive sorcery to spread fear. But we do not fear them. We fight for our homes, for our families, for our lives!"

Did she ever have a family, in the old world? he wondered, without knowing why. *Did I? It's hard to recall such things now. Is the past accelerating away from us ever more quickly?*

Omir shivered as if the cold dampness had found a way into his heart.

"We *do not* fear them!" Anya shrieked. She demonstrated more emotion in these fleeting moments, Omir mused, than she had shown in centuries of rule and countless, irrelevant meetings where they had each laid bare their hatred in so many different ways, subtle or violent.

An image of a smiling Garret stepping from purgatory to paradise formed in his head. He crushed it and listened as Anya continued to extol the people of Luudhoq to fight and to destroy the enemy when they inevitably rushed towards the city walls. They listened, eyes wide with fear. They would obey her. A few might lose their nerve and run, but it would not become a rout. The High Watchers nearest to the deserters would make sure that any such cowardice was dealt with gruesomely and publicly and crushed in its infancy.

Omir looked again to the High Watcher and asked, "Why did you fail to answer my question?"

"I heard no question," it responded.

That can't be so, Omir thought, but he also knew that High Watchers could not lie any more than they could turn against their makers. In the growing chaos of this world, they were a constant- they were the *one* constant.

But how could it not have heard him?

The enemy slowly approached the city walls. Their onward movement barely constituted a march, more a calculated crawl- cautious yet not overly fearful. Omir watched as they emerged from out of the mist, row after row of heavily-armoured *orkar* along with humans and some *luyan* fighters. Sunlight briefly glinted on chainmail before the sky clouded over again. He scanned their ranks to see if he could identify any of the witches from the reports that had filtered back to him over the last few tennights, but he could not.

This must be all of them, he thought. *We've had no reports of any separate groups hoping to assail us from west or east. They hope to simply overcome us in one wave from one place. Or do they hope to frighten us into sudden capitulation?*

Omir suddenly became aware that Issele stood nearby. He hadn't even seen her approach, although Issele did possess that curious capability. He noted her grim look and asked, "What is it?"

"We're being attacked from the west." Issele shook her head in disbelief. "We left a number of militiamen guarding that side, and I've received reports of our... *experiments* that we deposited in the marshlands, assailing the walls." She looked meaningfully at him. "*Your* experiments."

Omir took a deep breath. How could those creatures have suddenly emerged from out of the mists? The implants in each and every one of them should have destroyed any who dared to step beyond the defined edge of the Bonemord. Why had that not happened? Not one of them had escaped previously- they would all have known about it sooner or later- and he recalled the meticulous testing that he and Stephan had done within the Bonemord centuries ago, with the first few dozen of them.

A prickle of unease went through him. *It's all unravelling. We're stranded on threads which are coming apart.*

"What are they armed with?" he asked.

"Nothing much, as you might expect. Many have been shot down by the archers positioned on the western walls. But others have managed to scale the walls and kill a number of the men there and take their weapons. There are even reports that some have vanished into the city itself. They'll be found, of course, but in the meantime they'll do nothing but cause further panic. I will go and secure the area. I'll take one of the High Watchers with me."

"You will not," Omir said flatly.

Issele stared at him. "Shall we do battle here and now, you and I, in front of our subordinates? In front of our enemies? And undo Anya's fine words to the meat sacks milling around in the dirt below?"

She would, he realised as he looked into those darkly beautiful eyes. They had always held so much rage. He wondered how Issele had lived for all these centuries without simply catching fire or exploding. She *would* fight him, and it would all be for nothing. Issele could not be reasoned with, and in any case what was one High Watcher? Let her go into the western quarter and preoccupy herself with hunting down whatever desperate monsters had come lurching out of the fog. He and Anya would do as well without the stupid woman.

"Very well. Take one and be gone," he said dismissively, and turned his attention back to the approaching army.

A short while after Issele had departed, a great roar sounded from amongst the enemy, accompanied by the pounding drums and the blowing of horns. *Barbarians,* Omir thought contemptuously.

He watched as the archers set along the top of the city walls drew back their bows. Other men on the battlements dragged barrels of boiling pitch nearer to the edge of the walls in anticipation of attempts to scale them. Behind and below, in the streets and in the nearer buildings, defenders prepared their weapons.

But for Omir, an entirely different battle awaited. He had finally discovered the location of the witches and renegade Watchers, and in his mind's eye he leapt over the battlements and across the grassland, through the cold morning air and on towards the unsuspecting foe.

IV

Issele marched through the deserted streets, the lone High Watcher at her side. A cold fury coiled within her, aimed not at Omir- for whom she held only contempt- but at the

235

creatures that had breached the west-facing walls of the citadel.

Impulsive and irrational woman that she was, Issele had not paused to consider why this had happened now alongside so many other unexpected events. Phaedra had put forward her ideas about the disintegration of order, of ripples that created other ripples but Issele hated Phaedra more than she hated any of the other five and she had no time for her theories. "She was nothing. A *mathematician,*" she fumed to herself as she turned off the main road that headed towards the harbour, and instead began to walk down towards the distant western walls.

As she drew nearer and reached a point where the road sloped gradually down towards the western edge of Luudhoq, Issele paused. The situation had deteriorated. The walls had been partly pulled down in places, and a number of the monsters picked their way through the rubble. She wondered how they had managed to bring down the walls. Scores of militiamen lay strewn amongst the rubble. Some had been cut to pieces or beheaded. A few of the monsters carried those heads with them like trophies, swinging them by the hair as they lumbered through the gaps in the wall and into the city streets.

"I have a suggestion," the High Watcher spoke up.

"Then speak," Issele answered impatiently.

But it did not. Issele turned and peered at the impassive features. A cold feeling stirred within her. "Look at me." She felt an odd sense of relief when it obeyed. "You said just now that you had a suggestion."

The High Watcher did not respond.

Issele had no idea what to make of that, but an instant later she had put the anomaly to the back of her mind as she watched the filth from out of the Bonemord invade her city.

Accompanied by the High Watcher she made her way down the hill and eventually to the end of the road where it opened out onto the wider highway adjacent to the remains of the wall. Issele watched for a moment as the nearest group of creatures- most of the others had already disappeared further into the city warrens- stopped and looked at her. Whatever their deformities and compromised intelligence, Issele nonetheless saw recognition and hatred leap in their eyes. *They know me,* she realised. *They know who I am, even though I took no part in the creation of these wretched, irrelevant beasts.*

Putting that peculiarity to one side she addressed them, raising her voice. "I am Issele of the Seven. You creatures have no business in the city of Luudhoq. Your place is in the Bonemord from where you came. Remain here and you will die."

The largest of them, a hulking, muscular beast with sloping, hunched shoulders, stepped forward and uttered a barrage of sounds that might or might not have been words. His mouth did not work properly, and one half of his lumpen, twisted face had begun to waste away, revealing a hybrid structure of metal and bone. *A failed Watcher,* Issele thought contemptuously. *So many of them were, as I recall.*

It occurred to her that they might have discovered a great deal more about the monsters they had made, if the strange far-seeing properties of the Water Halls had been used more often. But it was far too late to think about such things now.

The Bonemord beasts had insufficient wits to realise the peril in which they had found themselves. Instead of retreating back over the rubble they rushed at Issele and the High Watcher. Issele had half-expected them to, and as the creatures bore down on them she concentrated on the largest, who had uttered the rallying cry for the others. In a moment his feet no longer touched the ground, and he was lifted into the air by an unseen force. As he bellowed with rage and fear, the others drew to a sudden halt, their dismay obvious.

"I warned you," Issele whispered. "I gave fair warning to you all."

The Bonemord creature's body slowly ripped in half from the top of his head down to the base of his torso, and the two pieces fell to the ground just in front of the others, spraying gore and internal workings across a dozen paces.

"Kill the others," Issele said to the High Watcher. "Slowly."

Leaving her subordinate to its grisly duties she set off along the road that ran roughly alongside the city wall, determined to locate as many as possible of the other marsh beasts that had entered the city. There might well be hundreds as the High Watcher had reported, but that didn't matter. She would find them, and then she would find an interesting way to destroy every single one of the miserable creatures.

From the shadows of a narrow alleyway some distance away Gahelyn watched and waited for Issele to make her way up the street and disappear from sight before he turned to his companions. He had no need to remind them what he intended- during their journey to the western edge of Luudhoq he had spoken of his simple plan- but one of them nevertheless asked, "Is it even possible?"

"I can't say," he confessed. "But whether or not it works, it's time for the end. What else is left for us? What life?"

The five Watchers made their way in silence along the road and left behind the brutal sounds of the battle between the people of the Bonemord and the High Watcher.

Issele sensed the Watchers approach a short while later, and turned slowly to face them. *Ah, now their treachery is plain to see,* she thought. *None of them defend the city. They skulk in the back streets and hide around corners.* At the same time she demanded, "Why are you not defending the north of the city?" But already she knew that these five had no intention of fulfilling that duty. If anything they hoped to accelerate Luudhoq's downfall.

We should have had them all destroyed days ago, she thought. *Why didn't we? Much as I hate to admit it, Phaedra was right about that.*

Her adversaries spread out in a semi-circle as Issele regarded each in turn. None of them spoke. "Move against me and you will all die," Issele promised them. But not one of the Watchers looked as if they cared. *Chaos,* she thought. *The unravelling. Random behaviour. What happens now? A mass suicide?*

"Do you not realise how lucky you are," Issele asked them all, "to no longer be human? You have lost nothing by your transformations. One might say you were chosen."

She no longer knew or cared whether or not she believed her own words, and a moment later it no longer mattered what she thought or had said. The Watchers rushed at her in the same instant.

Issele moved as a blur, smashing into one of them with as much force as she could bring to bear, while she brought up a shield of force as strong as a stone wall to stop the others. Her fist tore into the Watcher's stomach. The Watcher fell to the ground as the others surrounded her, attempting to use the powers they had been given to slow down her movements and attack her mind at the same time. A rage came upon her, and Issele brought down the Watcher nearest to her by nothing more than force of will. He clawed at his face as it began to fall apart, blistering as unbearable heat ravaged his features.

Issele began the task of blocking their attempts to confuse and obliterate her thoughts. "Fools!" she shouted once her defence was complete. She could feel the invisible, impregnable fortress of her own power surround every part of her body and mind. Together with the simmering fury that continued unabated, it made her feel like an empress, to be revered or feared. "What madness runs through you that makes you think you can defeat me?!"

But they *were* quite mad, she reminded herself as she regarded each of them in turn. That was precisely why they had all decided that they could overcome one of the Seven- and ultimately, what purpose could that serve? The Watchers had become servants of chaos.

Issele suddenly felt the strangest sensation inside her head, as if something attempted to create knots in parts of her brain. Furiously she worked to locate the source of the disruption, and was horrified to find that she could not, nor could she prevent it from happening.

Rage beyond anything Issele had ever thought herself capable of now enveloped her. She lost control of her own powers, and they leapt from her, carving straight through two of the Watchers in a flash of light and other, unseen energy that consumed them in an instant and turned them both to smoke and ash. A third who stood too close to them burst into flames.

But as the explosion of incandescent fury faded, Issele felt that strange scrabbling around in her head again. She tried to ignore it, but the invasion became unbearable. *Get it out,* a voice whispered urgently to her. *You have to get it out. It's the only way.*

No! she screamed silently, her baleful eyes fixed upon the lone remaining Watcher. *It has to be him. He is doing this. Kill him, and the illusion will end. It's a trick, nothing more.*

But the first voice proved to be more compelling. *Remove the intruder and you can kill the Watcher at your leisure,* it whispered. The voice didn't sound like hers, but she listened regardless.

Issele's fingers pressed against the side of her head as she considered the two choices over and over. Her vision had faded, but she still saw the single Watcher in front of her, standing unsteadily. His unflinching gaze remained fixed upon her. Issele's fingers trembled, moved away from her head, and remained held in place.

Something is wrong, an inner voice screamed. She channelled what energies she could muster at the Watcher, but no sooner had she done that than the need to remove the foreign entity from inside her head returned, stronger and more urgent than ever. *Remove it first,* the voice whispered. *Dig it out, and then deal with the Watcher. You can torture him slowly, over days.*

Issele's fingers stabbed straight at her head from both sides, again and again, moving so quickly that they fractured and then punctured her skull with their sheer speed and power. She scratched desperately at her skin, pulling it away in strips to reveal the bloodied, cracked bone beneath. Within moments Issele of the Seven became little more than a tattered skeleton.

The task of locating and crushing the alien invader within her head had consumed her utterly. Issele stabbed her fingers through her eyes and deep into the tissue beyond. Her screams cut off abruptly as those searching digits damaged part of her brain.

With that disruption her defence against the last of the Watchers suddenly vanished. Gahelyn, who had sown the seed of paranoia within Issele's mind, staggered forward. *Now is my only chance,* he thought. *She must be destroyed utterly before she can recover.*

The blow from Gahelyn's sword cut straight through Issele's head. She fell to the ground, and he crushed her skull with a stone taken from the breached western wall, grinding bone and flesh against the unyielding surface of the cobbles.

Knowing that even now the objective might not be complete, Gahelyn grasped as much as he could of the woman's brain and took it with him as he limped slowly and painfully away, barely aware of where he was going. Heat rose through his palms and finger tips, sufficient to cook and burn the strands of meat he carried. His hands burned along with Issele's remains, and flesh and scorched blood dropped hissing to the ground as he dragged his way along.

Despite the terrible agony, Gahelyn smiled.

Three people from the Bonemord found him a while later, slumped against the wall of a narrow side street. His head nodded back and forth, and they saw a dull flicker in his eyes, which faded from blue to grey to an almost colourless sheen before- just briefly- they returned to an intense, almost oceanic blue. His mouth opened to shape some words, but his new companions didn't hear them- or perhaps they simply could not understand.

But on some low level they understood that he was a little like them, as they gathered in sombre silence around his ravaged and broken body.

Suddenly Gahelyn's eyes widened in abrupt revelation. The Bonemord people drew back, cautious of the sudden change, a last flare of energy from the dying creature.

"I *remember*," he whispered. "I remember now. I was..."

His mouth closed and gradually the life fled from him. The Bonemord people remained at his side. They stared almost reverently at him until finally his head tilted back for a final time and his hands fell open to reveal a smear of black smouldering char, once part of Issele of the Seven.

V

Kian and Anlerran fell to the ground as one, clutching their heads and screaming.

Amidst the panic, Kelandra guessed at a glance what had happened. Instantly she gave the order for all their archers to fire in the direction of Omir on the battlements. The resulting barrage was not enough to wound Omir- none of the arrows reached him, although a dozen or more temporarily felled two of the High Watchers nearest to him- but Kelandra's strategy was simply to disrupt Omir's onslaught sufficiently to allow the witches time to gather their defences against a second attack, which they did with Elluron's help.

An answering volley of arrows arced through the low and grey sky towards them, although most fell short.

Garrok loomed nearby. "We need to ram the walls now," he said. "This stand-off does nothing. They will neither negotiate nor surrender. We cannot engage in a battle of wills with the Seven. And what happened to the messenger?"

Kelandra shook her head. "I have no idea, Garrok. But my instinct tells me that we may see much more that's unexplainable before the day is done." She looked at Elluron, who had already linked hands with the witches. All three of them stood with heads bowed in silence. "Let's make the onslaught as brief as we can. If we break through the walls quickly enough, the city folk may yet lose heart. At the moment they fear their masters more than they fear us. We need to change that."

Garrok needed no further encouragement. He shouted the order to his nearest commanders, who relayed them to the men who had built two vast battering rams over the last tennight. These had been constructed from stonewood gathered from woodlands during their journey south and hardened further by the ironmasters. Kelandra wondered if those tools, impressive though they were, would be enough to break through the walls and gates and into Luudhoq.

As she watched and then turned her attention back to the city walls, Kelandra found herself beset by doubts. During their approach she had sensed three of the Seven busying themselves in the defence of Luudhoq. She had also detected a fourth of their number, but further away, perhaps deep inside the Sanctum. She and her companions had received rumours that one of them- Stephan- had gone to the Border Wall some time ago, but the scouts they had sent to that area- people with some talent in the Powers who should be able to sense one of the Seven easily enough- had returned without having located him.

And in any case, Kelandra reasoned, where were the other two? No one had been able to detect them. Might they suddenly materialise in the midst of the battle? As far as she was aware, even the Seven hadn't learned how to move themselves physically from one location to another at will, but there were many things that she didn't and never would know about her former masters.

Kelandra shook her head in irritation and worry. Too many unknowns remained for her liking. Too many variables were at play. But decisions still had to be made.

A number of the *orkar* began pushing the two battering rams towards the city walls. The air grew thick with arrows and bolts aimed at them, but the majority of these burned to nothing in the air and fell as metallic ash- another impressive use of ironmastery. *So much I'll never have the time to understand,* Kelandra thought as a hundred or more tiny fires briefly lit up the sky.

The great stonewood rams rumbled over the grassland, the wheels making deep tracks as the heavy vehicles approached the city walls. Somehow they gathered momentum during the approach, as the *orkar* that pushed them strained every muscle in their effort to send them hurtling towards the walls.

One of the Seven lurked somewhere nearby in the city, probably just behind the walls. Kelandra could not tell who it was, but only a member of their vile septet could have unleashed the sudden, bright onslaught of power that shot from somewhere behind the main gates and towards the oncoming *orkar* and their siege-breaking machines. For a moment that ripple of almost invisible force caused her view of the city to distort.

Those pushing one of the rams abruptly stopped, and their bodies writhed as if they were nothing more than puppets pulled in one direction and then another. Kelandra heard screams and roars of agony as smoke rose from some of them. The abandoned ram carried on regardless, and was near enough to the wall to smash into it. The stonework cracked in a few places but did not break. Meanwhile the *orkar* who had been attacked staggered and fell. Some of them burst into flames. Others remained still on the ground, tendrils of smoke rising from their twitching forms.

But whatever force had been unleashed by the unseen sorcerer, it had affected only one group of *orkar* and therefore only one ram. Perhaps these men sensed the urgency and importance of their own effort in light of their comrades' demise, for they redoubled their effort to urge the ram onwards and now ran at speed alongside the hurtling vehicle. A couple of them were felled by arrows as the protective power weaved by the ironmasters faltered. But there was no stopping the ram, which hammered into the city wall with an impact that made the ground shudder.

The wall still did not crumble, but more great cracks appeared. Kelandra waited for the defenders to panic, but inexplicably they didn't.

Then the ground itself groaned and began to shake.

As she beheld this sudden phenomenon, Kelandra grew certain that it had nothing whatsoever to do with the impact of the vast weapon against the city wall.

It's an earthquake, she thought, barely able to believe it. *What were the chances of that happening at this exact moment? When was the last time Luudhoq suffered an earthquake? Long before my time. A century ago, perhaps longer. Could it be that the sorcery unleashed by both sides somehow caused it?*

The rumbling and shaking grew ever louder. The *orkar* who had driven the battering ram against the wall ran as best they could away from the city walls. Not a single archer fired upon them. Chaos erupted as huge cracks now began to appear in the ground itself. Riders and infantry alike on both sides were thrown to the ground.

Kelandra was thrown to the ground by a sudden movement beneath her. When she picked herself up she stared in shock as a wide abyss opened in the earth, in the middle of the *orkar* and northmen. Two dozen or more fell into the chasm and were lost, as the throng of panicked infantrymen moved fearfully away from the rip that had formed in a jagged line across the land.

Finally the earth lay still and the vast rumble of destruction died down, but the effects of this cataclysm had not yet fully played out. The proud, high walls of Luudhoq crumbled. The stonework collapsed and brought down a multitude of defenders with it. Vast clouds of dust rose from the city as the perimeter was reduced to rubble in moments. A few of the command towers beyond the wall, and some buildings in the distance still stood, but the defences had been breached simply by a natural phenomenon.

The defences have been breached, Kelandra reminded herself, and her thoughts came together with sudden, urgent clarity. She ran to Garrok, and called for Teryn, commander of the northmen to come to her as well.

"Attack now!" she urged. "Everyone, swarm into the city! With any luck the people of Luudhoq may even think that the earthquake was our doing. They may scatter or lay down their weapons. There will be no better chance!"

"What if it happens again?" Teryn's face was ashen. Perhaps he had never known such a thing as an earthquake before. "What if the remaining buildings of the city come down upon us?"

"Less than half still stand," Kelandra retorted. "It's a risk we need to take. This is the best chance we have."

Garrok nodded in agreement, and bellowed his orders to the divisional commanders, who swiftly relayed them. Teryn ran to convey the same to his smaller force.

"What were the chances of that?" Elluron said at her side.

"Who knows? But the odds have evened out a little," she pointed out.

"Along with much of the city. Perhaps Aona seeks to slay all the combatants rather than have them slay one another."

Omir watched with cold, considered detachment as panic spread amongst the ranks of Luudhoq's citizens. Those who had not been crushed under the rubble had become a witless body of crying, shouting creatures, broadcasting their panic to the oncoming enemy, who had shown the foresight and intelligence to mount their attack as soon as the earthquake had ceased.

Without Watchers to keep them in check and with the High Watchers engaged in fighting the hordes that now poured over the piles of broken stonework, many of Luudhoq's citizens simply fled. Omir turned his fury on those he could, and killed them from a distance. He stilled their hearts or snapped their legs, and watched as they writhed helplessly, their screams drowned out by the terrified sounds of so many others.

Some were caught by the enemy and tried to surrender or pleaded for their lives, but they were cut down either by *orkar* or northmen or in a few cases by the High Watchers, who recognised the terror of their subjects as treachery. *The mayhem is in full swing,* Omir thought, *and everyone can smell blood in the air.*

He strode down the steps that wound around the outside of the command tower. In places the earthquake had caused parts of the stonework to fall away, but enough remained for him to reach the ground easily.

Omir walked towards the heat of the battle. The cacophony had become absolute, to match the sheer bloody mayhem. *Orkar* and northmen died in their dozens as they fought the High Watchers, their bodies strewn thickly over the rubble of the city walls. Archers and pikemen from the city militia fought alongside the High Watchers, but many of them were cut down by the enemy. Omir saw one *orkar* man with a two-handed sword hack straight through the belly of a militiaman and cut his body clean in two.

He glimpsed Anya for a moment, felling anyone and everyone near her. She stood a couple of hundred paces away towards the rear of the city's main entrance square, in the way of the frightened citizens who tried desperately to flee. As far as he could tell, she also no longer discriminated beyond ally and foe. *Everyone is an enemy,* Omir thought as he breathed in the harshness of blood and steel and listened to the ring of blade on blade, and the dying screams of men and women whose entrails decorated the cobbles or fallen stonework. *They all deserve to die. Every one of them.*

Omir took a sword from a fallen Luudhoqian militiaman and hacked and slashed at everyone and anyone he could find, carving a bloody trail through the protagonists. Even the *orkar* reacted with dismay, although they neither fled nor even backed away. Cowardice wasn't in these brutes' character, Omir reminded himself as he made his way towards where the High Watchers had made their stand. He paused for a moment, already coated in blood and gore. Some of it was his own, but he could barely feel his wounds.

The fighting began to spread to other areas as a group of northmen pushed their way through into the streets and created more space near to the remains of the city wall. Omir became vaguely aware that thick clouds had gathered overhead, dark and low. Rain began to hiss down and mingle with the blood of the fallen, to form rivulets that poured over the rubble and masonry and across the cobbles. He wiped blood from his face and laughed as he found himself face to face with an *orkar* warrior. "Do you know who I am?" he shouted.

His adversary did not react. The large eyes set into that monstrous countenance regarded him carefully as they circled each other. On a whim, Omir cast the sword aside and opened his hands. He grinned at the creature and beckoned.

Whatever surprise the *orkar* man felt, he showed no emotion. He charged Omir in a move that was half brute force and half lightning speed. The *orkar* could move quickly when they had to.

But Omir was quicker. He moved to one side and aimed a punch into the swordsman's midriff that surely pulverised his innards even through the thick hide armour. The grotesque face contorted in agony, and as the *orkar* spat blood and bent double, Omir punched him on the side of the head. The *orkar's* skull cracked and he fell to the ground like a stone.

The rain intensified to a dull, all-pervasive roar, and the light worsened further as rumbles of thunder rolled across the leaden sky. It might have been dusk except that Omir knew it was still early afternoon. The battle around him took on an almost surreal, shadowy quality as the deluge became louder even than the battle. Omir saw combatants frozen by flashes of lightning that tore through the darkness. Everything else had become faint noise and indeterminate shadow. He looked around for someone to fight, but was perturbed to find that he could distinguish none of the figures in his vicinity. The battle had melted away to become little more than a dance of silhouettes.

Three figures appeared. They stepped over the mangled remains of the city gates and picked their way through the corpse-strewn entrance, heading directly towards him. One was a man in his middle years- no, not a man but something else, Omir decided in an instant, although he had no idea what sort of creature he might be. Next to him walked a young woman with long dark hair, and next to her another woman- a *du-luyan* whose feral orange eyes stared intently at him. Although everything else nearby had become muddied and oddly dreamlike, he could see these three in perfect detail, and he realised who and what they were. With a predatory grin he waited as they drew nearer. This would be an altogether different kind of battle.

No longer could he sense anyone else nearby. Perhaps the High Watchers and the enemy fighters had all moved elsewhere, in expectation of what would likely be a seismic confrontation.

"You took your time," Omir remarked, observing that the three Descendants had some kind of protective force field around them. No matter. He would smash his way through it. He wiped back his soaking hair. "I expected you to hide until the slaughter was done."

The three of them moved slightly apart from one another, and their invisible shield expanded and moved with them. The light, oddly warm breeze that had accompanied the deluge lessened to almost utter stillness, and the temperature dropped as the storm receded and the rain abated. His boots crunched over something as he took a step forward, and he noted with surprise that it wasn't bone or fragments from the broken stonework, but thick frost that had grown upon the cobbles. Was this their doing? he wondered. At the same time he explored the nature of the shield that protected them and wondered if they would need to relinquish their hold on it if they attacked him.

Had it got darker still? Omir thought that it had. He could still hear faint booms of thunder, as if the storm had moved elsewhere. But the sky was now almost as dark as night. *Trickery,* he thought, but he saw uncertainty in the expressions of his foes. *This is not their doing,* he realised.

Omir suddenly caught a glimpse of something *through* them, as if his enemies had become translucent for a moment. Whatever that strangeness was, it disappeared as quickly as it had shown itself.

He now beheld his enemies as silhouettes, framed against the broken arch of the city gateway, a starlit sky behind them. They each appeared taller and more angular than they ought. *It really is night-time,* he observed. *But how can time have passed so quickly?* He strained to hear the distant sounds of battle, but he could hear nothing at all.

Enraged, he launched an attack on the half-man, putting all his energy into the assault. The enemy should have crumbled to ash where he stood, but instead his shape became larger still, towering almost as high as the remaining ramparts of the city wall as if he had somehow absorbed all of the force thrown at him and assimilated it into his own being.

Impossible, Omir told himself, but his courage suddenly failed him, and he ran.

He fled at speed through the curiously empty streets and squares, deep into the city, where still he encountered no one. He did not even recognise some of the areas through which he ran. They bore a certain resemblance to areas that he would have known, but their relationships to one another had changed. Streets joined and turned differently. Hills rose where once the lie of the land had been flat. Squares and open areas were now fed by different roads. Statues and fountains that ought to have been present in many of these places had either disappeared or been replaced by entirely unfamiliar structures. A river cut through the city, but Omir looked to the stars and deduced that *this* waterway ran west to east instead of north to south. Narrower and faster than the Fhaarluy river with which he was familiar, it was spanned by short, arched bridges every hundred paces or so, for as far as the eye could see. He wondered madly if some great power had been released by the earthquake, a force that had the ability to restructure reality itself.

This is not Luudhoq. The thought embedded itself in his mind and would not be silenced. On an impulse he looked up to the clear, cloudless sky once again, and felt certain that the stars had rearranged themselves while he looked at the river.

He took a deep breath of the painfully cold air and told himself that he had simply been ensnared in a web of sorcery that operated on a vast scale. But he could detect nothing of that sort. There were no tell-tale signs to betray his environment as an illusion. It felt real.

Don't believe in it, he warned himself. *If you believe, it will hold you here forever.*

Nevertheless, as he eventually made his way over one of the bridges and stopped to look at the river below, he half-expected the entire structure to disappear and send him down into the watery depths to be carried wherever this river went. He even wondered if it simply went on forever or travelled in an eternal circle, bearing water pointlessly through this silent, alien city.

Omir reflected that this was the first time he had fled anyone or anything since the disastrous last days of the old world. Then, he and his compatriots had watched helplessly as their technology ran swiftly out of human control, not only spreading with terrifying speed but learning exponentially as it spread. Evolution that in previous ages would have taken many millennia hurtled towards its inevitable conclusion in a few months. Now the sorcery wielded by those who came to destroy them- and perhaps by the world itself- had risen like a black wave to ruin everything they had created over a thousand years.

Every time we try to impose order, sooner or later it breaks down, he thought. He stared into the shadows of a nearby alleyway and wondered why they flickered against the brickwork of the walls. Their behaviour was more like that of flames. *Our utopia in the old world became a horror on a universal scale. Now a very different enemy- or perhaps a different face of the same enemy- has done the same.*

For a short while he became lost in the idea that this universal enemy might be a great destroyer of all things, a mechanism to hasten the demise of life itself- an embittered God that had withdrawn in disgust from its creations and decided to bring the cosmic experiment to a halt, crushing everything into the darkness from which it had emerged. How else could the obliteration of entire worlds across the universe have been allowed to happen so swiftly?

How were we allowed to begin the chain reaction? he asked himself. *Why were we not stopped? Because it saw what would happen if and when our endless thirst for interference reached the tipping point? Because it didn't care what would happen from that point onwards- the long night-side and decline of our existence?*

And as for Aona- this world presented a very different face to that chaos, but was it not the same?

Suddenly he wondered what had become of Anya. He remembered he had seen her just before he confronted the three sorcerers. Then she had gone- or perhaps *he* had gone, spirited away to this empty shell of a city.

And he had no doubt that it was empty. He could normally sense the presence of the others, but not here. Issele, Phaedra, Anya- he could detect none of them.

He raised his head to the thin strip of sky above the alleyway, and noticed that the sky had changed once again.

Now he saw no stars, nor clouds, only a faint green-tinged gloom.

The tendrils of darkness in the alleyway appeared closer and larger now, but beyond them, somewhere further in Omir saw a faint, bright light. It moved like a lantern or a torch held by an invisible entity. He observed it for a moment and it occurred to him that this illumination must lead him to a way out of this silent nightmare.

Omir stepped into the alleyway and walked towards the light. His boots made no sound on the smooth stone. The shadows leapt on the walls as if repelled by his presence, and somehow he drew strength and courage from their behaviour. *I have power even here,* he thought. *These things would have already destroyed me if they could.*

After two hundred paces he had drawn a little closer to the light, although it still floated tantalisingly in the distance. The ground had begun to slope downwards a little. When he looked up he saw that the buildings on either side of the narrow walkway extended for what might be leagues up into the gloomy sky. Both structures were dotted with windows, and behind some of these he saw faint movements and heard muffled sounds, as if beyond these panes of glass some semblance of normality might exist.

I could break one and climb through, he thought, but every time he considered the idea he found that his head turned once again so that all he could think of was the still-distant, wavering light that called to him through the blackness.

Omir began to walk more quickly. He felt that he recognised the source and purpose of this illumination. It came from a distant place- distant in both space and time. *It's from long ago,* he thought as he frantically picked up the pace. *If I can reach it, if I can go back...*

Soon he was no more than a dozen paces away, and the light now appeared as a doorway, half-ajar, through which the strange illumination poured. But as he strained towards it, he felt himself begin to sink through the stone on which he walked. Furiously he redoubled his efforts, but the more he struggled the further he sank. When he looked down a moment later he could see nothing below his knees.

Screaming his despair, Omir reached out his arms imploringly to the light. It was so near now that had he not started to sink into the very ground he walked on, he could have touched the doorway, even walked through it.

Slowly he sank into an absolute darkness from which he knew no escape would be possible. Nor would even death be granted, he realised in horror as he stared through the doorway at a world coming slowly into focus. He would be assimilated by this nightmare, yet he would never die. He would become, eventually, one of the shadows that lingered and flickered around the extremities of this place- ephemeral, silent, eternal- and remembering what he once was until the end of time itself.

VI

Anya wrenched the *orkar* man's head from his body and stared disdainfully at it for a moment before casting the trophy aside. All around her, bodies lay mangled, crushed, burned and butchered in the strange dusk. Some of them were her own handiwork. Others were victims of some other creature or force, but she had no idea who or what.

She wiped blood from her face and limped along the street, no longer able to hear any sounds of fighting in the city. Sorcery had been let loose, Anya decided, and whether it was something fashioned by the barbarian witches or by the world itself, she neither knew nor cared. Sooner or later, things would go back to the way they were. She ignored the changes in her environment with the same iron determination she had used to make the best of centuries of existence.

Anya concluded that whatever had happened, it was not in fact the result of sorcery created by the witches and their cohorts. Clearly something far more powerful had created this environment, but sooner or later she would emerge from this illusion or the effect would simply disappear. *Circumstances are too volatile for anything to exist for longer than a short while*, she reasoned.

As she made her way through the quiet streets, Anya saw some remarkable things. At the corner of two intersecting roads the body of an *orkar* fighter half-emerged from the brickwork of one of the buildings, held in place and fused as one with the material as if physical laws had broken down for a moment and allowed the two to combine or to occupy part of the same space at the same instant. Blood dripped from the creature's wide-open eyes and its mouth stretched wide open as if in continued astonishment.

Elsewhere small sinkholes had opened up. Anya thought at first that these might be a product of the violent earthquake, but they looked too circular, too perfect. Anya counted five in one of the city parks she crossed. From one of them she heard faint cries of anguish, although even when she stopped to concentrate on the sounds she still could not determine the nature of whatever made them.

Anya made her way across the park. On the other side she saw that the sky appeared lighter. Not only that but she could once again hear the sounds of battle faintly in the distance. She smiled to herself and hastened towards the noise.

Within a short while Anya found herself in the vicinity of Luudhoq's northern quarter once again. She now recognised the streets, the buildings, the alignment of everything that made up this area. Confusion and chaos reigned as far as she could see. Fighting continued here and there, but had descended into small melees. *There should be many more people here,* Anya thought, but then she realised what might well have happened to them as she recalled the *orkar* she had seen embedded in the wall of the building. *People may have been swallowed up in their thousands,* Anya thought. *They took an involuntary step into the shadow world and paid the ultimate price, perhaps without even knowing.*

She strode towards a group of *orkar*, intending to destroy them before she reached their vicinity.

Then she drew to a halt as a sensation of sudden fear gripped her.

Nothing had happened. Her powers would not be summoned.

Slowly the behaviour of the *orkar* changed. Fear became disbelief. But as she struggled to contain her own astonishment at what had happened, one of the *orkar*- a female dressed in a grey robe and more lightly armed than the others- turned to her comrades and said something in their own language, accompanied by a few quick gestures.

As one they strode towards her. *Die,* Anya thought savagely, and she renewed her efforts. But again nothing happened.

She thought quickly. *This must be some temporary effect. The city has become engulfed in chaos, with holes appearing in reality itself, through which people have stepped. Soon enough, order will be restored.*

But for the first time in centuries, her courage failed her.

Anya turned and ran as quickly as she could, but a bolt buried itself in her back and she fell to the wet, gleaming cobbles of the street down which she had fled. As she gasped in agony and tried to get to her feet, she heard the footfall of the *orkar* group, harsh against the stone. They did not sound hurried.

As they reached her, one of them kicked her over onto her back, and Anya gasped in pain as the bolt embedded itself a little deeper. They gathered in a semi-circle around her prone form, and even now she saw doubt in their eyes.

Merinne stared down at the woman. It was hard to believe that this was truly one of the Seven- an empress of southern Harn, a creature of legend, hated and feared in equal measure for so many centuries. She looked like nothing more than a plain, middle-aged, slightly overweight human woman.

And that's all she is now, Merinne thought. *Somehow her powers have failed.*

Hylar, the commander of the unit, turned to her. "Are you certain this is her?"

Merinne nodded firmly. "I saw her earlier and I felt the effects of her sorcery. In some ways not unlike that which some of us wield ourselves, but far more powerful. But it seems her great powers have abandoned her."

"We have seen many strange things today," one of the other men spoke up. "Who is to say that they won't return?"

Hylar nodded in agreement. "We'd best make certain they don't have a chance." Stepping forward he regarded Anya in silence for a moment, then drove the blade of his sword through her mouth and twisted, breaking the woman's jaw.

Merinne winced despite herself, and as if he had sensed her discomfort Hylar glanced back at her. "You may go if you wish, Merinne."

She glared at him. "I'll stay until I know she's dead. That way I can report truthfully to Lord Garrok."

Merinne grasped the Powers, ready to pin Anya down and hopefully stop her from killing the *orkar* men if she somehow did regain use of her sorcery. Maintaining the serenity and concentration required for this was not an easy task. Hylar and his men beat, savaged and tortured Anya of the Seven for a long while. At first she uttered barely a sound, but towards the end her anguished, almost animal-like cries uttered through her broken mouth cut through Merinne so much that she almost abandoned her defence of the men and walked away.

Finally Anya lay dead, a lump of unmoving flesh on the cold, wet slabs. The men had about themselves a sense of dazed bewilderment. They cast hurried, almost blank looks at the dismembered ruin they had made of the woman. The carcass was unrecognisable.

Merinne relinquished her hold on the Powers with a sigh. "How did that advance our cause?" she asked coldly.

Hylar walked slowly over to her. "Don't forget who and what that was," he said, gesturing at the body parts. "Do you think the people of this city will thank us for their liberation, no matter the manner of our victory?"

Merinne said nothing, but Hylar was not done. "I am a monster after all," he said with a smile.

The *orkar* men and ironmistress continued on towards the heart of the city.

Kelandra, Ildoron, Kian and Anlerran entered the city at dusk, through what had once been the arch of the main gate. The fighting was mostly done, but not all their enemies had been vanquished. From behind the ruins of a building stepped one of the surviving High Watchers.

The Powers had seethed within Anlerran and Kian ever since their entrance into this place, and now they surged forth, unstoppable and uncontrollable. As the High Watcher raised an arm to defend itself, the unliving countenance watching them intently, a torrent of the Old Powers slammed into it. Anlerran could *feel* the creature's inner workings groan and shriek inside the cold body that housed them.

Even through the rage and the roar of the Powers that ran through every part of her, Anlerran saw Kelandra and Ildoron dart to one side, two impossibly fast blurs of movement. The High Watcher turned to face them for a moment. Something that either or both of the Watchers had done had made it indecisive. A sudden, more detailed vision came to Anlerran of the creature's insides, so complex and unearthly that she couldn't hope to understand them. Yet she could still bring the elements to bear upon the sorcery that held it together. Part of the creature was made from some kind of metal, and she concentrated her powers on those areas, and caused them to heat or cool, or change in subtle but important ways.

The High Watcher had no emotions to betray. Yet it must have recognised what she attempted, for a searing pain cut through Anlerran's head. She stumbled backwards and lost her concentration. For a moment the agony was unbearable, as if someone cut through her brain with a hot knife. Her vision blurred, but Anlerran could still see the creature stare directly at her. Ildar's pale illumination made it look even more ghastly, a nightmarish alabaster statue with black holes for eyes.

The agony intensified and then cut off suddenly as Ildoron leapt and pulled at the creature's head with all his might. The High Watcher flung him aside and his body made a sickening crunch against the half-standing wall of a nearby building, dislodging more rubble and dust. But whatever Ildoron had done during that brief moment had damaged it somehow. The High Watcher staggered as it moved forward, and the two witches redoubled their efforts to destroy it as Kelandra stood to the side of the High Watcher, silent and still, her arms outstretched. Whatever forces she brought to bear, they had the effect of slowing the creature's responses. Anlerran felt a chaos of conflicting energies in the air all around them. They swirled throughout the hall and made the air painfully hot or freezing cold from one moment to the next.

Something snapped inside the creature- an almost impossibly thin thread of metal. Other tiny structures, some of them far too small to be seen normally with their own eyes, bent and twisted and finally broke under the immense pressure.

Suddenly the High Watcher lashed out and the sheer force of its assault cut through the Powers. Kian sagged to the ground suddenly, her hands pressed against the cobbles as she tried to right herself.

A crack appeared in the creature's head, then another. It took one slow step forward and stopped. Something that looked like frost had started to form all over its body.

Kelandra swiftly drew her longsword and swung in a low arc at the High Watcher. The effect was instant and spectacular. As if it had been fashioned entirely from glass the High Watcher shattered into a myriad fragments that scattered throughout the area. Parts of its body that none of them could hope to describe slid, rolled and thumped across the floor. The largest piece that remained was about half of the head, which Kelandra stamped on and ground into glistening, metallic dust under her boots.

Without saying a word she went over to Ildoron, and after a moment the others followed. He was unable to move, and blood trickled from his mouth. Kelandra knelt at his side, and touched his wrist, then behind his ear, then finally his forehead.

"You... did it," Ildoron whispered.

"*You* did it," Kelandra said quietly. "If you hadn't weakened it to begin with..."

Ildoron half-smiled at that, then his expression changed. His eyes had a faraway look to them. "Wish I could..." he whispered. "Wish I could... remember..."

His eyes glazed over, and his body became still.

VII

An eerie silence had descended on Luudhoq by the following afternoon. The half-ruined city gleamed in strong, low sunlight as Garrok, Elluron and Kelandra convened and passed a spyglass between one another to observe and contemplate.

Throughout the city, they saw groups of people picking through the rubble of poorly-constructed buildings that even here had fallen, desperate to find missing loved ones. As the afternoon wore on towards evening they worked by the light of lamps or torches which were less than adequate for the task. Children and infants wept disconsolately or sat shivering, their faces dark with dirt and misery. Men and women pulled at bricks and fallen masonry, bent and exhausted in the face of an all but impossible task. Some stopped and stared fearfully every time *orkar* or northmen or *luyan* walked past.

"You're certain that the Gate was destroyed?" Garrok asked Elluron.

The *half-illeagh* nodded wearily. He had not slept for days. "Perhaps the earthquake affected it. Either way, it was easier than expected. I'm sure the others will not be."

"It appeared where Yui said it would?"

"It did."

Kelandra took another, longer look at the city landscape with the spyglass. "Much remains to be done. There will be Watchers somewhere within Luudhoq. They took no part in the fighting, but I cannot say where their loyalties may now lie or if they have any at all. A few of the High Watchers also retreated deep into the city. Their intentions will be...

more obvious. They will work out a way to continue killing us until they themselves have been destroyed. Perhaps they will work together, perhaps not. Either way, they must be hunted down."

"And what of the Seven?" Elluron reminded her. "To our knowledge, only two are known to have perished- Anya and Issele. I myself saw Omir turn and run from us when the cataclysm happened and the barrier between us and the Green Road began to break down. What if he roams that place?"

"The others have also yet to appear." Kelandra frowned as she pondered the puzzle. "Stephan was known to have left the Border Wall and headed somewhere, but no one knows where. Garret and Daniel cannot be found. Phaedra, according to the witches, remains somewhere within the Fortress of the Seven. Waiting for us, presumably."

"Merinne reported that Anya lost the use of her powers before she was killed," Garrok pointed out. "If that has happened to her surviving comrades then they too will be in hiding somewhere."

"Perhaps. But no trace of them has been found. It could be that they've fled to some other part of the land, in which case we cannot rest even if the *marandaal* are vanquished. Perhaps the Descendants, linked together, may be powerful enough to determine if they still live."

"Every enemy that still hides within Luudhoq must be rooted out and dealt with," Elluron said. "We don't have the resources to uphold law and order until the *marandaal* are dealt with, let alone leave the city at the mercy of the enemy."

"There will always be enemies in Luudhoq," Kelandra said. "And everywhere else."

She wondered once again what had happened to the rest of the Seven, and if the witches and warlocks had the power to discover their fate.

VIII

Stephan raised the spyglass and took a long, satisfied look at the land masses slowly coming into view in the distance. Kyransa, the largest and tallest of the islands, lay to the left. Through the spyglass he caught a tantalising glimpse of thick forest, rugged mountains stretching sharply towards a cloudless sky, and long, sand-covered beaches.

Finally he passed the device back to the ship's captain. The man still looked fearful, as well might anyone who was returning to their homeland with the new lord of that place. Stephan had revealed his identity two days ago, responding to the captain's initial doubt by crushing one of his sailors to death by sheer force of will. His comrades were still valiantly attempting to scrub away the stain of his existence from the fore deck. Stephan had enjoyed the exhilaration, the rush of excitement from abandoning his self-restraint and pouring every ounce of bright, joyous hatred into the ending of the man's life. The sheer horror on the faces of those who had witnessed it had gratified him further. It had been a long time since he had let himself go- on such a scale, at least.

"Would you care to be captain of my personal ship?" he asked suddenly, speaking in Kyransan for no other reason than that he enjoyed practising the language.

"I... I would be honoured, my Lord." The captain bowed low. Perhaps a little *too* low, Stephan thought, giving him a sharp look. Humility was one thing, but he didn't care at all for fawning sycophants. *He'll learn,* he thought. *Or he'll die.*

"Good. This will be my ship, which means you get to keep your job." He smiled as he turned and looked back north across the many leagues of ocean. No trace of the land mass of Harn and Aphenhast could be seen from this distance, even with the spyglass. "I have some good news to tell you," he remarked. "I'm sure you people fear the *marandaal* as much as the Harnians do. But I have a theory I'd like to share with you. I don't believe the *marandaal* can cross oceans, nor do I believe they can fly. If they could, Harn would have fallen long ago. Something has stalled their progress even across the land."

The captain had already revealed himself to be an intelligent man. He nodded thoughtfully.

Stephan allowed himself the luxury of contemplating how he would rule over the South Ocean Islands, and wondered at the same time how it could be that he and rest of the Seven had satisfied themselves with southern Harn and never attempted to take Aphenhast or the South Ocean Islands. *Something drew us to Luudhoq, and in its own subtle way kept us there,* he thought. The idea made him uneasy for a moment, but then his thoughts returned inevitably to the joy of conquest and the mechanics of rule.

His ruminations were interrupted soon enough though, by a heated conversation on the deck. Stephan scowled in irritation and made his way over to the captain. "My lord, the ship is sinking!" the captain blurted out as he approached.

"If it's taking in water somewhere, then find and fix the leak," Stephan said quietly. "Are you truly a ship's captain, or an idiot?"

The captain cringed but persisted, "No water is being taken in, my lord. There is no leak. It's as if the ship is being pulled slowly under..."

"By *what,* fool?" Stephan retorted, but the captain just shrugged helplessly.

Stephan strode to the rail and leaned over. The water *was* noticeably nearer, although that was not what made him temporarily forget everything but what he could see in the water.

Under the surface, moving as if at one with the currents of the ocean, Stephan saw a patch of intense light—something more brilliant than the sparkling of the sun on the ripples of water. As he watched it moved, changed shape and became still. Stephan concentrated and tried to determine its nature, but he could not.

As he finally tore his gaze from the phenomenon he noticed that the ship had sunk further, and a great rage came upon him. It crushed his cold logic and rational thought. "You *know* these waters!" he screamed at the ship's captain. "How many times have you sailed this route?! I *command* you to stop this ship from sinking further. Fail and you die!" He turned immediately to the other men within earshot. "All of you! I command you!"

But when he next looked over the edge of the rail he saw that the water had risen again and was now much closer. At the same time he heard an immense cracking, groaning sound. The ship was being crushed on all sides. Stephan knew for a fact that water had now begun to pour into the vessel, accelerating its descent into the ocean.

The end came more quickly than he could have imagined. The water rose swiftly, and with the ocean came the light. Stephan raged against his fate even as he drowned, pulled into the shining depths. He screamed until his lungs filled with water and his vision faded.

Even as he descended into blackness he could feel an insidious presence, all-powerful and unstoppable, and in his final moments he still thought he could hear himself screaming his hatred, denying his own mortality even as his body was slowly crushed under a vast mass of water, pulled towards an abyss that had never known sunlight.

IX

When Phaedra woke to the sounds of battle within the grounds of the Fortress, her first sensation was one of wonder.

She knew immediately that her powers had fled, spirited away as if something had stolen them in her sleep.

But as she got up and walked over to her mirror, she felt certain that her immortality and ability to regenerate nevertheless remained.

"The ultimate cruelty," she murmured, tracing a hand down her cheek. "To be rendered humble, powerless and yet still... still *this*."

Her hand trembled with effort. She dug a sharp nail into her cheek and then watched disconsolately as the wound gradually healed and faded away in moments.

"Why?" she whispered, but nothing answered her.

A group of witches and northmen searching the grounds of the fortress found Phaedra sitting on a bench in one of the courtyard gardens later that day. A barrier fashioned from the Powers was swiftly built by the Descendants, and Phaedra turned to watch. She could no longer sense or feel their sorcery in any way, but she knew what they were doing. "There's no need," she murmured, but they either ignored her or didn't hear.

With their invisible web of sorcery in place they surrounded her, still wary of their powerless prey. Eventually one of them, a slim *du-luyan* girl, said to the others, "She cannot harm us. Her powers have gone."

"I told you," Phaedra said.

"The same happened with Anya," an *orkar* woman behind them spoke up.

Phaedra looked at her, suddenly interested. "Did they die? Omir, Anya, Issele? I've been unable to sense them for days."

The *orkar* nodded.

"In agony?" Phaedra could not help but smile. "Please tell me they died in agony."

"I'm surprised their fate means that much to you. Perhaps you ought to contemplate your own."

Phaedra laughed. "Really? I've done little but contemplate for months. Do as you will and be done with me."

One of the northmen- their leader, she guessed- asked, "What of the others? If they're hiding somewhere here then we'll find them."

"Oh, they're all waiting for the right moment to strike," Phaedra said nonchalantly, and then abruptly changed her mind. "I'll tell you what happened to them. Garret escaped from Aona, through a Gate that Daniel and I were hoping to create from our old machinery. It worked... but Garret found out about it somehow. Who knows where he is now? All I know is that it looked like a pleasant enough world. Daniel is dead, or as good as. You may come across his pieces if you explore the Sanctum sufficiently. And as for Stephan... I don't know. He went to the Border Wall, and then he left. I suppose he must have run away, but my instinct tells me something has happened to him as well. I considered doing the same, a long time ago- but what's the point?"

They stared uncertainly at her, clearly unsure as to what to believe. After a while they conversed quietly and one of their number dashed away. He returned a little later with more people. The rebel Watcher was Kelandra amongst their number.

"Well," Phaedra said. "This is quite a gathering you've arranged for my benefit. I hope you all have time to enjoy the moment of your victory. A moment is all it will be. The *marandaal* cannot be stopped."

But instead of replying to her jibe they talked quietly amongst themselves for a long while. Phaedra waited as patiently as she could, ill at ease as Kelandra kept her steady gaze upon her. Phaedra decided that the coldly satisfied look in the Watcher's eyes had little to do with the fall of Luudhoq and the demise of the Seven.

"You could decapitate me and crush each part," she said helpfully when she could no longer bear the waiting, "and take all those parts to the four corners of the world..."

"We thought about that," Kelandra interrupted. "The Descendants have together determined that you are the last of your kind, Phaedra. A special fate therefore awaits you."

Phaedra laughed. "Impressive! How could they determine that? Although that said, I *did* point out that Garret is long gone from Aona and Daniel is no more, so I can assure you that you only had one of us to look for, if you thought Stephan was still alive."

"Linked together, there is very little that they cannot achieve," Kelandra remarked.

"The people thought of you all as immortal," the human witch said.

"Well, it would appear that nothing lasts forever." Phaedra smiled as she regarded each of them in turn. "You know, I sometimes wondered what might make an end of us."

"You made an end of yourselves," a man further back said quietly. Phaedra could not decide whether he was human or *luyan* or something entirely different. "Did we?" she rejoined. "I think you ought to take more credit for your work. I had several visions of your hordes as they poured from out of the north, bringing a mad darkness with which to fight us- and the *marandaal,* I suppose. The starspawn as you often call them. They're not from the stars, though. Not precisely."

"Then where are they from?"

"Your own legends tell of a single world from which they spread, and that much is true. It's a dead place now, baked and barren like most worlds. Actually it was well on the path to absolute ruin even before the dawn of the *marandaal.* But once upon a time..." Phaedra laughed suddenly. "You're familiar with many of the miracles and wonders that Aona harbours. Let me assure you, the world from which we came had its own share of those. Had you seen such things. none of you could have made sense of what you witnessed. We created something that I suppose you would call a *great magic.* But what is that except a profoundly complex set of rules and patterns that no observer can truly understand? I've seen your people perform deeds that anyone in the old world would have described as sorcery- whether they believed in such a thing or not. Certainly I can't hope to comprehend them. This world will forever be a mystery to me- and more now than ever before." Phaedra sighed. "Well? How should I meet my end?"

"That's something we have discussed. The Watchers have thought of a fate upon which we've agreed."

"They have? Well, I'm sure a suitably grisly end has been devised."

"We're not going to kill you," someone else spoke up.

Phaedra looked at her and laughed.

"You will be incarcerated within a tower," the man or part-man creature who had addressed her before said. "You will be held securely in place as we build it around you. The tower will have no way in and no way out, and no windows. The darkness inside it will be absolute, to match the darkness of your poisonous heart."

"Oh, how poetic," Phaedra spat back, but her lip trembled and her cheeks paled further. Next to the half-man, Kelandra stood with arms folded, a faint, hard smile of satisfaction on her face.

"When complete, it will be perhaps fifty hands thick. We will do whatever is needed to make it indestructible."

"I might escape," Phaedra warned. "My powers might return. What then, if I find a way out? How is the era of the Seven truly at an end if one of their number still lives and is even at large in the world?"

He did not appear to have heard her. "Perhaps, over time, Aona herself may grant you peace and allow you to die naturally, as once she granted you a powerful gift that you maligned and abused for many centuries. But you will be sealed away for eternity, and none of us here, nor our descendants, shall know how long you truly persist in your miserable prison."

"You should *kill me*," Phaedra asserted. Her voice shook, and she renewed her plea. "If you don't, I will escape my prison sooner or later, and slaughter thousands before you apprehend me. Luudhoq's streets will run with the blood of its subjects. Yes. You need to kill me."

But the dreadful detail continued unabated. "The tower will be protected with sorcery created by six who are strong in the Powers. None of them shall intimately know the weaves of the others. The spell and the construct shall merge as one and be impossible to break. It shall persist for as long as Aona herself."

"Perhaps until the end of time itself," Kelandra added. "That would certainly be my hope."

Phaedra bowed her head. Had it been possible, the horror of her situation might have crushed the life out of her. *Until the end of time,* she thought blackly. *And it may well be. Until the sun swallows the world, or if it doesn't, then until all heat and light and movement have dissipated, until energy itself is no more and the Existence folds back on itself.*

"Allow me to make amends," she pleaded. "To the people of Luudhoq and wider Harn. I will do anything. Anything at all!"

"You have had a thousand years to think on the atrocities committed by the Seven against their long-suffering subjects," the half-man reminded her. "Your fate has been decided. An example will be made. You will languish in your construct, which is to be known forever more as Phaedra's Tower."

The last of the Seven half-laughed and half-wept. "I will have a tower named after me?! Oh, the *immortality* of it all!" Suddenly her hands reached to her throat in a desperate attempt to tear it out. Kelandra and Alturus stepped either side of Phaedra. Silently they forced the woman's desperate fingers away from where they might cause harm, until her arms stretched out to her left and right.

She screamed continually at them all, but no one could understand any of her words. Her noise continued even as they bore her away to be shut in darkness for all time.

X

The sight of Phaedra's naked terror as she was dragged away to her incarceration pleased Kelandra- insofar as she felt pleasure of any sort. She waited awhile to watch as a spell was weaved to keep the last surviving member of the Seven in place and helpless. Then she turned and headed towards the south-east of the city.

Kelandra walked for a long while, oblivious to the soft, early spring rain that began to fall. Her progress was certain and she did not stop once to check her directions. She knew where she was headed. The place had been shown to her in a dream three nights ago- the only one she remembered ever having had- and the images of it in her mind had not dimmed over the ensuing days. If anything they had become more vivid than ever.

Sometime in the late afternoon Kelandra stopped abruptly, her gaze drawn towards an area of waste ground and rubble which had had long been left to grow wild with thickets of bramble, ivy and undergrowth. Here and there throughout this abandoned place the remains of old buildings could be seen, often no more than two or three rows of stonework, reclaimed by many seasons of vegetative growth.

The Watcher stepped off the road and into this wilderness. Although everything that had once stood here had been destroyed many decades ago, she nevertheless recognised this place, and as she took in the sight of what little remained more memories trickled forth. She recalled the route from here to the nearby shops and the old Harbour View market, which had long since ceased to be held. In her distant past before she had become a Watcher, she had walked this way many times.

We would shop every fourth-day and ninth-day, she recalled as she walked further into the jungle of ivy and thorn and desolation. Rain pattered on the leaves and dripped from

271

the brim of her hat. *First we would head to the market, and then to the herb and vegetable shops and the butcher's on the way back. On every tenth-day I would leave him with Father for most of the day, and walk to the local Guild for my studies- history and geography. I hoped to qualify for my diploma.*

Kelandra stopped suddenly and almost stumbled forward. She reached out a hand to steady herself and it caught a thick, wickedly-barbed tendril of mature bramble that wound around a pillar of stones, perhaps the corner of one of the houses that had existed here. Blood stained the green rope of thorns within a moment, but Kelandra remained quite oblivious to the fact. Her entire world had shrunk around one name, one face.

One child.

"Tomas," she whispered, as her hand finally relinquished its hold. "Your name was Tomas."

She wandered through the thick vegetation for many hours. The rain soaked her through. Finally she came upon an area where the remains of the walls- their dimensions, their relationships with one another and the spaces where once windows would have existed- all felt oddly familiar.

Kelandra began to tear through the chaos of thorns and weeds that proliferated here. She ignored the lacerations they caused her hands, and cleared the area as best she could. Just as the light had begun to fail, the Watcher saw a faint gleam of bones in the disturbed topsoil, and she reached out to pick one of them up. The bone was of a short forearm.

In itself the fragile remnant could not be proof of anything or anyone, certainly not the child of whom it had once been a part.

But as Kelandra knelt down in the gathering dusk and held this remnant, she simply *knew*.

IX - The Circle Revealed

I

At first the surrounding darkness appeared total, an emptiness made all the more desolate by the utter silence and the stillness of the air. But as time passed the faint glow of the sky became more noticeable, a directionless uniform tinge that emanated from the starless and moonless backdrop.

Vornen slowly picked himself up from the ground. His gaze took in the alien, barren landscape all around them. This land was flat, empty of all vegetation, and made from packed, dry earth through which a maze of cracks ran, like a desert formed from once-fertile land. Dotted around this derelict environment were the remains of buildings, their shapes and sizes as varied as the ground on which they stood was uniform. Some still stood half-intact while only fragments remained of others. A few climbed almost a thousand hands tall into the oppressive sky, while some had been reduced to little more than piles of stone and metal rubble. Together they appeared like an ancient city that had been reclaimed long ago by the desert surrounding it, the remains of civilisation shaped and worn away by the harsh conditions.

But no civilisation had ever existed here.

"We don't have much time," Alexia said quietly from behind him.

Ileana got to her feet and surveyed the desolation. "It's difficult to know how quickly we can get to where we need to be. Everything is different here, time included. Can you tell which direction it's in, Vornen?"

I can't detect it at all, Vornen almost said. But then, as he stood and slowly turned to face each direction in turn, he felt the faintest pull, as if a miniscule, invisible thread connected him to the Gate and had suddenly become taut. He turned again, waited until that insistent pull was at its strongest and then pointed in that direction. Ileana simply nodded and began to walk that way, and Vornen and Alexia followed her.

"How far, do you think?" Alexia asked him after a moment. Vornen shrugged. "Who knows?"

They threaded their way between the stark, ruinous buildings. None of them could have said how long they walked for. Both Vornen and Alexia noticed that Ileana consciously avoided the shadows cast by the buildings. As if sensing their unspoken question, she stopped at one point and explained, "They're not shadows in any normal sense. They're best avoided."

"There isn't anything in the sky to make shadows," Alexia observed.

Ileana smiled grimly. "Exactly."

During their journey, Vornen tried to measure the passage of time by counting the number of steps they took. He counted almost five thousand paces before they stopped to rest. The landscape looked much the same as where they had emerged into the Green Road, but if anything the buildings had thinned out. Perhaps they had almost reached the edge of this eerie, unoccupied metropolis.

As they ate and drank from the rations they had each brought, Ileana said, "This place has two sides. One living as it ought, and the other corrupted by disease. By the *marandaal* perhaps, or some other malaise."

"The *marandaal* can reach through the Existence to touch the minds of people in the waking world," Alexia agreed. "It shouldn't surprise us if they can likewise taint the Green Road. The Gate may well be their creation."

"Or it may be randomness," Vornen suggested. "The likelihood of disease is determined by factors, but it may also happen without apparent reason. I'm sure we've all seen that for ourselves. We're all just faint, brief glimmers in the Existence, and sooner or later we expire."

"The body and the affliction," Alexia mused. "These shadows and holes, and slivers of darkness and whole cities being eaten slowly away- supposing they're all symptoms part of it?"

An uncomfortable thought came to Vornen. "What if all of this has happened before?"

When the women stared blankly at him he explained, "Some sages maintain that everything we know- and for that matter everything we don't know- started from nothing, or a single point, and will eventually end up as nothing or as complete darkness, an absence of light and life and movement. But there are others who say that the Existence has neither a beginning nor an end, only stages which eventually repeat."

Ileana frowned in puzzlement but Alexia nodded thoughtfully. "I've read about some of these ideas. There are those who believe that everything that we witness, everything that happens to us, has occurred before in a different Age and will occur again in the future, and that's why some people dream of events that have not even happened yet, but then do."

"As if the lessons of any Age are never learned?" Ileana questioned.

Vornen smiled. "If only we could know how it all worked out last time. But would that not break the cycle?"

"I've read that such knowledge would simply alter or bend the path of the event," Alexia said, "so that it adjusts itself accordingly, and runs its course regardless. Perhaps the entire cycle would need to be known in order for someone or something to break it." She gave Vornen a considering look. "I didn't know you were so well-read."

"Neither did I," Ileana commented. "I can't remember seeing you so much as open a book."

"It was a long time ago," he said quietly. "I had a lot of time to myself."

"Judging by your accent, you're from the north of Aphenhast as well," Alexia said to Ileana. "Somewhere near Ethanalin Tur-morn?"

"I grew up there," Ileana admitted. "I always hated the place. I thought I'd be trapped there forever, until Vornen and Amethyst took me away from there."

A long silence followed before Alexia spoke up quietly. "We all had to leave people behind. I know the two of you had to leave Amethyst and Jak and that you've put your faith in me. You've both given up as much as I have if not more..."

A harsh keening sound started up amongst the ruins behind. The coldly industrial noise sounded unlike any creature they could imagine, as if ancient hidden machinery had started to work by itself, powered by whatever evil infected this place.

"What was that?" Vornen whispered.

"We need to go," Ileana said.

The companions hurried on across the parched landscape. Soon they had left the constructs of the silent city far behind. Ahead of them, the shapes of black and dismal hills rose into the distance. The air remained still and warm, almost like the lull before the violence of a storm. Finally, with the hills still before them they agreed to rest and take turns to watch while the other two used the opportunity to sleep.

Vornen fell asleep quickly. In the dream that soon came to him, he sat propped up against the wall of a building at the side of a busy city street. He couldn't have said which city this was or even which land. He could hear the faint buzz of conversations between people as they bought, sold, perused and walked along the unfamiliar streets, but he couldn't make out any individual words and their accents sounded unlike any he had ever heard. All the sounds around him were slightly muffled, as if an invisible barrier or distance existed between him and everyone else.

He looked down at himself, vaguely aware that his clothing stank. His bare feet, bruised and dark with dirt and caked blood, stood out like tombstones in front of him. *I'm a beggar,* he thought. *There's a surprise.*

"Well," a soft voice said, "look at you."

Vornen turned his head, and his heart skipped a beat as he saw his own self looking down at him. But this version was cleaner, better-equipped and shaved. He appeared to have been just passing by- one of hundreds of people who Vornen could see indistinctly some distance away. A faint memory of words that someone might have said passed through his thoughts, but he couldn't remember who had uttered them or when. *Something about what happens when you meet yourself,* he recalled.

"I'm dreaming," he murmured, as if in defence.

"That's always a difficult question to answer, or it would be if it were a question. *You* are probably dreaming, but I very much doubt that *I* am."

Vornen could think of nothing to say to that puzzle, but his apparition merely continued, "In the context of the dream, does it particularly matter?"

"That sounds like something I'd say after too much *kyush.*"

"Ah- that reminds me." His companion brought forth a pouch from somewhere and patted it gently. The heavy, almost dizzying aroma hit Vornen's senses straight away. A sudden thought leapt in his mind. *If I'm dreaming, then I can have as much* kyush *as I want and it can do me no harm.*

His likeness must have seen a look of desperation in Vornen's eyes, because he dangled the bag a little closer, a knowing smile upon his lips. "I gave it up, you know. But I can see that *you* didn't."

"You gave up *kyush?*" Vornen breathed in the heady fragrance, vaguely aware that his hands had started to tremble.

"No. I gave up struggling against life, the Existence and everything. I gave up that curious need to keep going when there was no longer a point to it. I traded in the pain and the misery for an eternity in the company of strangers, untethered to the concerns of the so-called *real* world. It's better here, so does it matter how real or unreal it might be? I'm never hungry, never tired- but most importantly of all, I'm never *afraid*. Imagine that- to exist without fear and pain. The *kyush* sustains me if I yearn to see this place differently for a little while. Nothing bad ever happens. However much I take out of the bag, there's always more. You see, this place is eternal, and so is everything it contains. Apart from you. You're just a visitor, I'm afraid. But you *could* become more than that. A smoke might help you see how that could happen."

Vornen, who had dutifully been imagining an existence without fear and pain, instead contemplated an unlimited supply of *kyush*. With an effort he swallowed down the saliva that had flooded his mouth, but he could not tear his eyes from the fat, aromatic pouch.

Unaccountably, he didn't beg for any. Instead he asked, "What do you mean by *here*? Where are we?"

"This is a place beyond the horizon. It isn't a *where* as such."

"Beyond the horizon... I think I said that before."

"You may well have done. Things do have a habit of repeating themselves. But that's not important. The sad fact is that you're still suffering, even though you don't need to. You don't need to go back to wherever you came from."

Vornen tried to clear his thoughts, which had become strangely muddied as if he had somehow ingested the *kyush* without knowing. *Where did I come from?* he wondered. *How can I go back if I don't know where I came from?*

The entire scene began to change, and gradually became insubstantial. Vornen's doppelganger scowled as if in frustration, stood up and walked away. Vornen heard something as he turned and looked at him. It sounded like *You'll return and sooner or later you won't want to leave,* but he couldn't be certain.

His eyes flickered open to behold Ileana looking down at him. For a brief while he wondered if he had stepped from one dream into another. "A deep sleep?" she inquired.

He sat up, still groggy as the final images from his dream fell away. "A strange one," he said. Alexia still slumbered nearby, and he wondered for a moment what she might be dreaming about.

Ileana pointed towards a valley between two of the dark hills on the other side of the earthy desert. "Look over there. Do you see how the sky appears lighter?"

Vornen looked. He saw a faint glow from somewhere within or perhaps beyond the valley, more pronounced than the deep and faint illumination of the sky. "What is it, do you think?"

"I'm not sure. A sign, perhaps. Is the Gate still that way?"

He allowed his thoughts to fade and his body to become still. He searched for the faint pull of the Gate, and remarked to himself that when he woke he hadn't felt the touch of that portal at all.

When he finally detected the Gate this time, the pull felt a little stronger than before, somehow more urgent. "It is," he said, and suddenly a dreadful thought occurred to him. What if the attractive force of the Gate became so strong that he was eventually driven towards it, his body dragged so powerfully towards that portal that neither he nor his companions could stop him?

He recalled the three Gates in Nisstar, which had forced him across a vast distance to that city, only for their hold on him to inexplicably vanish. What if this became stronger? If he was pulled through the Gate before Alexia had a chance to do whatever she needed to, what then? Would that destroy all hope they had? Was he even present here as the unwitting ruiner of hope, a tool of the *marandaal* or the evil that had infected the heart of the world?

"I know what you're thinking," Ileana said quietly. "I won't let that happen."

"Don't you remember when I had to leave you and Amethyst, in Aphenhast?" he rejoined. "I had no choice. If you'd stopped me, I would have gone mad eventually. I would have found a way to reach the Gates, or died in the attempt."

"It's different now," Ileana said, but she sounded less than certain. She lay down and closed her eyes. Vornen watched the girl as she fell asleep, and remarked to himself how much she had changed in the time that he had known her. The frightened, withdrawn creature who had accompanied himself and Amethyst as they travelled south from the frozen nightmare of Ethanalin Tur-morn was no more. She had become a resilient, brave young woman who had gradually come to terms with the sorcery she held within herself.

And she volunteered herself for this madness, he mused. *I should have expected it from her. But I certainly didn't expect it from me. How did Alexia convince us? Did Aona somehow work some magic into her words?*

Inevitably his thoughts turned to Amethyst, and it felt as if a heavy stone sank slowly through his stomach. *Gods, let us survive this,* he thought with sudden desperation.

He woke Ileana and Alexia when he judged that they had slept sufficiently- not that it was really possible to tell- and the companions walked on towards the still-distant hills. When they finally reached that area, they saw that grass and small shrubs clung to the landscape in places, although much of it looked barren and bare, dotted with rocky outcrops. They continued along a valley between the hills and after a while it opened out to the shore of a vast lake. An island emerged from the waters, perhaps five or six hundred paces away, and a tall, thin tower rose from its highest point. Light poured from a single arched window high up in the structure. It occurred to

Vornen that this had been the light they'd seen from a distance, rising above the shapes of the hills and into the starless gloom. The shoreline on the far side was indistinct, little more than a jagged, dark line.

"I remember this place," he murmured as they looked across the lake at the island, silhouetted harshly against the dim light.

"You ought to." Ileana glanced across at him. "We've been here before. The last time, you began to wade across towards the island. Is the Gate still there?"

He nodded. "Yes- but it's moved. It's below the tower. Far below."

"How far?"

Vornen shrugged. "I can't tell exactly. But it's... sinking, somehow. Going further down, deeper."

"Towards the heart of the world," Alexia said.

Ileana looked troubled. "We need to get across to the tower."

The water turned out to be no deeper than their knees for the entire distance, and its temperature was oddly lukewarm. The solid, smooth rock beneath their feet looked like polished sheets of marble. As Vornen looked down into the shallows he saw threads of light and small, indeterminate entities move through the water. When he placed his hand against the surface it rippled in response as if some vibration had been set off by his touch.

The island was composed of dark, glistening rock, jagged and uncomfortable to walk on. The three companions cautiously picked their way up to the tower, which was cylindrical and about thirty hands wide. They walked around its circumference but could find no obvious entrance. Aside from the window high up in the structure, through which the golden light escaped, the marble-like surface of the tower was so smooth that climbing it would be impossible.

"How do we get inside?" Alexia exclaimed in frustration after they had spent a while walking around several times, touched the surface in numerous places and explored the rest of the bleak little island.

Ileana stood facing the sea, deep in thought. "We wait," she said eventually.

Alexia walked cautiously over across the jagged rocks. "We may not have time," she insisted.

"But there's no other way." Ileana still stared across the lake as if she had spotted something across the watery distance, but Alexia could see nothing they hadn't already noticed. She turned to Vornen, who shrugged wearily. "Maybe we need to go back to the shore," he said after a while. "There might be another route."

Ileana shook her head. "If we wait, we'll be shown the way, somehow."

Alexia turned in frustration and walked back to the tower. She traced a hand across its surface as she walked slowly around. *I expect she knows how to survive this place better than I do,* Alexia reasoned. *After all, I almost became completely lost and trapped the last time I was here.*

"The tower is changing," Vornen warned them suddenly from nearer to the shoreline. He stared up at the structure, a look of bewilderment and unease on his face.

Alexia stepped quickly away from the cylindrical wall, almost stumbling over the rocks in her haste. She made her way down towards where Vornen stood. When she turned to look at the tower again she saw that it had inexplicably become shorter and wider, and a space had opened up at its centre. The shape of the tower continued to change, widening all the while.

"Ileana!" she called, but the girl still stood in silent contemplation, facing away and seemingly oblivious. Vornen walked across to where she stood and gently touched her shoulder. Ileana jumped and turned swiftly, confusion on her face. "Something spoke to me," she whispered. "It kept telling me to step back into the water, to let the water take me. I tried to ignore it, but I couldn't turn away."

The surface of the tower wall had stopped moving. Vornen and Ileana went to where Alexia stood, and then cautiously approached the space in the wall.

Without a word, Ileana stepped into the darkness and her companions followed.

After only a short distance they saw light up ahead. They walked through the archway at the end of the tunnel and into the pale illumination of the circular hallway beyond, the floor of which was made from clear glass. Nine exits stood at ground level, but above them another nine could be seen, then another nine, and another, and so on for as far up as they could see until the view disappeared into a faint haze- far higher than the height of the tower from the outside. When they looked down the companions saw a mirror image of the architecture above them through the glass floor.

"Which of these doorways should we choose?" Vornen asked Ileana.

"I think it matters only that we make a choice. Where is the Gate?"

"Below." Vornen peered down for a moment. "Far below."

"The only way out is through," Alexia said, and Ileana nodded. "All three of us suspected as much even before we came here."

They left the place through one of the archways almost directly ahead, walking uneasily across the glass surface of the floor. A stairway led down beyond the exit and spiralled deeply through the gloom. As the companions carefully descended, they saw that some parts of the spiral were lit up more than others, although they couldn't see where the illumination came from.

A long time passed. They rested occasionally, and a couple of times even slept fitfully and uneasily coiled in the stairwell, wrapped up in the suffocating silence and eternal dusk of this place. Days could have come and gone. As they descended the companions noticed that the stairs eventually became more and more worn. Some had even been broken apart in places.

"It's close," Vornen murmured at one point, as he stopped to lean against the central column of the stairwell. His surroundings swam before him as if they were no longer entirely solid and unmoving. At the same time he felt sure that his hand sank into the wall a little way. Abruptly he moved away from the cold surface of the column, only to stagger on the step and be steadied just in time by Alexia.

"Are you able to walk on?" Ileana asked, her eyes wide with concern.

Vornen smiled weakly as he took a few more tentative steps down the spiral. "I'm sure it will pull me as near as we need to get, if it ever comes to that."

A short while later the stairs came to an end and opened out into a vast chamber of rough-hewn stone and shadow. A faint glow came from the roof and floor.

"We're here," Vornen said. He took two faltering steps and then staggered to the ground.

The sides of the cavern began to pulse with a light that emanated from the rock face, as if something had been awakened by their presence, and in the centre of the cavern a column of light slowly formed, harsh and monolithic in shape.

Vornen got slowly to his feet. "It's somewhere beyond the light."

As Alexia looked into the light, whispering sounds began to echo through her mind. She couldn't make out any individual words, but she understood their meaning nonetheless.

Alexia turned and motioned for both Vornen and Ileana to come nearer to her. When they were close enough, she linked hands with Vornen and motioned for him to do the same with Ileana. She stepped towards the light and drew her companions with her, but as the three of them approached the light, its pull became far greater. Within a moment they were surrounded by it, and could see nothing but the all-consuming brilliance.

Then they lost one another.

II

Vornen stood alone in the light. The warmth and illumination poured down and up and swirled around him as if charged with a life of its own. It felt singularly alien but also familiar in a way he couldn't describe. He felt as if he ought to be frightened by it, but instead he felt oddly calm, almost emptied of any emotion whatsoever.

He closed his eyes, opened them again and looked around in shock, for the light, the cavern and the Green Road itself had disappeared.

He stood on open grassy ground, in the northern Plains of Aphenhast, an area he had known for his entire life.

This is impossible, he thought numbly.

Vornen's shocked gaze took in the long grass rippling in the light breeze, the distant, hazy blue peaks of mountains to the north, east and south, the occasional hills and distant settlements in between. He listened to the sounds of birdsong and the chirruping of crickets, the cadence of summer.

Then he saw a young boy sitting in the grass, facing towards the east and the distant peaks beyond which lay the desert realm of Alhar.

For a long while Vornen stood, transfixed and rooted to the spot. He felt exhilarated but also afraid, for not only did he know who the boy was, but he now remembered this day. He recalled sitting in that same place, doing nothing in particular. He had allowed his thoughts to wander and had just enjoyed being by himself, away from Ruan-Tor and its people. He even remembered somehow sensing that he was being watched. He had turned round to see if there was anyone there.

And there was, he thought numbly.

285

He began to walk towards his younger self, no longer able to control his body, helpless inside it. He despaired, knowing he was about to watch the entire scene unfold as if from behind some invisible screen, shielded and hidden. He had lost control of his physical self and become nothing more than a passenger.

The boy's head turned as the older Vornen approached.

Now I remember it all. Every word.

The boy stared uneasily up at the man with the iron-grey hair and hard, lined face. He decided at first that he didn't like him, and he reached instinctively for the longknife that lay sheathed on the grass beside him. But then he looked into the eyes of the stranger, and saw a gentleness there that stayed his hand. He wondered why the man looked familiar. "Who are you?" he asked warily.

"I can't give you my name," the stranger said quietly, and sat down beside him. The boy saw a strange light in his eyes. For a moment it felt as if he had seen through himself and into a different Existence altogether. *What was that?* he thought. But then a second, confusing question came to him. *When will I see it again?*

"One day soon, everything will change," the stranger continued as the boy stared at him, transfixed. "For you at first, but soon enough for the world at large. Visions and nightmares will come to you. You will find yourself drawn to certain places at certain times, and to begin with you'll have no idea why. Life as you know it will change utterly. Soon you will meet someone who you love so fiercely that it will be agony more often than not. As the years speed by your life will continue to appear worthless, as if you have become a conduit for a higher force that cannot be explained- a vessel without purpose. Often you will contemplate ending the misery. Each time you will find some inner strength with which to continue, although you won't know how or why. The morning will arrive and you'll be there to see it, still breathing, still there to witness the dawn. At times you will feel certain that some higher power is keeping you alive against your wishes for some unknown future purpose.

"Years later, you will be caught up in the final struggle that will decide the future of Aona. It may be that the light of life is crushed out and the Existence darkened forever without you. You will help heal the wound in Aona's heart. You will know how, because she is part of you and you are part of her."

Behind the eyes of his older self, Vornen's disconnected mind swam with images from the distant past. His parents, withdrawn and fearful as it became increasingly evident that their son had grown to become a slave to forces that no one understood. Suli, a fierce creature of love and darkness who had changed his world forever. His mentor Lord Vothangrane, who had forgiven him on countless occasions in the manner of a father. Even Rocan appeared, a man constrained by his self-imposed religion and morality and yet consumed with cold rage.

"But will I ever be happy?" the boy asked faintly. He glanced quickly towards the distant buildings of Ruan-Tor, and wondered suddenly if he stood a chance of getting back to the town if he scrambled to his feet and ran as fast as he could. "I don't want to be a hero. I just want to be happy."

The stranger said nothing at first. "I don't know the answer to that," he finally replied. "The future is never certain."

The boy could think of nothing more to say. He knew only that it was time for him to leave. Perhaps he should have run as soon as he saw the man approach. He wondered now why he hadn't done just that. He wished that he hadn't stayed to listen.

Quickly he picked up his longknife and slung his backpack over his shoulder, then headed back towards the town. The breeze sighed regretfully through the grass, and the boy did not dare to look back.

Nor would he remember this meeting until many years later.

The dark shapes of rustling leaves patterned Ileana's view. Beyond the foliage an azure sky stretched forever, dotted with wisps of high cloud. As if caught in an impossible dream, Ileana walked to the edge of the copse, where to her shock she saw the huts, hovels and other miserable dwellings of Ethanalin Tur-morn laid out before her, a grim and silent nightmare.

Why am I back here? she wondered, as panic rose through her. *This can't be real!*

Then she saw a little girl sitting on a rocky outcrop on the hill that overlooked the town, no more than a few dozen paces in front of her. Her hair looked lank and unwashed, her clothes thin and inadequate for this season or any other this far north. Ileana's heart almost missed a beat as she stared at the child, transfixed. *That's me,* she realised numbly. *That's me when I was maybe seven or eight. I used to come up here so often. I would try to pluck up the courage to turn and leave the town and never come back, but I was always too scared. I desperately wished I could run away but I never did. And my step-parents knew I would always come back. No one else would have taken me in even if they wanted to. I wasn't one of them, after all.*

I'm seeing through and into my past. But what if I can change it?

Am I really here?

Abruptly she began to walk forwards. Ileana would have cried out in shock had she been able to, but she could no longer control what she was doing. Instead she watched helplessly, a prisoner in her own body. Her older self slowly approached and sat by the seven-year old Ileana. Immediately the child jumped, startled, and tried to get away.

"Let me go!" the little girl shrieked as Ileana's older self grabbed her arm. *I remember this now,* Ileana's disembodied mind thought numbly. *I'd completely forgotten about it for all these years. How could I possibly not remember something like this? Was I meant to forget?*

"I have something to tell you," said the stranger quietly. "Something very important. Will you stay and listen? Please? It won't take long."

The child stared suspiciously into the older girl's eyes. She considered trying to suddenly pull her arm away- if she could- and run as fast as she could down the hill and into the town. But something stopped her. Perhaps it was the calm, knowing look in the eyes that stared at hers. Somehow she felt certain that this girl she had never met before knew everything about her- all the things that had happened and that might happen in the future.

"I know you're afraid that you might never escape," the stranger continued. "You come to this place often, and you think about running away from the town forever, but you know enough about the outside world to be afraid of it."

"I'm afraid to stay here as well," the little girl murmured.

"Yes. I know what happens to you. I know what the people who are supposed to look after you do to you. I know how much you hate them. But one day you will find a way out."

One day I will, Ileana silently echoed as she listened to the two of them. The words they uttered tore at her heart.

The child shook her head miserably. "I don't believe you. I'm here until I die. I wish I could die now."

"No. You're not. Six years from now, someone will come to take you away. You'll be afraid. You'll feel like a prisoner at first. But she will become like a sister to you. Your powers that you keep hidden safely away will grow..."

The little girl cringed in fear and stared at the stranger, alarmed. "How can you know about that?! *No one* knows about those things!"

"…and you will journey through the unknown heart of the world in order to save it from the darkness that surrounds everything."

The stranger looked intently into the eyes of the child, holding her arm gently. "She is a part of you, and you are a part of her."

Although Ileana hadn't remembered that meeting until now, she had always felt that little seed of hope that had been planted in her heart that day, without understanding how it had got there or where it had come from. *I still hated my life,* she recalled, *but I no longer felt entirely without hope.*

As if a spell had shattered like glass, the child broke free and ran headlong down the slope.

The surrounding light gradually dissipated, and shapes and forms materialised. Alexia found herself standing in a library whose four walls were all lined with books, leaving room for nothing else but the doors at the centres of each wall. In the middle of the room stood a long slate table.

She stared around in mute confusion for what felt like an age, until finally she realised that she stood in one of the libraries within the Palace in Darkenhelm.

How can I be here? she wondered. *Why am I here? Surely the* marandaal *will be bearing down on the city. This place might soon no longer exist.*

Once she had overcome her initial bewilderment, Alexia cautiously walked to one of the doors that led out of the library and turned the handle. Another library lay beyond, and after a short while it dawned on her that this room looked identical to the first one. She read the titles of the books closest to her, and then walked back into the other library. As she wandered alongside each of the walls she realised that each wall was stacked with the same books in the exact same order. *Each wall is exactly square,* she noted as she opened each central door in turn and observed the room beyond. *I'm not in the Palace at all, but somewhere else. How far does this* maze extend? If every room is identical then does this whole place simply go on forever? Does it even matter which of these libraries I'm in? I must be somewhere within the Green Road still, but why has this puzzle been created?

It occurred to her that a clue might lie in one of the books. But it would take a vast amount of time to look through every book in even one of the rooms, and Alexia knew that time had started to run out.

As she walked around the perimeter of the room she was in, one of the larger volumes caught Alexia's eye. She tried three times to read the title embossed on the spine, but the words blurred whenever she looked directly at them.

This is the one, a voice whispered in her head, although she had no idea what that meant.

Alexia tugged the book free from the bookcase with an effort, and placed it on the slate table. The title on the spine remained blurred, as did the words on the front cover. Alexia peered closely, then tried to look at it from further away. Finally she tried to read it by glancing from the corner of her eye in an effort to trick the illusion. But no matter what method she employed, the words remained illegible.

Finally she opened the book. But she saw neither words nor drawings inked upon the pages. Instead she beheld images that moved, as if she stared through a window into an ongoing scene.

Alexia knew her history as well as anyone and soon she realised, through a number of scenes that swiftly followed one another, that this was a retelling of the First Age in its entirety. The slavery of the Younger Races under the *choragh* after the *illeagh* finally chose to part from their dark cousins. The various failed and futile uprisings over long and miserable centuries, which crushed by ever more vicious means. The first incursion into Aona by the *marandaal,* and the great war between them and the *choragh,* who used the Younger Races as channels for their power. The death of many hundreds of thousands of people in the mud of a hundred battlefields. The eventual destruction of those *marandaal* that had invaded, and the closure or destruction of the Gates. The emergence of the First, who had learned how to secretly wield the Powers under their own control during the latter days of the conflict. The struggle between the First and the *choragh*, who had given greater sorcery to those loyal subjects strong enough to bear the burden. The eventual overthrow of the *choragh* by the forces of the First- a combined, united army of humans, *luyan, du-luyan* and other races, some of which had long since died out or faded from the world.

Finally the story of the First Age slowly disappeared from the pages before her. The last thing Alexia saw was the gradual construction of places such as Mirkwall in Aphenhast, and in Harn the city that would one day become Luudhoq, a place run by the Descendants of the First and those who came after them, until the arrival of the Seven.

Her hand reached out to touch the corner of the right hand page. She meant to turn to the next page, but a strange fear momentarily gripped her and she found herself unable to summon the necessary courage at first.

When Alexia did eventually turn the page, instead of being presented with more recent events she instead found herself propelled further into the past- a time that was virtually unknown.

During this era, the *choragh* and *illeagh* were one. No Younger Races existed over which they might hold dominion. Aona revealed herself to be a primal, natural place throughout, rich with vast, thick forests. Because the Younger Races had not yet arrived in Aona, no settlements had been built. The land existed perhaps as it already had for many millennia, unspoiled by the artefacts and fancies of civilisation.

How did the Younger Races come here? Alexia wondered, and in a moment the answer was revealed to her. Gates appeared, dotted around the world, and through them ventured the races that she knew- humans, *luyan, du-luyan, crommari, ko xkoth, orkar* and others that she had never seen before and knew of only through ancient history texts she had studied in Darkenhelm. Each race came only with their own people, and they emerged from different worlds to one another.

Through the portals Alexia caught glimpses of some of those places from a great distance, beautiful orbs hanging in empty space- as if a god's-eye overview of each world had been created for her eyes alone. Each and every one looked different. On some she observed the clear demarcations of land and ocean, whereas the surfaces of others were partly or wholly obscured by a coloured haze. She noticed that about half of these worlds had one or two moons, several had three or four, and a small number had as many as ten.

As she observed, Alexia found that other questions came to her. How could it be that all these people had access to powerful sorcery such as that which created, opened and directed Gates? Or had Aona somehow created these portals, linked them to the worlds where all these races had existed, and somehow enticed them here? If that was so, then why? It struck Alexia as a cruel trick on a truly cosmic scale, to lure the Younger Races from across the known Existence only for them to spend countless centuries of misery and terror under the *choragh*. It made no sense to employ sorcery of such unimaginably vast power for such a purpose, and yet it appeared that that might have happened.

Why would Aona allow such suffering? she wondered. Or could this be the grim work of some other, unknown entity- or a dark side to Aona? After all, did the Powers themselves not have two opposing sides? And were the Powers and Aona not, in one sense, the same thing?

Alexia watched helplessly as the people of all these races gradually spread from where they arrived in the world. Whether in Harn or Aphenhast or Alhar, or the South Ocean Islands, they made their way to neighbouring territories.

As these scenes eventually faded away to leave only blank paper, Alexia prepared to turn the page again, to witness an even earlier Age, but again she paused. Could there be any real purpose to this? Was she supposed to know such things? Ought she try to find out a way out of here as soon as possible instead?

Finally she judged that she had found the book for a reason. It had been waiting for her, she decided. In its own way, it had called to her. The sorcery or illusion that blurred the title was evidence of that call.

Alexia turned the page and allowed new scenes to form and play out through the window into the past.

But she understood nothing that she now observed.

Alexia had expected to see a world devoid of even the elder races and creatures, the peaceful paradise that she had always imagined the world before known history to be like- a lush and unspoilt vista much like the time of the single higher race that had given rise to the *choragh* and *illeagh,* but without even those beings.

Instead she saw odd, murky images from an entirely different reality. Almost all of them appeared to be from one city landscape or another, suffused with grime and fog. So alien did it appear that at first Alexia wondered if it might somehow be a window through to the unearthly cityscape of the Green Road through which she had wandered and become lost.

But she saw people here and there, and the more she looked the more she saw. However, much of what she observed made no sense at all. She beheld a city so vast that it dwarfed any in the known world, home to millions upon millions of people. She saw strange machinery, and vehicles that appeared to move themselves without the need of horses or oxen. She saw buildings that towered far taller than any she knew or had heard of.

Then she saw caught glimpses of people who she recognised.

"No," Alexia whispered. "This isn't possible."

As she struggled to make sense of what had been revealed to her, the pages of the book began to slowly crumble away at the edges. The more she tried to hold them together the more they disintegrated, until they became nothing but dust. Desperately she tried to recall the things she had seen, certain that this last scene was the most important of all those she had witnessed. She committed parts of it to memory, or thought she did, but meanwhile the book continued to gently fall apart, and some of its fragments fell to the ground as fine dust while others rose into the still air as smoke.

Alexia felt fear grow within her, as if something terrible was about to happen now that the book was no more, its unknown message transmitted to her.

She walked quickly towards one of the doors that led out of the library, so fearful that she almost broke into a run. She glanced back at the table and fine scattering of dust only once. Again she tried to remember the detail of the scenes she had witnessed, but by the time she reached the door they were like faded remnants from a dream, and thus they remained.

To her surprise, when she opened the door she saw not another library beyond but a passageway that led off into the distance. Alexia made her way swiftly down it, and a while later she came within sight of the end of the passageway. When she looked back, only another dead end faced her, but it was nearer than it ought to have been. She turned around again, and found that the *other* end was also nearer than it had been before. Panic rose in her heart as the wooden walls pressed in on both sides as well as the ends of the corridor. She saw that the walls were covered with holes. *I'm being watched,* she thought, certain that she could feel the eyes boring into her.

She touched the wall, then pressed against it as it yielded slightly to her touch and began to give way. She ripped desperately at the material. It was rotten, she noticed as she pulled and gouged pieces from the wall. Behind the structure stood an older, damper, darker wall. Alexia sank her hands into the loathsome surface, aware of the ends of the corridor still being drawn nearer by some entirely hidden mechanism or magic.

Finally she made a cavity big enough to step through into, and she almost threw herself into that chasm.

The cold darkness wrapped itself around her, and bore her away and down, into an unseen ocean. Alexia screamed, but her voice could make no sound in this closed but eternal hell. She could see nothing, but the icy touch of the liquid through which she travelled wrapped itself around her very being. It seeped through her clothes and the pores of her skin.

Dimly aware that she had arrived on a physical surface of some sort, Alexia gradually found that she could see once again. The familiar green-hued glow of the sterile sky faintly illuminated her surroundings. She lay upon a small island of jet rock, and a sea of dark water surrounded her. But the water began to recede even as she stared around, and she saw two other islands nearby. A figure lay on both, and although Alexia could not make out their details in the gloom, she knew who they were.

She called out their names, but her voice remained silent. Despite this, after a short while they both stirred. Wordlessly the three companions stared across the growing chasm left by the rapidly receding water, isolated and cast adrift from one another.

Soon the water had receded out of sight, leaving three impossibly tall columns of rock which formed the three islands on which the companions were stranded.

We can't stay here, Alexia thought suddenly. *We'll lose everything if we do. But what choice do we have?*

She knew the answer as soon as the question formed in her mind.

All we can do is fall, and trust.

She stood up and made her way over to the edge of the little island. The darkness, a step or misstep away, felt almost suffocating as she stood tremulously on the threshold of possible oblivion. She tore her eyes from the black emptiness that spread beneath her and looked to her companions. As if they sensed that she was trying to communicate with them, Ileana stood first, then Vornen a moment later. Alexia pointed to herself, then to both of them in turn, and then down. Vornen stared at her, then finally nodded. Ileana did likewise, and they both approached the edges of their islands, dark shapes against the faintly lit rocks, standing at the edge of what might be infinite darkness.

Now we can only hope, Alexia thought. *Hope that Aona saves us when we fall. She had faith in me, or else I would not be here. Now I need to have faith in her.*

She lifted her hand into the air as they looked to her, showing three fingers, then two, then one.

Then she stepped off the edge and into the abyss.

Alexia could not be certain how long she fell for. Finally the terror she felt ebbed away, replaced by visions of the life she had lived that flashed swiftly before her eyes. *Just as Phain once told me happened to people,* she thought for a moment, before that notion was also snatched away. Her childhood and adolescence loomed in her memories, a bright and sharp recollection of a time spent hidden away and forever trapped, unable to live the life that she had been meant to live. *It took the destruction of everything to set me on that path,* she thought. *The life I had, my family, eventually my city. I lost everything to reach this point.*

Not everything, came an immediate answering thought, as images of Phyqor and Yui swam before her. Sudden desperation filled her heart. *I can't lose them as well!*

But even those images faded as her consciousness darkened to nothing.

Alexia's eyes flickered open and she shut them again as brightness tore into them. The place in which she found herself was coloured entirely white. Ahead of her, that same illumination poured towards a doorway of utter darkness.

The Gate, she thought numbly.

Vornen and Ileana stirred nearby, and three of them stared wordlessly at the portal. Each of them felt its immense pull. It tore at every fibre of their being and gradually dragged them nearer to its core without any need for them to take a single step.

Alexia tried to speak to her companions, but she couldn't utter a word. With an effort she moved her head to look at them and was shocked to see that they were bathed completely in the indescribable brilliance from which this room had been made. She could see almost no detail whatsoever of their forms.

Am I also like that? she wondered, dumbfounded, and she reached her hands up to touch her face.

As if a single thought occurred to them in the same instant, the three reached out and their hands found one another. Alexia heard a voice whisper inside her head: *We are part of her, and she is part of us.*

As they stepped into the blackness of the Gate it surrounded them and then gradually dissipated, replaced by a profusion of colours that slowly changed into recognisable shapes and places. They walked through a vast sphere, and wherever they looked the surface of the sphere mapped out the lands and oceans of Aona. As the three of them stopped, Alexia stared around, transfixed. She recognised Harn, Aphenhast and then Alhar to the east. Where once cities had stood in Aphenhast, now dark smears spread upon the surface of the land. She wondered how many hundreds of thousands of people, perhaps millions, had perished in those places.

She looked towards Harn. To the north-west the land continued on for hundreds of leagues through the Wilderness, and to the south of that, the Western Ocean continued for possibly thousands of leagues before it eventually reached another land mass.

Then they saw something miraculous happen. Specks of light began to appear throughout Harn and Aphenhast, and a few in the empty realm of Alhar. *The light of Aona reaches the surface,* Alexia thought. It happened when we stepped through the Gate. *We made it possible for Aona to reach through her own heart and destroy her enemies. We've unleashed hope.*

Instinctively, Alexia reached out to hold her companions' hands, and as they formed their small circle, she managed to say one thing.

"Don't let go."

A moment later, everything vanished.

X – The Raging Earth

I

For days after the conquest of Luudhoq a low, exhausted silence hung over the city. Patrols carried out by *orkar,* northmen or what remained of Luudhoq's militia who had sworn allegiance to their conquerors, regularly found groups of citizens hiding wherever they could- often amidst the rubble and sagging walls of ruins, or in the warrens of alleyways that ran throughout the south and east, far from where the fighting had taken place. Some had even made it as far as the harbour in the vain hope of finding a ship from one of the South Ocean Island nations waiting, but the harbour had lain empty for many days, the sailors and merchants of the southern realms having listened intently to the rumours of coming war and abandoned all thought of trade. Other people had tried to flee the city, and a few had succeeded, although the new rulers of Luudhoq had moved swiftly to secure all the entrances and exits from the city.

Everywhere one looked, survivors huddled together. Many of them were refugees in their own city now that their homes had fallen or been left unsafe. Most had lost members of their families. Some- those who wandered blank-eyed and silent on their own- had lost everything, even their own sanity.

Garrok had observed all this and far worse during his walks through and around Luudhoq. He had seen many people turn to thievery, thinking that they would never have a better time to steal given the breakdown of law and order. He had seen quarrels break out between people or between families, sometimes over trivial matters, and quickly escalate to bloody fights that often ended in death. Numerous reports had come to him of beatings and rapes, and some of them, though he did not want to admit it to himself, involved some of his own men.

The ghost of Wistport, he had thought, recalling that in the aftermath of that violence and depravity he had wondered to himself if Wistport was itself the ghost of a far earlier battle where the *orkar* had arrived with largely noble intentions but had become partly lost in the red haze of battle and the opportunity to commit atrocities with the eyes of commanders looking elsewhere.

Show me a side in any war that committed no such unspeakable deeds, he thought sourly, looking out from the shelter of the command tent as rain continued to fall. But the words gave no comfort. Words never did. All he knew was that if the right situation presented itself, people of any race would seize whatever opportunity they could to commit those deeds they had always been afraid to contemplate when law and order had been present.

Images from the battle and its aftermath still played through his mind- scenes of those who had been crushed or maimed by the earthquake, those who had been forced into fighting to defend Luudhoq and subsequently cut down by the High Watchers or even the Seven. And then, although he had not seen most of them, there were the countless masses who had been caught up in the chaos in every part of southern Harn once the origins of the Watchers had been revealed.

All of this, Garrok thought, *and we're to blame for much of it. Oh, it made sense to sow that seed, but who could have known the extent to which it would cause mayhem?*

He wondered why, once the truth of their nature had been revealed, the Watchers of Luudhoq had not turned on the people of the city- why, indeed, they had not seized upon the revelation as swiftly and madly as their brethren outside the capital. Most of the Watchers within Luudhoq had simply disappeared. Not a single one had stood against them as far as he knew. Some bodies had been found, but not even a half of their number had been accounted for yet. He would have asked one of their own Watchers, but had seen none of them for days.

Garrok's thoughts drifted almost like the low misty cloud that drifted over and through the city landscape. Occasionally the murk would lift a little to reveal the broken buildings, insubstantial and blurred dark shapes against the lighter grey.

I thought that all this would be easier, he mused. *Not the battles themselves- they were every bit as difficult as I expected, and I know what to expect from warfare after all these years- but easier to deal with. Odd, really. I've left no one behind in Uythar. Not like Korrinn, who left a family behind in Ai-Haar. I'm my own man and I owe nothing to anyone. Many of my own people are surely envious of that position.*

Sudden anger overcame him. Southern Harn remained an ugly patchwork of chaos, and far more unpleasant challenges still awaited them all, not least of which would be ensuring that a force would be in place to defend the eastern border of Harn against the oncoming *marandaal* that had destroyed Aphenhast. *We won't have enough people to deal with all of them,* he reminded himself. *We can only do what we're able to do, in the full knowledge that it won't be enough.*

He saw Elluron walking through the thick mud of the camp, heading towards him. The half-*illeagh* carried himself wearily and looked older than he had only tennights ago. Garrok wondered idly to himself how old he really was.

We should convene a meeting today, he thought, and remembered that he hadn't seen Kelandra for days. "Where is Kelandra?" he asked as Elluron drew near.

"She left as we incarcerated Phaedra of the Seven," Elluron said. "I don't know where she went. I haven't seen her since. Nor have I seen Alturus."

Garrok shook his head in puzzlement. "Have they all disappeared? Every one of their kind? We will have need of Kelandra's expertise."

"No doubt she will return when she's done whatever she needs to do."

Garrok shrugged tiredly. "We'll see. In the meantime, the two of us need to decide our next step. I understand that Yui was entirely correct about the Gate in Luudhoq."

"She was," Elluron agreed. "To within fifty paces, apparently."

Garrok frowned, a sudden unrelated thought occurring to him. "What about the Luudhoqians themselves?"

"What about them?" Elluron blinked.

"There are hundreds of thousands of them. Some of those must have sorcerous abilities, even if they're weak. Not unlike how many of our own people were found to have a certain dormant capability in the Powers. It may be that we can link some of them as we did with the others."

The half-*illeagh* shook his head. "Many died when we did this before. Some groups were able to link, but the cost was terrible."

"We need them," Garrok said stubbornly.

Elluron sighed. "Perhaps we should see how many we can find. But we need to be more careful than before."

"Sooner rather than later," Garrok said pensively. "Send out that boy Jak again, with an armed escort. His ability to detect even tiny sparks of the Power has served us well before."

II

Jak woke slowly, his mind muddied by an unpleasant dream in which he had been trying to find Ileana in a maze of dark tunnels which gradually became narrower and lower the more he walked through them. His eyes opened to the harshness of dawn only for him to close them with a grimace and a grunt of discomfort. He rolled over on his side, wishing that the blankets afforded a little more warmth.

At Amethyst's request he had moved his and Ileana's scant belongings to the tent she had been sharing with Vornen. *So I can keep an eye on you,* she had explained, but Jak reckoned it was simply because there wasn't much sense in them staying apart and being even more miserable than they already were.

And because of the knife as well, he thought, and felt the heat of shame rise to his cheeks. Would he really have tried to kill himself? At the time he had thought so- the guilt and misery of a hundred deaths had been too much to bear- but now he wondered if he would have been too fearful, as he held the blade to his wrist or his throat. His father had believed that self-murderers languished in the Seven Hells forever after they died, and Jak had grown up believing the same thing.

In truth he was glad of Amethyst's company. He liked her, even if she could be ill-tempered and prickly at times.

He tried for the hundredth time to imagine where Ileana, Vornen and Alexia might be within the Green Road. Jak was an imaginative boy but even he struggled to understand what the Green Road might look like, and how the three of them could still be within Aona but not here in the world they all knew.

"I miss you," he whispered, wondering if by some curious, magical mechanism Ileana might somehow still be able to hear him, even if it was through a dream or just a thought entering her mind. *I've seen so many things I thought were impossible in the last few months,* he reminded himself. *Would that really be so incredible?*

"Are you feeling sorry for yourself again?"

He turned quickly and looked across the tent to see that Amethyst had sat up and dressed without him even noticing. "No," he said quickly, aggrieved that he had been heard and equally aggrieved that he hadn't caught a glimpse of Amethyst as she dressed- not that she would have allowed him to look at her while she did so.

"Good. Because she wouldn't want that." Amethyst strapped her belt and sword and pulled her boots on. "Get dressed and ready, Jak. We'll go for a walk."

"Why? We haven't had breakfast."

"I intend to find out what the plans of our esteemed leaders are, if I can," Amethyst said, glancing impatiently back at him.

A short while later they headed out through the camp and towards its centre. It was there that they saw Elluron, who called out to them. "I may have need of Jak," he said to Amethyst as they came to stand together. "We need to determine how many fit and healthy survivors within Luudhoq hold the Powers, even if they're weak." He glanced at Jak. "The same as you did before, although I hope we might find many more this time."

Jak's heart sank. "Is there no one else who can do this?" Amethyst asked.

"We've found no one who can sense such tiny amounts of the Powers."

"As you wish then, but I'll go with him."

Elluron smiled. "I wasn't planning to send him on his own, Amethyst. He'll have an armed escort. Probably northmen- they'll elicit respect but rather less fear amongst the people of the city than the *orkar*."

"Nevertheless, I'll go with him."

Elluron nodded. "So be it. Break your fast if you haven't already, and I'll arrange for Teryn to loan me two dozen of his men. We may need that many- I don't expect anyone who Jak finds to be at all happy about his discovery."

By noon the mist had lifted and a pallid sun hung in the cold sky. Jak and Amethyst, accompanied by a contingent of fighters from Darkbrook, were admitted through the remains of the north wall and into the city. The rubble from the earthquake had been cleared days ago, but remnants of the once-fortified area could be seen everywhere around.

Within Luudhoq's walls miserable scenes awaited them. Although most of the survivors had been moved to areas that were safer, some small groups still remained here and there. Amethyst and Jak saw groups of *orkar,* northmen or other factions patrolling the streets. They encountered little resistance but plenty of animosity. He knew from the things his father had told him when he was growing up that there was no love lost between the people of Luudhoq- and the south in general- and those folk north of the Unbuilt Wall. Now these people had lost their city, and perhaps their homes and even their families. With the Seven and the High Watchers no longer ruling over them and the Watchers either dead or roaming the south as outlaws or vanished altogether, they were without government for the moment.

Jak wondered briefly what had become of his father. Harqan had been dismissed by Inerdyr and sent back to Fhaarluy, and since then Jak had been so caught up in other events that he had thought about him only briefly. He felt a measure of shame and guilt about that, and resolved to go home to see his father once all of this was over. *If I survive,* he added darkly.

With a pang of unease he found himself reminded about how close their home in the forest was to the Border Wall.

"Keep your wits about you," Amethyst said, giving him a sidelong glance. She tapped her fingers restlessly on the pommel of her sword as she added for good measure, "You spend too much time daydreaming. Now is not the time to be doing that."

Jak scowled and threw her an aggrieved look.

"There," he said suddenly, and turned to the nearest of the northmen. "The man and woman just there by the corner." He gestured towards them quickly, and the two were quickly apprehended. They tried to struggle at first before they capitulated. "We haven't done anything," the man protested. Jak felt their frightened eyes upon him, and looked away.

Two of the northmen were assigned the task of taking them towards the encampment outside the city walls. They returned a short while later and they all continued on through the streets.

Jak found a total of forty people that afternoon who he felt reasonably sure had some residual talent in the Powers. As the day wore on he felt even worse about pointing them all out so they could be taken away, some of them with their families in tow. At least a dozen of them tried to run when the northmen went to apprehend them, and two somehow managed to evade everyone and disappear down back streets or alleyways.

I hope none of them die, he thought fervently. But he knew that some would.

III

The following day, the larger contingent of the force outside Luudhoq began their journey east towards the Border Wall. Most of the *orkar* ironmasters went with them, along with about half the northmen of Darkbrook and Uythar led by Teryn, and most of the Descendants, who tentatively began instructing and teaching the city folk who Jak had found.

Neither Kelandra nor any of the Watchers appeared.

Less than a tennight later they reached the vicinity of the Border Wall, and drew within sight of the defenders before stopping on the windswept moorland. The force spread out for leagues to the north and south, although both Garrok and Elluron admitted that it would be impossible to monitor every part of the wall in the south. Reports filtered back to them that *kin* far to the north had also massed on the frontier.

The day was bright but bitterly cold, and the wind swept from the east over the Border Wall. Lura stood halfway up the slope where the command tent had been erected, and watched the scenes to the immediate east. A number of High Watchers patrolled the battlements of the vast wall, their attention fixed solely on whatever might come from out of ruined Aphenhast. They had made no attempt to attack the force that had gathered just within Harn. Their orders had been simply to await the *marandaal* and defend Harn from them as and when the time came.

"They will be overrun," Iyoth said at her side. Lura jumped and cursed under her breath, causing him to laugh. "Do you enjoy creeping up on people?" she scowled.

"Enjoy? I wouldn't say that." He shrugged. "It did help though, given the kind of work I did." He glanced at the greatsword strapped to her side. "How do you find your Powers-enhanced blade?"

Lura glanced uncertainly at the pommel and touched it lightly with one hand. "It makes me faster and stronger than I ought to be, certainly at my age. If it can help to damage the *marandaal* then so be it. As to how I *find* this weapon... I find it unnatural, truth be told. Some obstinate part of me prefers to rely only on my innate strengths, less though they are these days."

"Hmm. I feel much the same way." Iyoth fell silent for a short while. "I don't think I ever want to lift a weapon in anger again, if I'm still alive when this is done," he said finally.

Lura stared speechlessly at him.

"Are you so shocked?" Iyoth sighed. "Well, I suppose you and everyone else would have a right to be. I'm simply tired of bloodshed, tired of death. It's perhaps a little late to come to such a conclusion, but there we are."

"If we survive..." Lura said suddenly, but he swiftly placed a finger to her lips. "Let's keep any plans for when they can be realised," he said quietly. "Agreed?"

Lura nodded. "As you wish."

But as she looked again towards the Border Wall, her thoughts were suddenly no longer of the oncoming enemy but of a distant, almost unimaginable future for which she had never dared to hope.

A dozen leagues to the north, the character of the Border Wall became noticeably different. The clean lines of the vast stone structure were rougher here, and in places some of the stonework had tumbled down. Vegetation snaked its way around the stones, slowly reclaiming the wall. Further north the state of the structure worsened further, but the witches who rode alongside the unguarded wall to inspect the area knew that the more ruinous it appeared the stronger the natural defences in the vicinity would be.

"It's started to rain," Anlerran observed, glancing up into the gloomy sky as a couple of fat raindrops streaked her forehead. The earlier brightness had disappeared as clouds massed from the north and east. "That's good. Maybe we can soften the earth the other side of the wall when the enemy comes for us. Whatever their strength, they still need to travel across the ground. They can't fly."

"And the wind is stronger," Lumi spoke up behind them. "Might that also help?"

"You're learning," Anlerran said with a faint smile. "Use whatever tools you have available, and it might make all the difference. Invoke the elements that best suit the situation."

Kian had been riding a little way ahead. She halted her horse and turned to look back at her companions. "They'll come soon," she said. "Sometime this morning. I can already sense them."

"Let's go back," Lumi begged. A contingent of ironmasters had travelled north with them along with Elluron, and Lumi had been chosen to go with them alongside Arin and Ryn.

Anlerran glanced at the girl. Although she hadn't said so explicitly, it was clear that she wanted to make sure that she was with Arin and Ryn when battle was joined with the starspawn. She smiled and nodded. "I think we've seen enough."

As the three of them made their way back, Anlerran found herself thinking of the *illeagh*-summoning device that her father had kept since their time deep within the Rhunin. *It's time at last* she thought, and said as much when they returned.

Everyone nearby watched pensively as Elluron took the cylindrical device from his robe, held it before him, and with a sudden movement broke it in two. Those who witnessed the act either shrank back as if expecting the *illeagh* to somehow materialise from the two pieces, or looked all around, perhaps thinking that they might swoop down from the clouds, or out of the earth.

The cold breeze blew; the clouds rolled past. In the distance, they heard faint shouts from defenders who had scaled the Border Wall and now saw the first of the *marandaal* in the distance.

The *illeagh* did not come.

IV

Lightning sizzled through the air, stabbing at the earth and driving great dark clods into the air. Cracks and deep holes appeared in the ground. A continuous dull roar echoed back and forth, unbearable in its monotony. The sky filled with low, heavy clouds, some of them almost black. It became impossible to tell if these conditions were the work or consequence of the *marandaal,* or their enemies, or Aona herself.

The Border Wall shook violently and cracks appeared in its structure for many leagues along its length. Great pounding noises could be heard, as if huge and heavy objects struck at the other side of the structure. In a matter of moments the vast stonework had collapsed.

Where the High Watchers still guarded the border in the south, they stood upon or near the remnants of the wall, in obedience to the last orders given to them by their human commanders whose bodies lay strewn everywhere near the rubble. If the High Watchers knew of the sorcerers in their midst then they did not act upon that knowledge. Their attention was focussed purely on the *marandaal*. A few even appeared to absorb and then channel the lightning, firing great streaks of it towards the brilliant shapes of the enemy.

The invisible protective area that the witches had created about themselves swayed, buckled and even opened up in a couple of areas before healing itself. The Powers surged in a torrent from each of them, combining and heading straight for the nearest of the *marandaal*.

Kian and Anlerran became one and the same as they allowed the eruption of forces within them to spill forth and wreak what havoc it could amongst their enemy. They directed this violent energy as best they could. The air where the *marandaal* continued their steady advance thickened, so that a sudden weight bore down on their shimmering forms, forcing them to stop.

They used the natural conditions of the battlefield to what advantage existed. The soft earth of early spring already lay heavy with moisture, and they directed more from elsewhere, turning the ground to thick, deep mud wherever the *marandaal* advanced. They directed violent forks of lightning from out of the low sky, to stab through their enemy, momentarily rendering them incapable of attacking anything nearby.

Explosions ripped apart whole areas of the Border Wall's remnants as if that structure, impregnable for so many centuries, was now nothing more than earth to be kicked aside.

Mayhem ensued. Hundreds of Hastians who had gathered in desperation on their side of the wall and who had survived the massacre as the *marandaal* approached, now scrambled through and over the rubble. Most of them died, caught up by further explosions or forces that simply cut them to shreds or pulled them apart. A few made it as far as the Harnian defenders and continued to run for their lives.

Lura gripped the pommel of her greatsword, in awe of the sorcery that flooded not only through the weapon but into her from the blade. It felt as if tiny creatures writhed through every part of her body.

She took an involuntary step forward, then another. Several more strides she took, each one longer and yet somehow faster than the last. *I'm at its mercy,* she thought, terrified. *The blade pulls me into battle, to destroy or be destroyed.*

Lura barely remembered the chaos into which she was pulled. As she walked faster and faster it seemed to her that the world slowed down. Close up, the *marandaal* appeared like a thousand miracles in one- ever changing their shapes and colours. The Powers poured forth from her blade as she attacked them, but Lura felt something else at the same time- a dark, malignant force that swept through her and the blade as one.

After a while she sensed Iyoth beside her, and even through the pain and terror of her enslavement, Lura smiled to herself.

V

Far to the north, higher *kin* gathered, in the foothills of the Daymorn mountains at the eastern edge of the vast forest of Mordenglen, and even further to the north where the high moorland swept down towards the great frozen swamps of Huurin. The *choragh* joined them, dark spectres that moved amongst the *kin* like ephemeral shadows, extolling their subjects to fight until their dying breath.

Meanwhile the bestial lower *kin* had already been sent forward, and surged across the landscape to engage with the starspawn. Some had surrounded and even brought down their enemy. Many others lay torn apart on the battlefield or had been obliterated so completely that nothing visible remained of them. Smoke drifted up towards the storm clouds, acrid tendrils or plumes that dissipated in the damp gloom. But more creatures of the Old Dark rushed to take their place, and a few of the *marandaal* were leapt upon and torn to oblivion by these frenzied creatures, the light of their existence slowly extinguished under a howling cacophony of dark and bloodied shapes.

Ferrin and his companions stood beyond the wall, facing the rolling grasslands to the east of Mordenglen. One of the *choragh* swept into view nearby like an utterly black, flickering flame, and Ferrin, Ithia and Leon immediately bowed low, their foreheads touching the ground. Jaana did likewise a moment later, gesturing frantically for Lyya to do the same. As Lyya also bowed down, pressing herself against the cold damp ground, she could sense the *choragh* drifting silently nearby, a dark ghost seeping through the rocks and the trees. She pleaded with herself not to scream.

The *choragh* passed them by with neither message nor instruction.

Ferrin was the first of the companions to pick himself up. He looked all around and stared in disbelief as colours and shapes filled the sky. They swarmed from out of the north and flew towards the oncoming *marandaal*. At first he had no idea what this dazzling swarm of movement might be, but as he watched he suddenly realised. Even then, he struggled to believe what his eyes saw.

Illeagh, he thought numbly. *They've returned.*

He continued to watch as the flashes of colour and insubstantial shapes rose higher into the sky, suddenly darting leagues away north or south, covering great distances in a moment. *What does this mean?* he wondered. *Why have they appeared only at this late hour?*

No matter that late hour, the *illeagh* were no less effective than their dark brethren and the swarms of *kin* that still battled the *marandaal*. When they attacked the enemy, the result was a devastating explosion of colour and a noise that Ferrin could not hope to describe, but which he thought for a moment might even be a scream of rage from the heart of Aona herself. The ground split apart in places, or great cavernous holes opened up to swallow the *marandaal* as the defenders surrounded them.

"The *illeagh*," he said simply to his astonished companions. "Ancient cousins of our Lords. They were thought gone from this world forever."

He began to walk towards the chaos, and the others followed.

Jaana felt the Powers wash over her like a dark wave as she strode towards the oncoming starspawn. Her body crackled with energy, and she looked up towards the seething clouds, directing the vast natural forces towards the shimmering beings that bore down upon them. Explosions cut through the air. Lightning stabbed the ground. An all-consuming rumble came both from the sky and the earth as the fabric of the world was being torn apart. Jaana felt nothing but the well of hate from which she drew her strength, and which the Powers fed upon. She was vaguely aware that some of her companions had fallen, and even as she directed her sorcery towards the enemy she felt a pang of fear- not for herself but for Lyya. The *luyan* woman was still unused to her *kin* abilities. Where was she?

Jaana looked to one side for a moment. Then a sudden flare of brilliance cut through her vision and she was picked up and hurled through the air. The last thing she saw before her consciousness faded was the darkening sky cut through with colour and violence, and the last thing she heard was the sound of her bones breaking as she hit the ground.

A finger pressed softly against her lips. "Don't try to talk. There's nothing more to say."

I know that voice, was Jaana's first thought. *I must be dreaming.*

Her eyes flickered open, wide and bright as a sudden wave of agony shot through her. She could feel the blood pulse slowly out of her body, a ghastly warmth between the shaking fingers of her left hand. Nothing could staunch the flow. She had landed on something sharp and it had torn straight through her body.

"Am I... will I..." Her voice shook so much that she could not utter any more words, but she already knew the answer.

She opened her eyes again, and saw her mother looking down at her.

"There can never be rebirth without death, nor hope without rebirth." Her mother smiled and stroked a strand of hair away from Jaana's face. "Do you remember the first time I said that?"

The memory came to her eventually- a faint recollection from when she was five years old, and tearfully mourning the death of their dog.

"Yes," she whispered.

It could have all been different, she wanted to say. *I can't remember how I became who I now am. I lost my way, Mother. I spent my whole life losing my way. I wasn't strong enough to be who you wanted me to be.*

Then another instant of crushing pain caused her vision to fade a little more. Yet still she could see her mother's face. Desperately she tried to reach out, in the manner of an infant needing to be held.

The last thing Jaana felt before the world faded away was her mother gently picking her up. *It's time to let go,* a voice from somewhere told her. *It's time to let go and be at peace.*

Lyya watched numbly as Jaana's arm fell back and her head moved to one side. She half-ran, half-stumbled to her side, but needed only one look to know that she was beyond saving.

Lyya stared at the look of permanent wonder in Jaana's eyes. *That's how she used to look,* she thought. *Before the world and its desperate cruelty ate into her very being.*

She kissed her upon the lips, feeling the last of her lover's warmth escape into the wintry air. Her tears fell upon Jaana's cheeks, and when she finally raised her head, convulsing with grief, it looked as if they had both wept.

The battle had become a dull roar in the distance, as if the sounds of rampant chaos had faded out of respect for her silent farewell. Lyya stood up. *Our love remained,* she told herself fiercely. *No matter what we became, no matter what she made me become, and no matter the eventual result of this bloodshed- it persisted in our hearts. And for what?*

An incandescent rage began to seethe within her. The howls and shrieks of dying *kin* filled her ears, but Lyya paid no mind to the baying of the hordes. She walked towards the east where the glow of a dozen *marandaal* rose into the dusk, and as she neared the Great Enemy the roar of the Old Powers rushed through every fibre of her being, an unstoppable river of dark fury.

On she strode, until finally she broke into a run, heedless of the crackling forces tearing through the sky and cutting deep troughs and channels in the ground. Energy poured from her as she flung herself into the hateful brilliance of her foes and fought with every ounce of rage she could bring to bear.

Lyya did not know how many she weakened, perhaps even destroyed, before the light consumed her.

VI

Far to the south, a light began to leak from out of the earth itself in dozens of different places. It became stronger until no one could look directly at it. A great rumbling sound, louder and deeper than all the other sounds combined, emanated from out of the earth to accompany the brilliance that emerged from the ground and poured towards the *marandaal,* tearing through them all.

When finally everything lay still and the shaking of the earth had ceased, no *marandaal* remained, and in the north the *choragh* and the *illeagh* alike had also vanished.

Not all the Gates that opened across the land were reached in time. Thousands died as *marandaal* stepped from out of those portals. But as the Gate within the Green Road closed forever, everywhere in the land great chasms opened up to allow freedom for Aona's light. In Anvar, those *marandaal* that had emerged from the Gate were set upon by *kin* and their masters that had gathered nearby, but the *marandaal* would nevertheless have destroyed them had Aona's light not emerged from deep within the earth.

Those few *kin* that survived were rendered powerless soon afterwards, the great sorcery of their masters slowly dissipating, and many became little more than empty shells. A vast, deep silence fell over the land.

Days later, at the encampment north of Luudhoq, Amethyst listened to the scarcely believable reports of what had happened. *They did it,* she thought, almost overwhelmed by pride and fear. *Whatever happened afterwards, the three of them somehow destroyed the Gate and saved us all. I don't know how, but I'm certain of it.*

She did not dare hope, but two days after that, she and Jak saw two figures approach with the onset of dusk, and even before they could be made out in the gloom Amethyst knew who they were. Such was her joy that for days afterwards she

317

almost failed to notice the continually haunted look in their eyes, the impression that they held some terrible secret or knowledge that could never be explained or told.

In time that almost otherworldly chill faded, and over the tennights and months that followed, neither Amethyst nor Jak thought anything more of it. Neither did Phyqor and Yui speak to Alexia of the subtle, indescribable change that she had undergone. The look of exhausted relief in her eyes on the day she returned to them had been tempered with grim determination, as if the miraculous completion of her quest had somehow brought about another. They waited as patiently as they could for her to speak about what she had done and seen. But she would not, or perhaps couldn't, even when Yui eventually pleaded with her to tell her story.

"One day," Alexia said finally, many days later. "But be careful what you wish for."

XI – To Sleep At Last

I

After days, tennights or perhaps an eternity in the sterile peace of the Endless Shore, spent looking out across the void-black sea or sleeping, Ilumor woke to find that he had been returned to the world of the living.

He could not bring himself to fully believe in his environment at first. He sat up and observed the cool thickness of the trees around him. He breathed in the sharp, pine-scented air. He listened to the light early spring breeze rustle through the grass.

Ilumor managed to stagger to his feet. His legs almost gave way but an unseen hand held him upright.

"Let me die," he whispered. Then he repeated the words over and over in a barely audible jumble. The dead weight of his head would not raise itself, but his eyes tried to shut out the light that poured forth from more places within the woodland than he could hope to count.

One task remains before you sleep, Ilumor.

He wept with exhaustion. Tears fell through his half-closed eyes, but he could find nothing to say. He could not reason with her. He could not argue. His only choices were to obey or to summon some token, futile resistance, be punished and tortured and then obey.

In the city of Luudhoq, there stands a structure known to the people there as Phaedra's Tower. You will go there and undo the weave that holds the prisoner within that tower. It has been fashioned with the Powers. Complex though that structure is, you will be able to open it.

Then you will sleep.

"How can I do this?" Ilumor managed to ask, but no reply came, and when he opened his eyes the day had already passed. The forest lay dark before him, and the boughs sighed in the wind.

He walked for many leagues, south and south-west towards the city. A tired and sombre mood pervaded every settlement through which he travelled. The struggle against the *marandaal* had been won, in the sense that they had been vanquished and the Gates destroyed. But hundreds of thousands had died, and a number only slightly greater than the dead grieved for those who had not lived to witness the days after the victory.

Ilumor sat in gloomy taverns or guest-houses, barely noticed by anyone around him. He watched and listened. He heard suspicions raised about those people who had been discovered to possess talents in the Powers, suspicions that over the following days he heard less of, as it became evident that those same abilities had waned since the destruction of the *marandaal.* In most cases they had faded to nothing.

She used them, he realised. *Everyone had a purpose and a price. Everyone was a smaller or greater cog in a vast machine.* But he swiftly pushed that thought to one side, still fearful of the familiar agony that could strike without warning at any time.

Ilumor found himself idly listening to the rumours being voiced with regards the new ruling Council. Apparently the members of that Council- and no one seemed to be quite sure how many of those there were- squabbled and fought one another for supremacy. Again, that did not surprise the once-lord of Mirkwall. He remembered it had happened many centuries ago, in the area that was now called Aphenhast. He even held a vague memory of a struggle for power in the long-abandoned desert realm of Alhar. *They built great castles there, and temples that scraped the sky itself,* he thought, the faint recollection brushing through his mind as he sat and listened to rumour and counter-rumour.

When he finally reached the northern gates of Luudhoq, dusk had fallen. He observed the still early stages of rebuilding, and stood for a while outside the walls, listening to the curious sounds of combined celebration and grief that came occasionally across the breeze from some distant place. He felt certain that if he stood still for long enough then he might eavesdrop on every voiced emotion throughout the land and beyond.

Those labourers assigned the task of repairing the damage done during the struggle for the citadel and the earthquake- which included *crommar* brickworkers, he noted with surprise- were about to finish their day's work. The guards at the temporary gate looked Ilumor over but had nothing to say as he passed through. He wondered if everyone was allowed to pass freely in and out of the city nowadays. Did the new rulers of Luudhoq think that now the *marandaal* had been vanquished they had no more enemies to fear? Or had he simply been gifted with the ability to blend in so much that he barely existed at all- a man of no consequence who was noticed by the people no more than they would notice their own shadows?

Ilumor made his way along the city streets. He had no need to ask directions to Phaedra's Tower. Now that he was inside the city, he felt the hum and pulse of the vastly intricate sorcery that had been used to create this unique prison. Soon he caught sight of the tower's sharp spire reaching into the darkening sky, taller than every building nearby- no matter that it held only a single prisoner.

If this prison does indeed hold the one known as Phaedra of the Seven, he thought, *then why does Aona will me to release her? How can that serve the interests of the world?*

He cared nothing for the fate of the world and its people, however. His attention was focussed only on the task assigned to him, and the promise of a final sleep.

He saw no one near the tower. Perhaps the people of Luudhoq feared its contents, or perhaps luck remained resolutely on his side and would until the task was done. Ilumor walked the final few steps up to the structure, now certain that no one would disturb or even witness what he was about to do.

His hands pressed against the stone and he closed his eyes. Immediately the intricate, complex beauty of the tower's protective sorcery spread out before him like a hierarchy of infinitely strong, interwoven webs. But after a while he realised that although he could not destroy it, he *could* move the components aside without needing to change their structure in any way, effectively bending them. These manoeuvres allowed him a way to reach into the wall of the tower and slowly remove blocks from it. As each brick was removed and set to one side, the position of the remaining ones in the wall remained unchanged.

Soon he saw before him the astonished visage of the prisoner.

"You are Phaedra of the Seven," he murmured.

Phaedra took a gulp of cold air blown in from the dark courtyard beyond, and peered at her rescuer's oddly bright eyes. She couldn't even tell what colour they were, yet she found herself drawn to the strange light that flickered somewhere behind them. Something about that luminescence spoke of destination, and peace. *There's my Eden,* she thought suddenly. *There's my paradise world. Not an undiscovered planet hanging in the void, but an inner place.*

"Have you come to rescue me or put an end to me?" she asked. "It must be one or the other."

"She told me to take you with me. Then it will end for us."

Phaedra frowned in puzzlement, but a moment later she suddenly understood *everything,* and the knowledge rendered her speechless. In that instant she knew not only who and what he meant but also why he had come to take her from this prison. Finally, after all these uncounted decades and centuries, after a myriad hateful sunrises and sunsets, and being woken by the soundtrack of her own misery each day, she had been granted the peace she craved. No matter that she hadn't deserved it.

"Thank you," she whispered. Tears rolled down her cheeks. She held the stranger close, and as she pressed her head to his chest she heard a raging tumult like a vast waterfall, and felt the heat of the unexplainable light within him. *"Thank you!"* She spoke not only to him but also to the great force that had compelled him to release her.

"Sometimes she is cruel," he told her, no longer fearful of a violent response. "Powers know she has made me suffer. But there's a reason behind it all, no matter which part of the plan we belong to."

"Why could we not know such truth when we lived?" Phaedra murmured.

"What punishment would that be for the likes of us," he rejoined, "to live through hell and be comforted by the knowledge that our hell is not eternal?"

Ilumor rebuilt the portion of the tower's wall that he had taken apart. Phaedra watched in fascination as the blocks were put back in place and he passed his hands over them to seal the structure in such a way that it appeared untouched.

"How will you spirit me away from here?" She looked quickly around, half-expecting her jailers to materialise out of the cool evening air.

He didn't reply, but his hands linked with hers and their fingers entwined. For a moment Phaedra found herself reminded of a time in her childhood, so long ago that it was barely the ghost of a memory- a simple time when a simple friendship had meant everything in her world. *I don't even recall his name,* was her last thought before the cityscape around her slowly melted away.

She looked up at the glittering night sky. *Are the stars getting closer?* Phaedra thought. Dreamily she looked down at herself. Somehow she could still feel her companion's hand holding her own, and yet she no longer saw or even sensed her own body as they drifted through the space between realms.

II

For a long while after the *marandaal* and the Gates vanished from the world, those who had survived to see victory felt only a curious, tired emptiness- a relief tempered by sorrow. No celebrations were held. Too many people had died and the horrors remained fresh in everyone's minds. Almost all those who had fought and survived had lost close friends or family members. Some had lost everyone.

In time, people made their way back either to the towns and villages from which they had come, or in some cases, to Luudhoq. Many held out tentative hope for a new life of some kind, although they wondered to themselves what would replace the rule of the Seven in the south and if the Free Territories would retain their Wardens as upholders of law and order.

The alliance that had originally been created by Ruhal Dalmorn- a man who would in time be consigned to the footnotes of history- drifted naturally apart, its purpose complete.

The losses suffered by the *orkar* were great, and Garrok made a point of counting and noting each one. He gave the sombre details of each man and woman to Korrinn for writing into a book of remembrance- something that Korrinn could not recall any *orkar* lord ever authorising before. The survivors expressed surprise and even some misgivings about the decision. It was not their way, some would say in private. Were they not a race of warriors? Was death not simply a part of life, the inevitable end of every path?

With the grim task complete or at least up to date, Garrok became withdrawn and elusive as the remnants of the *orkar* force made their way back towards the middle southlands of Harn. Korrinn recognised the mood, or thought

324

he did, and in any case wisely said as little possible to his lord, allowing him however much time he needed to reflect on the death and carnage that had been wreaked upon their people.

Garrok refused to attend the first meeting of the new Council of All Harn which had been set up, and so Korrinn attended by himself as the sole representative of their people. He observed that tensions already grew between the various factions who held some claim to power in the Council- the people of Darkbrook, Targmal and lower Uythar who had given much, the Wardens of the middle north who had suddenly found a voice following Inerdyr's demise, the *luyan* and also the few *du-luyan* who still lived, and men and women who claimed to represent the people of Luudhoq, or Waylorn, or a number of other vanquished southern cities. Lords and ladies, landowners, members of one forgotten ruling council or another. Anyone with ambition and ruthlessness who still possessed the money to finance it.

Korrinn listened to them quarrel over details of government and territory, grimacing as pain from wounds incurred in the battle for Luudhoq occasionally flared up. The jostling for position in this poorly conceived hierarchy mattered little to him. Soon his people would return to Uythar and Ai-Haar and there they would maintain their own nation as they always had. He left at the end of the meeting without saying anything and perhaps without being noticed.

Three days later, as preparations to leave their temporary camp and head north were well underway, Korrinn went to Garrok's tent early in the morning to deliver a message about a summons to a second meeting of the Council, knowing that he would once again be sent as representative.

When he was permitted by the sentries outside to pass inside, Korrinn ducked under the folds of the tent and peered through the gloom.

The single lit lantern near the back gave only a poor light, but it was more than enough for Korrinn to see, once he walked closer, that the lord of the *orkar* had slit his own throat.

Korrinn crouched down by Garrok's body for a long while, even after he had shouted to the guardsmen to bring healers- as if healers could perform miracles. He could scarcely believe the amount of blood that had been spilled. It had soaked much of the man's garments and the mattress beneath. It had stained the grass nearby. The air in the tent hung heavy with the bitter odour.

We all are shaped differently by the ravages of war, he thought a little later, as he stood back to watch the healers sit and try to coax back the life that had long since fled. *Was he plagued by nightmares that made him relive all his battles? Or had he simply nothing more to live for, his task fulfilled? I know he had no surviving family, no lover, no children. Is it easier for those who leave behind no one, to slip away into the final darkness?*

Korrinn walked out into the glare of the warm spring morning. He thought, as he did every single day, of his wife and daughter who he had left in Ai-Haar. Later that day, after Garrok had been cremated and a commemoration made, the *orkar* readied themselves for the long journey north. Korrinn saw that the nervous young messenger from the Council of All Harn had still not left-presumably because he had not been given orders one way or the other. "Go tell your masters that the monsters are leaving," he said. "Be gone."

Korrinn watched as the messenger rode away. "Time we left," he murmured to no one in particular.

III

The season turned and the days grew longer. For tennights the chill winter winds had been replaced by warmer spring breezes from out of the south and south-west. Flowers bloomed and crops began to grow.

Communities gradually rebuilt and repaired themselves. The process proved to be long and painful. The Unbuilt Wall was no longer spoken of, the administrative line removed from the plans and policies of those who governed. The boundaries between north and south became blurred. No Watchers remained to guard the line now. It was assumed that they had all disappeared, gone to their deaths in some hidden place.

As the Descendants of the First and the *kin* had known before anyone else, the *choragh* and the *illeagh* were no more. The great struggle against the *marandaal* had extinguished them, and soon after their extinction those *kin* who still survived, whose use of the Powers had derived from their masters the *choragh*, also faded from existence. Some merely lay down and died; others became maddened by a kind of overwhelming grief as their powers waned and eventually expired. Those who had retained much of their outward humanity became pariahs and outcasts, reviled in every corner of the land through which they hopelessly stumbled.

All that was magical, fearsome and inexplicable had started to fade from the world.

During the early days of this gradual return to the natural order of things, three tennights after the vanquishing of the *marandaal* a gathering was held in a great hall within the former Fortress of the Seven in Luudhoq, partly to herald in the governing council which had finally been agreed amongst the races and communities of both north and south, and partly for the leaders of Aona's defence to quietly commemorate the many who had fallen in the pursuit of that victory.

Nia watched the ceremony and speeches by the various leaders and representatives from a corner of the hall. She allowed her gaze to drift amongst those who had been invited, and she reflected on each of them as she did so. *I know something about most of these people,* she thought, *but none of them truly know me, nor would they care to. Still, I've been more useful to their cause than anyone would ever have expected.*

Kian and Iyoth stood near the front of the gathering, Anlerran and Lura to either side of them. Anlerran and Kian were close friends, of course, and Nia was too observant and too good a judge of character to fail to notice a closeness between Iyoth and Lura as well. *Good luck to Lura,* she thought absently. *I think I understand her as much as anyone does, although I've barely exchanged more than a few words with the woman.*

Nia smiled to herself at that curious sentiment. Lura didn't need her good wishes, and neither did anyone else.

She looked to Phyqor, Alexia and Yui. *The child fought her inner darkness- and she may even have defeated it. I have tried to fight mine, but maybe I should simply embrace it. Does it matter to the wider world?*

Nia shook her head. To ask herself such questions was pointless.

She continued to look around the hall, and soon located Vornen, Amethyst and Ileana. *Another family,* she thought morosely. *They're everywhere if only you look for them.*

That immediately made her think of Arin and the two children, Lumi and Ryn. *Stop it,* she told herself sharply. She didn't know what had happened to the three of them. She had caught sight of them briefly a couple of days ago, but they might no longer be anywhere in the city for all she knew.

Nia had learned the tentative plans that most of her former companions had. Kian intended to eventually head east into the remains of Aphenhast and reclaim Mirkwall, and as far as Nia was aware Iyoth and Lura had decided to go with her. Nia couldn't work out quite why Kian wanted to be the ruling lady of such a place- by all accounts a desolate swampland forever surrounded by a magic mist that never cleared. The *kin* had claimed it, but Kian- along with the other Descendants of the First- was confident that the *kin* were no more, or had at least started to fade from the world.

Phyqor and Alexia had abandoned their plan to return to Darkenhelm. The city had been all but razed to the ground. So little of it remained that the few survivors of the invasion by the *marandaal* had apparently drifted away to other places, leaving behind a smouldering ghost and bodies rotting slowly in the spring warmth. Nia had heard that the three of them hoped to live in Luudhoq. *I planned to leave anyway, but now I'll make certain I go elsewhere,* she thought. *Their hatred- and especially Yui's - won't die any time soon. Why should it? I would feel the same, if I were her.*

Nia smiled grimly as she looked around at everyone gathered and contemplated their sheer number of plans and hopes. One thing was certain in life, she knew. Matters never, *ever*, turned out how people wanted them to.

Her weariness at life in general and her discomfort at the situation soon became too much to bear. She preferred to forget rather than commemorate.

Nia placed her cup of wine down on the nearest table she could find and quietly slipped out of the hall through one of the exits where less people were gathered.

She was about to turn right to head towards the nearest north-facing exit when a movement to her left caught her eye and she spun swiftly round to see Kelandra step from the shadows near the wall.

"Kelandra," she murmured. "I had wondered where you'd got to." *Will she kill me?* Nia wondered. *The code of the Watchers has disintegrated. Surely she no longer considers herself bound by it. She may well be the last of her kind. Is this the moment of her revenge?*

The Watcher looked steadily at her. Nia silently marvelled at how *human* Kelandra's eyes appeared, no matter her inner workings.

"I drowned in a nightmare at first." Kelandra's voice was soft and reflective. "I knew the truth but at the same time I refused to believe it. Then the pieces of my past came back to me- without warning, and savagely for the most part."

Nia did not dare to say anything.

"I found the remains of the house where I lived with my son, so many, many decades ago. I recognised the place. I found a few of his bones. I now even remember the day they came and took me away and killed him. It plays over and again in my head each day."

"I wish I'd never discovered the truth," Nia said disconsolately.

"The truth will eventually give me peace. Besides, I helped you find the things you did- after all, I had you sent down into the sanctum."

"Then let's share the blame, if you like." Nia shifted uncomfortably. "What will you do now?"

"I will disappear." Kelandra regarded her thoughtfully. "I hope *you* find peace, Nia- one way or another."

"Likewise, Kelandra."

"It's interesting how some facets of being a Watcher linger on. I still cannot cry more than a single tear, any more than I can sleep." The Watcher smiled faintly, turned and walked away. Nia watched her for a short while and then continued on her way.

I'll be far away from all this by nightfall, she thought, *and perhaps further still by the time anyone realises I've gone.*

But her heart sank when, as she reached the archway that led out into the sunlit courtyard, a voice called out to her: "Nia!"

Nia closed her eyes tightly for a moment. *Powers give me strength,* she thought. *I wanted only to be quietly away from here, without any awkward farewells.*

Eventually she turned to see Anlerran walking towards her. The girl had about her that look of heartfelt compassion that Nia still found humiliating for reasons she couldn't fully understand. *She'll be one of the well-loved leaders of the land if she chooses to be,* she thought. *The people will spin folk tales about them all and send those heroic stories echoing down the decades until the myth bears little resemblance to the reality that was.*

"Had you hoped to ride out of the city without so much as a farewell?" Anlerran asked.

"I detest farewells even more than greetings," Nia admitted. "It's easier to leave without a word, although I suppose I shan't be doing that now that you've decided to see me off."

"You don't have to leave," Anlerran persisted. "You're one of us."

"Oh, I do." Nia shook her head. "I never wanted to set foot in Luudhoq again. I attended this gathering only out of morbid curiosity. This place is a hive of bad memories for me, besides which I have no one here. What reason then do I have for staying? I can be alone wherever I wish. And I am most certainly *not* one of you." She took a deep breath. "I hate the whining sound of my own voice. I just can't bear to be in Luudhoq any longer, Anlerran. There's the simple truth. I don't want to be sworn in to your ruling council or whatever form of government you intend to set up- if you even had me in mind for a position."

"We had as a matter of fact. You know this city and its people. Don't you wish to help rule and re-shape Luudhoq?"

"After all I've done? Hardly. I've already been responsible for too many things in this city. I've long lost count of the deeds I've done in the name of the Watchers."

"Where will you go?"

"I have no idea. Does it matter? I may find myself a map and a stone, and shut my eyes as I cast the stone over the map."

"That sounds like madness," Anlerran commented with a smile.

"It sounds like freedom to me." Nia paused and then added uncomfortably, "Good luck to you, Anlerran."

"Thank you. But is there nothing I can do to persuade you to stay?"

"Nothing. Farewell."

"Fare you well also," Anlerran said sadly.

Nia turned and walked out into the yard. Soon she had walked beyond the fortress gates and headed down the road towards the nearest stables, where she used some of her silver- her share from the treasure troves of the Seven- to purchase a horse and tackle. She headed slowly through the streets of Luudhoq, and as she rode Nia reflected on how swiftly life had started to return to normal- shopkeepers, traders and everyone with a job to do or a service to provide seemed to be out and about. Here and there, the broken walls and rubble of fallen buildings could still be seen, but everywhere she looked new buildings were being constructed. *Maybe it should all be remade,* she thought.

Eventually she reached the northern edge of the city, and a short while later the gates of Luudhoq had closed behind her forever.

When she happened to look back on Luudhoq after a while, Nia saw two other riders in the distance heading along the same road out of the city. She waited a while longer, wondering with irritation if someone had been sent to again plead with her to remain in Luudhoq. *I won't go back,* she thought fiercely, and considered riding ahead or in a different direction, as swiftly as possible. But she waited.

As the newcomers drew closer she realised with shock who they were. In fact there were three of them. One of the riders was Arin and the other, on a smaller horse, was Lumi. The *luyan* boy Ryn sat in the saddle behind Arin. As they drew to a halt nearby, he grinned at her and then said to Arin, "I *said* it was her and you had to go now before she disappeared."

"Eyes of a hawk," Arin said, and nodded approvingly. "Well done, Ryn."

"I'm not going back to Luudhoq," Nia said. She noted with alarm that her voice trembled.

"Neither are we," he remarked.

"Then where are you headed?"

"Into the west," Lumi said. "Maybe Telith, if it isn't completely destroyed. Maybe somewhere further."

"Anlerran told us that you'd left," Arin admitted, "and then Ryn spotted you from afar. So we left rather sooner than we had planned, although we had little to stay for." He shocked her with the words he uttered next: "How lonely do you wish to be, Nia?"

Nia could think of nothing to say. She could barely think at all.

"There's nothing for us in Luudhoq either," Arin continued. "We came after you for a reason. I think you know what that reason is."

"I might. I might not." She could not stop her voice from shaking.

"I thought to convince you to stay, when you left me the first time," he continued softly. "I would have protected you from your enemies. I would have done anything to keep you safe. I desperately wanted you to stay, Nia."

She looked away, tears in her eyes.

"After we parted company for the second time, I knew something for certain," he continued. "I was equally certain that *you* knew it also, but of course you would never admit it."

"Please," Nia begged him, "don't say it."

"Are you so frightened of a simple truth after everything you've been through?" He rode right up to her. "Reject me now," he said, "and we'll ride away. You won't see me again."

Having uttered that warning he leaned forward and kissed her on the lips, long and lingering. Nia almost swooned in her saddle. Perhaps she would have done had his arm not encircled her.

"You're a fool, Arin." She looked into his eyes, wiping tears from her cheeks even as more fell.

"A happy fool," he retorted. "Shall we travel together?"

"I suppose we'll have to see how we get on," Nia said.

As they rode away north-west, she stole a look at Arin and then at the children- who grinned back at her- more times than she could count. *Do I now have a family?* she wondered, barely able to believe she had dared ask herself the question.

Eventually she allowed herself a smile of her own. It was born of something that Nia felt quite unused to- hope for the future.

TWENTY-FIVE YEARS LATER

I

Soft rain fell and glistened on the cobbled streets as the city folk hurried through the early morning gloom, wrapped up in their cloaks or robes as they headed towards their places of employment, or engaged in errands. For them, this would likely be a day structured like any other, a snapshot of time that involved rising with the first light, work, eating, meeting with employers or friends or both, returning to families and eventually to sleep- a short cycle amongst other, greater ones. A day that for most would soon be lost amidst the ensuing months and years as time ground away at the fleeting significance of life.

Alexia turned from the window. A single thought occupied her mind. *I have to begin it today,* she decided. *I don't even know how I'll begin, but I can't put it off any longer. My memory of the things I foresaw remains fresh in my mind still, after all these years- but for how much longer? I must write about everything I witnessed while I still can. There can be no real future without a history, even if centuries pass before the truth of what happened in the aftermath of our victory is revealed. The history I write, the story of the great war against the* choragh *and the* marandaal *and of what happened in the years afterwards, will surely be destroyed if it's found. It would without doubt be a forbidden text.*

But it would be protected, she reminded herself, and therein lay the hope. Yui had said she could weave sorcery into it to make the book indestructible, and Alexia had no reason to disbelieve her. After all, Yui was one of the very few people in the known world who still had use of the Powers- and yet she had to keep them a secret from everyone except Alexia and her father. Several times over the years she had been interrogated, asked again and again if she still

335

harboured any such talent, however small it might be. The authorities had tested her with methods both blunt and subtle, but somehow she had fooled them all- the greatest powers in the land.

Phyqor appeared in the doorway and crossed the room. As they embraced, Alexia smiled up at him and silently reminded herself how lucky she was. She had a husband who in her estimation had grown only more handsome with age, and Yui had blossomed into a beautiful and loving young woman who was both a true friend and a daughter to Alexia. It was astonishing given her ordeals as a child.

Perhaps Phyqor saw something of her pensive thoughts in her expression. He asked her, "Will you begin it today?" He had voiced the same question every day for the last tennight.

She nodded. "I've put it off for long enough. Once Yui has weaved the protective spell, it will be ready for me to begin. The truth must never be destroyed, Phyqor, no matter what. Truth is power, and perhaps one day it will be our salvation- or that of distant future generations. I will write a history, but much of it will be of events that haven't yet happened and which the three of us will never live to see."

"The Watchers knew many truths that were never shared with the people. Isn't that what you said once?"

"The Seven imparted something of their knowledge when creating them. An insight into the Existence itself. But all the Watchers are long gone. Some say that they were destroyed by..." But she stopped as he placed a finger to her lips. "Don't name them," he whispered. "The rumours may be true. Never name them. It's said that they will always know if their names are spoken."

A short while later, Yui arrived. She asked the same question as her father and received the same answer. "What will you call it?" she asked.

Alexia thought for a moment. "The True History of Aona. I can't call it anything else."

Phyqor turned to his daughter. "Are you certain that your use of the Powers can't be detected? You know the penalty- even for us."

"I'm absolutely certain, father. You know I would not risk this otherwise." She squeezed his hand in reassurance and then turned to Alexia. "Is the book ready?"

Alexia brought forth the book from one of the shelves across the room. Heavy and thick, it consisted of a thousand blank pages. Alexia laid it on the table and the three of them contemplated it in silence for a short while, lost in the enormity of this moment. Finally Yui placed both her hands on the volume and closed her eyes. Moments passed, and nothing appeared to happen. Phyqor and Alexia exchanged quizzical glances. Yui did not move.

Eventually a faint glow appeared around all the edges of the book at the same time. Alexia glimpsed lines and symbols that appeared on its surface momentarily. They flashed into existence and were then gone.

Finally Yui opened her eyes, straightened and removed her hands from the book with a sigh. "It's done," she said quietly. "Nothing can now destroy this book. The web of Powers is as complex as it can possibly be. Even I would find it impossible to work out how to undo the knot, or even find it."

Alexia reached out cautiously to touch the book. "But I can write as much as I need into it?"

Yui nodded. "Of course."

They gazed at the book for a long while, and each of them wondered what might happen to it over the long centuries. How would the truth eventually be used?

II

Two months passed. Alexia wrwote almost constantly, and paused in her efforts only to sleep, bathe and eat, although she spent as little time as possible away from her work.

Phyqor and Yui observed that she became withdrawn and almost obsessive about her task during this time, such that they feared for her health. She lost considerable weight. Her hair turned from darkly luxuriant to thin and greying. She held about her a look so haunted that both her husband and his daughter even wondered if it might be better to intervene and stop her.

But they could not. Both knew the importance of Alexia's work, although they feared that the task- and the nightmares that her newly-sharpened memories gave her- would prove her undoing before that work was done.

She suffered periods of such self-doubt and suspicion that she even tried to destroy the book herself. It encountered the flames of the hearth, boiling water, the edges of daggers and knives, but Yui's words proved to be true. Nothing that Alexia tried in her less lucid moments could destroy the book, nor could it disrupt or shroud the words that had been written thus far. But one curious effect that everyone noticed was that the words that Alexia had written became oddly blurred and impossible to read. "They are not meant to be read by anyone alive today, or possibly a century or more from now," she told them. But Yui, for all her knowledge of the Powers, could not explain how those words, written by Alexia's hand, had worked about themselves an additional web of protection that had nothing to do with her own.

Finally the book was completed, and Alexia wept for hours from sheer relief.

"I need to ask something else of one of you," she told them the next day. "The book may be indestructible, but the authorities may yet discover it, and that would be the end of us three. It must be taken somewhere as safe as can be. I think you will dislike the location I've chosen and one of the people who should be its guardians. One of you must go to Rannik…"

Yui somehow knew who she meant immediately, and shook her head. "She cannot be trusted, Alexia."

"But I know that she *can*. I've seen things I thought I would never be able to describe, and I'm certain that one day everything will depend on her descendants. Everything will change long before then, but the book will restore balance in the world. Yet for now, they must simply keep and protect it. It cannot remain here."

"I will go," Phyqor said reluctantly. "If you're certain about this, then I'll take the book to them."

"No." They looked to Yui in surprise as she continued, "I'll go. I brought this spell into being. I can hide it so the book appears to be ordinary to others. Besides which, it's time that I met her again." Yui noticed their looks of misgiving and added, "To make peace."

The following day Yui rode to the city gates in the northern quarter and did her best to remain calm and composed as the guardsmen demanded to know her reasons for travelling outside Luudhoq. She made up a story about how she planned to visit some old friends who she hoped to convince to come and live in the capital. The guardsmen searched her saddlebags and gave only a cursory glance to the rather dull and tired-looking book they found stuffed amongst her rations and blankets. Finally she was allowed beyond the city perimeter.

Yui rode north-west for a tennight. She stopped at settlements along the way and slept in guest houses where they existed. Fewer people than ever lived out in the countryside now. Most had been encouraged to migrate to Luudhoq, which continued to expand relentlessly. Yui observed some of the people she met and concluded that most of them lived in fear. Although the authorities rarely left the citadel, leaving only token militiamen in place in the larger towns, on the occasion when they did nothing good happened. The few who remained in these settlements were suspicious of her accent, which had long since become Luudhoqian. She kept as low a profile as possible, and eventually reached the town of Rannik in the far west without any incident.

Rannik, like many other places across the land, had become virtually a ghost town. Many of the trades that had once thrived here had long since gone. Much of the town lay desolate, with houses and stores in varying states of ruin as nature gradually reached out her tendrils to reclaim the land and cover the sorry remains of human endeavour.

Yui asked about a dozen different people where she could find the remote dwelling she was looking for. Only the last of them gave her an answer, and to her mind the man appeared evasive. "The woods north of the town," he mumbled.

The woods north of the town- an area called Oakenglen- turned out to be much larger than Yui had thought, and as she rode slowly along one forest track after another she took to choosing them at random simply because she had no directions to follow and no signposts existed to any locations here.

The day grew long. Soon after the sun dipped below the treeline the early evening air became cooler and Yui decided that she had spent long enough on her task today. She decided to head back to the town and see if any hostelries remained open where she might find accommodation. Tomorrow she would see if anyone might be willing to volunteer more detailed directions. With a sigh of frustration she turned her horse gently around and headed along a track that led south towards Rannik.

A short while later a *luyan* man stepped out onto the track, about a hundred paces ahead. Yui slowed her horse gradually until they were just a short distance from him. The man had pale, green-tinged eyes and yellowish translucent hair. He was about her age, perhaps a little younger. As she warily returned his look, Yui felt certain that she had seen him before, although they had never spoken to each other. "Ryn?" she queried, scarcely able to believe her luck.

He nodded. "And I know who *you* are. Why have you come here?"

Yui carefully explained why she had travelled all the way from Luudhoq. Ryn listened with initial suspicion which soon became worry. "We want nothing to do with this," he said abruptly as soon as she had finished.

"At least take me to Arin and Nia," Yui pleaded. "They deserve to make the decision for themselves. You can't make it for them."

Ryn did not seem pleased with the idea, but he sighed and nodded in agreement. "We'll take the short route. You'll need to dismount and lead your horse," he said. Without further ado he strode across the track and onto a grassy path that Yui hadn't noticed before. She wondered if they had hidden the routes that led to their home, or at least made them difficult to find, using the Powers. *It wouldn't surprise me if they'd retained their abilities somehow,* she thought, casting a thoughtful look at Ryn's back as he pressed on along the path.

As they walked, Yui's mood grew pensive at the thought of meeting Nia again. She recalled their long-ago talk in the field by the army encampment. Although she had never admitted it at the time- or since for that matter- Nia's words that day had deeply affected her. She had made the decision to locate the Gates because of what Nia had said.

Yui suddenly felt immense regret and guilt well up inside her. She almost never thought of her distant childhood now, but recent events had forced that time closer in her mind. She recalled the rage and hatred that had almost consumed her during those dark days, the result of Nia's trickery and then her torture by the Seven.

I almost lost myself, she thought. *I would have done, had it not been for my father.*

Many years have passed, and it shouldn't matter now. But I have to make peace with Nia if I can.

Nevertheless, Yui's apprehension only increased as Ryn led her on into the heart of the forest. She felt as if she might be headed into a trap of her own making. Ryn took many different paths, and she tried to memorise the routes he took but for some reason she couldn't. She felt certain that sorcery ran through this whole woodland. Perhaps Nia's family had created it as a means of protection from the wider world.

Finally they reached a clearing where a rambling country house stood. Ivy covered much of the walls and smoke drifted up into the cool evening air from one of the chimney pots. Ryn led Yui to a stable adjacent to the main building, where they led her horse into a spare stall. As they approached the main door into the house afterwards, it opened and a woman with long blonde hair looked out from the doorway. "Good evening, Lumi," Ryn said. "I think you can guess who this is."

Lumi's eyes narrowed suspiciously as she looked Yui up and down. "Why are you here?"

"I asked her the same thing," Ryn said before Yui could reply. "She wants to speak with Mother and Father. Something about a book."

Yui was ushered inside and through to a large living room. As she sat at the central table Yui looked around at the great wooden beams and roughly ornate yet rustic furnishings. *Were it not for my family I would prefer to live in a place like this rather than Luudhoq,* she realised.

Ryn went to fetch Arin and Nia while Lumi sat two places away from Yui. As she observed the woman's forbidding expression Yui wondered again if Alexia had made the right choice. Would these people be able or even willing to protect and conceal the book? She was about to ask them all to accept the burden of a terrible responsibility, one for which they would certainly not thank her.

"This is a beautiful house," she commented after a moment, for no reason other than to break the uncomfortable silence.

"It's our home," was all Lumi said.

Footfall sounded in one of the corridors and Ryn reappeared with Arin and Nia, and to her surprise a young man and woman, both dark-haired and blue-eyed. *Their natural children,* Yui thought as she looked at them.

Arin was approaching old age now although he still walked with a sturdy and upright presence. Nia had changed less than Yui thought she might. She exuded a calm confidence that didn't waver as her eyes met Yui's.

Once everyone was seated, Arin looked to Yui. "Ryn has given us what he knows of your story, but we would hear it again from you."

Yui recounted once again her reason for coming here. She told them what little she knew of Alexia's visions within the Green Road, then the long years she had spent planning to write the book- which was both the history and the future of the Age in which they lived. She described the spell that she had placed to protect the book, and the months that Alexia had spent writing into it.

Finally she brought forth that book, and the effect on all six of them was instantaneous. It was as if they somehow caught a glimpse of its contents and also the web of sorcery that shielded it from harm. But Yui felt certain that they also instinctively sensed their own roles in this great play, and even felt the faint echoes of roles their descendants might play down the many decades and centuries. In time, she realised, the book itself would determine the parts to be played by its many protectors. She had cloaked it in sorcery, Alexia had written the chronicle of their Age and Ages to come into it- but the resultant tome was far more potent than they could have imagined.

What have we done? Yui wondered, suddenly fearful.

"It must be kept hidden until the time comes for it to be discovered," she told them.

"And how will we know?" the young man asked.

"More than likely you won't. Neither will your own children or grandchildren. Alexia herself said that many centuries may have to pass before the time comes. She asks only that you keep it hidden. I know that you've used some powerful weave of sorcery to help make yourselves undiscoverable here unless you want to be found. Do the same with the book."

Arin fixed her with a level stare. "We trust nothing that comes out of Luudhoq, and for all your past heroism we have little reason to put any trust in you."

"My family are no friends of those who rule the Citadel, nor their underlings. The very act of writing this book would be seen as treason. We risked much by bringing it into existence. But one day it will be the saviour of everyone-salvation in the hour of greatest darkness."

Yui was left alone with her thoughts while the family went to discuss the matter in private. Logs crackled and spat on the fire. Outside the light breeze had stiffened to a wind that sighed through the trees and rattled the windows. Yui wondered suddenly what she would do if they refused to accept the responsibility. They could not be forced, after all. But neither could she return with it to Luudhoq.

Abruptly the door opened and Arin walked in by himself. "The hour is late and the weather has worsened," he remarked, just as the first few raindrops of the night pattered on the windows. "Rannik is no place for anyone on their own, and I'm sure you'd rather not have to use the Powers to defend yourself. You can stay here for the night. We have a spare room. I'm sure you're hungry as well."

Yui tried to hide her surprise. "Thank you," she said eventually. "Have you decided..."

He shook his head. "Not as yet." His expression darkened. "We must all agree. I think we will, but there are matters to think about."

Later that evening they dined, and for a while everyone's mood became lighter. Afterwards Yui was shown to the guest room, which although small proved to be comfortable. She slept well and didn't wake until mid-morning.

When she went downstairs she saw that the door to the main room was open. She peered around it and saw Arin sitting in one of the chairs at the table, the book in front of him. "It's been decided," he said. "We will do what you ask, and when the time is right we will explain to our descendants the importance of what we do. They in turn will pass it on to theirs. At least, that will be our instruction and our hope."

Yui nodded, immense relief washing over her. "One day, someone may come for it. Someone who can unlock its truth." She paused, uncertain. "I would like to speak with Nia before I go, if I may."

"Good. It's about time, I would say. She's out in the back garden at the moment."

Yui found Nia tending to vegetables, and waited for a moment until she happened to glance round. "Yui," she said quietly.

"Thank you for taking the book," Yui said awkwardly.

"I didn't want to," Nia admitted. "Truth be told, none of us wanted to. But the damned thing reached to us somehow. Even I could feel it, and I don't have a scrap of talent with the Powers. What needs to be done must be done, I suppose."

"I wanted to apologise as well, even if it's so many years late. I doubt that we'll meet again, but I want to make my peace with you."

Nia looked at her, the gardening forgotten as she knelt on the earth. "You were a child," she said finally. "And you had been wronged."

"When you told me I should use my ability to find the Gates that day, it changed everything. I would never have done it if you hadn't spoken to me."

Nia shrugged. "I honestly don't know what came over me. I just talked without knowing what I was doing."

"Well, you did as much as anyone to save us."

"Do you think we're saved?" Nia asked softly. For a moment the morning sun rolled behind a cloud and the surrounding forest appeared, Yui thought, darker than it ought, as if some presence out in the woodland mirrored the woman's thought.

"Let's not speak of it." Yui changed the subject. "You seem content with the life you have."

"I am. I have a home and a family, and I want nothing else. I have to say I'd be a lot more contented without that damned book, but that's not your fault." Nia shivered. "I wish you luck, Yui- but if I were you I would leave Luudhoq and take your family with you- and head as far away as you can. No secrets can be kept for long in that place. It was always that way."

"I may do that. Farewell, Nia."

As the sun climbed higher in the sky, Yui left their homestead. She took a route suggested by Arin, which led to a wide grassy path which she thought she recognised. It would lead her back towards the southern edge of the woods.

A short while later she drew her mount to a halt and out of curiosity she looked back in the direction from which she had ridden. But the path now looked different, as if her passage along it had changed its nature in some subtle way and drawn a veil over her progress, to ensure that no way back existed.

III

The three women met as they always did, at the bottom of a long-forgotten spiral staircase deep within the place that had once been called the Fortress of the Seven. Attuned both by habit and by a sensitivity to the behaviour and movements of their compatriots, they appeared from separate entrances within a moment of one another. The cold grey light of the new day diffused listlessly through the single window in the wall by which the stairway commenced its ascent.

346

They happened to look out through the window, which by chance afforded a view of the structure known as Phaedra's Tower. The three of them had discussed their opinions of this place on numerous occasions over the years.

Anlerran had pointed out that the tower, which had such powerful sorcery woven into it that surely it would last until the end of time itself, served as a cautionary reminder to the people of Luudhoq of the time when the Seven had ruled over them. She argued that for as long as the tower stood, every citizen would know how and why it came to be, and would pass the story of its making- and the woman incarcerated within- down the generations.

Kian had voiced her reservations about keeping the last surviving member of the Seven alive and incarcerated for all time, not because she held any sympathy for her but because she feared what might happen if the tower's magic failed and the vengeful woman within was released- no matter the supposedly absolute power of the sorcery weaved throughout the building.

Ileana had simply stated that Phaedra ought to have been publicly executed after her capture. *The tower may work against us, deifying her,* she had warned. Privately she also looked to the tower from time to time when on her own, and thought on occasion that something was not quite as it ought to be. But she never figured out how or why; the moments passed, and she never spoke of her odd misgivings.

Today, like every other day for many years, they had nothing to say to each other on the matter of the tower. They had not spared their prisoner a thought for a long time.

In familiar silence they climbed the spiral. The three women might have spoken in years gone by, but now they conversed only when matters of law or judgement had to be discussed. It was not that they considered the banal talk of common folk to be beneath them, rather that they had exhausted its possibilities long ago.

Today the dull and cold atmosphere had lowered their mood further, and so they barely looked at one another before they commenced the ascent. Not only did they not wish to speak, but they had no desire to look into one another's eyes. Long ago they had learned how to read expressions so clearly that the emotion itself might as well have been written on the countenances they observed. Eyes held no mystery to them.

Only as they finally reached the set of chambers where the staircase emerged did they exchange the briefest of glances.

They opened a door, then another in the room beyond. A powerful sorcery had once spread throughout this set of chambers, but with the demise of the Seven that strange magic had gradually dissipated. Yet even now some unexplained resonance remained.

They stood, as they had every day for the last twenty years, before the mirror that occupied much of one of the walls.

All three women knew that eventually they would raise their heads and look themselves in the eye.

It was here that they would listen to the music box, whose sounds of a world long departed- a world they themselves had never known- tore unaccountably at their hearts. It was here that they would force themselves to observe, as the music rose to a crescendo and faded away in lament, their eternally youthful features, smooth and free of blemish.

At first glance the three women remained a picture of the bright hope from twenty-five years ago when they crushed the starspawn and saved all Aona from an eternity of cold darkness.

For none of them had aged, and their powers had only grown. They looked as one now; stony, regal and radiant, a collective beauty worshipped throughout the known world.

Only in their eyes might the sharpest observer find something at odds with such splendour. Here lay a despair so great and so dark that it might draw in whomsoever saw and recognised it- into the inner night of the saviours' immortality.

349

Please also take a few moments of your time to review this book on Amazon and Goodreads and any other book review websites- even if it's just a few lines!

For a FREE fantasy novel, exclusive stories, articles and other goodies, subscribe to the author's newsletter: https://www.simonwilliamsauthor.com/freebies.php